ON THE WINGS OF FREEDOM

ON THE WINGS OF FREEDOM

by Malanna Carey Henderson

ON THE WINGS OF FREEDOM

Edited by Lorna Collins
Cover design by Larry K. Collins

ISBN-13: 978-1676062820
ISBN-10: 1676062823
ASIN: B082SD7ZM4

CONTENTS

DEDICATION..1

ON THE WINGS OF FREEDOM............................3

CHAPTER ONE On the Wings of Freedom 5

CHAPTER TWO Richmond...............................17

CHAPTER THREE Twin Oaks 29

CHAPTER FOUR New York 41

CHAPTER FIVE A Family Legacy.......................55

CHAPTER SIX A Holiday Celebration 64

CHAPTER SEVEN The Inquest..........................76

CHAPTER EIGHT Carrie's Fate 88

CHAPTER NINE Cole West.............................100

CHAPTER TEN Pinkerton Investigates 109

CHAPTER ELEVEN The Underground Railroad 115

CHAPTER TWELVE From Freedom to Slavery..123

CHAPTER THIRTEEN A Quaker Woman Gives Solace 129

CHAPTER FOURTEEN An Unwelcome Visitor ..134

CHAPTER FIFTEEN The Wait........................143

CHAPTER SIXTEEN Steal Away Home 149

CHAPTER SEVENTEEN The Reverend Jones ...160

CHAPTER EIGHTEEN Insurrection 169

CHAPTER NINETEEN Frank's Education 174

CHAPTER TWENTY I Shall Be Free 186
CHAPTER TWENTY-ONE Moses Delivers......... 195
CHAPTER TWENTY-TWO A Hidden Camp....... 203
CHAPTER TWENTY-THREE A Safe Haven 209
CHAPTER TWENTY-FOUR Love Finds a Way... 223
CHAPTER TWENTY-FIVE News from Virginia.. 234
CHAPTER TWENTY-SIX The Philadelphia Elite 237
CHAPTER TWENTY-SEVEN Captured 247
CHAPTER TWENTY-EIGHT Extradited 255
CHAPTER TWENTY-NINE Mason's Sacrifice 263
CHAPTER THIRTY Pinkerton Investigates........ 269
CHAPTER THIRTY-ONE A Plan for Liberty....... 276
CHAPTER THIRTY-TWO The Sexual Politics of Slavery 281
CHAPTER THIRTY-THREE Carrie's Trial Begins 285
CHAPTER THIRTY-FOUR The Prosecution Presents its Case 294
CHAPTER THIRTY-FIVE Family Ties 308
CHAPTER THIRTY-SIX The Wild Valley Ranch 315
CHAPTER THIRTY-SEVEN The Defense Presents Its Case.. 321
CHAPTER THIRTY-EIGHT Carrie Testifies 328
CHAPTER THIRTY-NINE An Unlikely Witness . 336
CHAPTER FORTY The Trial Ends 345
CHAPTER FORTY-ONE There Are Many Kinds of Freedom... 349
CHAPTER FORTY-TWO Olivia's Story............. 352

CHAPTER FORTY-THREE A Plan of Action 361
CHAPTER FORTY-FOUR A Secret Revealed......364
CHAPTER FORTY-FIVE Dayton's Story 371
CHAPTER FORTY-SIX A New Beginning...........377
EPILOGUE 388
STEAL AWAY HOME.......................................395
ACKNOWLEDGEMENTS 397
ABOUT THE AUTHOR 398

DEDICATION

~~ To Gigi, my daughter,
the bravest woman I know
To my granddaughters, Alize and Lexi.
I am so proud of you all,
much love and happiness always.
To Steward, my loving husband. ~~

ON THE WINGS OF FREEDOM

By Malanna Henderson

On the Wings of Freedom
We will fly, grandmother, you and I.
No need of scratchin' for food at master's table.
You've got your own table now,
eating hearty, off fine bone china.

No need for downcast eyes, filled with shame or fear.
You've got your own eyes now, full of smiles, free of tears.
No need for slow-treadin' feet, leading to a path of dread.
You've got your own feet now,
moving happy, steppin' fast.

No need of draggin' a body, exhausted with work.
You've got your own body now, restin' long, risin' late.
No need for calloused hands,
that labor in master's fields.
You've got your own hands now,
rose-scented, aloe soft.

No need for a borrowed bosom, to suckle master's child,
Or comfort master's head.
You've got your own bosom now,
to suckle your babe,
And comfort your man.

No need of carryin' a fallow mind,
governed by others to serve their kind,
You've got your own mind now,
to read and write, to create and delight.
Now, I am free to see you all the time.
Nothing's between us now: no state boundaries,
Or Mason-Dixon lines, no slave chains, nor prison bars,
No laws or customs can keep us part.

On the wings of freedom,
We will fly, grandmother, forevermore.

CHAPTER ONE
On the Wings of Freedom

New Year's Eve, 1859
New York, New York

"She may have a year, possibly two. It depends upon how fast the consumption takes hold." Dr. Nicholas Albert's words stabbed Carrie's heart like a knife. She had to accept the inevitable. Her mother, Sarah, was dying.

"Jonathan, it's time for me to have that talk with Carrie."

Carrie watched as fear crept into her father's eyes. She had seen that same expression only one time before: the night her mother gave birth to her last child. She'd never forget the look on her father's face as he held his stillborn son.

The grownups told each other the umbilical cord had strangled the baby. It had happened nine years before, when Carrie was nine and her brother, Sam, was four.

A prickly sensation crawled over her body. Whatever her mother was about to tell her filled her father with dread. How could things get any worse? Sarah's decline hadn't been hidden from Carrie or Sam.

Sarah's clammy hand grabbed her own as she sat on her mother's bed.

The red, swollen eyes repulsed Carrie. Ashamed, she looked upward and studied the patterned wallpaper. The soft blue color soothed her with its trim of bluebells and irises. Not ready to watch her mother suffer, she scanned the elegant room. The sturdy oak furniture, framed pictures, and free-standing mirrors placed the Bennet family in the upper middle-class stratum of colored society. The location of their four-story brownstone in Brooklyn Heights underlined their status.

"Mother, calm yourself. Whatever you have to say won't make any difference. You'll always have my love."

"I hope you'll still feel the same after I've finished. I knew this day would come. I've always intended to tell you, but it never seemed to be the right time. Now, my time has run out. Please don't hate me for what I am about to reveal. I was trying to protect you."

"Mother, there is nothing you can say to make me hate you." Carrie couldn't imagine anything worse than her mother dying.

Sarah's gray eyes held her daughter's. Carrie was aware of their similar appearance. "I wasn't born free in New York City as I led you to believe. I was born in Richmond, Virginia, enslaved to a wealthy family who owned a tobacco plantation called Twin Oaks."

"M-m-mother w-w...?" She choked on her words. What was her mother saying? Was her life a lie? She didn't want to hear any more. Was she enslaved to the Johnson family too?

"The master, Ebenezer Johnson, was my father. His wife, Roslyn, is Senator Eldridge Walker's sister. They visited Twin Oaks, in December of 1840, when I was fourteen. Another visitor, Preston Johnson, my father's twenty-year-old nephew had arrived a month earlier. He attempted to seduce me with whispered endearments and little gifts, but I refused to respond.

"One night, he caught me alone in the hallway and pulled me into his chamber. When I wouldn't give in to his demands, he put his hand over my mouth to muffle my cries and raped me. Afterward, he apologized. When he loosened his grip, I fled. I told my father, Master Ebenezer, but he wouldn't look at me. He never looked into my eyes again, and he did nothing to protect me. It happened a few more times." She looked away for a moment.

"Finally, Preston Johnson left. Jonathan was a free man, a cabinet maker, whose talent took him to many plantation households. Whenever he had work to do at the Johnson plantation, he found time to talk to me. He seemed kind. After a while, we fell in love. I was afraid to tell him what had happened to me, but finally I did. He still loved me. Jonathan didn't have enough money to purchase my freedom, so the Walkers loaned him the amount. When Mr. and Mrs. Walker left for New York, we came with them. We were married in the church, and you were born free in New York City."

Carrie exhaled the breath trapped in her chest. Her heartbeat filled her ears. She knew what her mother was going to say. She dreaded hearing the truth. *Please don't say it.*

"Preston Johnson is your father. I was pregnant with you when I left Virginia."

"Oh no, you're saying Daddy isn't my father? How could you have kept silent all of these years?" Her voice rose in anguish. Her mother had lied to her for her entire life. She turned away from her mother and rose from the bed. She swayed as if intoxicated. She stared at the painting of her family on the wall. Now, she saw it as if for the first time. Why hadn't she noticed it before? Her mother's complexion was café au lait, and her father's a dark chocolate. Sam's was copper, but her complexion was ivory with a touch of gold. Her hair was chestnut brown, which streaked blonde under the summer sun. Everyone else's was pure black. People often mistook her for white, and yet she had never questioned her parentage.

"Carrie, you were born free. I didn't want the shame of slavery to touch you. Never wanted you to know the humiliation I suffered. My own father saw me as his property and not as his daughter."

Carrie started to tremble.

"I have one more thing to tell you."

Carrie clutched her skirt and stared at her mother.

"My mother, your grandmother, is still alive. She's enslaved to the Johnson family at Twin Oaks. I begged her to come with me but she refused to leave my sister, Mary, behind."

Carrie put a hand over her chest and breathed deeply. "You have a sister?" Her voice sounded hoarse in her ears.

"I had many brothers and sisters, but, except for Mary, all of them were sold. I didn't know any of them. I never forgave my mother for not coming with me."

"Couldn't you have saved money to buy Mary's freedom?" Feeling weak, Carrie held onto the edge of the dresser for support.

"After she tried to escape, her master vowed never to set her free. It's the master's prerogative whether or not to set free anyone held in bondage."

Anger surged through Carrie's body. She paced across the floral-patterned carpet. Tears threatened to fall, but she blinked them back. "I don't know you anymore. I don't know my father either."

Sarah raised herself on her elbows. "Jonathan is still your father. He raised you and has loved you as his own since the day you were born. Please do not hate him. He's loved us both and has provided a good life for us. Do not blame him for being the only father you've ever known."

Sarah collapsed back onto the bed.

Carrie rushed to her side.

She sat at the edge of the bed and became alarmed by her mother's feverish eyes and moving lips, which yielded no sound. Carrie leaned down to catch the words and felt Sarah's hot breath against her ear.

"I could die in peace, if only I could see my mother once more. I must beg her forgiveness. Can you forgive me?"

Carrie nodded, despite the wedge between them. "I promise you, Mama, I will find a way to bring my grandmother to you." Tears spilled down her cheeks.

~~~

A series of whistles blasted from the train and snapped Carrie Jane Bennet out of her reverie. She'd never felt so strange in all of her life. She was not a Bennet, but a Johnson. She opened her eyes and stared out the window of the southbound Richmond, Fredericksburg, and Potomac Railroad train. A blur of tobacco plantations raced past, a reminder that America's wealth rested on the backs of African slave labor. Her destination was Richmond, Virginia where the Twin Oaks plantation still bent the back of her grandmother.
~~~

She reached into her reticule and extracted a white, beaded necklace with an amulet as its centerpiece. Carrie caressed the ancient bird in flight carved from ivory.

The train lurched, and the necklace fell from her hand. It zigzagged across the floor. Carrie rose from her seat and almost tripped over her skirt as she snatched up the heirloom. In haste, she sat down and secured the charm around her neck.

As the train rolled into the Richmond Depot, Carrie rose and placed her hand on the wall of the car to steady herself. She gazed out the window at the passengers lined along the track waiting to board the train and caught sight of her own reflection. A pink tint fanned her cheeks and aquiline nose. Her glossy hair was pulled into a chignon. Her face was oval like her mother's, but her jawline was square. She had noticed the difference before, but now she knew the significance. A worry line formed between her pale gray eyes. *There's nothing to worry about. Mr. Johnson agreed to the purchase.* She thought she looked refined in her olive-green traveling suit and matching bonnet, accented by a white ostrich feather. At eighteen, Carrie's figure mirrored her mother's. From a distance, people often mistook them for each other as both were slender and walked with grace.

Carrie turned to look at her two companions, Senator Eldridge Walker and his wife Laura. Her anxiety eased. The elderly couple had fallen asleep in their First-Class compartment, reserved for whites only.

When Carrie had made plans to visit Richmond, she knew her fair skin tone would provide her with a measure of protection. People would assume she was white. Aside from the usual pickpockets and muggers, free people of color were in more danger of being kidnapped by slave catchers since the Fugitive Slave Law of 1850 had eliminated free states as havens for escaped slaves.

Carrie looked at the vibrant Miss Laura and thought of her own mother's faded beauty and vitality, stolen by her illness.

"Miss Laura, Mr. Eldridge, we're here." She nudged her chaperones awake. "We're in Virginia." She shook Mrs. Walker's shoulder again, and her eyes fluttered open.

"I've never seen the bird before, Carrie." Miss Laura squinted through her rimless spectacles to get a better look. "It's lovely." The elderly woman rose and pushed a few gray strands under her black teardrop hat.

"It once belonged to my grandmother, who was kidnapped and brought to America on a slave ship when she was only seven years old."

"In all the years I've known Sarah, she has never mentioned her mother's past." The retired senator from New York straightened his clothes. He grasped the wolf-headed cane from the floor and employed it to rise from his seat.

"My mother never spoke of her time as a slave, but now since she's ill, she's told me her little-known family history." Carrie's hands shook a little.

"What did she tell you?" Mrs. Walker's eyes widened with interest.

"Grandmother was born in the Kingdom of Dahomey in West Africa." Carrie fingered the talisman. "Her father made this. Her name was Aisha, and she believed its power protected her through the Middle Passage. Mother gave it to me before I left. We hope it will help me bring Grandmother safely to New York in time."

"Carrie, Sarah always referred to your grandmother as Olivia." Mrs. Walker frowned.

"Aisha was her African name. After Ebenezer purchased her, he named her Olivia."

Once the travelers retrieved their luggage, they were fortunate to find empty seats in the station's waiting area. Carrie sat down heavily and sighed as she massaged the back of her neck.

Traveling had been a gruesome affair. They had boarded the Baltimore and Ohio Railroad train in New York for Washington, D.C. Next, they'd caught the Potomac Steamboat to Aquia Creek, where they boarded the RF&P train to reach their final destination.

Since it was New Year's Eve, throngs of holiday visitors crowded the station. Carrie scanned the travelers for Henry Mason, Mr. Johnson's trusted butler, who was to drive them to Twin Oaks. Mr. Johnson had described him in a letter as "a dark-skinned, amicable fellow, about twenty-five years of age, who stands well over six feet."

The train had arrived a few minutes early. While the Walkers chatted about the New Year's Eve ball to be held at Twin Oaks that evening, Carrie composed the first line of a poem in her head. "On the wings of freedom," she whispered. Her journey to emancipate her kin would be the subject of her next book of poetry.

~~~
~~~

Mason steered the Brougham out of the way of a careless horseback rider. The young man galloped by and yelled a racial epithet. Mason let the insult roll off him like sweat on a hot day. The frightened horses were soon under his control. Moments later, he walked past the mercantile into the alley.

Mason was careful to avoid detection as he ducked into the rear door of *The Richmond Enquirer.* His second visit might raise suspicions since he had already collected a bundle of newspapers for his route. Even though his master kept half his wages, the money allowed him to have dreams few slaves could imagine.

He passed the editorial offices and stopped when he heard the familiar whir of the printing press. Mason rapped on the door in a staccato rhythm, and then twisted the knob. He greeted Jimmy with an enthusiastic handshake. Gray-haired and bearded Jimmy, who passed for white, had proved to be a valuable resource for agents of the Underground Railroad.

Jimmy's deft fingers set type for *The Richmond Enquirer.* He extracted an envelope from the back of a desk drawer and handed it to Mason.

"These ought to last you for a while," croaked Jimmy in a voice salted with age.

Mason smiled and thumbed through the counterfeit bills of sale. His master's family crest was already imprinted on the documents. With the help of a blacksmith, he had been able to have a discarded broken seal repaired for such a purpose. He slipped the envelope in the back waistband of his trousers under his coat, while his eyes rested upon the wall clock. It was two-thirty in the afternoon. In half an hour, he'd pick up Olivia's granddaughter and his master's uncle and aunt.

Moments later, he stood in line behind Dotty Wilson, the chief prosecutor's widowed sister, at the counter of the mercantile.

"Will you tell that colored boy to move back?" She turned her head and glared at Mason. "I can feel his breath on my neck."

Mason waited two feet behind her.

"Excuse me, boy, did you aggravate the Widow Wilson?"

Mason turned to see the speaker. Captain John Pierce, a decorated soldier, womanizer, and brother-in-law of his master stood at attention with clenched fists.

"Not at all, Captain Pierce." Mason spoke in a monotone. *Don't let them know what you're thinking.*

The door swung open and a brown-skinned girl of thirteen entered. When she saw Captain Pierce, she stiffened, turned, and crept toward the door.

"Aren't you going to buy something, Annie?" The captain stepped in front of her. He was so close she almost lost her balance. His voice adopted a playful lilt, which caused Annie to tremble, as her tears welled.

"No sir." Annie's voice quivered and her eyes dropped to his spit-polished boots. "I came in here by-by mistake. I bes' be goin' home now, sir."

"Remember our little talk, Annie?" A smile tugged at his lips as his stare swept her form.

"Please, sir. Let me pass."

"I'll take you home, Annie." Mason jerked his head to the right and Annie ran behind him. "I'm going to the train station, and your place is on the way."

The captain's blue eyes flashed with contempt. He shook his head and flung his blond hair behind his shoulders as his chest heaved. The soldier craned his neck to look into Mason's face with slits for eyes.

"I heard you were on your way to pick up the Walkers and that colored gal of Olivia's. Whaddaya doing here?"

"I had to pick up a few notions for Missus Susan while I was out this way." Mason pulled a piece of paper out of his breast pocket.

The captain snatched the list, scanned it, balled it up, and threw it on the floor.

"Well, I've picked up a few notions about you myself. Let this be a warning, boy: He who walks on dangerous ground is sure to lose his footing."

Without preamble, Pierce flung open Mason's coat and patted him down, missing the envelope. He marched out of the mercantile, red-faced.

Mason's anger rose and fell like a wave. *Don't let them know what you're feeling.*

~~~

Entering the waiting room, his eyes rested upon a young woman with a rosy-golden complexion engaged in conversation with an elderly white couple, whom he recognized as his master's aunt and uncle. *She must be Carrie.* She was not conspicuous in the segregated area. Across from Carrie sat a white woman about her own age, their features excluded, they were like a pair of bookends.
~~~

A solution to a puzzle appeared to him as clear as spring water.

CHAPTER TWO
Richmond

The City of Richmond charmed the New Yorkers. They marveled at the Virginia State Capitol Building, a Greek Revival monument to government, whose white columns gleamed in the sunlight. Designed by Thomas Jefferson with the assistance of Charles-Louis Clerisseau, it was completed in 1788.

An array of restaurants, gothic-style churches, art galleries, hotels, and theaters comprised the bustling downtown business district. Christmas spirit adorned trees, wreaths, windows, and doors with bright red holly and pine cones. Street vendors hawked their wares. The voices of holiday carolers floated upon the winter breeze.

It was Carrie's first ride in a Brougham. Popular in England since 1837, she knew it was a favorite among the wealthy. She smiled and sank into the plush, diamond-pleated burgundy satin seat cushion. She surmised Mr. Johnson's was custom-made, hence its four-passenger capacity, with two fold-away seats designed for children. She smiled as she observed the rich russet leather interior.

The cobblestoned streets gave way to the countryside as dusk heralded the end of the day.

"Whoa." Mason yanked the reins. Several raucous pigs raced across the road with two boys in hot pursuit. The scene drew laughter from everyone.

When the carriage pulled to a sudden stop, the senator gripped the head of his cane.

"Mama, remember the Christmas we visited Twin Oaks in 1840, and teased Eb about his mutton chop whiskers? He left in a huff and said he preferred the company of his livestock." The senator chuckled.

"But we knew the barn was where he kept his secret stash, and he got all corned up." Mrs. Walker winked at her husband.

"He had a powerful hankering for corn liquor."

"What happened when he got back? I've forgotten."

"When Eb returned, Ros was right huffy because he denied he had been drinking. He may as well have acknowledged the corn. What else could have caused his strawberry nose and his birdlike hiccups?"

The couple's laughter caused Carrie to smile.

The gleam of Mrs. Walker's wedding band reminded Carrie of the ring in her jewelry pouch and its meaning. Marriage.

Carrie recalled the fuss Frank's sister made about her wedding dress. She had insisted on wearing white. A white wedding gown was a new trend, which had been started by Queen Victoria in England and had spread to America. Mrs. Turner, being ever practical, bought a lovely lavender gown instead.

Frank Harding Turner had insisted Carrie wear his engagement ring while she considered his proposal. "Don't reject him yet," her mother had advised, as she admired the ring on Carrie's finger. She'd put off her decision until she returned home. Although Frank was considered a good catch, his traditional views would stymie her creativity. "Writing poetry is a waste of your time," he often said. His opinion had dissuaded her from seeking a publisher, once she'd finished her first volume of poems. Moreover, she'd have to resign her job as well. He couldn't abide a wife who worked. But marrying Frank would please her dying mother.

The senator dabbed his eyes with a handkerchief. "I never understood how my sister could have married Eb, a slaveholder. Hypocrites all, who claim to be Christians, and Sarah—" His hazel eyes, narrowed. "Our last visit changed me. I went from being an anti-slavery sympathizer to an active abolitionist. And the next time we saw them, Ma, they were laid out in their funeral clothes, dead from consump—"

Mrs. Walker nudged him and nodded toward Carrie, who frowned when she heard the name of the disease which afflicted her mother.

The Senator's voice assumed a light tone. "It'll be good to see his boy, Robert, again. I wonder how he turned out."

"He was a studious young man," Mrs. Walker recalled. "Do you think Ebenezer's sister-in-law, Betty, is still living with the Johnsons?" Eldridge shrugged his shoulders.

"Oh, dear, she must be seventy, if she's a day. Which of Eb's brothers was she married to, Eldridge?"

"Herbert, he was a year younger than Eb. They had a son, just the one, named Preston."

Carrie lurched forward. She opened her mouth to speak, and then held her tongue. She sighed and then sank back against the seat.

Mrs. Walker and her husband exchanged glances.

"Generous of Robert to have taken her in," opined Mrs. Walker. "She was a hard pill to swallow, as I remember, strict and old-fashioned, but had a soft spot for Robert and Susan."

"It's December thirty-first." Carrie sat up straight. "It's Clarice's birthday. I hope they picked up her birthday cake from Ida's."

"Is Clarice a child at the orphanage?" The senator raised his eyebrows.

"Yes, she's frightfully intelligent and my favorite. Oh, did I tell you? I've been nominated for headmistress."

"Well, congratulations, Carrie." The senator nodded.

"Thank you. I'll be the first person of color to hold the position at the Colored Orphans Asylum of New York, and it's all due to Mrs. Mary Murphy. She recommended me to the board."

"We'll help, dear. I'll continue to collect used clothes." Mrs. Walker patted her hand. "Carrie, back in the 1830s, there was a colored woman's society named the African Dorcas Association. Ever heard of them?"

"Yes, they made clothing for colored children who attended school, since a lack of proper attire was the chief reason most were absent. They were ashamed to attend in rags."

"Well, Carrie, I've contacted the former president, Mrs. Margaret Francis. A former member's daughter, Lorraine Castle, is interested in reviving the organization."

"How wonderful." Carrie clapped her hands.

"And I'll raise funds for capital improvements. The building could use a fresh coat of paint." The senator smiled.

"As always, I can count on you both."

"You've worked hard to give the little dears an education, clean beds, and nutritious meals." Mrs. Walker patted her hand.

"I teach homemaking skills and basic reading, writing and arithmetic, but I've persuaded Mrs. Murphy to allow me to add French and American History classes."

The sight of the silhouette of a ragged colored boy running across a field in the moonlight jarred Carrie. Wealth and poverty, she knew, lived side by side on the plantations. Slaveholders, who starved their slaves and let them labor in tatters, still enjoyed respectable reputations.

Robert Johnson's letter had revealed a kind-hearted gentleman. But would she find him a paradox? Or did he show any humanity toward the enslaved people on his plantation?

Soon, Mason made a right turn off the main road. Carrie's eyes widened as the grand Georgian structure came into view. Her exclamations prompted Mason to relate details about its history.

"Twin Oaks was built in the late 1700s, and is a close replica of George Mason's Gunston Hall. Master Johnson's great-grandfather visited Mason and declared it to be the most beautiful home he had ever seen. He hired the same English architect, William Buckland, and master carver William Sears to design Twin Oaks."

"Was George Mason one of the signers of the Constitution?" Carrie asked.

"No, he didn't sign it because it didn't have a Bill of Rights. He's the author of the 1776 Virginia Declaration of Rights and the Virginia Constitution. Jefferson re-phrased Mason concept of inherent rights to 'inalienable rights' when he wrote the Declaration of Independence."

"I'm impressed. Mason, you know quite a bit about American history."

"It's my passion, Miss Carrie."

Riding toward Twin Oaks, Carrie wondered if her grandmother's freedom was only hours away, or would calamity upend her plans? All the answers were inside The Big House, a source of hope and dread.

Mason drove past two enslaved male sentinels, who stood at each side of the black-iron gate.

Carrie asked about the two oak trees, which framed the residence, the source of the plantation's name. Their trunks, wide as thatched huts, were crowned with bony branches. They reached skyward like gnarled fingers.

"The trees are over one-hundred-years old," Mason offered.

~~~

"Welcome, Uncle El." Robert Johnson shook the senator's hand. Next, he hugged his aunt, Laura. She held his face in both her hands and studied him for a moment. Carrie thought him handsome in his white tie and tails. Gray peppered his dark hair, and faint lines framed his eyes and mouth. However, his sparkling gray eyes and sprightly bearing made him appear more youthful than his years.
~~~

"You must be wearied from your travels. Lulu will show you to your rooms so you can freshen up."

Awestruck by the interior, Carrie had walked arm in arm with her female companion as she crossed the threshold of the manor through the garden entrance. Inside the foyer, she stepped away from the others and peeked into the ballroom and admired the iridescent chandeliers, lit with hundreds of candles. Women and men in formal dress were sprinkled amongst those attired in splendid masquerade costumes, all of which declared them members of Richmond society. Carrie felt as if she had walked onto a stage while a play was in progress, and she didn't know what her role should be. However, she forgot her awkwardness as the pageantry unfolded before her.

A manservant dressed in tails announced the costumed guests as the characters they portrayed as they entered the ballroom. Robin Hood escorted Queen Marie Antoinette. When Little Bo Peep and her companion were announced, gasps filled the room. She entered on the arm of the Headless Horseman, complete with his head under his arm.

Mrs. Walker touched Carrie's arm. "I want you to meet Mrs. Johnson."

"I'm sorry, I didn't mean to be rude, but the ballroom and the costumes are exquisite. I've never seen anything so magnificent."

"It's been years." A lovely woman Carrie assumed was Robert's wife, Susan, had joined them. She gave his aunt and uncle perfunctory kisses on their cheeks.

"It has." Robert patted his uncle's back.

"I thought Aunt Olivia's granddaughter would be with you." Robert's eyes swept passed Carrie.

The senator's eyes twinkled.

"Did she come in through the side door?"

His remark stung like a hard slap. Carrie looked down and bit her lip. *People of color were not permitted through the main entrances.* The side doors were designated for merchants, servants and the enslaved.

Before Carrie could respond, several guests in blackface, dressed as slaves and minstrels entered through the side door. One male, impersonated Thomas Dartmouth "Daddy" Rice, the white comedian, who popularized the song and dance called, "Jump Jim Crow." Carrie had seen posters with his image in New York.

His female companion asked him, "Why did we enter through the side door?"

He laughed. "All darkies have to enter through the side door, Jim Crow included." He stepped ahead as if he were dancing and drew laughter from his friends.

Carrie's blood froze in her veins. Rice's caricature of a clumsy, dimwitted slave called Jim Crow was a vicious insult.

A swell of whispers permeated the room, and all eyes turned to the handsome blond man in military dress as he stood at the entrance.

"Captain John Pierce," announced the manservant.

The newcomer strode across the room with a swagger in his step. His shiny boots clacked upon the polished wood floor.

Carrie noted smiles from some and contemptuous stares from others. He cast his arrogant gaze about until his eyes rested upon her. The flirtatious sparkle in them was unmistakable.

He slapped Mr. Johnson heavily on the back. "Happy New Year, Rob, old boy." The scent of corn liquor pervaded his person.

Mr. Johnson winced. "John, I'm glad you could make it."

"Happy New Year, Cousin." Mrs. Johnson pecked his cheek and greeted him with a jubilant smile.

Carrie felt a small hand tug her own. She looked down, and her eyes beheld a pretty little girl of about seven years. The bodice of her dress was embedded with semi-precious stones. The image of the ragged boy she had seen in the field came to her mind.

The girl addressed Carrie. "You're the most beautiful lady I've ever seen, next to Mommy, of course." The child's eyes shone, and her dark curls danced around her shoulders.

"My opinion, too, Polly." The captain stepped forward.

"Oh, Captain Pierce." Polly grinned. "Are we going to have our dance?"

The captain lifted Polly and kissed her plump cheek. He twirled her around before setting her on her feet.

He advanced toward Carrie with military precision.

Before she had time to react, he'd bowed and kissed her hand. Alarmed, Carrie attempted to withdraw it, but the captain's grip remained steadfast.

"Her beauty has captured my heart, Rob. I believe I am about to meet the belle of the ball, and she's in street clothes. Rob, I'm in love."

Carrie's heart hammered in her chest. She looked down at their hands, and then, he released his grip. Her cheeks felt warm. Embarrassed, she looked away.

Mr. Johnson stared at Carrie and stepped forward. "Forgive my ardent cousin, Miss—er—" He looked into her eyes.

She was sure he recognized their similarity to his own and watched realization wash over him.

The senator stepped forward. "Robert, may I present Carrie Bennet? Carrie, Robert Johnson, master of Twin Oaks."

"Carrie Bennet." Amusement lit Mr. Johnson's eyes.

Carrie nodded.

The senator continued his introductions. "And Carrie, this is Susan Johnson, mistress of this domain. Mrs. Johnson, Carrie."

"How do you do, Mrs. Johnson?" Carrie curtsied.

"My God, is it true?" Mrs. Johnson stepped back to appraise Carrie. Her stare hardened as her lips pressed into a line. She threw her husband's aunt and uncle an angry glare.

Carrie guessed the mistress's thoughts ran akin to: *Yankees. How dare they walk this pale-skinned nigra through a main entrance?*

"Carrie, may I present Captain John Pierce." The senator appeared oblivious of the hostility from his hostess. "Captain Pierce, Aunt Olivia's granddaughter, Carrie."

The captain's jaw had dropped at the first introduction to Mr. Johnson. Now, with his mouth agape, he stood like a statue.

"It's a pleasure to meet you, Captain Pierce." Carrie nodded.

"The—pleasure—is—all—mine, Carrie." There was fire in the captain's eyes as he whispered his response.

Carrie moved closer to Mrs. Walker.

"And this young lady, Carrie, is our youngest, Polly." Mr. Johnson nodded toward the child.

"Hello Polly." Carrie held out her hand. "It's so nice to meet you."

"Likewise, Miss Carrie, I'm charmed to make your acquaintance." The child shook Carrie's hand then made a perfect curtsy, which brought a smile to Carrie's lips.

"Just call her Carrie, Polly." Mrs. Johnson smiled even as she corrected the child.

"Would you like to see my doll house?"

"Oh, I'd love to very much, Polly. I'm a big girl, but I still like dolls."

"Me, too." Polly's dimples appeared.

"Aunt Olivia's granddaughter?" The captain circled her at a steady pace. "My Lord, those gray eyes should have spoken to me sooner."

Gone was his chivalry. Carrie felt stripped naked by his perusal. Their eyes locked, and she shuddered.

Now that he knows I'm colored, he doesn't have to hide his lust under the cover of propriety.

She grabbed the amulet around her neck. To her dismay, she found the charm in her hand as the beads slipped off the broken string and scattered across the floor.

Polly hurried to retrieve the beads and deposited them in Carrie's palm.

The child looked around and pointed. "There's one near Aunt Betty's chair." She walked a few feet into the ballroom where an elderly woman, whom she presumed was Aunt Betty, sat conversing with a younger one. Carrie hadn't noticed the women, earlier.

Aunt Betty wore a mint green ball gown, decorated with several tiers of ruffles at the sleeves and hemline. The iron-gray curls framed a square jaw. Red spots appeared on her wrinkled cheeks. Her gray eyes narrowed as Robert and Carrie approached. Polly picked up the bead and handed it to Carrie.

She must have heard the exchanges. I must be the cause of her creased brow and red cheeks.

"Carrie, you must meet the matriarch of the family, my Aunt Betty."

CHAPTER THREE
Twin Oaks

At six o'clock, as Carrie finished the first stanza of a poem, "On the Wings of Freedom," she heard a knock on her chamber door.

There stood Mrs. Walker, in her dressing gown, her hair in disarray, with a colored ladies' maid holding a ball gown.

Mrs. Walker entered and began without preamble. "Carrie, remember how you dressed my hair for the governor's ball last year?"

Carrie nodded.

"You must help me now."

The maid looked distressed. "I'm sorry you weren't happy with what I did, ma'am. Please say nothing to the misses." Her wide eyes begged forgiveness.

"Not to worry, child, you can place the frock on the bed." Mrs. Walker placed a hand on her shoulder. "Do fetch my toiletries and the rest of my clothing. Carrie knows what to do."

The maid curtsied, and exited.

Carrie raised an eyebrow. "Her reaction to letting you down makes me wonder how Miss Susan treats the enslaved people here."

Miss Laura nodded. "I saw definite fear in her eyes."

~~~
~~~

Carrie had entered her lovely chamber only a half hour earlier. The rose-colored wallpaper, trimmed in green leaves, gave her a sense of peace. How she longed for a nap. The late hour forbade the ladies from resting. The ball was in full swing, and Mrs. Walker was expected to attend.

As for Carrie, she had to prepare herself to meet her grandmother in the slave quarters. Just thinking about it made the hair on her neck rise. Would her grandmother agree to leave Virginia, even though her daughter, Mary, was still enslaved? Carrie had taken a gamble traveling south, but fulfilling her mother's dying wish precluded all worries.

~~~

Carrie invited Mrs. Walker to sit at the vanity. The maid knocked and entered. She placed Mrs. Walker's corset, stockings, petticoats, and hoop skirt on the bed, along with the beauty case and jewelry box. Mrs. Walker thanked the maid before she bowed and exited the chamber.

Before Carrie arranged Mrs. Walker's thick gray hair, she began to massage her companion's shoulders. She felt the tension melt away under her fingertips.

"Ah." Mrs. Walker sighed, as she began to relax. "How I wish I could enjoy this luxury for an hour, but time will not allow."

"Where's the senator?"

"He's asleep. As soon as he entered the chamber, he lay down and fell asleep instantly." She chuckled. "He was snoring so loud, I was afraid he'd disturb the revelers. It will take him no time to dress. I'll wake him when I'm ready."
~~~

Carrie retrieved the beauty case and set it on the vanity. She took out the comb and brush and began to remove the tangles in Mrs. Walker's hair.

"Are you efficient at tightening corsets?"

"Yes, thanks to my mother. Of all the cumbersome clothing we women wear, I detest corsets the most. However, crinolines are not far behind."

"Did I ever tell you what happened to me?"

Carrie shook her head.

"While I attended a ladies' tea, I stood near the fireplace to admire a portrait. My dress caught fire. I extinguished the flames, but none of the women helped for fear their own gowns would be engulfed."

"Oh, thank God, you weren't burned."

"Miss Amelia Bloomer has given us an alternative."

Carrie felt shocked at the mere mention of the name. "Miss Laura."

Mrs. Walker's grin spread across her face. "They're hidden in the bottom of the highboy. When Eldridge is out, I strut around the house in them."

Carrie laughed. "Papa wouldn't hear of it."

By the fiftieth stroke, Carrie had smoothed Mrs. Walker's hair to a silken state. She fashioned the locks into an elaborate updo. She deemed it most becoming. Carrie passed a hand mirror to Mrs. Walker, who complimented her talents with oohs and aahs of delight.

Mrs. Walker laid down the mirror. "What is your impression of Aunt Betty?"

"She seemed embarrassed and angered by my presence."

"As well she would be. She's your grandmother. Aunt Betty is Elizabeth Johnson."

Carrie's heart skipped a beat. She took several deep breaths as she processed this new information. "Preston's mother is the woman you were discussing in the carriage?"

Mrs. Walker nodded.

Carrie shook her head. "Of course, Betty is a common nickname for Elizabeth. I should have known who she was when I met her, but it hadn't dawned on me."

"She'll never warm up to you. If the stories I've heard about her are correct, you'd best steer clear. Grandmother or not, she's extremely protective of the Johnson family name."

"Miss Laura, please...."

"You can't see Grandmother Olivia without your amulet. There's bound to be some ribbon in my jewelry box that will do."

Carrie nodded. She had to know the answer to the burning question her mother had planted in her heart. "Miss Laura, please tell me about my father."

Mrs. Walker looked at Carrie and frowned. "What did your mother tell you?"

"Before I left, she confessed many things. I'm n-not a Bennet, b-but a Johnson. I haven't felt like myself since."

"Bring a chair and sit by me."

Carrie lifted a chair with pink upholstery and sat it beside Mrs. Walker.

The older woman patted her hand. "You mustn't judge your mother too harshly, Carrie. She was trying to protect you."

"Her reason hasn't dulled the sting of betrayal I feel or the anger, which burns inside me. She asked me if

I could forgive her. I told her I did, but I wasn't sincere. I did so out of fear. She appeared much weaker after we talked."

Mrs. Walker closed her eyes. "Your father was tall and handsome with a boyish grin, a square jaw, and glossy chestnut hair. He had a fondness for animals. Nursed Robert's favorite horse back to health after Ebenezer ordered it shot. Robert idolized him."

"When did you meet him?"

Mrs. Walker clasped Carrie's hands. "When Eldridge and I returned from our honeymoon in Paris, we visited Twin Oaks. Sarah was my personal maid. I soon grew fond of her. I discovered Robert was teaching her to read and write.

"It was the summer Preston came to visit from North Carolina. He was Robert's first cousin. Whenever Sarah was in sight, his eyes fastened on her. Eldridge feared his intentions and touted Christian morality, but Preston grew angry. He said it wasn't against the law if he fancied her, as long as Uncle Ebenezer didn't object.

"Legally, he was correct. Sarah's fate was sealed. I learned some masters offer slave women as hospitality to male visitors." Mrs. Walker cringed and shook her head.

"I'm sorry to say, Carrie, since then, nothing has changed. Never roam about the estate without me or Eldridge with you."

Any sense of safety Carrie might have hoped for at Twin Oaks was shattered.

"I tried to protect Sarah. However, Preston had his way with her, and she became pregnant. Robert is your uncle since Ebenezer fathered both Robert and your mother. Sarah's pregnancy made her more vulnerable. As her child, you could have been sold if she'd stayed in Richmond."

Mrs. Walker looked at Carrie and smiled. "We learned of a carpenter, Jonathan Bennet, who was in love with Sarah. He had planned to buy her freedom, but he didn't have enough money. So, we loaned him the rest and brought them to New York. He set up shop as a cabinet maker and paid us back within the year.

"Your parents were married at the First African Methodist Episcopal Church. I had one of my Parisian gowns altered to fit Sarah. Eldridge gave her away, and I felt like the mother of the bride." Mrs. Walker's smile brightened.

Carrie flung her arms around Mrs. Walker's neck as her tears gushed. "I love you, Miss Laura."

For the first time, she noticed the door was ajar. The rustling of petticoats was followed by a blur of mint green.

~~~

Cole Bartholomew West studied his face in the mirror and judged it handsome. The Irish and Native American lineage from his mother produced his jet-black hair, high cheekbones, and hazel blue-green eyes. They appeared green but sometimes looked blue, revealing his emotions. His father's English ancestry contributed his square jaw and high brow.

On his dressing table lay articles intended to transform him from a nineteenth-century lawyer to an eighteenth-century pirate. He donned a bandana and pulled it back from his eyes, which glittered against his suntanned skin. He tied his hair back with a
~~~

leather thong. On his left earlobe, a silver earring glinted.

For the ball, he'd raise the ghost of Edward Teach, the legendary pirate Blackbeard. Jonah fashioned a red-stained bullet wound on Cole's right shoulder.

"Are you almost finished?" Shirtless, Cole's muscular physique was revealed. It resulted from the occupations, which shaped his life. Nicknamed "the Philadelphia lawyer" by the press, Cole tried cases, raised cattle, and bought and sold horses on the Wild Valley Ranch.

"Keep still, Cole." Jonah made final adjustments. The men had grown up together on the ranch.

At thirty, Jonah, a Negro, was three years older. He'd been born free to parents Stuart West had emancipated.

A score of years back, the senior West had converted the original one-room structure into an expansive ranch, nestled in Northern Virginia. Beautifully landscaped, the estate boasted an elegant thirty-room mansion situated on seven-thousand acres of land.

"Man alive." Cole appraised his appearance in the glass. "Jonah, this is terrific." He considered the buccaneer shirt, which lay across one of the matching rosewood Belter chairs. "I wish we didn't have to ruin the shirt."

"Got to." Jonah assessed his handiwork. "If you intend to portray Blackbeard, a man who was hunted down..."

"...in 1718...."

"...and died of a gunshot and twenty-five stab wounds, you must."

"It's a sure-fire way to end up cold as a wagon tire. Jonah, did you know it was our own Lieutenant Governor, Alexander Spotswood, who financed the coastal defenses, which finally captured and executed Blackbeard?"

Jonah shook his head. "No, I didn't know." He chuckled. "So, it was a Virginian who brought him to justice. Well, ain't that something?"

Cole laughed, paused, and then grew silent.

"There you go." Jonah took a step backward and shook his head. "You *will* go to the party. Been mopin' around, workin' like a slave your pappy forgot to free."

Cole returned a weak smile. "Sometimes, I think of her and—" His throat tightened. The image of her lifeless body claimed his memory.

Jonah patted him on the shoulder.

Just a year before, Cole and his wife, Amanda, had arrived at the ball in a cutter. He was dressed as a country doctor while Amanda wore frills as one of the F.F.V. (First Families of Virginia). Once a respected title, it was now used to label social climbers as "Fast-Flying Virginians." Some Southerners took offense.

Amanda had ignored Cole's advice and voiced her opinions at the party. She ended with, "Slavery keeps the devil busy."

They were ostracized, and Cole's businesses had suffered.

Mrs. Johnson had advised Amanda to make a handsome donation to the historical society, and the esteemed matron hosted a tea in her honor. Although it took time, the young couple had reclaimed their social status.

He missed her.

To complete his costume, Cole added a cutlass, a knife, a holster with two pistols, along with a black beard, styled in five long braids. For a final touch, Jonah ripped the sleeves and drew Blackbeard's flag on Cole's right bicep with charcoal. The flag pictured a horned skeleton holding an hourglass in one hand and in the other, a spear-pierced heart, which rendered three blood drops. Jonah drew these in some cherry juice he had acquired in the kitchen.

Now the toughest, blood-ripping old pirate who ever lived was ready to haunt the ball.

~ ~ ~

The full moon and star-studded sky created a perfect backdrop. Jonah drove the Landau through the gate, guided by the glow of oil lamps.

A footman greeted Cole, who sprang from the coach and handed him a gratuity. He readjusted his cutlass.

A window hinge creaked above, and Cole's eyes followed the sound to the third story. In the lamplight, a beautiful young woman pushed open the double windows.

"Did my heart love till now? Forswear it, sight. For I ne'er saw true beauty till this night. Look Jonah, the loveliest girl I've ever seen is up there."

Jonah stared at the woman in disbelief and laughed. "Cole, you're the darndest—"

Cole looked up again. An elderly woman leaned forward and closed the windows. "I swear on my mother's grave, Jonah. A beautiful *young* woman was up there."

"Are you drunk on Blackbeard's potion?" They had toasted the New Year over a glass of rum. "I hope you didn't lace it with gunpowder as he did."

"She was there."

Cole entered the ballroom, and conversation halted. At six-foot-four-inches, like Blackbeard himself, he towered over most men. He spied Mrs. Johnson and commenced a bit of playacting.

"A king's ransom you'll fetch, milady. You're in the custody of Blackbeard." He flexed his bicep which made the horned skeleton on the pirate flag appear to dance.

Mrs. Johnson laughed and stood on tiptoe to kiss Richmond's most eligible bachelor. She fingered the bullet wound through his torn shirtsleeve. "It looks so real."

~~~

Carrie awoke and stared at the rose-colored wallpaper. She found the canopied four-poster comfortable and admired the large trunk at the foot of the bed. The decorative carving of rosebushes on the lid matched the cornices, which surrounded the high-ceilinged chamber.

Where was she? The orchestra below answered her question: Twin Oaks. Captain Pierce invaded her thoughts, but she prayed him away.

Her Saratoga trunk stood in the corner. She heard the case clock below ring nine times. She had only meant to rest for an hour. A pang of annoyance surged. Mrs. Walker hadn't awakened her as promised. Her likely reason: "The poor dear is so tired. I'll let her sleep."

"Oh, my neglected grandmother, I must hurry," Carrie said aloud.
~~~

She recalled an ugly pirate beneath her window. The wealthy indulged their every whim. She, too, was guilty. Hadn't she slept while her grandmother waited?

Carrie grabbed her corset, and then decided against it. She was confident her trim waist wouldn't betray her. With her bell-shaped crinoline in place, she donned a peach-colored evening frock. The modest square-cut bodice, trimmed with lace, flattered her assets.

In her haste, Carrie swept her hair into a topknot with tendrils. Inside her case, she found her amulet. She smiled as she remembered Mrs. Walker securing it with a thin black ribbon. She tied the ribbon and centered the charm.

Won't Grandmother be astonished to see the amulet she wore while she crossed the Middle Passage?

She slid the engagement ring onto her finger as a mere adornment and hoped it would discourage the captain if he should cross her path again.

Carrie pushed her feet into high-heeled slippers and threw her sapphire cloak over her shoulders before she grabbed two small gift packages.

When she reached the bottom of the staircase, the music beckoned to her. She couldn't resist another look. Emboldened, she opened the door a crack and peeked inside.

Carrie felt like a child who'd glimpsed a forbidden adult world. What a sight. The holiday ball was like a magical moving canvas. The dancers, dressed in colorful costumes, swirled around the room to the lush strands of Franz Liszt's "Mephisoto Waltz" under a blaze of candlelight.

As she closed the door, a man stuck his black boot in the opening and pushed passed her. Carrie gasped and turned to run. Captain Pierce seized her arm.

"Captain, no."

"Not so fast, my sweet." His voice stilled her heart.

"Come on in and join us."

CHAPTER FOUR
New York

New Year's Eve, 1859
New York, New York

Jed "Killer" Calhoun punched the fugitive with all his strength. As the prisoner keeled over, he grabbed Jed's red bandana. Dennis "Big Red" McPherson yanked Jeb by the collar. "Shit, Dayton's gonna be pissed if you kill him." McPherson's hair color and three-hundred-pound frame earned his moniker.

The third slave patroller, Scott Bancroft, checked the injured man. "He's dead." His voice conveyed wonder.

Freedom had come to the fugitive at last in death.

~~~

Two stylish gentlemen exited the Fraunces Tavern at nine in the evening. Frank Harding Turner and Calvin Davis hurried down Pearl Street under the glow of oil lamps in lower Manhattan. They had celebrated the milestone in their lives with shots of whiskey.

The next day, Frank would join his father's law firm. The senior Turner had defended the mutineers aboard *La Amistad* in 1839, before John Quincy Adams took the case. The following Sunday, Calvin would preach his first sermon at his father's church.
~~~

"Mama's gonna have a conniption fit." Calvin grinned. "We're late for church. What did you think of Lucretia Mott?"

"Men of color deserve the vote before women." Frank frowned. "Carrie would have said men of color and women shouldn't vie for rights, which ought to be guaranteed them in the first place. God, I miss my woman." He sighed.

"Your woman? You're a stick-in-the-mud, and she's a reformist. Little chance of a wedding."

"She's accepted my engagement ring."

"Only because her mother...."

Three men sprung at them as a red bandana fell to the ground.

~~~

"Robert, may I have a word, please." Betty Johnson looked up into her nephew's pearly-gray eyes and saw confusion.

"Why certainly, Aunt Betty. Let's go into my study where we can have some privacy."

The elderly woman eased herself into one of the leather chairs opposite her nephew's desk. He sat down and poured a snifter of brandy. He offered her a glass.

"I never take spirits. You should know that by now, Robert."

"You look upset. A sip of brandy is good for the troubled
soul."

"My husband never approved. What is that gal, Carrie Bennet, doing here?"

"She's come to buy her grandmother's freedom."
~~~

"You've agreed to emancipate Olivia?" Anger tightened her lips and put a frown on her face. "It might set a dangerous precedent, Robert. When the other planters hear of your actions, they won't be pleased."

"Aunt Betty, you need not bother yourself with the affairs of Twin Oaks. I do appreciate your concern, Auntie, but the opinions of the others have never governed my actions. I'd like to see Aunt Olivia free and comfortable in her old age. I'm glad she has kin who can care for her. She was my mammy and midwife to my mother. Had it not been for her, I'd have never been born."

"I understand, dear, but recently, there have been escapes from the Mayfield plantation and from this one. Emancipating slaves at this time will only encourage others to run off, too."

"Leave it, Auntie, I'm not changing my mind."

"Tell me, Robert, is the chit here to make a claim on my grandson's estate?"

~~~

Carrie ceased to struggle as the captain pulled her into the ballroom. When Pierce steered her toward Mr. Johnson's circle, she saw panic steal the smile from his face.

"Captain Pierce forced me in here," Carrie whispered through clenched teeth as she reached him. "I was on my way to visit—"

Pierce interrupted. "Gentlemen, may I present Rob's niece, Miss Carrie Bennet from New York City." He winked at his brother-in-law. Carrie's cheeks suddenly felt warm.

Mr. Johnson froze.
~~~

"Carrie, may I present Frederick Wilson, of the Mayfair Plantation."

The gentleman bowed and kissed Carrie's hand.

"She killed her master. Claimed he threatened to attack her again." Conversation drifted from behind. Carrie turned her head and saw a young man with a scrapbook standing before a tall man in black and white attire. She glimpsed the headline of an editorial from the *Glasgow Weekly Times*: "Celia v The State of Missouri, by Lucius Dayton."

Pierce continued introductions. "Miss Bennet, meet Francis Weatherspoon of the Morning Star Plantation."

Mr. Weatherspoon's hazel eyes twinkled.

A red-haired man with handlebar moustaches greeted her next, Mr. Murdock, a land merchant.

"Would you please autograph your article in my scrapbook, Mr. Dayton?"

"Of course, young man."

Carrie turned to see a man she presumed to be Mr. Dayton scribble his name in the book.

Mr. Wilson whispered he'd like his host to introduce Carrie to his bachelor son ahead of Weatherspoon's.

Mr. Johnson appeared flummoxed.

Carrie heard the request, too, and wanted to disappear.

Next, Pierce turned to Mr. Dayton and introduced Carrie.

Mr. Dayton's eyes widened at the sight of her.

Can he tell I'm colored? Can the others?

She recalled seeing a blonde woman thrown out of a tony store at Coney Island. Someone had recognized her as a Negro. Carrie had missed the sign in the window, "*No niggers or dogs allowed,*" as well. Had someone identified her, she might have been the one left sprawled on the street with her hair across her face and her clothes ripped by the angry mob.

Dayton's surprised look faded. "I am charmed, my dear. Richmond will never be the same since you've graced it with your lovely presence." He bowed and kissed her hand. "Miss Bennet, may I introduce my party to you along with their masquerade characters?"

Carrie nodded.

His friends smiled as they waited their turn. Isaac Cartwright, Justice of the Peace, dressed as a prince. Marvin Sellers, another justice, represented a woodcutter. He'd donned a homespun shirt, vest, and breeches. A toy axe was sewn onto the back of his waistcoat.

Sheriff Benjamin Coffe attended as the court jester.

The young man, who held the scrapbook book, was introduced as Jeffrey Bowles, a law student.

"I never dress up," Mr. Bowles explained when Pierce asked him about his attire.

"Edward Stevens, our coroner, has braved public ridicule, and dressed as an old woman." Dayton chuckled.

Carrie suppressed a giggle. The little man wore eyeglasses on his bulbous nose, while his huge ears dislodged the gray wig and white ruffled cap on his head. He wore a checkered gingham dress and white apron.

"The only Yankee in our little group is Doctor Carolyn Ashley from Boston. Fresh from her European travels, she's dressed as Little Red Riding Hood, a character in a children's story popular in France."

Carrie assumed the character's name came from the bright scarlet-hooded cape the doctor wore.

"It's a pleasure to meet you, Miss Bennet. A female doctor, you are a rarity, indeed. What inspired you, doctor?"

"My father was a physician. I often helped him after school. He had an office in our home. I never wanted to do anything else." The doctor's pretty face was framed by a mass of blonde curls.

"What a beautiful costume." Carrie smiled in admiration.

"I found this red cape at the last minute. Yours is similar."

Dr. Ashley's cloak was identical to hers except for the color. Both wraps were lined in white silk.

"As for me...." Dayton gestured to his clothing with a sweep of his hand. "I'm dressed in Puritan garb as John Hathorne, the chief judge in the Salem Witch Trials of 1692."

"Yes, the great-great-grandfather of author Nathaniel Hawthorne. I enjoyed *Goodman Brown,* but reviled *The Scarlet Letter."* Carrie frowned. "I found fault with Hester's decision to protect her lover, who left her, to face the harsh punishment of bearing a child out of wedlock alone."

"Which was her choice." Dayton nodded.

"He could have offered her the protection of marriage." Carrie felt her ire rise just speaking about the plot. "Why is it Hawthorne only punished the woman for moral indiscretions?"

"She paid the consequences for defying moral authority." Dayton raised an eyebrow.

"As I said, I find fault with Hawthorne." Carrie refused to concede.

"This is the chief prosecutor of Richmond County you are sparring with, Miss Bennet." Bowles smiled at Dayton. "She's shown more mettle than most women you've interrogated, Mr. Dayton. Miss Bennet, he's reduced many of your gender to tears during cross-examination on the witness stand."

Without preamble, Pierce placed a hand at the small of her back and abruptly spun her around to his brother-in-law's circle.

Mr. Weatherspoon addressed Carrie. "My dear, you must honor me with a dance."

Carrie stalled as her eyes searched for her companions. Mrs. Walker noted her worried look and started over.

"Sorry, Francis, me first." Pierce took her hand. "Shall we, my sweet?"

"Please, Captain Pierce, I—"

"Say no more. I always aim to *please* the fairer sex." He ushered Carrie onto the dance floor.

"Excuse me." Mr. Johnson hurried to catch up with Pierce and grabbed his shoulder. "John, what are you doing?"

Mrs. Walker arrived out of breath and implored Pierce to release Carrie.

He smirked at her and then turned to his brother-in-law. "Rob, I would prefer not to embarrass you. If your friends knew her identity, I dare say—" Pierce raised his eyebrow. Then he ripped Carrie's gifts from her hands and thrust them against Mr. Johnson's chest.

The older man's face turned scarlet as he gripped the packages.

Next, Pierce snatched Carrie's cloak from her shoulders and draped it across Mrs. Walker's shoulder. He circled Carrie's waist with one hand and spun her onto the dance floor.

She spied Mrs. Johnson's stricken face as Pierce led her around the floor as a *Viennese* waltz soared.

The mistress of Twin Oaks hurried across the room, most likely to ask Mr. Johnson to help put an end to her cousin's shenanigans.

Carrie heard people compliment Robert and his wife on their beautiful niece.

When Mr. Johnson addressed his wife, Carrie was within earshot. "John's gone too far."

His wife's response chilled her veins. "They're oohing over a colored gal, Robert." Her harsh laughter rang out.

Her husband glared at her with steely gray eyes.

A talented dancer, Captain Pierce glided Carrie across the floor with ease. He made sure to stay within his cousin's vision, so he could relish her response to his unorthodox antics.

Carrie followed his lead, as some couples retired to the sidelines to watch them.

"How's your social life, my sweet?"

Carrie ignored him.

"You may as well play along. All eyes are on us. Are you married? Let me see. Aha, there's a ring. He looked at the gold band with a half carat aquamarine stone. It looks expensive. How could a colored boy afford it? Is it a fake or did he steal it?"

She cocked an eyebrow. "The gem is real. My fiancé is a grown man and a lawyer."

Carrie thought about Frank's proposal. Was she being fair to him—to herself? Could she forsake her dreams and submit to a conventional marriage?

He whistled. "He's educated like you."

Carrie frowned.

"You speak like a book. It was an easy guess. By the way, I saw Ira Aldridge, the colored Shakespearean actor, in *Hamlet* and *Othello* in London."

Carrie's eyes widened.

"Are you surprised? Some Negroes do possess remarkable talents, my sweet." Pierce's eyes swept her body. "Do you like the theatre?"

"I've attended the Winter Garden Theatre."

"That reminds me, dear, how excited I was to see a production of *The Octoroon* there. You could have been cast in the lead role. She wasn't nearly as beautiful." He started to caress her hand.

"Captain, please let me go."

"Look around you, *Miss Bennet*, every woman would like to trade places with you." He ceased rubbing her hand.

"I regret that none has." She scowled at him.

The captain laughed. "What lofty goals do you have in Gotham City?"

"I'm a teacher. I-I-I was just promoted to headmistress."

"A credit to your race."

"Do you mean everyone else is a *discredit* to my race?" The venom in her voice shocked Carrie. *I shouldn't have spoken so harshly to a white person.*

"No one of your race has ever spoken to me like that." The amusement on the captain's face drained.

A pang of fear hit the pit of her stomach.

"You're trembling." Concern showed on his face, and then vanished. "You know, I could have you whipped for what you said."

"But, I'm free."

Mirth crept into his eyes. "Really? May I see your pass?"

Fear struck Carrie. She was reminded of stories about free colored people kidnapped into slavery. "I was born free in New York City. I don't need a pass."

"I wouldn't be so sure, if I were you." He paused and then smiled. "I have other plans for you." His blue eyes twinkled. "You're intelligent, bold, and witty. I can prove to be a companion with considerable charm. I value the society of women of color beyond the bedroom, unlike other southern gentlemen. If you consent to be my lover, I'll spoil you with a house and servants. Who knows, I may give up life as a rolling stone."

"No thank you, Captain Pierce. I—am—not—for—sale." Her anger mounted. She struggled to free her hand, but the captain held on tighter.

The music stopped, and lively applause reverberated.

Captain Pierce bowed. "Curtsey to the crowd." When she didn't respond, his grip turned painful. "Curtsey."

She did, and the applause swelled.

Mrs. Johnson's high-spirited laughter sailed above the din.

Pierce seemed delighted to have entertained his cousin with his mockery of social decorum.

"Thank you for the dance, my sweet. But most of all for the chance to feel a real woman in my arms, unhampered by a corset. Words fail me in—"

Carrie snatched her hand from his and moved away from him. His mocking laughter followed as she sought the companionship of Mrs. Walker.

~~~

Captain Pierce leered at her retreating form. "I'll have you, my sweet. You belong to me. It's just a matter of time until you're all mine."

Mr. Johnson rushed to Pierce's side. "I won't tolerate your mistreatment of my mammy's granddaughter. Promise me, John, you'll steer clear of her."

"Don't be so serious. It was entertainment for me—and your wife. 'Sides, I gave *Miss* Bennet a chance to dance at the finest ball in Richmond. No colored woman can boast of the same. She can savor it in her schoolmarm's memoirs. Damned unkind of her not to have thanked me for it. There's a matter I need to discuss with you, Cousin Robert, about Carrie Bennet."

~~~

Moments later, a pretty maid brought Carrie a message from Mr. Johnson. He wanted to see her in his study in half an hour before she met her grandmother.

"I'll need to go to my chamber to get my reticule. He must be ready to give me my grandmother's emancipation papers." Carrie smiled at the Walkers.

"Don't forget to come and get us before you see your grandmother. It's been many years since we've seen her." The senator reminded Carrie.

Carrie retraced her steps to her bedchamber with the maid at her heels.

"I'm Lulu, Miss Carrie, before I take you to Massa's study dere is some folks working in the kitchen who wanna meet you."

Carrie smiled. "Why, of course, I'd be delighted."

She followed Lulu down the stairs and into the basement, where the winter kitchen was located.

The aromas struck her before she entered, and her stomach churned. A six-foot-long wooden table occupied the center, where people busily chopped, stirred, and minced. The holiday menu, written in calligraphy, rested on a music stand near the hearth.

In time, everyone looked her way, and all activity slowed like a clock winding down to the minute.

A girl with flour dusting her hands nudged a woman who had been reading the menu. The woman of about fifty, who seemed to be in charge, looked her over.

"Are you Olivia's granddaughter?" Her ginger-colored skin contrasted with her blue bandana. The food stains on her white apron ran helter-skelter like an artist's palette. Carrie nodded, and the woman smiled.

"Yes, ma'am, she surely is." Lulu beamed. "Ain't she pretty?"

"Well, come on in, child, and give Auntie Violet a hug. Your grandma and I have been here as long as those oak trees out front. Thanks for bringing her, Lulu."

Carrie complied and inhaled the faint scent of English lavender. The kitchen staff crowded around her.

"I'm surprised to see a menu setting on a music stand. You can read Aunt Violet?" Carrie peered at the menu.

"I was taught to read by Master Robert years ago. My, did he get a scolding from his daddy, Master Ebenezer. When Missus found out, she started writing the menus and leaving them on a stand for me. Said it was easier for her, and she could practice her calligraphy."

Carrie nodded. "I see."

"This is Louis, second butler to Mason." Auntie Violet indicated a young man.

"Dat's when dey can find me." Louis chuckled. The wiry fellow moved forward with the agility of a smooth dancer to shake her hand.

"Here is my granddaughter, Ella. I've taught her nearly all I know about cooking so she can open her own restaurant someday. Am I'm crazy to have a dream like that, Miss Carrie?"

"There's a colored woman named Ida who owns a bakery shop in New York City. So, Auntie Violet, your dream is not impossible. Don't give up and maybe—"

Louis nodded. "If de Lord sees fit, your dream will come true."

"Ain't you something'?" Auntie Violet shook her head. "You're the very one who told me my dreams are too highfalutin'. Now because Carrie's here, you want to show off." She wacked him with the dish towel she had in hand.

Everyone laughed. Ella, a plump young woman with bright hazel eyes, smiled and wiped her hands on her apron before shaking Carrie's hand.

When Senator Walker and his wife appeared, their gaiety vanished, and they all donned an air of artificial formality.

Mrs. Walker put her hand on Carrie's shoulder.

"How did you find me?"

"Another maid told us where Lulu had taken you."

Auntie Violet nodded toward the Walkers then addressed her staff. "Let's get this late supper out to the guests." Auntie Violet passed the formally dressed men the food platters, and they exited.

"Carrie, I'm sorry about John." The senator placed a hand on her arm. "Had I been a younger man—" The sentence hung in the air as he assumed a boxer's stance. "I would have taught the fool a lesson."

"Oh, I'm fine now. Thanks to these kind people, I've recovered my wits."

The senator handed Carrie her packages, and Mrs. Walker placed Carrie's cloak across her arm.

Lulu told the Walkers she'd come for them after Carrie had met with Mr. Johnson. The couple thanked her and returned to the holiday festivities.

CHAPTER FIVE
A Family Legacy

Carrie trailed Lulu down the hallway to Mr. Johnson's study. Her heart raced. This was the purpose of her journey—to free her grandmother.

Carrie knocked on the door. She inhaled the clean scent of wood polish.

"Come in."

Twisting the brass doorknob, Carrie entered.

Seated behind a handsome mahogany desk sat Mr. Johnson. His eyes rested upon a document. He looked up and smiled. "Have a seat, Carrie. I'll be finished soon."

Carrie sat in one of the butter-soft leather chairs across from the desk, and laid the gifts on the other. Her gaze circled the study. In addition to the desk, it held a scarred coffee table and a bear rug with angry eyes and sharp teeth. Antlered moose and elk heads jutted from the walls, except for one, which was bedecked with Mr. Johnson's prized gun collection, ensconced within a glass case.

Wainscoting panels covered the lower half of the remaining walls, but the upper half depicted a vista of an English hunt. The flickering light from the fireplace animated the figures.

A party of men in blood-red coats and black trousers sat upon mounts with shiny coats of snow, chestnut, and midnight. They dashed over green hills, under a pale blue sky, after a beautiful red fox. A stroke of the painter's brush blurred its bushy tail. Some hunters took aim.

The fox never had a chance. Sadness enveloped her.

"Here is your copy of the manumission document, Carrie, which frees your grandmother. I'll file this copy in the courthouse next week." He placed it in his wall safe.

"Thank you, Mr. Johnson." She read the single page, dated December 31, 1859: *I, Robert William Johnson, master of the Twin Oaks Planation and owner of a female slave, Olivia, about seventy years of age, declare from this day forward that she is forever free.* Robert's elegant signature and family crest seal authenticated the record.

Her hands shook as she placed the precious document in her reticule. Her eyes filled as she extracted five-hundred and sixty-five dollars. She handed the money to her grandmother's former master.

Olivia, as a skilled midwife, had garnered a price higher than most aged enslaved women.

Mr. Johnson offered his handkerchief to Carrie before he opened a wall safe behind him and inserted the bills. He closed the safe and turned toward her.

"I have something for you, too." Carrie dabbed her eyes with the handkerchief, and sniffed. She handed him one of the gift-wrapped packages.

"Why, this is unexpected, Carrie, and very thoughtful." He tore the festive paper with unabashed delight, as Carrie smiled.

A Charles Dickens novel emerged, which caused the wrinkles around his eyes to deepen with joy. "He is one of my favorite authors."

He turned the crisp pages of *A Christmas Carol.* "A first-edition, and signed, too. This gift will increase in value with time. Thank you, my dear."

"Your aunt and uncle brought home several signed copies after attending a recital of Mr. Dickens on a London stage." Her emotions gathered around her throat like a tight collar. "Mr. Johnson, I want to thank you for—for...."

"You're quite welcome, Carrie. Now, off to your grandmother. It's getting late for her, it's after ten. You must be anxious to see her and give her the good news."

"Yes, indeed. Furthermore, I look forward to spending some time with my relatives in the quarters."

"Take good care of her, and do drop me a line to let me know how she is getting on. Is there anything else I can do to make your stay more comfortable?"

Carrie paused. "Your wife's cousin, Captain Pierce—"

The color rose in Mr. Johnson's face and neck. "He has my wrath for his bombastic behavior toward you. My dear, I heard he's already left the premises. You have nothing to fear. Anything else?"

"Yes, the captain asked me if I had a pass. Mr. Johnson is one necessary?"

"Not if you're accompanied by me or any of my family members while you're away from Twin Oaks. I don't expect you'll be out alone. However, I should scribble something for you and seal it with my family crest, which names me as your guardian—just in case."

He quickly wrote the pass and handed it to Carrie.

"Oh, I nearly forgot." He turned his eyes upon the half-filled whiskey glass on his desk. His fingers began a steady drumbeat before he spoke. "Preston Johnson died several months ago—a heart attack."

Carrie's heart fluttered. *My father? My biological father?*

There came an urgent knock on the door.

A well-dressed Negro man entered. "Massa, your Aunt Betty says she has to speak to you, now."

"Excuse me, Carrie, I must see what Aunt Betty needs." Mr. Johnson rose.

"Of course, Mr. Johnson."

"We'll talk tomorrow."

~~~

"She been feelin' mighty poor." Lulu escorted Carrie through the servants' quarters of the house to her grandmother's room.

This news alarmed Carrie. Her mother was sick, and now her grandmother.

Lulu seemed to notice the concern on her face. "It's only the flu, Miss Carrie. She be all right in a week or so, Doctor say. Den she can travel."

Carrie was crestfallen.

"I thought she had a cabin in the quarters."

"No, Miss Carrie, she been in dis room ever since I can remember."

Lulu and Carrie entered the room, followed by the senator and his wife. They found Olivia asleep.

Carrie gazed at the woman, who was an ancient version of her mother. Olivia's skin was the color of a
~~~

Brazil nut. Her long, gray hair was twisted into two plaits. Carrie was astonished to see a patchwork quilt with a pattern similar to one her mother owned covering Olivia.

"We'll visit her tomorrow." Mrs. Walker spoke in a whisper.

"I'm anxious to get a taste of that holiday cake." The senator placed his hand on his wife's arm. "Can we bring you some, Carrie?"

"Don'tcha worry none 'bout Carrie, ma'am." Lulu looked at Mrs. Walker. "We going to the quarters, and dere'll be a feast."

Satisfied Carrie was content, the couple left.

"I'll bring in some soup and leave it by her bedside. She likes dat. Would you like some, too, Miss Carrie?"

"Yes, Lulu. I'm famished."

"You's what?"

"Hungry."

"I jest bring you a little. Dere be plenty at Joshua's." Lulu, mimicked high society and waved her hand, adding a bit of humor. "You can stuff yourself, right proper."

Carrie took note of the slightly used furniture as proof of Mr. Johnson's affection. There was a decorative round tin set upon the chest, along with grooming implements. A few wooden sculptures graced a wall shelf. Among them were statuettes of a royal African family, antelopes, and a few female warriors. Carrie wondered if they were her grandfather's creations alone or perhaps her grandmother created some, too.

Sarah told her they were descendants of the Fon people or Dahomey from Benin, an area noted for its mining and artisan community, often called Black Sparta because of its military society. Some believed their women warriors gave rise to the legend of the Amazons.

"Carrie is dat you?"

The young woman knelt by her grandmother's bedside. She held Olivia's rough hands in hers. "Yes, Grandmother, I'm here. I'm so happy to meet you." Carrie's eyes filled. "When you're well, I hope you'll accompany me to New York. Mother wants to see you very much. She needs your forgiveness." She swallowed hard. "Promise me—" Her voice gave way, as unexpected sobs erupted.

"I promise." Olivia answered without hesitation. "I done forgave yo' mama years ago. Now, we all be together in New York. Dere is no need to get yourself all worked up. My other chillen done died or been sold away. Alls the chillen I got livin' is you, your mama, and Mary and her family. Now, dry your eyes."

She beckoned Carrie to come closer. "Mary, Joshua, and deys chillen be taking dere freedom tomorrow."

Carrie felt the old woman's breath on her cheek.

"Mason done seed to it. She be 'way from dat ole' devil, Lucius Dayton, or should I say Lucifer Dayton."

"Lucius Dayton, the Chief Prosecutor of Richmond County?" Carrie's eyes widened.

"De one and de same."

"I see why he was surprised when he looked at me. He must have seen the family likeness."

"You seed him? He saw Mary in you. He's da cruelest, along with Cap'n Pierce. Not sure who's more dangerous. A nigga girl gone missin', a few years back.

When dey found her, she named de cap'n 'fore she died."

"What happened to him?"

"Nuttin'. Dere laws protects dem, not us. Dis is a dangerous place for colored folks. Oh, you wearin' my charm dat I brought over here from Dahomey." Olivia's voice lifted in awe as she looked at the ivory amulet with dreamy, wet eyes. She touched the talisman at Carrie's neck and closed her eyes.

"Sometimes, when I close my eyes, I can still hear de rush of de Atlantic Ocean slapping against de slave ship and feel de ocean's sway. I was just a little girl, a frightened chile, trapped in de belly of de ship. I slept in a tight space between two dead wimmen. I clasped de charm so tight my palm bled. I prayed, and I survived."

Olivia opened her eyes and smiled at her granddaughter. "You is de reward of my survival, and now you come to free me. It proves de power of dis charm." Olivia turned over the amulet in her rough hands. "I gave dis to your mama when she left for New York. My father made it for me, and the conjure man blessed it. He named the bird *Huriya*, the Arabic word for freedom. Dat's why I's alive today."

"Mother kept the charm in a locked box of mementoes she hid in a drawer of her bureau. I had never seen it before the day she gave it to me for my journey. She said the charm would protect me and liberate you from slavery. Grandmother, how did you manage to hold on to it while you traveled on the slave ship?"

"When the slavers lined us up to be examined, me and da other chillen would pass our keepsakes from one to the other." A crafty smile lit up her face. "So, when our turn came, we'd be empty-handed."

Carrie smiled.

"How is your mama?"

Since Olivia had agreed to leave Richmond, Carrie saw no need to reveal Sarah's condition. She didn't want to worry her grandmother.

"She told me about Preston. I feel like a ship at sea lost in a storm, with the wind pushing me this way and that, not sure where I can find solid ground."

"You needn't worry yourself none. We's family. We's gonna all be together, and white folks nowhere can mess dat up. When you get as old as me, you'll see family is all dat matters. Dere's a lot of things I wants you to have. De figurines and de quilts."

"Mama has a similar one." Carrie touched the quilt, smiling at the similar picture of a white bird against a blue sky, soaring above the green ocean. "The bird on the quilt reminds me of the charm."

"It's da same one. I made dem both."

"When you're well, Grandmother, we'll be flying on the wings of freedom toward home." Carrie reached for her grandmother's weathered hands and held them. "I have the most wonderful news." Carrie extracted the manumission document from her reticule. "I have bought your freedom from Mr. Johnson."

With Carrie's help, Olivia sat up and peered at the document.

"See, Grandmother? This paper says you're free." Carrie pointed to the phrase that released Olivia from slavery.

Olivia looked heavenward as her eyes filled. "Chile, I can't read, but dem words look like gold to me.

Freedom at last is mine. I prayed many years for dis day." Tears rolled down her wrinkled cheeks. Carrie put her arms around her grandmother.

The door opened, and Lulu stepped in with a young girl. She carried a tray with soup bowls and spoons and set them on a table near Olivia's bed.

The young girl bounded to the chest and opened the ornate tin.

"Put dat back, Janie." Lulu started toward the girl.

Dodging Lulu, Janie ran out of the room in a flash.

"Dat child just earned herself a whuppin'." Exasperation showed on Lulu's face.

"Would you like a piece of candy?" Olivia looked at Carrie and pointed to the tin.

"No thank you, Grandmother." Carrie walked to the chest and looked into the tin. It contained pieces of chocolate candy. Carrie picked up the card. "Who are these from, Grandmother?"

"We don't know." Lulu shook her head. "Musta been one of de ladies Olivia midwifed for. Dere's no name on de card."

Carrie wondered why the donor wished to remain anonymous. The note read: *"Good deeds earn good rewards. Happy New Year."* It was signed: *A Well-wisher.*

CHAPTER SIX
A Holiday Celebration

Olivia's eyes shone like stars as she caressed the silver-plated daguerreotype of the Bennet family.

As they chatted about the picture, Carrie saw her grandmother's eyes start to close. "I'm going to visit the quarters when Lulu returns. Get some rest now, Grandmother." She held the old woman's hands. "Happy New Year."

Olivia was asleep in minutes.

At eleven o'clock, Carrie followed Lulu to her Uncle Joshua's cabin in the slave quarters. Lulu informed her Joshua held the highest rank among the elders, who governed the enslaved community. Carrie felt a sense of pride about her uncle's prestige amongst his society. As she entered the quarters, she eyed the rows of small wooden A-frame cabins with a single chimney. Her uncle's cabin was the largest. Although plain, she admired his attempt to dress up the tidy, two-room cabin, which he shared with several men his age. Wooden vases of holly and fern sat on the rustic tables and counters. Inside, she witnessed the ecstatic salutations between Johnson's slaves and those from neighboring plantations, who arrived in wagons. A hush fell over the crowd when fair-skinned Carrie appeared.

Lulu announced, "Dis here is Aunt Olivia's granddaughter, Carrie."

Suspicious looks melted into warm smiles and handshakes.

Carrie spotted Mason with a dark-skinned man near the holiday table, laden with food. Was he her Uncle Joshua?

"How lovely you look." Mason nodded and turned to Lulu. "Thank you for bringing Carrie."

Lulu nodded and then disappeared into the crowd.

After introductions were made, Joshua looked her over. "You are your mother's twin."

"Where's Mary?"

"Mary lives on de Dayton place." A sad look crept into her uncle's eyes before he looked away.

Carrie watched him go. "It must be hard on him. He must miss her very much."

In a low voice, Mason repeated their history. "They had jumped the broom when she was fifteen and he was eighteen. Within a year, Mary had borne twin boys, who were sold on their fifth birthday. Mary and Joshua were grief-stricken. One evening, Massa Eb entertained an important visitor who wanted to purchase Mary. Unwilling to separate the family, Massa refused. However, he offered Mary to his guest as a compromise. The man was Lucius Dayton."

"At the ball, he seemed the perfect gentleman." Carrie raised her eyebrows.

"Oh, he do be dat. Another evening when Dayton spent the night, Mary was ordered to his bedroom. Joshua got all corned. He slipped into the Big House and barged into the bedroom. He stood in the doorway with clenched fists. Outraged, Massa Eb sold Mary, his own daughter, and his grandchildren to Dayton."

"What God has joined together—"

"God's left out *altogether.* The laws don't permit slaves to marry, you know. By controlling their reproduction, those who trade in human flesh can boost their economic prosperity and fracture families. Nothing can be counted on here. Plantation life is full of uncertainties."

"Mary." Joshua ran to the door.

He twirled her around, and her ash-brown tresses flew in the air. Mary's golden complexion shone in the candlelight. Once she was on her feet, the family huddled together, sobbing.

"God bless us all." Mary looked around the room. Her hazel eyes shone as she looked at the young woman standing by Mason. "You must be Carrie." Before Carrie could answer, Mary hugged her. "Dese here are my children. Li'l Joshua is five, and Matthew's eight." She kissed his head. "Dese here, are my twins. Mary and Sarah are two years-old. One is named after me and de other after your mama. We were always apart. I pray dey never be."

The boys had tan complexions, but the girls appeared fair like Carrie with blonde hair and blue eyes, sired by Dayton, Carrie guessed. Only a mole near little Mary's mouth differentiated the sisters.

Carrie enjoyed the holiday fare. It included rabbit, smoked ham, red-eye gravy, roast chicken, mixed greens, sweet 'taters roasted in ashes, ash cakes, and sweet potato pie. Some masters were generous to the enslaved during the Christmas season. They often gifted them with extra food, liquor, and small tokens.

Their usual fare was corn meal, lard, some meat and vegetables, and perhaps molasses. Some were allowed to have vegetable gardens.

Jugs of corn liquor were passed around while the musicians tuned their instruments. When Carrie heard "Silent Night," her clear, melodic soprano filled the room. Soon a multitude of voices swelled in reverent harmony.

Afterward, Mason prayed for universal emancipation.

Exuberant music ripped through the air, and the children started "cuttin' a pigeon wing" while the adults, "shook it to the east and west, and shook it to the one who they loved the best."

A crowd of young men pushed one of their friends forward, and he asked Carrie to dance. She accepted, and his friends shouted their approval.

After a time, Mason cut in. "Having fun?"

"Very much." Carrie grinned and nodded. "Mason, Grandmother Olivia is free. I have her papers in my bag. When I told her, she was so happy."

"What wonderful news. Mission accomplished. Now, I could use your help with another."

Carrie's eyes sparkled. "Grandmother told me you're aiding Mary's family in their escape."

"She promised to keep quiet." Mason frowned and then explained his strategy. He implored Carrie to request the use of a carriage for a shopping trip. He planned to conceal the fugitives inside, meet his partner, whereby the fugitives would transfer to another carriage. His partner would then drive them to a safe house. From there, they'd travel north by boat and train as servants to a white agent.

"Why on New Year's Day?" She frowned.

"Slaves are sold or hired out on New Year's Day."

"What a cruel way to begin the New Year, by separating families."

The fiddler's voice rang out. "Cake walk time."

Carrie grabbed Mason's hand and got in line.

The dance was popular among people of color in the north and south. Sarah told Carrie the "cake walk" started as a ridicule of whites dancing the minuet. Slaves added steps as the dance circled the plantations until a unique dance style developed.

Carrie and Mason won a cake, but the top prize went to Joshua and Mary. Exhausted, Mary dropped into a chair.

"You and Joshua are excellent dancers." Carrie grinned.

"We been dancing long enuf. We win every year, but for '53. Dat's when Celia and her partner done beat us."

"Celia?"

"Yeah. She da one dey hung back in '55. Kilt her massa. Tired of having to give in all de time. Her ol' Massa Newsome brought her to Virginia from Missouri when he visited ol' man Dayton. The poor chile had a bad time of it. She was only seventeen and pregnant when we met her."

"Ah." Carrie leaned back when an old woman stuck her head between them.

"Ole Jessup be walkin' through tonight." The woman's eyes blazed. "Be raining hard. He gonna wash dem sins away." Her face was inches from Carrie's. "Stay in yo bed *tonight.*"

The woman moved away from Carrie and Mary. As she walked across the room, the crowd parted, their eyes riveted to her crooked form as she delivered her warnings.

Mary's eyes stretched in fear at the old woman's words. "Dat's the conjure woman. She da one born in Africa and brings us word of de African spirits. Best listen to her warnings, Carrie. Stay in yo' bed tonight. I'm gonna do what she say."

Mason walked over to Carrie. "I promised Mrs. Walker, I'd bring you back to the ball to toast the New Year. The clock will strike midnight in ten minutes."

~~~

As servants circled with trays of champagne glasses, Mr. Johnson tapped a spoon against his for silence. The case clock in the corner read a quarter to midnight. "Let us lift our glasses to toast the New Year with family and friends. Another year has passed. Some of us have gotten richer. Some of us have gotten fatter." This elicited much laughter. "Some of us have new additions to our families, and some of us have experienced loss. May God bring us all good health and fortune in the New Year."

"May I?" Cole addressed Robert, who nodded.

Cole raised his glass. "To Robert and Susan Johnson, the finest couple in all of Virginia, who so generously invite us, the mudsill of Richmond—"

Laughter echoed.

"—to their beautiful home, year after year. May they enjoy health and happiness in the New Year."

"Aye, aye." The guests raised their glasses.

Twelve chimes rang.
~~~

"Happy New Year," resounded throughout the room.

Carrie laughed. She wondered if the young man who gave the toast was the same pirate who'd stood under her chamber window. She clicked glasses with the senator and Mrs. Walker and they wished one another Happy New Year.

~~~

Carrie stood in her backyard. A perfect blue sky canopied the sun-drenched garden. The green leaves and colorful flowers glistened. The "Wedding March" began, and Jonathan appeared. Arm in arm, they walked along the bridal path, festooned with pink and white roses. Their sweet fragrance filled the air.

She could see the groom, but the glare from the sunlight blocked his face. She adored her white bridal gown. Its lacy bodice and crinoline skirt flowed to her toes, and it dazzled in the sunlight.

Oh no. What's happening?

As she moved forward, the gown transformed. It changed from white to ivory to pale gray to dark gray to black. Spots appeared on her shoes. Blood drops. Looking backward, she saw a trail of blood, and ice ran through her veins.

Boom. Boom. Thunder exploded like cannonballs firing in the sky.

Carrie sat straight up in bed. *The dream, what did it mean?* She looked out the window into the night. Lightning flashed. Rain flecked the window panes.

"Ole Jessup be walkin' through tonight." Jessup, Mary explained was a powerful African rain spirit, who
~~~

washed sins away with his hard-driving rain, sometimes flooding whole villages.

Someone knocked on the door. She heard the clock downstairs chime. Tired from the busy day, she had retired shortly after midnight. She had fallen asleep immediately, but felt as though she hadn't gotten much rest.

Frightened, Carrie donned her dressing gown and beheld a slave boy outside her door. "What are you doing here at this hour?"

The small boy rubbed his eyes and then thrust a piece of paper at Carrie. "I'm s'pose to give you dis." The child turned and disappeared down the hall.

She read the bold scrawl: *I need help tonight. Meet me in the barn, now. Mason.*

Is it time to transport slaves on the Underground Railroad?

Carrie was eager to answer the call to freedom.

She threw her winter frock over her shift, donned her dark cloak, and put on high-button boots. Slipping out the side door, she darted to the barn. The rain quickened its pace as a gnawing question loomed.

Was there a change of plans?

Carrie opened the creaking door and stepped inside. The sudden pungent odor of horses and sweet-smelling hay assailed her nostrils. Languid footsteps across the floor planted the seed of suspicion.

"Mason. It's me, Carrie."

"Over here." A masculine voice came from a figure across the room. She could barely distinguish a man in the darkness. The rough scratch of a match echoed, and the scent of sulfur permeated the air. A small flare grew from the kerosene lamp, which hung from a post behind him.

Her heart stopped.

This man wasn't Mason. Blond hair fringed the collar of his uniform. A blurry white hand extinguished the match as her worst fears were confirmed.

Captain John Pierce had set this trap for her, and she had come running.

Thunder cracked, ripping the clouds open. Torrential rain beat its frenzied dance upon the roof. Carrie sprang for the door and swung it open. The rain came down in a sheet and rendered her sightless. Strong hands forced the door shut. Chilled to the bone, her teeth chattered.

"It's nice of you to meet me on such short notice, Miss Bennet."

As she retreated, he advanced. His back, straight as a flagpole, and his measured footsteps attested to his military discipline.

"How d—dare you send me this false note, Captain Pierce?" She brandished the note and thrust it back into her pocket.

"Still the feisty quadroon I fell in love with at the ball. We can get better acquainted. 'Sides, a southern gentleman would never let a lady go unescorted in this weather. My sweet, you've given me the proof I've needed." A sudden maniacal laugh burst from his throat.

Fear oozed from her pores. As she backed away, her backside grazed the handle of a scythe sitting on a table. *Proof? Of course, by coming to the barn, I have identified Mason as an agent of the Underground*

Railroad. If caught, he could be flogged, maimed, sold or worse—burned alive.

"The planters in the area are furious about the theft of their property. I've always suspected Mason, and you have just confirmed my suspicions. Never fear, my sweet, I shall keep secret what a ready, able, and *lovely* accomplice you've been. I'm sure you can find a way to reward me for my loyalty."

Without preamble, Carrie snatched the scythe and hurled it at his head. The captain ducked. As stealthy as a cobra, he pounced.

She dodged him and ran across the barn, throwing the lamp from its post unto a small mound of hay.

"You little fool." Captain Pierce cursed.

He grabbed a water bucket and doused the flames. Frightened, the horses reared up as the barn door banged shut.

Carrie ran toward the manor as lightning guided her steps. *"Stay in yo bed tonight."* The conjure woman had been right after all. As she rushed through the storm, her wet cloak flapped in the wind. Its soggy hem twisted around her ankles. She fell.

Struggling to stand, Carrie felt strong hands lift her. Captain Pierce flung her across his shoulder and continued toward the house. The rain lessened its onslaught.

The captain has come to his senses.

Once they reached the huge oak trees, the captain set Carrie on her feet. She turned toward the manor, but he grabbed her and punched her in the stomach. He dragged her under the oaks.

Captain Pierce pushed her face-down to the ground. She yelled for him to stop, but the howling wind swallowed her cries. He leaned on her back, pulled up her skirt and ripped her pantaloons.

"Noooo. Please. Don't." She cried as loud as she could.

"You're in my territory now, *free woman,* where I can exercise my rights as your master. How dare you deny me, as if you were white?" With difficulty, he thrust himself inside of her, claiming her virginity.

Pain exploded between her legs.

The deafening rain, like an accomplice, smothered her screams.

After he climaxed, he flung her over on her back. The shock of the rape paralyzed her. She stared at the branches overhead. Interlaced like fingers, they reminded Carrie of a steeple. His fingers flew to unfasten her cloak. The soldier clutched her bodice and ripped it down past her breast. She felt the ribbon around her neck snap. The pelting rain on her skin, called her back to life. "Don't."

"I'm not through with you yet, goddammit."

He clamped a nipple between his teeth, shooting needles of pain through her breast. She pulled out a fistful of yellow hair.

"Ow." The captain slapped her, and the vicious blow galvanized her into action.

Her fingers roamed the earth and grasped a sturdy stick. Gripping it like a knife, she aimed at his back. He raised his head, and in one motion she drove the sharp stick into his left eye. As he rolled off her, high-pitched screams tore from his throat. She spied her ivory bird gleaming in the moonlight and grabbed it. A spasm seized him, while Carrie scrambled to her feet.

She pushed the front door open and almost collided with Lulu.

"Carrie is dat you?"

"Lulu, the captain knows about the Underground Railroad. Tell Mason to run now."

Carrie rushed toward the study.

Lulu's eyes grew wide at the sight of blood drops trailing Carrie down the hallway.

Jovial voices floated from the study. Carrie dashed through the door and beheld the mistress and master of Twin Oaks. She framed them in her memory like an old photograph to mark a time before the impending scandal and grief altered their lives.

She knew she must look like an apparition. She arrived like a storm upending a perfect day. Her rain-soaked garments clung to her body and dripped on the carpet. Her cloak was caked with mud. Her leather boots were drawn and wrinkled like aged skin.

She moved farther into the room where they could see her face. She heard them stammer, shriek, and cry out.

Her hair clung to her cheeks in spidery strands. She felt the skin around her eyes swell. Her right cheek burned with the blow from the captain's hand. She gripped the bird of freedom in the pocket of her cloak.

"Miss Bennet, What the devil? What's happened? Where were you?" Master Johnson grabbed her by the shoulders and searched her face for an explanation.

"In the b—barn—under the oak trees." She stammered.

The tempest outside his window had followed her inside.

CHAPTER SEVEN
The Inquest

She sobbed. “He—attacked me. I—I—I struck him.”

“Where is Pierce?”

“Under the oak trees. His eye—”

Stevens jumped up from his seat. “I’ll accompany you, Robert.”

Mrs. Johnson stumbled behind her husband. Everyone left, except Mrs. Walker, who led Carrie to the sofa. “Oh, my child, what happened? Your face—”

Heavy footsteps approached, no longer hurried, yet ominous. Fear ran through Carrie like fire devouring a dry field.

The men entered, their faces, white, solemn, accusing. Eyes wide with horror stared at Carrie.

“He’s dead.” Mr. Johnson’s soft words had the effect of a shotgun blast.

She felt her face drain of its color, and then she cocked her head to one side. “He can’t be. He was alive when I left him.”

“You killed him.” Stevens held a thick, blood-stained stick in his hand. A din of accusations assaulted her.

“Quiet.” A voice exploded and silence ensued. The Chief Prosecuting Attorney of Richmond County, Lucius Dayton, assumed his official demeanor. “We must conduct an inquest. According to Robert, this young lady is Aunt Olivia's granddaughter."

"What?" Francis Weatherspoon's jowls shook. "I thought she was white. She's a...?"

"It's true. I am." Carrie's eyes darted from one accuser to another. She bit her bottom lip.

Why should I feel responsible when others mistake me for white? But, she had always felt she was somehow at fault.

"Had that not been the case, none of this would have happened. He raped me because he knew no law would hold him accountable."

Susan Johnson rushed at Carrie with her fingernails raised like claws. Her bloodshot eyes stared out from a red, swollen face.

Robert grabbed his wife by the waist and lifted her feet off the floor. She raged like a tigress, clawing the air between herself and Carrie. "You killed my cousin, and I'll see you hang."

Dr. Ashley hurried to Mr. Johnson's aid. "May I give her a sedative?"

"Yes."

"Someone, please bring my doctor's bag. It's in the closet."

The two struggled as they forced the hysterical woman upstairs. Jeffrey retrieved the medical bag and climbed the stairs, two at a time.

"An inquest? At this hour?" Mrs. Walker looked aghast, as she responded to Dayton's suggestion. "It's after one in the morning."

The prosecutor looked around. "The sheriff and coroner are present, as well as two justices, and our chief witness. Stevens, you've examined the body.

Sheriff Coffe, you've already examined the crime scene."

"There has been no crime." Mrs. Walker put an arm around Carrie to comfort her.

Bowles hurried down the stairs.

"We don't know what happened for sure." Mr. Dayton turned to Carrie. "You can testify, and the experts will state the facts. Do we have a quorum?"

Wilson, Weatherspoon, Bowles, Sellers, Stevens, and Cartwright affirmed aloud.

Justice Cartwright stood. "I'll serve as judge."

Dr. Ashley and Mr. Johnson returned.

Robert Johnson looked around. "What's going on?"

"Lucius suggested we conduct a formal inquest," Dr. Stevens explained.

"Is it necessary?"

Justice Cartwright nodded. "We'll get to the truth. First, there must be a written affidavit."

"All right, I'll see to it." Mr. Johnson walked to the secretary.

Lucius Dayton addressed Carrie. "You've alleged Captain Pierce attacked you. We must first verify your accusation."

"I'll examine her." Dr. Ashley walked toward Carrie and put a hand on her arm.

"Thank you." Carrie was grateful the doctor was a woman.

"Very well, get on with it while we get the papers in order."

Mrs. Walker turned to the doctor. "I'd like to accompany her, if there's no objection."

Dr. Ashley nodded.

The women climbed the stairs to Mrs. Walker's bedchamber.

"Don't change your clothes, yet," Sheriff Benjamin Coffe called after them. "They're evidence."

"They don't believe I've been raped," Carrie whispered to Mrs. Walker.

"Don't worry, Carrie, this is just a formality. Once there's proof you were attacked, this should end." Dr. Ashley opened the door.

~~~~

A short time later, everyone reassembled. Justice Cartwright read the affidavit, while Justice Sellers took notes for the official record.

> *I am requesting a formal inquest be conducted to investigate the circumstances surrounding my cousin's death. The chief witness, Carrie Bennet, a free Negro woman, was in the company of Captain John Pierce before his demise.*
>
> *Robert Johnson, Master of Twin Oaks Plantation,*
> *Richmond, Virginia, in the Year of Our Lord,*
> *January First, Eighteen Hundred and Sixty.*

A chair was placed in the center of the room. Everyone looked solemn, except for Bowles. He smiled, and then covered his mouth with his hand. Carrie guessed he was happy to watch his idol, Lucius Dayton, practice law.

The coroner took the oath first. Edward Stevens, still dressed as a woman, presented a surreal contrast to the solemn proceedings.

Lucius Dayton stepped toward him. "Dr. Stevens, please describe the deceased's injuries."

"The captain suffered a stab wound to the left eye. Had he lived, he would have been blind."
~~~~

"Is this the weapon used?" Dayton held up the blood-stained branch with contempt.

"Yes, it is. When I first saw the body, he was lying on his back. His head rested upon a rock. Blood trickled from his head, and the bloody stick lay by his left side."

"Is it possible to tell whether he fell or was pushed down?" Lucius Dayton continued his inquiry.

Stevens shook his head. "It's impossible to determine."

"So, a man in the throes of severe pain could have been pushed back with force by someone as petite as Carrie Bennet, which could have caused him to strike his head. Or she could have struck him with the rock and then positioned his head in such a way as to make it appear he had fallen upon the rock?"

"It could have happened either way." Stevens nodded.

"Dr. Stevens, do you know which injury caused his death?"

"The head injury from the rock. I've seen people with arrows or knives stuck in their eyes, and they survived. I'm going to have to ask for your indulgence." He snatched the wig off his head. A chorus of laughter rose. "This contraption is hot."

"I have no further questions of this witness." Dayton turned his back on the doctor.

Carrie stood up and asked Judge Cartwright if she could question the witness.

Dayton objected, but the judge acquiesced.

"Dr. Stevens, please describe the state of his attire."

The doctor hesitated for a moment. "Pierce's clothes were muddy and in disarray."

“Were his pants buttoned or unbuttoned?”

“Unbuttoned.”

“Yes, they were unbuttoned. There was no reason for his pants to have been unbuttoned, but they were, because he raped me.”

“He could have been taking a piss.” Dr. Stevens glared at her.

His response drew laughter.

“In a thunderstorm?”

“Certainly.”

Crestfallen, Carrie returned to her seat with her head bowed.

Mrs. Walker put a protective arm around her shoulders as Dr. Stevens vacated the witness chair.

“Dr. Carolyn Ashley, please take the witness chair.” Justice Cartwright administered the oath and held out a hand toward the chair.

“Dr. Ashley, what was the result of your examination of Carrie Bennet?” Dayton peered at her.

“I examined Miss Bennet, and I can confirm she was raped and she appeared to have been a virgin.”

“How did you determine she may have been a virgin?”

Dr. Ashley raised an eyebrow. “Mr. Prosecutor, I wasn’t aware you had a medical degree.”

Dayton shot her an angry scowl.

“I know a rape when I’ve seen one, having examined other rape victims. Carrie’s injuries are consistent with forced intercourse. She has lacerations in her private area, where she is bruised and swollen. Considerable blood is present. He was brutal.”

“Strike that last sentence from the record, Sellers,” Dayton bellowed. “It’s prejudicial to the deceased.”

Dr. Ashley challenged Dayton's motion, but Cartwright ruled in her favor.

Dayton flashed Cartwright a nasty look and then turned to the witness. "You've testified that you've examined women who've cried rape before. Afterward, what was their emotional state?"

"They were angry, humiliated, frightened, filled with shame, and sometimes, self-loathing."

Dayton hammered on. "How about revenge?"

Dr. Ashley said some had felt vengeful, but only one had acted on her feelings, the nineteen-year-old slave, Celia. "In 1855, she was convicted of first-degree murder in the death of her master."

Dayton asked her to describe the crime.

"She struck him on the head with a blunt object, cut his body in pieces, and burned the remains in her hearth. She had borne him two children and was pregnant with the third when she slew him. You're acquainted with the details better than I since you were the prosecutor, Mr. Dayton."

He grinned.

"Dr. Ashley, did Carrie mention the inquest while in your presence?"

Dr. Ashley nodded. "Carrie feared her accusation of rape wouldn't be believed."

"That will be all, Dr. Ashley."

Dayton turned to Carrie and called her to replace the doctor in the witness chair.

Carrie rose from her seat as if in a trance. She repeated the oath and sat down.

"Carrie Bennet, what was your state of mind when you stabbed Captain Pierce?"

"I was in shock. I was in pain. He had raped me and said he wasn't through." She shook at the memory. Her hand went into her pocket and clasped the ivory amulet.

"Will you please describe the details of the attack?" Dayton gave her a hard look.

"He ripped my clothes, raped me, and then said, 'I'm not finished with you yet.' I kept pleading with him to let me go. I yanked his hair, and he slapped me—" She took a deep breath. "So, I searched the ground for something to strike him with. My hand touched a stick. I intended to jab at his back, hoping he'd release me, but he raised his head, and I stabbed him in the eye instead. He screamed and rolled off me. I ran into the house. I didn't know he was dead until Mr. Johnson told me. I didn't see him fall, and I didn't push him. I ran in here to tell Mr. Johnson."

"Why would you do that?" Lucius Dayton raised an eyebrow.

"I wanted to tell Mr. Johnson what had happened. Captain Pierce made an indecent proposal to me at the ball. Mr. Johnson seemed concerned for my welfare. I understood it to mean he was offering me protection while I was in his home."

"When Captain Pierce attacked you, did you feel your life was in danger at any time?" Dayton paced before her.

Did he mean I had no right to protect myself, short of the threat of death? "I had a right to defend myself against rape. How could I know whether he meant to kill me afterward or not? Dr. Ashley proved I was assaulted. It was natural for me to defend myself. You imply that by doing so, I've committed a crime."

"Oh, but you're mistaken, Carrie. Captain Pierce, if he did force himself on you, committed a trespass, not a crime."

"A trespass? But rape is a crime." Carrie stared at Dayton.

"Only if the woman is white. You see, our laws do not recognize the legal status of a free Negro woman. In the eyes of the law, all Negro women are presumed to be slaves. Thus, if rape occurs, it is a trespass against the property rights of her master."

"So, where does this leave me? I have no master. I am no slave."

Carrie's eyes traveled past the fireplace and then rested on the wallpaper. The fire crackled. Its flickering light danced between the shadows cast upon the hunting party. Carrie could almost hear the pounding of the horses' hooves as they chased the red fox. For a moment, she was transfixed.

"Be that as it may, for a woman of color, slave or free, in common law, there is no middle ground. Your actions led to the death of a decorated hero in our community. When you came here tonight, you told Robert Johnson you struck Pierce. You confessed you struck him with the rock. People blurt out the truth when they are under duress and have no time to concoct a story to hide their guilt."

"No, I struck him in the eye with the stick." She clutched her skirt.

"But the correct word is stabbed." Dayton looked amused. "You stabbed him with the stick. It would be natural to use the word stabbed instead of struck."

Carrie repeated when she used the word struck, she meant she had stabbed him with the stick.

"Would an articulate woman, such as yourself make this mistake? I think not. When speaking about injuring a person with a rock, it would be natural to use the word struck. So, I contend, you stabbed him with the stick and struck him with the rock. Isn't this true?"

"No. It is not true."

"Where did you say you were attacked when you first entered this room?"

Please don't ask me.

Dayton reminded the witness. "And I quote, 'in the barn.' This encounter started in the barn."

"It was not an encounter."

"Miss Bennet, for once, we agree on something." Dayton's face was inches from hers. "It was not an encounter. The word would mean you met him by chance. But it was pre-arranged." He stood up and walked away. "Why were you in the barn?" He pivoted, faced her again and yelled. "Why did you meet the captain in the wee hours of the morning in the barn?"

Carrie dropped her gaze to her lap and wrung her hands.

"I submit you went to the barn to meet him for a tryst. It got out of hand. You ran. He had his way with you. Being a prideful, educated, *free* woman, you sought revenge and stabbed him in the eye. He was at your mercy. Your lust for revenge still unsatisfied, you struck him on the back of the head with the rock and arranged his dead body to corroborate your story. Aren't those the facts, *Miss Bennet?"*

"No. His death was an accident. If I had intended to kill him, why would I have run here? I would have gone into hiding."

"You came to plead your case to kind-hearted Robert Johnson in the hope he would explain away your guilt to the authorities. You ran to Mr. Johnson to save yourself, not Pierce. Otherwise, you'd be on the run with the hounds and the law snapping at your heels." He stood ramrod straight. He gave her a wide grin.

Carrie asked the judge if she could speak. Judge Cartwright nodded.

She stood before the others and implored them to believe her words. Her intention was not to kill Pierce but to end his assault. She left him alive. She surmised he must have risen and fallen upon the rock after she stabbed him in the eye. No other explanation was plausible.

Dayton applauded her summation. "Answer one simple question. Why did you meet Captain John Pierce in the barn?"

Carrie couldn't explain without the Underground Railroad being exposed. Her silence felt like an anchor, weighing her down with guilt. Carrie pulled her cloak tighter around her body.

Bam.

Lucius Dayton slammed his hand on the desk, and Carrie jumped. "Why were you in the barn, Carrie Bennet, a tryst gone awry?"

"That's not how it happened."

"Then inform us."

"I have a right to defend myself against rape." Carrie held her ground. Her eyes fell upon the blurred red fox. *Run, run, run for your life.*

Justice Cartwright waited for Carrie to answer. When she didn't, he shook his head. "I think we have heard enough to come to a conclusion. Does anyone have any more questions for this witness?"

The room was silent.

"Carrie, wait outside the door until we summon you." He turned toward the jurors. "Gentlemen...."

CHAPTER EIGHT
Carrie's Fate

The scrapbook, which contained the article about Celia, lay on the table. The door opened, and Sellers summoned her.

Carrie walked on heavy legs. She spied the red cloak inside the open closet door. *Red was the color of blood, the color of passion, the color of freedom.*

Justice Cartwright announced their decision to bind her over for trial.

Carrie's legs buckled and she slumped against Mrs. Walker, who led her to a chair. Coffe informed her she'd be arrested.

"A trial?" She screeched. "I was protecting myself."

Dayton reminded her she could defend herself at trial. If she needed one, he could appoint an attorney.

Carrie informed him she could hire her own counsel. She asked Cartwright her fate, if convicted.

"Murder carries the death penalty."

Dayton's eyes gleamed as he provided an alternative. "Or, you could be sentenced to a life of slavery."

A death sentence would be a blessing. Carrie remembered the words of Supreme Court Chief Justice Taney at the Dred Scott trial. *A Negro man 'had no rights that a white man was bound to respect.' Well a Negro woman had even fewer.*

"The poor dear's in shock." Mrs. Walker patted her hand. "May I accompany her upstairs to help her change her clothing?"

The sheriff nodded.

~~~

Dayton looked away from Doctor Ashley, who decried the outcome of the inquest. He looked around and noted the rest of the men avoided her stare—all but Robert.

The doctor frowned at Dayton. "This isn't over yet. I'm not surprised Robert voted in Miss Bennet's favor. I certainly would have done the same had I been allowed to have a say."

The doctor sighed. "Robert, may I have some apple pie for my husband? He'll swear it'll cure what ails him."

Mr. Johnson nodded and escorted her to the kitchen pantry where the baked goods were stored.

Wilson and Weatherspoon said their goodbyes.

"A damn shame about Pierce." Dr. Stevens shook his head.

"You know he was quite a devil with women. Remember the Gwendolyn Mathers scandal in '58?" Dayton laughed, as he poured drinks. "It was rumored she left town in the family way by Pierce. Susan Johnson managed to arrange a hasty marriage." He handed out drinks, and then sat down in an armchair.

A door closed, followed by the sound of horses moving away from the house. "There goes Dr. Ashley's carriage." Bowles glanced out the window, but it was too dark to see much. "How could she leave without saying goodbye?"
~~~

"She's a Yankee. Never met one yet who had any manners." Stevens lit his cigarillo, and sat in an overstuffed chair. "The real crime would be to waste a fine piece of feminine flesh by hanging the Bennet gal."

Dayton nodded. "She'd pull a handsome price on the Fancy Girl market. Some old gentleman would love to keep her in frills and lace."

Fifteen minutes lapsed. The sheriff finished his drink and started pacing. The clock in the hall struck a few minutes after two.

"Women always fuss over their looks. Don't be impatient. Sit down." Sellers smiled.

Bowles left the room but returned in a moment. "My scrapbook is gone." He glanced around the room and shrugged. "No worries. I'll check tomorrow," he said on the way out, bidding the men goodnight.

Mrs. Walker looked befuddled as she entered the study. "Has anyone seen Carrie?"

"What the devil do you mean?" The sheriff turned to her.

"We were in my room. When I awoke, she was gone."

"When you awoke?" Dayton leapt up.

"We prayed, and I dozed off. I thought she came down on her own."

"Benjamin, you left *her* in charge of the prisoner."

"I didn't think she'd run off. She's ignorant of these parts and scared as a rabbit." The sheriff sounded uncertain.

"You *didn't* think." Dayton started for the hall.

"What's going on?" Dr. Ashley entered holding a cloth-covered basket. Mr. Johnson followed.

"How long must I wait for your man to fetch my carriage, Robert?" The doctor walked to the hall closet. "Where's my cloak? I'm sure it was here."

The men froze.

"A scared rabbit, eh? More like a fox." Dayton frowned. "The little fox has run—in Carolyn's carriage, and draped in her red cloak."

~~~

Euphoria surged through Carrie as the carriage flew from Twin Oaks. Goose flesh spread across her arms.

In the eyes of the law, rape isn't a crime where I'm concerned.

She hugged Bowles' scrapbook to her chest and felt a kinship with Celia. Overnight, she had become a fugitive *and* a thief. Stuart West might be her salvation. True, he had lost Celia's case, but how many abolitionist lawyers lived in Richmond?

When the carriage reached Dr. Ashley's home, Carrie decided to bribe a servant to find out where Mr. West lived. She was glad she had brought her reticule. The coachman extended his hand, and she alighted from the carriage, her face shielded by the hood of the cloak. He didn't know her identity, so he couldn't be implicated.

"Carrie."

Startled, she looked up and beheld a familiar astonished face. She clasped his hands.

"Oh, Mason." She sobbed. "How did you know it was me?"

"I noticed how the cloak swept the ground. Dr. Ashley's taller."

"I've gotten you in trouble."
~~~

"How was I to know it was you in the doctor's carriage? Is what I'll say. Her driver took ill, so I volunteered to drive her home. He will spend the night in the quarters at Twin Oaks. I'll say I never saw your face. I dropped you off, settled the horses to the barn and returned to Twin Oaks on my own horse, Blaze, who was tethered behind the carriage."

Carrie became aware of the horse, who stood behind the carriage. She quickly described her situation.

"Where will you hide?"

"I'm going to convince Mr. West to defend me."

Mason stared at her. "The law to protect you has yet to be written."

"I'll retain Mr. West and turn myself in. If I run, I'll look guilty and shame my family."

"You could die for your principles, Miss Bennet." Mason's eyes widened with incredulity.

"I won't run." She sighed.

He gave her directions to the Wild Valley Ranch. Mason saddled one of the horses in the doctor's barn and advised her to ride beside the road, but to stay in the woods for cover. "When you get to West's house, slap the horse's behind, and she'll head home."

"Henry, since I'll see Mr. West, I don't need Bowle's scrapbook. Please take it back to Twin Oaks."

~ ~ ~

Early the next morning, Carrie awoke and rose from her straw bed in the loft of the barn. Before she fell asleep, she discovered a childhood phobia had returned to haunt her. She was once again afraid of the dark.

Men's voices intruded upon her thoughts. She looked out of the small window of the loft. Fear clutched her as she noticed the lawmen's shiny badges in the sunlight. She recognized Sheriff Coffe. The night before, her frantic knocks had gone unanswered, so she had found refuge in West's barn. Her reticule lay beside her in the hayloft. The sheriff was talking to a man. She surmised from his dress the fellow was a ranch hand. Their conversation drifted her way.

"What does she look like?" The ranch hand's baritone boomed across the field.

"Some say she can pass for white, a brunette."

"Here's a sketch of her." One of the lawmen passed the ranch hand a paper. "Those are the prettiest lips I've ever seen. They look like a bow. She's busty and right pretty, too."

"Shut yo' mouth, Larson."

"It's what you done told me."

Please don't search the barn.

She ducked when she saw one of the lawmen look toward the barn. Soon, she heard the horses' hooves grow faint and sighed. Carrie peeked out the window again. She saw the ranch hand turn toward the barn, and her heart pounded. Even from a distance, Carrie could see he was handsome.

Bigger than Pierce, she feared the consequences if he discovered her. She swung the cloak over her shoulders. Carrie slipped the reticule over her wrists and climbed down from the loft. She spied a bucket of water. Near the door were shelves laden with tools. The nail at the end of one shelf was loose.

Carrie formed a plan.

He entered the barn, spotted her, and froze in his tracks. His hypnotic blue-green eyes flashed with danger under dark dramatic brows. His strong build sent fear through her body.

She grabbed the pail.

Realization came too late. He jumped backward to dodge the freezing water and fell against the shelves, which came crashing down. He was buried beneath.

He didn't move, and she ran.

The door to the house was unlocked. She walked through the first floor and called for Mr. West, but no one answered. The rich furnishings stunned her. In the parlor, an ornate case clock read fifteen minutes after six. Heavy gold frames held oversized canvases. Vibrant shades of red, green, and gold brought the landscapes of the American frontier to life. Carrie recognized the works of Bierstadt, Cole, and Moran.

The aroma of baking bread called her to the kitchen. There, she found a dish of creamy butter and a covered bowl, which contained about a dozen biscuits. A glass of water stood on the counter. She grabbed a biscuit, buttered it, and stuffed it in her mouth. She savored the next buttered biscuit before she gulped down a few sips of water. Some spilled down her chin.

Upstairs, she found a dozen bedrooms. A door in the middle of the hallway led to a staircase.

"Mr. West?" When no answer came, she climbed the stairs.

She stepped into a rectangular foyer which had been converted into an office. Law books lined built-in shelves. She was awed by a series of articles framed on the wall, above the secretary, most about Celia's case.

In addition to the one authored by Dayton, several were from various publications and written by Stuart West.

The door at the end of the foyer opened into a luxurious bedroom. She recognized a Chippendale chair and ottoman next to the bed. The four-poster canopy was framed by transparent curtains of golden green, which dominated the room. Inside, a matching silk comforter, swollen with down, tempted her to lie down and wrap herself in luxury. A gilded mirror adorned one wall from ceiling to floor. She turned to avoid it.

Carrie was thrilled to discover the modern water closet with an indoor commode. The built-in tub, filled with warm water, beckoned to her.

On the dresser lay a silver vanity set and perfume bottles. Four beautiful crystal cherubs adorned the dresser. Carrie studied several silver-framed daguerreotypes on the wall. A wedding portrait showed a white groom and Native American bride in traditional attire. Another one depicted the couple holding a chubby-cheeked boy with his father's complexion. Carrie surmised the man, who looked to be about forty, was Stuart West.

Carrie peeked at her reflection in the mirror. Her appearance shocked her. Little wonder the ranch hand was speechless when he saw her. Mud streaked her clothes and hair. Her leather boots were ruined—like her. Even Frank wouldn't marry her now.

The room held two armoires. One contained women's apparel. She grabbed a tan shirt and threw it on a nearby chair. She peeled off her clothing. She discarded the cloak and frock and finally the shift. She threw it across the room. Captain Pierce's scent still clung to it.

Standing bare-breasted before the mirror, she examined herself. The imprints of the captain's fingerprints had turned a purplish-blue on her cheek. Dried blood settled into the corner of her torn mouth. Bruises smudged her back and chest. Her left nipple was still tender from the captain's bite. Anguish filled her at the sight of her torn pantaloons smeared with her virgin blood.

The door banged against the wall. The bold ranch hand stood in the doorway with clenched fists. Blood trickled down his face. His piercing turquoise glare struck fear in Carrie's heart.

She covered her nipples with her arm, and then flung an angel at him.

He caught it in midair and returned it to the dresser. A perfume bottle sailed at his head before she scrambled across the bed to get to the door. Again, he caught the object and set it on the dresser.

Within seconds, he pounced on the bed, throwing her on her back, pinning her under his weight. His hands wrapped around her wrists like a steel vise. He held them above her head.

She screamed. "Get off me."

"How dare you ambush *me* when I was going to help you?" His angry face reddened, and then his eyes traveled downward and fastened onto her breast. His jaw dropped and his arousal pushed against her thighs.

Carrie thrashed around as his ragged breath warmed her face. She struggled to free herself. Sobs erupted from her throat. "Get off."

He jumped up with lightning speed and sat on the edge of the bed with his back to her. Carrie rose and sat on the bed with her back to him. She'd folded her arms across her chest.

He let me go.

"You have no reason to fear me. I'm an agent of the Underground Railroad, for land sakes." Then his voice dropped to a whisper. "*She doth teach the torches to burn bright.*"

"What did you say?"

"I'm not the enemy. I'm going to help you."

She exhaled a labored sigh. "I should have awakened Mrs. Walker and asked her to come to the barn with me. Perhaps he wouldn't have attacked me. I should have chased down the slave child to find out who had given him the note which summoned me to the barn, but all I thought about was helping my poor enslaved kin."

"Miss Bennet, what happened to you was not your fault."

The man's words flooded her with relief. She hadn't realized how much she had blamed herself.

"I'm sorry about what happened to you. I knew Captain Pierce, and I have no doubt he abused you."

"He did more than abuse me. He raped me."

"I didn't mean—but the law would overlook what happened."

"I was a virgin." She sobbed again.

"I'm sorry. Was it premeditated?"

"What?"

"The attack, did he plan to meet you alone?"

She nodded. "Yes, and I fell right into his trap."

Cole stood, picked up the shirt from the chair and placed it around her shoulders. He grabbed a skirt from the armoire and handed it to her. Then he turned his back.

Carrie dressed herself. “Why does a ranch hand have the run of the house?”

He laughed. “I'm the owner.”

“You're too young to be Stuart West.”

“You're right. I'm his son, Cole.”

“Oh. I'm sorry I ambushed you.”

“...and left me for dead.”

“...and left you for—no, I didn't think you were dead. I was afraid, I thought—”

“I know what you thought. No harm will ever come to a fugitive, slave or free, who comes here. Didn't you see The Faithful Groom, the statue outside? When the groom's lantern is lit, it's safe to seek refuge.”

She told him she hadn't noticed. “You can turn around now.”

He chuckled and rubbed his head. “You got me good, making that stuff fall on me. I was just about to fix the shelf this morning. You should put some salve on your bruises. I'll get it for you.”

He started for the bathroom and then swayed.

She rushed to him and grabbed his arm. “You'd better lie down and let me help you. Your head wound is bleeding.”

He sat on the bed. She felt a wave of guilt when she saw the open wound. “Mr. West, it's worse than I thought.”

He chuckled. “I'll live. Please, call me Cole.”

“But we've just met.”

"Under the circumstances—" He extended his hand, "It's nice to meet you, Miss Bennet."

She hesitated, and then grasped his hand. She felt reassuring warmth from the gentle handshake.

"You may likewise call me Carrie." She took off his boots, and he swung his legs onto the bed and lay back. She found first aid products on a bathroom shelf.

As she leaned over him to dress his wound, she realized his lips were inches from her chest. She moved back, glanced down, and saw a sheepish grin on his face. She blushed. She assumed he was imagining her breast beneath the shirt. After all, he *had* seen her nearly naked.

"I noticed the tub filled with bath water."

"I prepared a bath for your arrival, m'lady." He waved his hand toward the bathroom with a theatrical flourish.

Carrie looked puzzled.

"The bath was mine, of course, but now that you've arrived, my unexpected guest, you're welcome to it."

Carrie thanked him. "After I get cleaned up, will you take me to see your father?"

He looked away, took a deep breath, and stared at the wall. His attitude puzzled her.

"Listen, I *must* see him."

"Well you can't," he snapped. "I'm sorry, I didn't mean to shout. No one can see him because he's dead."

CHAPTER NINE
Cole West

The delicate scent of rose water announced Carrie's arrival before she entered the kitchen. Once again, he was struck by her beauty. The wavy brown hair, still damp from her bath, cascaded down her back. The blue gown complimented her golden-ivory skin tone despite the ugly purple and red bruises. Sorrow struck him as he recognized his wife's frock. Minus a hoop petticoat, the garment draped her body and flowed into a train at her feet. No one could have looked lovelier.

"I hope you don't mind. I borrowed this dress." She looked down.

Still enraptured, Cole shook his head.

Eggs sizzled in the frying pan.

"Cole, the eggs."

Smoke spiraled upward.

Carrie watched in horror.

Cole removed the pan from the flame. "This cook stove is quite handy. Mrs. Lindstrom, my cook, can bake, fry, and roast with half the fuel of an open hearth." He scraped the scrambled eggs onto two plates and added homemade sausage and biscuits on each plate.

He brought the plates to the table. Carrie was already seated. He returned to the stove, poured the coffee and carried the cups and saucers to the table.

He found Carrie scanning the papers he had left on the table.

“Here’s your breakfast, nosey,” he teased. Cole grabbed the papers and moved them to the countertop.

They said a quick prayer of thanks and began to enjoy their meal.

“I noticed, a few biscuits missing from the bowl.”

Carrie’s eyes darted around the room, then back to her plate.

“So, you’re the biscuit thief.”

She blushed. “I hope you don’t mind. I was so hungry. You’ve been very kind to me, Cole, despite everything. Thank you for the bath, and the clothes, and the breakfast. It’s delicious.”

“You’re welcome.” He smiled.

“Where is everybody, the servants, your wife?”

In an effort to hide a still raw nerve, he attempted to reply, but he couldn’t control the tremor in his voice. “The house servants are away on holiday, except for the ranch hands, and my wife is dead.”

“I’m sorry. How did she die? If you don’t mind telling me.”

Cole looked across the table at Carrie. “I returned home from my law office and called her name. There was no answer. I climbed the stairs and heard a commotion from the bedchamber. Amanda begged for her life.” He took a deep breath. “A boy of no more than eighteen held a knife at her throat. By the time I entered, she had fainted. I tried to coax the burglar into putting down the knife.” He looked down at his hands.

"I offered him cash to let her go. He did, but he dashed off without waiting. I checked Amanda, then snatched my Henry rifle from behind the bed, and raced downstairs. I ordered him to stop. He kept going, so I shot him before he stepped over the threshold."

"Why?"

"When I attempted to revive Amanda, I discovered stab wounds in her back. While I tried to persuade him to release her, the life oozed out of my wife and our unborn child."

"Oh, Cole, I'm so sorry." Carrie frowned.

Cole found Carrie easy to talk to. Once he opened up, he told her stories of his life in Virginia. He was an attorney by profession and like his father, a horse trader. Some of the animals he sold were wild. Often, customers paid extra for him to break the horses.

His mother was the product of an English father and Native American mother from the Powhatan nation. Named Little Flower, she died when he was young. Riding home from a visit to a sick friend, her horse was spooked by snakes. The carriage toppled over and she was pinned underneath. By the time help arrived, it was too late.

"I'm sorry, Cole."

"I wasn't more than four years old. I barely remember her."

"I saw pictures of your family in your suite. Do you practice law out of your home?"

"No, I have an office in town."

"Like father, like son." She smiled. "I teach at an orphanage for colored children in New York. I was the strongest candidate for the headmistress position. Of course, it's impossible now. I had ambitious plans for the children. My dream was to teach them to write stories and poems and add science and theatre to their curriculum."

"Don't give up on your dreams. Life is uncertain now, but your future can be bright again. Would the administration allow an academic curriculum?"

"Mrs. Murphy, the superintendent, did agree to my proposal to add French and American history classes. I think she was open to the ideas but we'd have to find and pay teachers from those disciplines, which would have been the greatest challenge."

"Education is the first step toward equality. Keep pushing for more opportunities for the children. If the status quo isn't challenged, change will never come."

"You think so, Cole?"

He nodded.

"Now that I'm a fugitive, I'm sure the administration will have nothing to do with me. A teacher's reputation is everything."

Cole shook his head. "Don't give up."

"I know I must not give up hope but my future seems so bleak." She looked down at her hands. Then, raised her head and sat up straight before she changed the subject.

"What was it you didn't want me to see?"

"While I was waiting for you to come down, I dabbled at a bit of poetry."

"How funny. I'm a poet, too. I've recently finished a volume of poems."

"Have you sought a publisher?"

"I've thought about it. I won a contest at school once. I had to recite the piece on stage. The only other time I was on stage is when I had the lead in a school play."

"Speaking of theater, I've been in a few plays, myself." Cole grinned. "I played Romeo at Yale. Shakespeare's still my favorite."

"Well, I played Juliet in a spring production at Oberlin. I'll bet you can't remember any of your lines."

"Man alive. You've got yourself a bet. Mmm... Oh, yes."

"O, speak again, bright angel!
For thou art as glorious to this night,
Being o'er my head,
As is a winged messenger of heaven."

Carrie gasped and said, "How beautiful. All I remember is...

"Romeo, Romeo, wherefore art thou, Romeo?
Deny thy father and refuse thy name.
For, if not I would something, something, something...no longer be a Capulet?"

Carrie and Cole convulsed in laughter.

Mischief darkened Carrie's gray eyes. "Cole, were you the pirate standing underneath my window at Twin Oaks?"

"'Tis true, m'lady. Blackbeard, t'was I." Cole answered in a rough, seafaring voice.

Carrie studied his face.

Cole caught her staring and smiled.

Carrie turned her head. She twisted the dress material around her fingers.

"My favorite passage is when Romeo sees Juliet for the first time," Cole said. "He's entranced by her beauty."

"Oh, she doth teach the torches to burn bright.

It seems she hangs upon the cheek of night.
As a rich jewel in an Ethiop's ear;
Beauty too rich for use, for earth too dear.
So shows a snowy dove trooping with crows,
As yonder lady o'er her fellows shows.
The measure done, I'll watch her place of stand,
And touching hers make blessed my rude hand.
Did my heart love till now? Forswear it sight,
For I ne'er saw true beauty till this night."

"That was wonderful." Carrie's eyes appeared flecked with silver as happiness washed over her face. She applauded with enthusiasm.

"I wasn't acting. You *are as lovely as a rich jewel in an Ethiop's ear*." He slid his hands across the table and touched her fingertips.

The smile fell from her face as her hands recoiled from his. Was there fear in her eyes?

"I'm sorry, Carrie, I didn't mean to offend you. Blame Shakespeare. I got caught up in the mood."

She looked down and then met his eyes. "No harm's done." She laughed and pushed her hair behind her ears, and wrung her hands. "I'll need an attorney. Will you defend me?"

"Are you guilty of murder?"

"I don't think so, but I may have caused his death."

"I need to know the circumstances of the attack."

Carrie did not answer immediately.

Cole offered her another cup of coffee, and she acquiesced. Carrie stared at the sugar melting in her cup, and then stirred it. She avoided Cole's eyes, took a deep breath, and began to relate the horrific events of the previous night.

Afterward, she sobbed as if she had just lost someone dear to her.

Cole moved to the chair next to her and offered his handkerchief. “It’s all right to cry, Carrie. It’s a good way to release your anger.”

Her tears slowed. “Will you defend me?”

“Of course, if it comes to that. I’ll need a retainer to make it legal.”

“Everything I own is at Twin Oaks. I—I have this ring Frank gave me.”

“You’re engaged?” Cole was aware of the tension in his voice.

“Not really.”

“If you don’t love him, why would you accept his ring?” Cole flexed his jaw.

“My mother’s dying of consumption.”

“I’m sorry.”

“She wants me to marry him. Frank’s an attorney from a good family. I told him I’d wear the ring while I decided.”

“I understand her reason, but you will have to live with your decision every day of your life, not your mother.”

“I didn’t want to disappoint her. This I could never part with.” She reached into her pocket and showed him her amulet.

“Is this why you have red marks around your neck? Was it yanked off during the attack?”

“Yes. I never want to be without it, so I put it in my pocket. It was the second time it’s broken. Miss Laura gave me a ribbon to replace the string it was on. I wish I had something to replace it.”

"I'll see what's in my wife's jewelry box. There's bound to be something you can use."

Cole extended his hand and she placed the amulet in his palm. Cole studied the charm and returned it.

"My grandmother hid this when she crossed the Middle Passage." Carrie recounted its history.

"I can understand why you would never part with this. It's a true heirloom. The ring will do."

Carrie turned around and twisted the ring from her finger. She stared at the gold band with an aquamarine stone in its center, and then passed it to him. "Your fee is?"

"This is sufficient. I'll take you to Julia Weeks' safe house. We can get an early start. Perhaps Tim can get you and the others out of Virginia before nightfall. Tim is Julia's son."

"I want you to defend me in court. I'm innocent, Cole. Running would appear to be an admission of guilt."

"I don't think you understand the scope of your predicament, Carrie." Anger colored Cole's voice. "I can't guarantee you a fair trial. Believe me, the odds are *against* you." He shook his head and frowned. "If I lose the case, you could hang. Are you willing to risk your life? I'm *not*."

Carrie dropped her head.

He raised her chin with his finger and looked into her eyes. "You've retained me as your attorney, and my advice is to flee by the Underground Railroad until you get to Canada. You should have had legal representation at the damned inquest." Cole's eyes darkened. "Damn Lucius Dayton. I swear he's the son of Lucifer."

"All right, all right, you've scared me."

"Being arrested for murder should scare you."

Carrie let out a deep sigh. "I'll go to Canada, but everyone will think I'm guilty."

"Listen, once you're safe in Canada, I'll work to get the charges dropped. There, you'll be safe from the hangman's noose."

Carrie nodded and wiped a tear from her eye with her finger.

He forced an easy smile to his lips. "Would you like another cup of coffee?"

"No, thank you. I'd rather take a nap. How far is the next safe house?" Carrie rose from her chair and grimaced.

"Are you all right?"

"The bruises still ache."

"They'll heal in time. Mrs. Week's place is a few miles north of here." Cole escorted Carrie upstairs.

"Cole, which one can I use?"

Cole walked down the hall and stopped before a door. "This is the prettiest one, Carrie." He opened the door to an attractive room with feminine touches. The wallpaper and counterpane depicted a garden of lilacs.

Carrie smiled.

CHAPTER TEN
Pinkerton Investigates

While searching for wood, Allan Pinkerton, a cooper, discovered the hideout of a notorious counterfeit ring. The incident launched his unique and distinguished career in law enforcement. He ultimately created the occupation of private detective and founded the secret service.

In 1855, Pinkerton organized the North-Western Police Agency in Chicago. Hired by the railroad to police the labor force and protect the company's property, he devised a spy network of undercover operatives, who posed as workers. Soon, the pilferage of ticket money was traced to a conductor.

Allan Pinkerton's career was imbued with controversy. He adopted a single eye as the logo for his detective agency, and it took on a double meaning. Railroad executives saw his spy system as a means of control. However, laborers found it deceitful since their ranks were infiltrated with spies.

He had worked on the opposite side in his native Scotland. Pinkerton had supported the new labor movement in Glasgow.

As a courageous conductor on the Underground Railroad, he used his detection skills and network of operatives to help transport slaves to freedom.

However, on January 1, 1860, at ten o'clock in the morning, the Scotsman stood outside the manor of the Wild Valley Ranch on another errand.

"Morning, Jonah." Pinkerton smiled.

Jonah laughed outright. The Scottish brogue never failed to amuse him.

"Good morning, Mr. Pinkerton. Cole's in the study. Help yourself to coffee and biscuits."

"Thank you." Pinkerton snapped the brim of his bowler hat before passing it to Jonah. He headed to the study and found Cole sprawled on a sofa with the newspaper in his lap.

"Good to see you, Allan." Cole moved the *Richmond Enquire* to the seat, stood and crossed the floor to shake his friend's hand. "When did you arrive? Have a seat."

The detective dropped into an armchair near an end table.

"Coffee?"

"Please."

Cole poured him a cup and set it on the table. Pinkerton drank deeply, and a smile of appreciation spread across his ruddy face. Then he twirled his great moustaches in delight, and stroked his bushy beard. Cole put two biscuits on a plate and set them on the table before he returned to the sofa.

"Yesterday afternoon. I washed up, ate, dressed, and went straight to the ball. Stayed until the end, so as not to miss a thing, I did. Saw you in your pirate getup. Enjoyed your bit of playacting with the mistress of the manor, I did. Nice touch, very nice touch. You may have missed your calling, my friend." He devoured a biscuit in seconds and then grabbed another. "Jonah makes the best biscuits in Virginia."

"I made them." Cole said. "I was expecting you."

Pinkerton looked amused.

"Are you any closer to discovering who killed my father?" Cole gazed at the gold-framed painting of his father above the mantel and frowned. He took a sip of coffee.

"I discovered a match for the bullet that killed your father."

Cole sat up. The cup rattled against the saucer.

"The bullet from your father's body is the same as those used by Sam Houston's troops in the Texas Wars."

"That narrows it down." Cole jumped from his seat and began to pace the floor. "Robert Johnson fought with Houston, and so did Captain Pierce. But Pierce donated his rifle to the Richmond Historical Society before the murder, with a lot of fanfare, of course. Did you get a chance to see the rifle?"

"Like any good ole southern boy, Johnson couldn't wait to show off his gun collection. Not only did he have an impressive arsenal, but he produced bullets for 'em all. I always keep the bullet that killed your father in my breast pocket. It paid off." He snapped his finger and patted his breast pocket. "When no one was looking, I compared the two."

"If Robert has his gun, and Pierce's is in the museum. Who's left?"

"I posed the same question to Robert." Pinkerton fingered his moustache. "Sherman Dayton, Lucius' son, was the only other man who served in these parts."

"Man alive. But what motive could Sherman have for killing my father? They didn't really know each other." He paused and sat down. His head snapped up. "Why, hell, yes. Of course, Lucius Dayton could have gotten hold of his son's rifle."

"According to Robert," added Pinkerton, "Sherman claimed his rifle was stolen."

"We have to find it. It's not possible to get a search warrant for Dayton's house yet, but I will when we find compelling evidence."

Pinkerton sipped his coffee. "Heard about the death of Captain John Pierce?"

"Yeah. Shocked the hell outta me. But he had it coming." Anger hardened Cole's features. He grabbed a biscuit from the plate and finished it in two bites.

"Some colored woman stabbed him. Name's Carrie. She's wanted for first degree murder. Patty rollers are on the highways, waterways, and train stations. Is there anything about it in the paper?"

"It made the front page," Cole answered. "The newspapers are crying for her blood. When the accused is colored, these papers are quick to print inflammatory editorials to rile the white community against all colored people."

Cole scowled and poured himself another cup of coffee from a service sitting on his desk.

"I met her at the ball as Murdock, a visiting land agent. Pierce introduced her as Robert Johnson's niece. The bloke had himself a joke of it." Pinkerton laughed. "She's a looker, too."

"She's the most beautiful woman I've ever seen." Cole's eyes sparkled.

Pinkerton stared at Cole with new interest. "You must have seen her there, too."

Cole shook his head to the contrary. "She's here, sleeping upstairs."

Pinkerton's jaw dropped.

Cole seemed unable to hide the excitement in his voice. "Found her in my barn this morning, right after the sheriff and his posse left."

Pinkerton dropped his voice to a whisper. "Wow. In a pretty bad state, I'll bet."

Cole nodded.

"Taking her to a safe house?"

Cole nodded.

"Know of anyone I can trust at the Johnson place?"

"White or colored?"

"Colored, I need to know what's happening on both sides of the fence." Pinkerton frowned.

"Why?"

"I stopped by Twin Oaks, on the pretense I'd left my hat and gleaned this bit of news. A woman named Olivia and a child named Janie were poisoned last night."

Cole appeared shaken as he asked what became of them.

"The child died, but the granny survived. Made her pretty sick, though. Frightened Robert something awful. It may not have anything to do with your father's death, but I'd like to look into it a bit to be sure. This one's on me. Olivia's your girl's grandmother."

"My girl?" Cole's face turned crimson.

"The eyes are the window of the soul, my friend. I know she's got ya in the bag." The Scot chuckled out loud at Cole's uneasiness.

"Okay, I admit I find her quite—beautiful." Cole shifted his weight in the chair. "Why would anyone want to poison Olivia?"

"It's what I want to find out. An odd piece of business, that. Nothing to do with your father, most likely, but I look at everything that rubs me the wrong way when I'm on a case."

"Henry Mason, Robert's butler. You can trust him. He's one of us."

"An agent of the Underground Railroad?" Pinkerton's eyes widened.

Cole nodded.

"Excellent." Pinkerton grabbed another biscuit.

CHAPTER ELEVEN
The Underground Railroad

Carrie stared at her image in the bedchamber mirror. They had decided to disguise her as Cole's teenage nephew. Jonah had supplied her with baggy brown trousers, a loose tan shirt, and a belt. The outfit was completed with a pair of well-worn black boots and leather gloves. The costume fit well enough, except for the three-quarter-length coat, which fell below Carrie's knees. All that was left now was to hide her hair.

She had pushed it beneath a hat Cole had given her when he appeared with a carpetbag. Seeing him made her uneasy. The unexpected conflicting emotions confused her. She was grateful to him for hiding her and caring for her needs. A sense of peace had started to settle within, but the journey ahead made her wring her hands.

"My, you do look like an innocent lad." Cole set the carpetbag on the bed. He pushed a few tendrils under her hat, and she jerked her head away.

She swallowed hard and felt her hands tremble.

He looked dismayed and took a step back.

Carrie looked away.

Cole cleared his throat. "Mrs. Julia Weeks lives at the edge of town. You'll wait there until your relatives arrive. I'm glad they will be with you. We'll take the carriage to Mrs. Weeks's place to keep you out of sight. Her son, Tim, will escort your family to the next safe house. It's almost noon. We'd better get on the road. I have to be in Philadelphia in a few days. I promised to be second-chair to Thaddeus Stevens, a family friend, at a court case. He has a stomach ailment, and may need my help."

"Mr. Stevens and men like him are a blessing to colored folks. I wish him a speedy recovery. Tell me what Mrs. Weeks is like."

"She's a kind, good-natured Quaker woman. The Weeks and my father worked together for years helping runaways." Cole paused. "When Tim arrives, we may never see one another again."

An awkward silence ensued. She couldn't ignore the sadness she felt. Cole was attractive, but she couldn't allow herself to trust him completely.

Carrie had finished packing her personal items, and included an extra shirt from Jonah.

Cole placed a few strange articles in her carpetbag.

"Why would I need pepper?" She raised an eyebrow.

"It's good for warding off bloodhounds." Cole frowned.

Carrie's nerves jumped at the thought of snarling dogs after her. She took a few deep breaths.

He added another item. "Ether is a good anesthetic and also acts as an antiseptic in case you acquire a few cuts. And here's my trusted Bowie knife." He unsheathed the weapon, and her heart jumped.

"A knife?"

"Yes. It's a good tool, both for protecting yourself and peeling fruit. Don't worry. I have another. You'll need something to surprise an enemy."

"God forbid I'd have to use it. I have no idea how to handle a knife, especially such a big one." A tear fell from her eyes which she quickly wiped away. "Maybe I'd be better off with something smaller." She glanced at Cole.

He looked startled by her sudden turn of her emotions. "Didn't mean to upset you, but you must be prepared for the unexpected. A small knife may not stop your assailant. But, you're right. You need to learn how to handle it. In some cases, it's better than a gun. It's quiet and inconspicuous. I'll show you how to use it now." Cole returned the weapon to the scabbard on his belt. He held out his hand, and after a pause, Carrie placed hers in his. He led her down the stairs and through the back door.

Cole faced Carrie and displayed the knife. The blade flashed in the noonday sun. He held it by the haft, in the middle of the handle. "This is where you want to grip it, where its balance lies." He went on to explain the difference between an overhand strike and underhand thrust. "Attack your foe by using the underhand motion. The enemy won't see your knife coming. People of small stature have an advantage with this technique. Overhand is good only if your opponent is already on the ground and of little threat."

Cole beckoned for Carrie to come closer and take the knife. He stood behind her and placed his hand over hers as she held the weapon. He guided her hand in an upward motion at a tree, which was a substitute for an enemy. "Aim for just under the breastbone. You must hit hard and upward to strike the heart. It'll kill within a minute or two."

She practiced several thrusts, increasing the pressure and speed each time.

After he was certain she was comfortable with the Bowie knife, he unbuckled his belt and slid off the leather scabbard. "You can take this."

Carrie took off her belt and handed it to Cole.

He pulled it through the loop of the scabbard and slipped the knife inside. "Now, you're armed."

Carrie took the belt and fastened it around her waist. She became aware of the extra weight.

Once Cole had replaced his belt, he led her back to the house.

They climbed the stairs to his chamber.

Carrie looked around and blinked back tears. "I can't believe how suddenly my life has changed."

Cole gazed into her teary eyes. "You can make it to Canada. You must have faith in yourself. Agents on the Underground Railroad will assist you in every way, with food, clothing, and a place to sleep. You'll have your relatives with you as well. Oh, and here's some money." Cole retrieved a wad of small bills from his shirt pocket and stuffed them into her bag. "Some folks might demand payment along the way. Tell me, Carrie, what brought you to Virginia?"

"I came to Virginia to free my grandmother from slavery. When my mother left Virginia, eighteen years ago, she asked Olivia to come, too, but she refused. She didn't want to leave Mary behind. Dayton, her master, promised never to set her free. So, Olivia stayed to protect Mary any way she could. Olivia wouldn't have been able to enjoy the benefits of freedom while her child was enslaved. My mother is dying from consumption. She didn't want to leave this earth without her mother's forgiveness. So, I promised her I'd bring Grandmother to New York. I felt so lost after finding out the man I've loved as my father, Jonathan, wasn't my real father. Preston Johnson is my biological father. He raped my mother. She bore me in shame."

"He raped your mother, and you just found out before you left New York?"

Carrie nodded.

"What a terrible shock."

"I'm still trying to come to terms with it."

"I'm sure you don't want to hear this now, but no matter how difficult it seems, you need to find it in your heart to forgive him."

Carrie frowned.

"It'll take some time, but it's the only real way to heal. To preserve a space for bitter feelings in your heart will leave smaller spaces for love to grow. It's in the past and can't be changed." Cole shook his head. "We both have conflicted feelings about our fathers."

"You do as well?"

He sat on the bed and gestured for her to sit in a nearby chair.

"Yes, when I was a younger man, I often avoided my father's requests to help run the Underground Railroad. I ran with the rich boys of slaveholding families. I believed in emancipation, but I still excused friends who owned slaves. Then, one day, the boys bragged about how they had abused slave girls. One expressed satisfaction about a slave who received forty lashes for some slight transgression. Their callousness shocked me. Then, it dawned on me. Was I going to be a man who condoned their behavior by my silence or a man like my father, who had the integrity to live by his principles? I knew I had to sever all ties with people like them.

"When I saw my father swinging from a rope on the porch, I was angry and filled with regret."

"Your father was murdered?" Carrie gasped.

"Yes, I found him after he had won a trial prosecuted by Lucius Dayton."

"The trial of Celia, the woman who killed her master?" Cole nodded. "I heard a law student, who attended the ball, talking about the case. I learned your father defended Celia. It's what brought me to the Wild Valley Ranch to seek your father's counsel."

"I'm glad it did. You know, I never told my father what a great man he was or how much I wanted to be like him. I never told him he was my hero. I've vowed to continue his work as stationmaster and conductor on the Underground Railroad. I'm legal counsel to the enslaved and all Negroes who need my assistance. I want to see them get a fair shake in court, 'cause there are plenty who conspire to leave them on the edge of society, with no legal protections at all."

He wrote something on a piece of paper. "This is Thaddeus Stevens's address. Wire me there." He tucked it inside her carpet bag.

"Oh, I almost forgot." His smile returned. He pulled a silver chain from his breast pocket and asked for her charm.

"Cole, I can't accept something so expensive."

"It's not very expensive, and now you can wear your heirloom again. Be sure to tuck it under your shirt." He extended his hand toward her. Carrie extracted the amulet from her pocket and placed it in his palm. He strung the bird on the chain and gestured for her to turn around. He placed the necklace around her neck and clasped it.

Carrie turned to look at him and touched the sleeve of his shirt. “Cole, I don’t know how to—”

“Don’t say goodbye yet. I’m going with you to Julia’s, you know. Just for the record, I hate goodbyes. You can borrow this chain for now, but I want it back later. It’s a guarantee we’ll see one another again.”

He turned away, and grabbed an object off the dresser.

“Here’s something to remember me by.” Cole smiled and handed Carrie a small leather-bound book of *Romeo and Juliet.*

Carrie opened the book and saw he had written an inscription inside the cover. Emotions flooded her. She turned her back to him to read it, but he came up behind her and recited the words. She lost herself in the resonance of his baritone voice.

My Kindred Spirit

My Dearest Carrie,

I’ve known you for less than one earthly day,
And yet you’ve pressed upon my grateful heart
A touch so deep ’twill never fade away.
Despite our bond, I know for now we must part.

An arduous journey, perhaps brings woes,
And fills your fragile heart with dread.
I shall fiercely battle those
Whose aims impede the noble life you’ve led.

For, like the gardener tending fertile fields,
A teacher sows the seeds of wisdom's fires
While those you fear bow down and weakly yield
The strength your spectral beauty thus inspires.

A lamp of Faithful Groom still lights my door
My kindred spirit waits, forevermore.

Yours Always,
Cole

"You've written a poem—a sonnet—for me. It's the most roma... No one has ever... Was it the poem you hid from me at the breakfast table?"

Cole nodded. "Yes, I can't explain it. The words flowed from my pen with little effort."

Carrie lowered her eyes and felt her chin tremble. She could hardly contain the joy she felt.

He lifted her chin with his forefinger and looked into her eyes. "Carrie Bennet, I think we might be kindred spirits. What do you think?"

"Yes, we might be. Kindred spirits with the souls of poets."

CHAPTER TWELVE
From Freedom to Slavery

New York
New Year's Day

"I think Sally's house is just around the bend, boys." Big Red McPherson's tongue, thick from liquor, caused his words to come out slurred. A loud belch escaped his lips, which sent the other men reeling with laughter.

"This sure beats sleeping on the winter ground on New Year's Day." Scott Bancroft's head dropped to his chest. His gentle snore evidenced slumber had crept upon him like a drug.

"Good ole Sally Bird." Jed 'Killer' Calhoun chuckled. "Now there's a smart business woman. Did I ever tell y'all how she got started?"

Silence followed.

"About ten years ago, she found herself a destitute widow and decided to take on boarders: twin sisters, Nancy and Janet Thompson. They fed her a story about being spinsters who had traveled with P.T. Barnum's circus as Jenny Lind's personal maids. Then one night, Sally heard some noises coming from one of the sister's bedchamber. She thought the girl was moaning in pain. When she barged into the room, a man scrambled off Nancy, opened the window, jumped to the ground butt naked, and ran like the devil carrying his clothes in his arms."

The men chortled.

"The girls were prostitutes. To their surprise, Sally kept quiet and charged them twice the rent. Thus, a businesswoman was born, and a failing farmhouse was converted to the best cathouse on the outskirts of New York City." He bayed like a wolf.

The slave catchers came upon the familiar clump of shrubs and evergreen trees, which marked the route to their refuge, as evening fell. They heard music floating from the house.

Jeb recognized the tune as "Camptown Ladies" and started singing.

Within minutes, the silhouette of Sally Bird's rambling old farmhouse came into view. Although the second story was dark, bright lights shone through the parlor curtains.

Jeb's vocals brought a tawny-colored boy of about twelve out of the house. He greeted the customers and led them to the barn. Big Red pulled Frank out of the wagon and chained him to the spokes of the wagon wheel, while Scott aimed a rifle at him. Then they left him and walked to the house.

A willowy, auburn-haired, caramel-colored girl of about fourteen answered Scott's knock at the front door.

Entering the foyer, the newcomers eyed the walls of the vestibule. Here, sketches of their semi-nude hostesses graced the red velvet walls. The soft glow from beeswax candles and gas lamps illuminated the opulent parlor. Plush sofas and chairs with dainty tables were the main furnishings. Colorful accent rugs added beauty to the gleaming wood floor.

Peals of laughter echoed from the ruby lips of two ladies who slurped from crystal glasses and laughed at every joke a balding gentleman uttered, as he squeezed handfuls of flesh on their thighs.

A young man who resembled the stable boy pounded an energetic ditty from an upright piano while two inebriated women danced around the room like marionettes.

Jed stepped into the parlor. “Where’s Tessie?”

A dull-eyed blonde of about nineteen stopped dancing and turned her attention to the new arrivals. Her tall slim frame was clad in an amethyst-colored, floor-length silk robe. It gaped open to reveal a lacy bustier. Her full breasts crested above the garment. A matching pair of short drawers reached her thigh, exposing long shapely legs. She squinted at Jeb, whose friends had left his side to seek their own female companionship. Once she recognized him, she waved. “Hey Baby, you’re back.” She frowned at Nelly, her dance partner.

Tessie walked on unsteady legs toward the slave catcher, her heels clicking on the wood floor.

“Thank the Lord for whorehouses.”

When Tessie reached Jeb, he doffed his hat, grabbed a handful of blonde hair and pulled her head back, kissing her hard on the mouth.

She struggled to free herself. “Jeb, you’re hurting me.”

With quick strides, Sally crossed the room and slapped Jeb on the back. “Jeb, let go of Tessie. You promised you'd be a gentleman the next time you came to visit. Don't let me have to get the sheriff."

Jeb released Tessie and stared open-mouthed at Sally. His eyes swept her figure from head to toe. The black and red shimmering evening gown fitted her plump, shapely frame to perfection.

Her long earrings bobbed beneath her elegant hairdo as she spoke tersely. "Don't look so surprised. Me and the sheriff are like this." She held up her right hand and crossed the first two fingers.

Tessie moved to Sally's side, and the middle-aged woman put her arms around the trembling girl.

"And I will, Sally. I will." Jeb looked down at his feet like a small boy who'd been reprimanded by his mother.

~~~

The dawning light began to spread across the sky. Frank opened his eyes, squinted, and lowered his head. Daylight had exposed his shame. He found himself on the floor of a barn, chained like an errant dog. The once-elegant three-piece suit, which verified his success, was torn and crumpled like well-used cleaning rags.

Hunger pangs stabbed Frank's belly. He licked his cracked lips and tasted the bitterness of dried blood caked in one corner. He tried to swallow, but his throat felt as dry as chalk. How he longed for any kind of sustenance.

A shadow fell across his manacled limb as the scent of floral perfume mingled with the odors of horses and hay. He heard the rustling of her petticoats as she crept across the floor. Raising his head, Frank looked up into the white face of a young woman.
~~~

As she neared him, she slowed her pace until she stood three feet away. Then, he noticed she was carrying a plate, steaming with hot food. The thin chain from a canteen dangled from her wrist. "Are you hungry?"

Frank, stupefied, couldn't speak.

"You must be. I'm sure those dumb bounty hunters you've been keeping company with didn't bother to feed you last night." She placed the tin plate on the floor and nudged it with her foot bringing it closer to Frank's unchained hand.

Her unexpected appearance stirred a spark of hope in Frank's heart. He opened his mouth to speak, but a dry cough was all he could manage.

The woman placed the canteen on the floor and pushed it toward him with her foot.

He picked it up with his free hand and twisted off the cap with his cuffed hand. He drank. The water flowed down his chin like grateful tears.

"I must go before my absence is noticed." She turned.

Overcome with gratitude, Frank felt a lump in his throat and struggled to find his voice. "Thank you, ma'am." His voice sounded like sandpaper.

"You're welcome." She began to walk toward the barn door.

Frank realized his opportunity. Hope filled his soul like a caged bird before an opened door. "My father is Attorney Turner at fifty-four Madison Avenue in New York City. Please get word to him."

She stopped and her back stiffened.

Frank heard a hiss as she drew a breath and held it.

"Tell him I've been kidnapped and on my way to the Dayton Plantation in Richmond. Please."

She stood still for a moment, exhaled, and made her exit as silently as she had come.

About an hour later, Jeb kicked the barn door open, stubbing his toe. "Dammit." His face reddened and contorted into a grimace.

He limped to where Frank lay, unlocked the shackles, and yanked him to his feet.

Once he stood, Jeb punched him in his stomach.

"That's for talkin' to my Tessie." He spat on the ground near Frank's feet.

Jeb didn't move out of the way quickly enough before Frank's fist made contact with his jaw.

Big Red and Scott arrived. Each of them grabbed one of Frank's arms. A quick jab to Frank's face split his lip and skinned Jeb's knuckles. The slave catcher raised his arm to land another when Big Red let go of Frank and grabbed Jeb's fist with his ham-sized one.

"Let me go." Jeb's face flashed white, then red, then white again, drawing laughter from Big Red and Scott.

The huge man let go of Jeb's hand.

Jeb shook his hand to relieve the numbness.

"Leave him alone, Jeb. He'll need his strength for the next stop." Big Red frowned. "Plus, we don't want him so broken he'll be no good to old man Dayton."

"We're going to hire you out, niggah." Scott smirked. "A fancy niggah like you with an education ought to fetch us a bundle. Old man Dayton never need know 'bout it."

The others laughed.

Where are they taking me now?

CHAPTER THIRTEEN
A Quaker Woman Gives Solace

Virginia

New Year's Day

Mrs. Weeks greeted Cole, as they stood in her farmhouse kitchen. "Now tell me about this young man with thee, Cole."

"Let me introduce Miss Carrie Bennet." Cole removed her hat. A cascade of wavy hair fell to her waist as Mrs. Weeks gasped in astonishment.

"Is she *the* Carrie Bennet? All of Richmond is talking about her."

Cole nodded.

Mrs. Weeks stepped back to appraise Carrie. "My, my, she is pretty, Cole."

The lawyer nodded with a broad smile.

"You've heard about me already?" Carrie frowned.

"Scandal travels fast. My son Tim told me about thee this morn. His wife is in the family way. Chances are he won't stay to eat with us but he'll return this evening to take you all to the next safe house."

Mrs. Weeks pulled a thick rug over the trapdoor. When Carrie and Cole reached the farmhouse, they had traveled through a tunnel from the barn to the kitchen. Cole told her the passageway had been dug by Stuart West, Tim, and Mr. Weeks several years before.

"That nosey widow, Dotty Wilson, is here again, Cole." The aged woman frowned. "She has kin over yonder and is liable to drop by at any time. Almost caught me with fugitives on her last visit. Just walked in, never bothered to knock. She's the prosecutor's sister, Carrie. She makes me jumpy. It's more than a body can stand. Come on into the parlor where it's warm by the fire. I'll get thee both a cup of tea. Supper is ready. We'll eat as soon as the others arrive."

Cole took a deep breath. "It smells delicious."

"Tonight's supper is chicken pot pie, corn, and a cucumber salad. I still have some of my chocolate cake left. I made two cakes the other day because Tim and his family came to dinner. Every year, his brood increases." She smiled. "The sixth one will arrive by spring."

Carrie walked into the cozy parlor and stood before the fire. Cole followed her and spread his fingers over the flames.

A portrait of a young couple hung above the mantelpiece. Carrie recognized the younger features of her hostess and guessed the man was her deceased spouse.

Soon, Mrs. Weeks bustled in and set the tea service on a side table. She filled their cups before her own and sat down in the rocker to enjoy the warm brew.

Carrie noticed a basket by the rocker full of cloth dolls. Curious, she leaned forward to get a better view.

"Mrs. Weeks these dolls are adorable. May I?" Mrs. Weeks nodded. Carrie lifted the basket and examined them. Their skin tones ranged from ebony to gold. Yarn fashioned their hair and buttons their eyes.

"It's my way of making the little girls who stop at my station feel welcomed," Mrs. Weeks said. "For the little boys, there are plenty toys for them to choose from, which my husband made."

The elderly woman pointed to a corner in the room where a menagerie of wooden animals stood along with wooden trains, wagons, and buildings.

"Mrs. Weeks, your husband was quite talented, and so are you."

"He helped Stuart with the tunnel, too."

Carrie glanced at the clock on the mantel. It was a quarter past one. She started to worry about her family and said a silent prayer for their safety.

Moments later, they were summoned to the kitchen by soft knocks. The sound came from the trapdoor. Mrs. Weeks rushed to the kitchen with Cole and Carrie at her heels. She moved the rug and swung open the trapdoor to reveal a circle of smiling, upturned faces.

Cole gave Tim a hand, and then the two of them assisted the family. One by one, the fugitives climbed up the ladder and into the kitchen.

Mrs. Weeks hugged Tim, a medium-sized young man with sandy hair and clear blue eyes, and introduced Carrie.

Carrie thanked him for his courage and dedication. Mary and Joshua did likewise before he left. He promised to return by nightfall.

"Thank God. Mary, Joshua, I'm so glad you're safe." Carrie's arms flew around them in a hearty hug before acknowledging the children. "Did you see Grandmother before you left?"

"Yes, she's better. Mason made sure we had a chance to say goodbye." Mary's tone turned serious. "Mama told me you killed Cap'n Pierce."

Carrie conveyed the specifics of the captain's demise.

"There's no such thing as self-defense for colored. We is always the guilty ones." Mary shook her head.

"Was Grandmother upset by the news?" Carrie wanted her grandmother to be proud of her.

"We all knows what kinda man Cap'n Pierce was, Carrie. Grandmother was happy you got him before he killed you. I told her we'd be together, and dat soothed her worries something powerful."

Mrs. Weeks interrupted their conversation and asked them to wash up for supper.

Afterward, everyone helped to set the table. The adults sat in the dining room, while the children ate their supper in the kitchen.

At the dinner table, Joshua and Mary sketched the details of their escape. Afterward, they spoke of their plans. Joshua's goal was to open a blacksmith shop, and Mary just wanted to make a beautiful home for her husband and children.

Cole praised the work of Thaddeus Stevens and the Radical Republicans for their fight to win emancipation.

"If more white folks thought as they did, slavery would have died a quick death a long time ago," Carrie surmised.

"They'll never abolish it without a fight. Slavery is a three-billion-dollar industry, and both the north and south benefit from it." Cole shook his head. The others looked astonished at the sum of money slavery provided for the country.

"Cole, has there been any progress in thy father's murder case?" Mrs. Weeks asked.

"The case is closed, as far as Sheriff Coffe is concerned. He's convinced Thomas, whom my father defended, killed him."

Cole related some of the details of his father's murder.

"I'm sorry Mr. Cole," said Joshua. "Lucius is a monster. He's been abusing my wife for years."

"Dere ain't a decent bone in his body," declared Mary.

When the tables were cleared, some headed upstairs to rest. Mrs. Weeks asked Cole to take the wagon to town and pick up some feed at the mercantile. "I have two wagons in the barn. You're welcome to either one. The feed is too heavy for me to carry. Most bags weigh at least twenty-five pounds."

"It would be my pleasure, Miss Julia."

Carrie approached Cole before she went upstairs to rest. "If you have time, please send this telegram to Miss Laura's New York City address. I'm afraid to contact mama directly. I've signed it with my middle name."

Cole scanned the note to make sure the code wouldn't divulge their whereabouts or the identity of the writer. "This will do. Rest easy, I'll send it."

CHAPTER FOURTEEN
An Unwelcome Visitor

As the fugitives rested upstairs, Mary offered to help tidy up. Mrs. Weeks washed and rinsed while Mary dried and stored the dishes in the cupboard.

The women were chatting when a noise from the parlor silenced them. Exchanging a worried glance with Mary, Mrs. Weeks pressed a finger to her lips. The Quaker woman dried her hands and stepped into the parlor. She stopped short when the face of Dotty Wilson peered at her through a gap in the curtains.

Mrs. Weeks yanked the curtains closed. "Mary, up the stairs. I fear she's seen thee."

Horrified, Mary climbed the stairs as Mrs. Weeks waited until she no longer heard Mary's footsteps. She opened door.

Like a gale, Dotty Wilson rushed inside. "Julia Weeks, I'm in the middle of baking a cake and ran out of sugar." Her bulging eyes darted about. "May I please borrow two cups? I've been asked to bake my blue-ribbon cake, the Richmond Glory, for Friday evening's church social. It was the pride of last year's event. Did you get a chance to taste a piece?"

"No, Dotty. We don't attend the same church. Please wait here while I fetch it for thee."

"Did I see a colored woman in your kitchen? The curtains were open, and I couldn't help but see."

"Thine eyes must have been playing tricks on thee." Mrs. Weeks turned back to Mrs. Wilson. "I do my own housekeeping, and the farm hands do the rest. Wait right here in the parlor."

In the kitchen, she started to fill a jar with sugar. As she screwed the lid on, she heard a noise and turned around. Dotty Wilson stood in the doorway eyeing the room, evident of recent company. Fear shot through her as Dotty's hand clasp a cup sitting on the kitchen table. Mrs. Weeks knew it was still warm.

"I haven't had time to clean up from entertaining the Society of Widows and Orphans."

Mrs. Week's hand shook as she extended the jar to Dotty.

"Dear Julia, I've always said, you are the soul of generosity." Dotty gave a wry smile, as she took the jar. "I've seen no one come in or out of your farmhouse. I guess those do-gooders travel by wings, eh?"

After the widow left, Julia rushed upstairs to tell Mary they must hide in the secret passageway.

"Joshua, wake up." Mary shook him.

"What in tarnation?" Joshua's face lined with worry.

"We have to get to da tunnel. Dat Wilson woman saw me through da curtains. She's liable to bring da sheriff."

Mrs. Weeks started dressing the sleepy children, who shared a room with their parents. She heard Mary, in another bedchamber, wake Carrie.

"Carrie, wake up. You kept the candle burning?"

"What's going on?"

"Some white neighbor woman of Miss Julia's done saw me through da curtains. She's liable to bring da law."

"I'm already dressed." She looked around. "Where did I put my carpetbag?"

In the meantime, Joshua dressed himself while Mary and Mrs. Weeks attended to the sleepy children. When they were ready, Mary put both boys over her husband's shoulders, while she carried Sarah, and Mrs. Weeks held little Mary.

Mrs. Weeks began to worry when she noticed Carrie hadn't come downstairs.

By the time they reached the kitchen, they heard horses stamping and men shouting outside.

"She must have had them lying in wait." Mrs. Weeks looked about. She heard Carrie descending the stairs and hurried to signal to Carrie to go back upstairs. She knew they had no time to escape. A man pounded on the door as Carrie raced back up the staircase.

"Mrs. Weeks, open up. This is Morris Wilson, your neighbor."

~~~

The butt of a rifle struck the kitchen window. Glass flew in all directions. A man jumped through and ran to unlock the front door. Two armed men rushed inside. They surrounded the family with guns drawn.

Frightened, the little girls and young Joshua started to cry. Anger creased young Matthew's face.

"Now, you all go sit down in the parlor until the sheriff arrives."
~~~

The speaker, Morris, was Dotty's brother-in-law. He ran his hand over his thinning hair as he followed the family into the parlor. "And don't try anything."

Mrs. Weeks recognized the younger man as one of Morris's sons. *Dotty must be thrilled*, she thought bitterly.

Joshua herded the boys into the parlor. Mary picked up a tearful Sarah and carried her on her hip. Mrs. Weeks followed with little Mary.

Once seated, Joshua confronted the lawmen. "We ain't runaways. We got free papers."

"Show 'em, then." Morris stuck out his hand.

"Deys upstairs," Joshua started to rise from the sofa, but Morris stuck his rifle in his face.

"You." He pointed to Mary. "Go get the papers. Ned." He turned to the young man. "Go with her."

Mary got up with little Sarah clinging to her.

Ned followed her upstairs.

A knock sounded at the front door. Morris turned the knob and admitted Dotty. Her eyes popped as she scanned the fugitives. "I knew it. Didn't I tell you?" She slapped her thigh and grinned. "When I saw that nigger through the curtain window, I knew Julia was breaking the law. She often bragged how she did her own cleaning. I had to come and see for myself." She looked at Mrs. Weeks. "Julia, you lied to me."

Mrs. Weeks remained stony-faced as she hugged little Mary.

"These darkies weren't going nowhere till nightfall. Benny's gone after the sheriff. He'll be here soon." She sat down in a rocker.

Morris eyed Mrs. Weeks. "Dotty was right about you, Mrs. Weeks. You've disgraced your husband's memory. I heard Sheriff Coffe and his posse are nearby tracking Pierce's killer. When he gets here, you'll be arrested along with these fugitives."

Julia Weeks sat straighter. "You're mistaken, Morris. These people are my guests."

Mary came down the stairs with Sarah.

Ned followed, holding Mary's carpetbag. He aimed his pistol at her back.

Mary sat the child down on a chair and extracted several documents from the bag.

Morris snatched them from her. He glanced over the papers and threw them to the floor. "These are forgeries."

"You're wrong." Mrs. Weeks spoke with confidence.

"I've seen emancipation papers. Master Dayton's seal isn't legible. We'll all just sit here till the sheriff arrives. He'll straighten this out."

Less than twenty minutes passed before they heard knocks.

Morris opened the door, and Benny Wilson, his younger son, entered along with Sheriff Coffe and his deputies Jedidiah, Lewis, and Larson. The sheriff greeted the men and tipped his hat to Dotty and Mrs. Weeks.

Morris brought him up to speed.

Coffe pulled several documents from his pocket. "I'm holding warrants for y'all's arrests," he looked around the room at the fugitives. "I'm gonna return y'all to Masters Johnson and Dayton."

"We've gotcha now." Deputy Lewis grinned.

"If you have a wagon, Mrs. Weeks, I'll need it to haul y'all to jail." Coffe looked toward the back door.

Mrs. Weeks didn't answer.

"Go check the barn, Ned, and see what we can borrow."

"Yes sir, Pa."

"Morris, I want to thank you and your boys."

"Weren't them, 'twas me." Dotty took a step toward the sheriff. "I knew something was up when I saw the colored woman through the curtains."

"Well, thank you for your attentiveness, Mrs. Wilson." She flashed a satisfied smile. "If there's a reward, it ought to be mine."

Coffe's eyes narrowed. The fugitives moved toward the front door with guns aimed at their backs.

Dotty caressed little Mary's cheek. The child recoiled and clung tighter to Mrs. Weeks.

"Git your hands off my child." Mary spat at Mrs. Wilson.

"You stole these children from Lucius." Dotty's face reddened.

"You ain't takin' my children back to slavery." Mary raised her voice.

Sheriff Coffe dug his fingers into Mary's shoulders. "You dare speak like that to a white woman. Remember your place, nigger."

Once they reached the bottom of the porch steps, little Joshua and Matthew started biting and kicking the lawmen. While the boys held everyone's attention, Mary sat on the porch steps, and then pressed Sarah's face against her chest as the child struggled.

Dotty realized what Mary was doing. "Stop her."

Several lawmen tried to pull the child from Mary, but she held on. Once they succeeded, Coffe slapped Mary, nearly knocking her off the stoop.

"Save her." Dotty pointed to the child.

Coffe sat on the steps and checked to see if the child was breathing. "She's dead." Sorrow colored his voice. "You'll hang," he shouted with a cold stare.

"Murderer." Dotty pointed a finger at Mary, whose face was wet with tears.

Mary sobbed. "Slavery won't get none of mine. Dat one's in the Lord's hands now, where Massa Dayton can't get her."

Jedidiah helped her to her feet.

Ned appeared with a wagon and hitched the sheriff's horse to the vehicle.

Coffe placed the dead child on the wagon floor with care and covered her with a blanket he found in the wagon. He grabbed Mary and snapped on handcuffs.

A deputy handcuffed Joshua.

Morris and Ned assisted the fugitives into the wagon.

~~~

Cole drove up to the farmhouse with the feed bag in the wagon bed.

"What are you doing here, Cole?" Sheriff Coffe looked surprised.

Cole jumped down from the driver's seat. "I came to see Mrs. Weeks before I left town." His voice faltered. "She's a family friend. What's going on?" Cole gasped and eyed the prisoners but didn't see Carrie.

"Mrs. Weeks has been harboring runaways." A sneer stamped Coffe's features. "Dotty Wilson found out, and her brother-in-law held them until I got here. We met Benny on the road while searching for Pierce's killer." He jerked his head toward Mary. "This one killed her own child."
~~~

"What?" Cole shook his head. "What are you going to do with the child's body?"

"There's a Negro burial ground nearby. We'll stop there first."

Cole advanced to Mrs. Weeks, who appeared ancient. Her shoulders sagged, and her skin looked ashen. He placed an arm around her shoulder and put his mouth next to her ear. "Carrie?"

The Quaker woman looked at him as if in a trance. She blinked, and then recognized Cole. She nodded toward the house.

"I'll do what I can for you and the others." He squeezed Mrs. Weeks's hand.

The sheriff patted his pockets. "Dadburnit, I only have two pairs of handcuffs. Mrs. Weeks, you'd better behave." He reached into a pocket and pulled out a wad of tobacco.

"Did she really kill her child?" Cole asked the lawman as pain gripped his heart.

"She did, right in front of us." The sheriff frowned at Cole. "We were busy with the young'uns kicking and screaming and didn't notice till it was too late. I gotta take these fugitives to the nearest sheriff's office. It be in Mechanicsville. There'll be a hearing in the morning, and then we can get back to hunting that murderess and collect the bounty money."

Cole stepped toward the sheriff. "I'll defend Mrs. Weeks if she's charged."

"Well, well, you're a chip off the old block after all." Coffe spat tobacco juice at Cole's feet.

"See you in court, Coffe." Cole turned his back on the sheriff. He set the bag of feed on the porch, and then went to the barn to retrieve his own coach.

The children cried and huddled against their father. When Mary reached out to Matthew, he recoiled, but her younger son hugged her. Joshua closed his eyes and recited the twenty-third Psalm as tears ran down his cheeks, while the wagon wheels rolled toward Mechanicsville.

Morris assisted Dotty onto the seat of her buggy, before he and his sons mounted their horses and headed home.

CHAPTER FIFTEEN
The Wait

Carrie crept down the stairs on unsteady legs and stopped at the bottom of the staircase. She felt like a frightened rabbit, frozen, too afraid to move or make a sound. She dared not peek through the windows to see for herself what was happening, lest she expose herself to the same fate.

By the cacophony she heard outside, something terrible had occurred. She strained her ears to catch the words. Cole's urgent voice mingled with the sheriff's and her heart lurched. Mary had killed her daughter.

Her family's capture and fear of returning to slavery had caused Mary to commit an unspeakable crime. She'd expected their journey to be unpredictable but never could she fathom it would lead to such a tragedy.

Now what? Once her relatives were returned to Dayton, she knew their punishment would be severe. Would he sell Mary's children? Would he flog her, tearing the skin off her back?

What will Robert Johnson do to Joshua? Would he sell or beat him? She couldn't imagine him in the role, but she knew nothing of his treatment of slaves who dared to run away. She'd heard of men who were hired for this purpose. Would Mr. Johnson send him there to be disciplined, his screams out of earshot of himself and his family, or would the overseer at Twin Oaks administer the punishment?

A loud voice, belonging to Sheriff Coffe, stated his intent to go to Mechanicsville to seek charges against Mary and Mrs. Weeks.

Carrie exhaled a long breath when she heard the horses' hooves grow faint and the wagon wheels roll away from the farmhouse. She was no longer in danger of being discovered, but it gave her little comfort. A cup of hot tea would soothe her jumpy nerves.

Once she held the saucer and cup in hand, she sat in the rocking chair. She rested her head against Mrs. Weeks's shawl and sipped the warm liquid.

The fear which gripped her heart and made it race was still present. She could hardly wait for Tim's return to take her to the next safe house. She didn't want to go there alone. Perhaps, she could stay with Tim's family until Cole returned or sent word.

Dark shadows grew inside the quaint farmhouse until the night settled and the moon cast its silvery shafts through the windows. Carrie trembled as she waited in the dark for Tim to arrive. Any light from Mrs. Weeks's farmhouse would cause suspicion. She heard noises from the secret tunnel and hurried to the kitchen. She pushed the rug aside and threw open the trapdoor.

Tim, holding a lantern, smiled up at her before he climbed the ladder and stepped into the kitchen. His eyes widened as he looked at Carrie. Alarmed, the smile slipped from his face. "Where's everyone?" His blue eyes scanned the room for his mother and the others.

"Oh Tim, they've been captured." Carrie wrung her hands. She recounted the horrific events of his mother's capture and those of her own family.

"Thou should stay with my family tonight, Carrie, instead of going to the next stop." Carrie nodded and gave Tim a grateful glance. She folded her arms and pressed them to her chest.

"Cole is with them, Tim. I'm sure he will do what he can to help your mother. I heard the sheriff say he was taking them to Mechanicsville, so he could have Mary charged with murder and your mother with harboring runaways. Cole will defend them."

"Thanks to him, I have some measure of hope. I pray my mother will survive this ordeal. She has grown frail as of late, but her constitution is strong. Do thou wish to bring anything with thee?"

"Only my carpetbag. It's here by the rocker. Had I been able to locate it in time, I would have been captured as well." Carrie moved as fast as her trembling legs would allow. Try as she might, nothing she did or thought could shoo away her fears. She advanced to the secretary, which stood against the wall, and scribbled a note to Cole. She found a pin in a side table drawer and used it to pin the note to the shawl, which lay over the back of the rocking chair.

With her carpetbag in tow, Carrie followed Tim down the steps into the tunnel. They crouched down and made their way through the dark path and into the stable. Carrie climbed into the wagon with Tim's help. She curled up beneath a few blankets piled in the wagon among a few burlap bags of feed and other foodstuffs.

~~~
~~~

Carrie guessed twenty minutes had passed before the wagon came to a halt in the barn. She threw back the blankets and sat up. She smoothed her shirt and rose to grasp Tim's hand before he lifted her down. They walked the short distance to the farmhouse and he opened a side door.

The room Carrie stepped into was immense. By the time her eyes grew accustomed to the candlelight, she saw it was divided into several areas, which comprised the main living space.

The kitchen had a large cook stove, fireplace, butcher block table, countertops and cabinets. An inviting fire glowed in the fireplace. Carrie counted seven Christmas stockings nailed to the mantelpiece.

A rectangle table stood in the middle of the room. The gleam off the dark wood shone under the chandelier, lit by eight broad candles. Straight-back chairs were pushed under the table. Beyond this space was a common area scattered with chairs of all sizes, and a pirate's chest, which Carrie surmised was filled with toys. Books, toy soldiers, and rag dolls were among the items which lay helter-skelter on a multi-colored rug.

Little children, playing in the area, scrambled to their feet upon hearing their father's arrival.

The children ran toward them, communicating a mix of warm and unintelligible salutations. A brown and white puppy raced alongside the children, wagging its tail and yelping a 'hello' to welcome them. Their attention was divided between Carrie and their father. Three ran to him, but the youngest ones walked up to Carrie and stared. Tim patted a boy's head. He favored his father. The youngsters were like stair steps. For the first time that evening, Carrie felt peace envelope her.

"Now children, let the lady breathe."

Carrie saw a young woman who looked as if she was only a few short years from childhood herself rise from her rocker in the kitchen and waddle over behind her brood. A shawl was draped around her shoulders. The ends folded under her hands, which rested upon her swollen belly.

"Thou are most welcome to our home." The traditional Quaker white cap covered an abundance of dark hair twisted into a bun, which had unraveled. Her eyes drooped with fatigue, but she smiled at the sight of Carrie. Tim gave his wife a loving look.

"Katie girl, don't worry thyself none, I will take care of our guest."

Tim introduced her to his wife and children. The eldest, Eliza was eight, Tim was seven, Katie was five, William was three, and Julia, two.

"Off to bed, children." Kate beckoned, and they followed her without delay. Some looked back at Carrie and waved. Little Julia stopped to pick up a rag doll from the play area before disappearing with her siblings through a door on the left.

Tim lit a candle and led Carrie through the door on the other side of the play area.

She saw several doors along the hallway. They stopped and entered a plain room with a single bed, a table, and a rocking chair. A window behind the chair was covered with heavy drapes.

Tim lit the logs in the fireplace, and soon warmth enveloped the room.

Carrie thanked Tim for the generosity of his family. Before he left, she asked for an oil lamp for her room. "I'm afraid of the dark." She shook her head. "A childhood malady I've seemed to have acquired again."

"You've been through a lot, Carrie. Once you feel safe again, the dark probably won't bother you. I'll get the lamp."

Once the lamp was sitting on her side table, Carrie undressed and slid under the sheets in her shift. She folded her hands and prayed for the safety of her family, Mrs. Weeks, and Cole. Exhaustion settled upon her, bringing a deep dreamless sleep.

CHAPTER SIXTEEN
Steal Away Home

The next morning, after breakfast, Tim left for work. He saw the oldest children to the school house and took the youngest children to the babysitter. He mentioned he'd stop by the telegraph office on his way home.

To pass the time, Carrie assisted Kate with some of the household chores. "I can hardly bear the wait until Tim returns. I feel certain there will be a telegram from Cole. Work keeps me from fretting about what's happening in Mechanicsville. I'll tackle this load for you."

Piles of laundry sat in baskets waiting to be ironed, folded, and put away.

Kate smiled when Carrie started in on the tasks.

"It's nice having another woman to talk to, Carrie. The only socializing I do is at meetings and playing with this little guy, Tidbit." The puppy dashed from the play area and stood wiggling on his hind legs, while its forepaws rested on Kate's knees.

Carrie laughed at the frisky pup.

Kate tickled him behind the ears, and then rose to feed him.

"I get lonely on days like this when Tim is working and the children are away at school. My granny, who lives near, tends to the youngest ones four hours a day. Otherwise, I'd never get any work done. I have you to thank for Tim's company. He works for his cousin, the local blacksmith, during the winter months until the planting season begins. Whenever we have passengers, depending upon the guests, he works part of the day or stays home all day to provide protection and comfort."

Carrie smoothed the lines of the skirt Kate had loaned her. She recalled her image in the chamber mirror after she had donned the plain Quaker attire. Her altered appearance had brought forth a hearty laugh.

Curious about Kate's religion, she questioned her hostess about the beliefs and practices of the Society of Friends.

The young mother's light blue eyes lit up in response.

Carrie learned Quakers were pacifists, who didn't participate in politics. However, their beliefs in social equality and reform challenged the political landscape in which they lived.

Prison reform, humane treatment of the mentally ill and the abolition of slavery were some of their ideals.

Carrie admired their sense of justice for all people. They had been forbidden to own slaves since 1758. Many were abolitionists and advocates for women's suffrage. In their religion, men and women were spiritual equals. Women were encouraged to speak in public at meetings.

"Quakers believe the presence of God is in everyone. Our support of emancipation has a long history. In 1790, we presented an emancipation petition to

Congress during George Washington's presidency." Kate finished pressing a shirt and picked up another.

Carrie took the garment and folded it. "James two, verse eight supports your beliefs: Love your neighbor as yourself. Verse eighteen states: I will show thee my faith by my works. What good is it if people say they have faith but do nothing to show it? If people practiced their faith, many of the ills which plague society would be solved."

It appeared to Carrie the Quaker community lived lives congruent with their religious beliefs, which held them accountable for their behavior. She felt some Christians of other denominations left their religion at the church door, so their actions wouldn't be burdened by the principles of their faith.

"I am so grateful to you, Kate, and your secluded colony, which has become a sanctuary for so many suffering under slavery."

"My folks and Tim's have lived in Foxwood Hollow all of our lives. This town was settled by Quakers in the early 1730s. It's named after George Fox the original founder of the Society of Friends. When most of the Quakers moved to Maryland, Richard Fox, a distant relation, founded this community."

"How fascinating."

A few moments before noon, Tim arrived from the telegraph office with the children and news from Cole. He read the telegram. The Mechanicsville court had freed Mary and dropped the charges against Mrs. Weeks.

Carrie clapped her hands in relief at the news and hugged Kate, who squealed as she threw her arms around her husband's neck.

"Mother is free. I'm sure it's because of Cole's help." Tim grinned at Carrie.

"I'm surprised Mary wasn't hanged," Carrie said in wonder.

The outcome of the trial brought her satisfaction, but Carrie knew the road for the fugitives would be a harder one to walk after their unsuccessful attempt to flee their masters. The possibilities were many. Some slavers maimed or forced a captured runaway to wear an iron face mask or shackle with bells, which announced their every move. Selling them to the Deep South where many fell dead from overwork on the sugar plantations was a common solution, as well.

She had heard about the Franklin and Armfield coffles whereby thousands were led on foot from Virginia to the slave auctions in Mississippi or New Orleans. Their wrists were handcuffed together by a chain running the length of one-hundred pairs of hands.

Carrie grew anxious as the day wore on and there was no sign of Cole. Mechanicsville was less than four miles away. She couldn't guess the reason for his delay. She felt it was an omen.

He finally appeared at Tim's farmhouse by dusk with Mrs. Weeks.

"Tim, I asked Cole to drive me here so I wouldn't be alone." She sniffled. "I need my family, son, to heal my heart and soul after Mechanicsville."

Tim welcomed his mother and hugged her. Tears glistened in her eyes.

Kate was quick to round up the children and get them ready for bed. Her eyes told Carrie she expected the talk to be serious, and wanted the children settled away from the conversation.

Like an oppressive heatwave, tension radiated from Cole and Mrs. Weeks.

Cole had walked into the farmhouse and never sought Carrie out. She reached for his hand, but his fingers didn't clasp hers, so she let go of his.

Why is he so sad?

His shoulders drooped like a man defeated. She was unprepared for his low mood since his telegram held good news. He appeared to be grieving. What puzzled her most: since his arrival, he had yet to look her in the eye.

Cole shook his head. "I am so sorry. I can hardly believe what I saw with my own eyes. It all happened so fast." He fisted his right hand and punched it into his open left palm. He cracked his knuckles before he took a seat at the table.

Tim brought out several decanters of whiskey and brandy, and a pitcher of water. He poured whiskey for his mother, Cole, Carrie, and himself before taking a seat.

"You read my mind." A slight smile curved Cole's lips. He gulped the drink and then poured himself another.

Carrie's hand shook as she took a sip from the glass. She coughed, and Tim was quick to offer her a glass of water.

I should have had brandy instead.

Cole exhaled a laborious breath before he spoke. "I'll start from the time I returned to Mrs. Weeks's farmhouse yesterday with the feed, and then go on from there." Cole plunged into his shocking monologue.

First, he gave a summation of the court hearings in Mechanicsville. Mary had murdered her child in front of the sheriff and his posse. Upon his arrival in court, he learned the judge had appointed an attorney for Mary to prevent him from defending her. The attorney argued for her life to be spared, saying her death would deprive her master of her labors. After all, the child was only a slave. The judge concurred.

Cole argued for Mrs. Weeks's freedom, saying a prison term would be an unusual punishment for a person of her advanced age.

He looked directly at Carrie for the first time. The sorrow she saw there frightened her. He moved his chair closer to hers. His eyes were glassy as he spoke.

"After we left the courthouse, we followed the others who had a head start. By two o'clock in the afternoon, I could see the wagon carrying the fugitives in the distance ahead, led by Sheriff Coffe and his posse. Mrs. Weeks sat next to me. She'd started to regain some of her color. After the trial, she fainted from nervous exhaustion. A doctor was called before we returned to Richmond, which was the reason for our delay.

"To my surprise, Mary and Joshua started to sing."

"I am very familiar with the song," Mrs. Weeks sat up straighter. "It's called 'Steal Away.'"

"I told Mrs. Weeks, it seemed strange to sing at a time when they were returning to slavery."

"I felt the same." The elderly lady kept her eyes fixed on Cole. "The original tempo is a haunting one, but they had sped it up. It was all wrong. They'd improvised a bridge, unusual for a spiritual. The traditional composition is one of verse and chorus." Mrs. Weeks shook her head.

"I tried to figure out what they were doing," Cole said. "I'd heard spirituals had double meanings, so I asked her about it."

"I explained the song's history to Cole. This tune is usually sung when slaves get ready to board the Underground Railroad. It's a call to folks planning to flee to a hidden meeting place in the woods. It's time to steal way to freedom. However, on the surface, it means dying and going to heaven."

She recited the words:

"My Lord, He calls me
He calls me by the thunder.
The trumpet sounds within-a my soul.
I ain't got long to stay here.

"Steal away (Oh!) steal away,
Steal away to Jesus.
Steal away, steal away home,
I ain't got long to stay here (no, no, no).
I ain't got long to stay here."

"These lines were added." Mrs. Weeks looked toward the ceiling as she recalled the words.

"When the bright stars glow,
It's time for me to go.
When the moonbeam gleams,
The path to glory seen.
And when the North Star shines,
I know its quittin' time.

And my Lord, he calls, he calls,
He calls me, he calls me,
He calls me, he calls me, home."

Cole continued the story.

"Ahead, we saw the family descend from the wagon and head for the river. I figured they would relieve themselves and the lawmen would take off their handcuffs.

"One deputy followed them while Coffe and the other two remained on horseback. Then, something went terribly wrong.

"Coffe and one lawman jumped down from their horses and ran to the river. The uneven landscape obstructed my view, and I strained to see what was ahead. I remember Mrs. Weeks squeezed my arm.

"As we got closer, we saw Mary and Matthew, her oldest boy. She pulled him down and held him under water as he fought her with vigor. Deputy Lewis attempted to reach her, but he stumbled. Moments later, the boy's body went limp."

Mrs. Weeks shuddered. "'Steal away to Jesus,' is what Mary shouted as she raised her face to the sky."

Cole shifted in his chair. "Lewis gained his balance and was within arm's-length of Mary. Joshua lunged at Lewis, but the lawman dodged and punched Joshua in the side. He turned around, grabbed Lewis by the neck, and both men fell. Larson arrived and attempted to help Lewis but was struck in the face. He struggled to stand but fell into the water. Moments later, both Joshua and Lewis rose. Joshua's uppercut felled the lawman.

"As Coffe approached Joshua with his pistol raised, Joshua snatched the gun out of his hand. He struck the sheriff in the mouth and threw the gun to Mary.

"Coffe scrambled to his feet and ran to his horse. Little Mary and little Joshua ran off into the woods. Mary fired at them, but missed. Jedidiah trembled and raised his rifle. He aimed at Mary and fired, but she moved quickly and dodged the bullet.

"Lewis rose from the water in front of Joshua. Mary turned toward the deputy and fired. The bullet struck Lewis. His body slapped the water hard, and a wave washed over Joshua. A stain on Joshua's shirt spread across his stomach. The bullet had gone through Lewis's body and hit Joshua.

"For a brief moment, husband and wife stared at each other." Cole's voice shook. "He smiled at her and they both mouthed in unison, 'I love you.'

"'Steal away to Jesus,' Mary screamed. Joshua's body fell hard and sank beneath the surface. Jedidiah stood motionless. Mary raised her gun and took aim. Her finger touched the trigger.

"A blast threw Mary's body several feet back before it plunged into the river and then rose to the surface. Coffe held a smoking rifle in his hand."

Cole shook his head. "When we got to the river, we saw Mary's body afloat. Mrs. Weeks was sobbing, and I put my arms around her. We sat motionless for a while in shock.

"Coffe saw the children hiding behind a tree and ordered Jedidiah to get them. Larson dragged Lewis's body out of the water and laid it on the riverbank. He sat a few feet from the corpse. He complained to Coffe, he feared he wouldn't get paid, now that all was left were two children. Coffe assured him, he'd be paid."

Cole took a deep breath. "Jedidiah led little Joshua and Mary, away from the river and lifted them into the wagon." Cole placed his hands over his face and lowered his head.

~~~

Cole had spoken in a quiet voice. At times, Carrie had to strain to pick up some of the words. She was horrified. Everyone around the table had sat in eerie silence as they listened to his narrative.

"What happened to their...." Kate's voice trembled.

"We buried them in a nearby Negro Burial Ground." Cole raised his face, and his eyes held tears.

Carrie jumped up from the table, gasped, and hurried to her chamber.

Cole was on his feet in seconds. He followed and found her sitting on the bed. "May I?"

She nodded and he sat next to her and put his arm around her. She laid her head on his shoulder. She struggled to hold back her tears.

"Go ahead. Let it out. Breathe. Shout. Cry. Just get it out." He handed her his handkerchief and she let the flood of tears run down her cheeks.

She cried out, took ragged breaths, and then continued to sob. When she was finally able to talk, she said, "I just met them, and now they're lost to me forever."

"I'm so sorry, Carrie. I've failed you and your kin."

"There was no way you could have prevented what happened. You didn't know their plans. The song, 'Steal Away,' was their final solution to end their enslavement if all else failed."
~~~

"I couldn't bear the thought of anything happening to you on the road. You have my word, Carrie. I will see you safely to Canada. I—I can't lose you—er I mean, I can't let anything happen to you. As long as I draw breath, I will do whatever I can to win back your freedom."

CHAPTER SEVENTEEN
The Reverend Jones

Carrie and Cole rose before midnight to continue their journey north.

Tim, Kate, and Mrs. Weeks had breakfast with them before they left. Kate packed beef jerky, biscuits, and cured ham for them to take along.

Ready to embark, the couple bid the Quaker family good-bye and thanked them for all they had sacrificed.

Once the horses were hitched to the carriage, Cole helped Carrie onto the passenger seat. His roomy Clarence horse-drawn carriage could transport several fugitives, if any waited at the next safe house.

They didn't expect to encounter anyone on the road at this late hour.

Cole told Carrie to climb into the carriage and hide under the blankets if they encountered danger.

Once again, she wore Jonah's clothing. She hid her hair under a woolen flat cap and pulled the brim down low over her eyes.

"Where is the next safe house, Cole?"

"It's about sixteen miles from here. It'll take us a day's ride."

"I traveled through there on my way to Richmond. It seems like a lifetime ago." Carrie looked at the path ahead in the darkness. The moonlight illuminated parts of the dirt road, which was lined with trees.

"We can rest at the Reverend Solomon Jones's farmhouse tonight. From his place we have a five-day ride to cover fifty-five miles to Fredericksburg."

"What's the reverend like?"

Carrie heard respect and joy in Cole's voice as he described the minister.

"Reverend Cornelius Solomon Jones was a passenger I helped escape to Canada. He was a free man who slipped into the slave quarters to preach and teach. One of the slaves overheard a plot to have him arrested, so Solomon had to flee. The quickest way I could get him out of Richmond was to book passage for him on a train, as my maid."

"How did he look?" Carrie grinned.

Cole chuckled. "He was the ugliest woman I have ever kept company with. His 'breasts' never looked right. While I helped him adjust them in the baggage compartment, the ticket man walked in and caught me 'fondling' my maid. From then on, each time the conductor saw me, he gave me a conspiratorial wink. To keep up the ruse, I always winked back." He laughed and Carrie joined him.

"Why did he return to Virginia?"

"He said he couldn't enjoy his freedom when so many of his people were enslaved. He believes it's his calling—to free the enslaved. He's now a stationmaster. He converted the basement of his farmhouse for passengers. On his property, he built a church where slave and free can worship together. He's being watched."

"I'm proud of people like Solomon—and you—guideposts to those who seek freedom." Carrie shook her head. "I know I've said this before, but I never thought I'd be in the same predicament as a runaway slave."

"You're not alone. I'm your lawyer, and your friend. I intend to keep you safe."

After two hours on the road, they rested the horses and stretched their legs for a spell. When they stopped a second time, Carrie suggested they eat the food Kate had packed in her carpetbag.

By mid-morning, they had reached the sprawling farmhouse. Two stories high, it had blue shutters and four huge chimneys. The usual farm structures dotted the landscape, and the steeple of the one-room church gleamed in the bright sunlight.

~~~

Cole's knock was answered by a teenaged boy, who slammed the door in their faces. Carrie and Cole exchanged glances.

Fear expanded in Carrie's chest. *I hope this is the right house.*

A few seconds later, a bear of a man carrying a pistol opened the door.

He frowned at the white man and boy who stood on his doorstep. In an instant, his face broke into a wide grin. "Come on in, my friend." Solomon's bass voice rumbled with joy. He pumped Cole's hand and laughed with glee. "Alma, they're here." Turning to Cole he said, "Got your telegram. We expected you long before now."

He apologized for his son who thought Cole was a lawman. The reverend introduced Edward to the newcomers before he instructed him to feed and take care of Cole's horses.
~~~

Solomon was as tall as Cole. His snow-white hair, considerable girth, horn-rimmed glasses, and heavy features made quite an impression.

Alma stepped into the hallway. Her slim frame was clad in a plain gingham dress under a long, starched, white apron. Her long braids framed a caramel-colored oval face. She wasn't pretty, but she exuded dignity and grace.

Cole greeted her and introduced Alma to Carrie.

Carrie smiled and shook her hand.

Afterward, Cole and Carrie sat with the couple and brought them up-to-date on their journey.

They both needed rest.

Solomon raised the lantern and led them downstairs to the basement, where the sanctuary for fugitives was located.

"Isn't there a hidden room on the other side of this wall?" Cole pointed.

Without responding, Solomon pushed aside two tall highboys standing at the back of the room to reveal an identical set of floor-length bookcases. He pulled a lever between the bookcases, which separated to reveal a sitting room with a sofa and desk. Six chairs circled a crude table with a colorful ceramic bowl as the centerpiece.

"Where will we sleep?" Carrie looked about.

The reverend indicated the closed doors located at each end of the room. "I trust you both will get a good rest."

Carrie hurried to open a bedroom door. The decorations were minimal but the bed and a pretty oil lamp on the side table was a most welcome sight. Personal touches made the small space cozy. A ragdoll lay upon a hand-stitched quilt. A crucifix hung on the wall above the bed.

~~~

"If you were my daughter, I wouldn't trust you alone with any man." Reverend Jones frowned.

Carrie stood by his side at the hearth and filled her plate with chicken, mashed potatoes, corn, and baked bread.

"Well, except for my friend Cole." Reverend Jones grinned.

"He's a gentleman." Carrie gave Cole a surreptitious glance. "He's proven it at every turn."

They joined Alma and Cole at the table.

Carrie answered her host's questions about her predicament and life on the run. She was about to recount the tragedy of her relatives, but her voice trailed. Cole laid a hand on her arm and gave them a brief account.

~~~

The husband and wife looked stunned after hearing the narrative.

Cole changed the subject and started to reminisce about the past adventures he'd shared with the reverend.

"I have a scrapbook, Cole, with articles your daddy wrote about his last trial. Carrie's case has some similarities." He rose from the table to retrieve the book from another room.

"I haven't read those since they were published. Perhaps, I'll get an idea about how to defend Carrie if she ever goes to trial."

Solomon returned shortly with a thick scrapbook. "I've been collecting newspaper clippings for years on many subjects." The reverend thumbed through the book until he located the articles and handed the book to Cole.

"Celia was on trial for first degree murder," Cole read. "It was a case of self-defense against rape. If a man is killed by a woman who's defending herself against rape, Missouri law exonerates her, as does Virginia law. My father tried to apply the self-defense law in Celia's case. However, he was unsuccessful in his argument that the law should include enslaved women as well."

"Imagine if it did." Solomon shook his head. "There'd be a dead man in every plantation home."

Cole looked up. "The irony is, the law doesn't extend its hand to *protect* enslaved or free colored women against forcible rape, but they are in the grip of its jurisdiction, and must adhere to unjust laws or be punished by them. I think I've found my strategy. I'll have to argue that a free colored woman must be allowed to defend herself against rape. She has no master and is not a slave. Thus, the law must apply to her as it does to free white women."

"Let's hope I can get to Canada before you have to argue my case," Carrie said.

While Cole read the articles about the trial, Alma handed her husband the newspaper. "There's something in here you should read."

~~~

Solomon scanned the article, and then looked up from the paper at Cole. "Buddy, do you remember Floyd? Floyd Nelson?"

Cole nodded.
~~~

Carrie and Alma looked on.

"He's formed a militia of runaway slaves. They say he murdered his master."

"My God. Floyd, a murderer?" Cole shook his head.

"The papers say he's a copycat Nat Turner."

"Please stay here until he's caught." Alma placed a hand on Cole's forearm. "More bounty hunters and slave patrols will clog the roads."

Cole shook his head. "I don't know. If it weren't for this case in Philadelphia, we'd stay."

"They're liable to search every free colored person's home, in a case like this one," said Solomon.

"What's Floyd's story?" Carrie looked from Cole to the reverend.

Cole turned to her. "Floyd once lived on the Mayfair Plantation. His wife refused to return to the fields after giving birth, so her food ration was cut. She was allowed to nurse her child every six hours. Not long after, the child died of starvation. Depressed, she starved herself to death. Soon after, the barn caught fire, and the master suspected Floyd. As punishment, he sold him to a Mississippi slaver."

Solomon continued. "After a few months, he escaped and led a murderous midnight attack. He and a few other escaped slaves headed northeast, killing along the way. The authorities expect his destination is the Mayfield plantation."

"I met the master of the Mayfield plantation, a Mr. Wilson, at the New Year's Eve ball." Carrie looked at Cole.

"Floyd ought to head to Canada or out West." Alma shook her head. "'Vengeance is mine,' sayeth the Lord."

"He may prefer to die fighting the man he blames for his family's deaths." The newspaper caught Carrie's eye. It was *The Liberator.* "May I?" She held out her hand.

An article caused her heart to leap in her chest. She recognized the drawing of a man with a full beard and close-cropped hair. The headline read: *New York Attorney Believed to Have Been Kidnapped by Slave Catchers.*

"Oh Lord." She bit her lower lip.

"What's the matter?" Cole inquired.

"Frank Turner's been kidnapped."

"Frank Turner. Is he the man you're engaged to?" Cole's eyes narrowed.

Carrie nodded and began to read aloud. "According to the article, Frank's boyhood friend, Calvin Davis, gave an eyewitness account: *'Frank and I were attacked by three white men. They beat us and left me for dead. When I awoke, Frank was missing. I remember hearing them say Frank would replace a runaway who had died in their custody.'*"

"Frank's a fugitive too. How uncanny. The world's gone mad, and we've been swept up in its fury." Carrie lowered her head and sighed. She turned the paper and saw another article, which caused her to cry out.

Cole moved closer, so he could read it, too.

There was a hand-drawn picture of her as well. Her heart fluttered. *The Liberator* quoted *The Richmond Times*: *Let us not be persuaded by the perpetrator's sex or beauty. Carrie Bennet is a killer who cut down one of Richmond's most revered citizens in the prime of his life. Nothing should satisfy a law-abiding public but the death penalty.*

"May I keep this?" Cole tore the article out of the newspaper and put it in his breast pocket. He turned worried eyes on the reverend.

"I think you've already made the decision."

~~~

As the noon hour approached, the couple gathered their belongings and prepared for their journey to the Fredericksburg depot. Alma provided them with basic comforts: food, additional articles of clothing, a warm quilt for the coach, and a flask of brandy.

Carrie prayed they would get to the train station without incident.

The horses fed and rested, Cole and Solomon hitched them to the carriage. Solomon promised to go into town in a week or so and retrieve Cole's carriage and horses at the livery.

Carrie hunkered down in the carriage on the way to the station. They thought it best she stay out of sight.
~~~

CHAPTER EIGHTEEN
Insurrection

An hour into their journey, Cole shouted down to her. “Hide yourself. There’s a group of white men ahead.”

Cole took a deep breath and squared his shoulders.

Carrie crouched down on the floor of the carriage and disappeared under the quilt. *If they’re a posse, are they after me?*

~~~

As the carriage neared the mounted men, their badges were evident.

“Whoa. Whoa.” One of the men jumped down from his horse and stepped forward. He waved his arms, signaling Cole to stop.

The carriage came to a halt a few feet from a dilapidated barn on the right side of the road, partially hidden by the thicket of trees. Another man approached and grabbed the reins from Cole’s hands.

“Hey, wait a minute.”

“Get down from the carriage.” The first man motioned to the ground. “We’ll need your help to put down this slave revolt. A band of niggers and renegade Indians have joined forces. They’ve butchered entire families. We suspect its Nigger Floyd’s gang.” He spat on the ground.
~~~

The lawmen appeared haggard and disheveled, but their eyes burned with the fervor of righteousness.

Cole threw up his hands. “I’m sorry, but I’m in a hurry to get....”

The leader interrupted him. “I’m Sheriff Metcalf, and your refusal is not an option. I’m deputizing you to help us haul in the renegades. If you refuse, you’ll be arrested. The Fugitive Slave Law requires you to assist me if I need extra hands. Now dismount.”

Cole took his time to reach the ground.

“Search the carriage.” Metcalf addressed the deputy. “He might be harboring runaways himself, for all we know. What’s your name, mister?”

“West, Cole West.”

The deputy approached the driver’s side of the carriage and yanked the door open. The quilt Alma had given them, which covered Carrie, came into view.

Cole’s heart did a somersault like a fish on a hook when the deputy snatched the quilt off the floor. He tossed it on the seat. The carriage was empty. Carrie had fled.

Cole realized she must have slipped out while the lawman was questioning him. His jacket was soaked with sweat from fear Carrie would be discovered. *Bless the girl. She’s gotten away.*

His heart beat like thunder from both fear and elation. He suppressed a smile.

The sheriff ordered Cole to get back onto the driver’s seat and follow him to the plantation. “We need your coach to transport our injured to the nearest plantation, while we fetch the doctor.”

As he rode through the melee, it appeared the whites had regained control. A few slaves and Indians stood chained together, while deputies with rifles stood on guard. More colored men were being rounded up and added to the chain gang.

Cole looked toward the plantation house just in time to see several slaves run from the mansion.

Boom. An explosion blew out the windows, scattering glass and wood as flames devoured the once-majestic home. The roof collapsed, and it was reduced to rubble in a cloud of dust and debris.

"Jeff and Henry, get the chain gang on the road before we're attacked again." The sheriff shouted over the din. "Now, let's put this rebellion down and chain the rest of the savages."

The lawmen obeyed.

Cole looked across the road to the barn where he thought Carrie might be hiding.

While the lawmen's attention was elsewhere, he jumped from the carriage and moved toward the shack.

As he crossed the dirt road, a mob of colored men emerged with a few white men in pursuit.

Once they caught up with the escapees, a vicious fight ensued. The colored men outnumbered their oppressors and overcame them with sticks, fists, and chains.

Cole was knocked to the ground as two colored men attacked him.

~~~

Horrified, Carrie watched the fighting from her hiding place in the shack. She lost sight of Cole but could see black clouds swirling in the sky as the acrid smell of smoke permeated the air.
~~~

Her thoughts were interrupted as the back door flew open, and a colored boy sprinted across the floor toward the front door.

An angry white man with a pistol yanked the boy by his shirt and slapped him. "Ya damn niggers," he bellowed. "You and the rest will pay for what you've done. I'm the overseer of this here place, and you've got an obligation to obey me. So, give up."

When the fugitive didn't obey, he punched the boy in the face, splitting his lip. Blood trickled down the teen's tattered shirt as he fell to one knee.

A noise drew the white man's attention, and the boy grabbed the pistol.

They wrestled for the gun. It fell and skated across the room. Carrie dashed for it, shocking both males by her appearance. They froze as she retrieved the weapon and waved it at both of them. The white man stepped forward.

"Let the boy go or I'll shoot."

The man stood still as if confused by her words. He appeared deceived by her fair skin and male clothing.

"Whose side are you on, boy? This nigger's a runaway." He turned toward the slave and raised a fist.

Carrie slammed the pistol against the back of his head, and he fell to the ground with a heavy thud. The boy stood up to his full height. Traces of childhood still clung to his round features and thin frame. Rage seized him, and he began to kick the unconscious man.

"Stop, stop. He can't hurt you anymore, and you might rouse him. You'd better get out of here while you can."

"Thanks sir—er miss." The boy vanished through the door.

Carrie looked out and saw Cole's body lying prone on the ground. He wasn't moving. *I must rescue him.* She hoped to do so undetected.

She tucked the pistol into her waistband and crouched low to the ground. The marauding men had moved on, leaving Cole and other white casualties sprawled on the dirt.

Soon she was at Cole's side. "Cole, can you hear me?" She held her face close to his, but he remained still. She attempted to rouse him, but she heard men shouting as they approached.

The din of the men's voices grew louder. Carrie had to flee before they saw her.

Once again hidden in the shack, she kept her eyes glued to Cole's form. An argument broke out among the men, as they neared Cole.

A few walked about examining the fallen whites. A long haired, bearded man knelt down and slashed each white man's throat. Carrie watched in horror as he approached Cole. *How can I save him without putting my own life in danger? I must save Cole.*

She aimed the gun and was about to squeeze the trigger when someone struck her on the back of the head, and darkness swallowed her.

CHAPTER NINETEEN
Frank's Education

Loud voices awakened Frank as he lay in the wagon. He opened his eyes to a starlit sky. The pain in his shoulder intensified with every bump in the road. He had tried to escape and had been shot. Jeb's fury at the prostitute's kindness was expressed by a bullet.

He sought out his captors. Frank's ears caught their slurred speech. He saw Scott raise a pint to his lips. How he longed for the warmth of liquor.

Where are they taking me now?

In order to distract himself, he recalled the passionate legal banter he had enjoyed with his father and proposing to Carrie. Heretofore, his life had been a testament to the power of freedom.

Frank wasn't like other free Negroes. His family was successful in the white man's world. Even so, his education hadn't shielded him from the bigotry he inherited because of his skin color. His achievements defied the doctrine of inferiority of blacks, which whites swore as fact. Wasn't he proof of the opposite?

Ugh. A spasm of pain ended his reverie. The wind ruffled the thin blanket, and his teeth began to chatter. He prayed, as he wove in an out of consciousness.

His fear heightened when he realized four other colored men shared the wagon. Were they kidnapped free men, like himself? Chained together, he wondered if their heads bowed from shame or pain. Poor devils, just like him, were caught up in the pathway that led straight into the fiery hell of slavery.

They're lucky if they're dead. Dead slaves have no value. Dead slaves feel no shame, feel no pain. The irony struck him as funny, and he almost laughed out loud.

"We're here." Jeb slowed the wagon.

Ahead, Frank saw a grand mansion. *This is where the devil, which possesses the power of life and death over me, lives. Edmond Dantès must have felt as I do at first sight of the Chateau e'If.*

Beyond the gate of the splendid residence, Big Red disappeared into a side door. He emerged a while later with a well-dressed white man of senior years.

Scott and Jeb gripped the chains and led the gang off the wagon. Other men appeared and relieved the bounty hunters of their prey.

The white man scowled as he looked at Frank, who lay on the wagon floor.

"Master Dayton, we had no choice. The niggah you sent us after fell ill and died. This niggah came along and—"

"Did Jeb kill my boy?" Dayton's eyes skewered Big Red's. "Did you take him to the Lumpkin farm?"

"Er—er." Big Red nodded. "'Spect you'll be adding to your nigga crop come summer, Master Dayton."

"'Spect I will." Dayton threw back the blanket and appraised Frank. "All right, he'll do. Is that blood I see?" Anger hardened his voice.

"He tried to get away, Master Dayton." Jeb's blunt fingers walked around his hat brim. "That nigger ran so fast there was no other way to stop him."

In a flash, Dayton's uppercut slammed into Jeb's ribs. He doubled over gasping and wheezing.

"You fool, you might have killed him. If you had secured him properly, he wouldn't have tried to escape. I bet you killed my boy, Willie. Don't expect to get your full pay for destroying my property or for taking him to the Lumpkin farm. Don't none of you try to cheat me. I can easily find out how much you were paid."

Dayton ordered his men to put Frank in the cabin next to Pap and his daughter, Black Hattie. "They'll tend to him. Then come 'round back for your pay. Except you, Jeb, I 'spect you owe me money. Matilda will get y'all something to eat. But first, take off those irons."

Frank wore an iron collar and iron handcuffs.

Big Red unlocked Frank's chains.

Moments later, Frank lay on a cot in a dark cabin. A creaking door opened, and the wind whistled past.

A young woman appeared carrying an oil lamp. Its amber glow shone on her chocolate complexion. She set the lamp on the table and pulled up a stool. "I's called Black Hattie."

"I've been shot. Please help me." Frank could barely get out a whisper.

A white bibbed apron covered her calico dress. Her head wrap was made of Kente cloth fashioned like a crown. "I's gon' ta help you. Don'tcha worry none. My pap be heah soon ta git dat bullet out. You hungry?"

Frank moaned and shook his head. He fought overwhelmed fatigue to stay awake.

A short middle-aged man entered carrying a tray of medical implements.

Black Hattie left and returned with a bowl of broth, as the old man examined him. The man introduced himself as Pap, Hattie's father. He stared at the sodden vest. He pointed out the fine cloth and detail of the design to Black Hattie. Pap sat on the edge of the bed and took off the blood-stained clothing to reveal a jagged hole in Frank's shoulder.

"Hattie, give him da leather ta bite on while I git dis bullet out."

She pulled a chair from the table and set it next to the bed. Black Hattie sat down before she grabbed the strip of leather off the tray and brought it to his lips.

"Bite on dat. Take a deep breath, mista, and hold still."

"Wait, Pap." Black Hattie retrieved a canteen. "Brandy." She lifted his head, and he drank.

Warmth traveled his length. Frank bit down on the leather while Pap dabbed whisky on the injury.

Frank groaned. Sweat appeared on his forehead. He struggled to stay conscious as Pap extracted the bullet.

Black Hattie bandaged the wound, and together they washed Frank's chest and arms and tended his bruises.

Pap announced he was going to get some clean clothes.

"Hattie, we ain't neva seen da likes of him 'round heah. Dem clothes suggests he ain't no slave."

After Black Hattie left, Pap dressed Frank in a homespun nightshirt. He pulled a pair of woolen socks on his feet and then spread several quilts over him. When he had finished caring for the stranger, he banked the fire and dropped into the rocking chair, tucking a quilt around himself. “We ain’t neva seen da likes of you ’round heah.” He shook his head.

Frank, aware of all that had been said, groaned and finally drifted off to sleep.

~~~

Daylight flitted through chinks in the slave cabin. When Frank awoke, Black Hattie was stirring a pot of broth, hanging on S hooks over the hearth.

“Where am I?” He attempted to rise but fell back against the pillows made of bundled rags.

Black Hattie hurried over and eyed his bloodied bandage. He noticed the bulge of her belly for the first time. He guessed she was about three or four months pregnant.

“Lie still, mista, while I change your dressin’. You on da Dayton plantation.”

“I’m Frank. Thank you, er—er—”

“Black Hattie.”

“Black Hattie’s your name?” Frank said, as he frowned.

“I’s called Black Hattie, ’cause dere’s a light-skinned woman named Hattie, too. She called Pretty Hattie. Dat’s so no one will mix us up.”

“To distinguish yourself, you could add a second name, like Hattie Rose or Hattie Mae. Calling her Pretty Hattie because she’s fair and you Black Hattie because you’re dark is absurd.”

“You think—I’m pretty?” Black Hattie leaned forward.

“Yes, you *are* pretty.”

She dropped her chin and looked up at Frank with coy eyes. “Thank you, Mista Frank. I *like* the name Hattie Rose.” She straightened and smiled.
~~~

"Well, call yourself Hattie Rose if you want to."

"How can I git peoples to go along wid what I say?" She frowned as she reached for several clean white strips of cloth on the tray.

"Say you won't answer to anything but Hattie Rose. They'll get the message." He winked and grinned.

Hattie Rose giggled and smiled, then covered her mouth.

"Don't hide your smile, Hattie Rose. It's beautiful."

Hattie Rose dropped her hand away from her mouth. She giggled again, showing even white teeth. Frank noticed how the curve of her high cheekbones lifted as she grinned. Her bow-shaped lips, darker than her face, were the color of a glossy plum. Her brows had a natural arch above her long thick lashes. Her almond-shaped eyes were shining.

"Hattie Rose, the way you've fashioned your head wrap is impressive. It looks like a crown."

"I'm a seamstress. I make all de dresses for da white ladies, and when I can get some extra cloth, for de colored folk as well. 'Cause, you know, we only get one outfit a year, and it don't last all year long. When Missy let me have some scraps, I make use of dem for folks in da quarters."

Yes, she is pretty.

"I bet you're hungry."

"My stomach's growling."

With Hattie Rose's help, Frank sat against a blanket she placed between him and the cold wall. His eyes took in the cabin. A rough-hewn table and four chairs occupied the center. A collection of wooden masks, decorated with shells and beads, sat on pine shelves. He admired the diamond-shaped designs Pap had carved into the packed dirt floor. Hattie Rose said it was his attempt to dress up the cabin.

Hattie Rose set a tray before Frank with a bowl of broth and a plate of ash cakes on wooden dishes along with utensils. She poured brandy into a cup from a canteen adorned with hand-painted pictures.

Frank studied the designs.

She described it to him as she sat in the wooden chair she had left by his bed. "Dis here canteen made from a buffalo horn. Pap helped nurse an Indian brave once, and he give Pap dis canteen. The pictures show da brave huntin' da buffalo. It's one of Pap's prized belongings."

The broth and ash cakes tasted delicious. Frank asked for more, and Hattie Rose filled his bowl several times.

She also poured more brandy. The liquor helped him relax.

Inside the cabin, he finally felt warmth and comfort.

"The child you're carrying—does the father live here, too?"

She frowned at Frank, and then dropped her gaze.

Frank inquired once more, but she rose, turned her back, and left the room.

~~~

As the days wore on, Frank's strength grew. By the end of the second week, the overseer came to see if Frank was ready to work.

He blustered through the cabin door on Monday morning with a bullwhip wrapped around his shoulder and under his arm. His other hand gripped a bundle. He yanked the covers off Frank.
~~~

Frank bolted upright and pulled the quilt up to his waist.

A pair of cold, green marble eyes stared at him. The blond hair was cut short. His dirty collar exposed a prominent Adam's apple. His lanky body slouched in a pair of baggy pants. His lips were set in a pink line. Porcupine quills of blond stubble peppered his chin.

He ordered Frank out of bed and led him through a series of exercises. Frank walked the length of the cabin several times and bent his knees. But he was only able to lift his right arm above his head. The left shoulder and arm were still sore.

Hattie Rose had cautioned Frank about the overseer, Mr. Green. Men like him, she said, weren't too far from slavery themselves. So, they used hatred and violence to put more and more distance between themselves and all Negroes. No amount of bloodshed or black misery could quench their thirst.

Frank saw something else in the overseer's eyes he couldn't fathom. Hattie Rose told him southern poor were often called "poor white trash" by their wealthy relations, who encouraged their better-fed and better-clothed enslaved household to do the same. *Divide and conquer*, Frank thought when she had explained this societal dynamic. It's the oppressors' long-standing policy of dominance and manipulation over others.

Frank vowed not to provoke the man. He didn't want to feel the lash on his back.

"You'll do limited work, fancy nigger, until you done healing." Green looked Frank up and down and then threw the bundle at his feet. "Dems ya work clothes. No more fancy duds for you, niggah. Get 'em on and meet me in the east field. Be quick about it, or I'll thrash ya. You'll call me Mister Green." He pointed to his chest. "Mister Green."

His thin bowlegs framed a swath of daylight on his way out of the cabin.

Jealousy, it was jealousy Frank saw in the overseer's eyes.

~~~

Frank's life became filled with backbreaking winter labor, a poor diet, and little rest. He mended fences, built cabins, slaughtered livestock, and cured hams. He avoided the social gatherings held on Saturday evenings, the slaves' time off, which extended to all day Sunday. Many wanted to hear about New York City, but he gave them curt answers. Some called him uppity, while others steered clear. It would take months before his shoulder was completely healed. Escaping beforehand would be foolish. There were other dangers on the plantation which could delay his time to leave.

However, he had one unforeseen obstacle: Hattie Rose.

Like the floral moniker she'd adopted, he saw Hattie Rose flower like a rosebud. Her confidence lit up every room she entered. He witnessed men noticing her beauty for the first time. Several young men told her she was as pretty and sweet as a rose. As Frank had predicted, everyone called her Hattie Rose, even the white folks.

She smiled more often.

Pretty Hattie felt displaced. She had been considered the prettiest girl on the plantation, inside or outside the Big House.
~~~

Hattie Rose's relationship with Frank grew. She mended his clothes and included him when she prepared meals for herself and her father. Frank, in turn, made renovations and repairs to the cabin she shared with Pap.

He often found reasons to walk along the moonlit paths in the evening and asked Hattie Rose to accompany him. As time passed, Frank realized his affection to Hattie Rose had gotten out of hand. By the middle of February, his feelings for her had deepened, and it frightened him. He was astonished to discover he had pushed back the date to escape so he could see Hattie Rose. This was exactly what he was afraid of, caring about someone on the plantation with whom he felt he could never leave.

He had to come to his senses. He devised a plan to withdraw from her emotionally. Instead of lingering in the cabin she shared with Pap after dinner, he said his good-byes earlier and earlier. He made an effort to avoid looking into those big brown eyes, so full of curiosity and warmth. He did his best not to stand too close, lest his urge to slip his arm around her waist or push an errant strand of hair underneath her headwrap overwhelmed him.

What if he asked her to go with him? She'd slow him down. Babies could be born anytime. Some came early. What if she gave birth on the trail and needed medical attention? Perhaps she was waiting for the father of her child to return.

By the end of February, their relationship had changed drastically. Fewer smiles passed his lips. The twinkle in his eye whenever they shared a laugh seldom appeared. Absent, too was his kind touch upon her hand or shoulder.

A wedge formed between them. Like a gust of wind, it pushed them apart in the opposite direction. He spoke to Hattie Rose but only to answer her questions. He no longer initiated conversations.

He knew she missed the smile he had beamed at her every morning when he first saw her. He ceased his flirtatious banter and initiating the funny jokes they had shared. He'd better keep his mind on devising a plan of escape instead of letting a pretty woman distract him.

Hattie Rose and Pap had been delighted when Frank volunteered to teach them how to read and write. The idea occurred to him the evening the word "dat" slipped out of his mouth. His offer was as much for himself as it was for them.

One day, while Pap and Frank were chopping wood, the older man expressed his concerns. "Frank, you've made such a difference in our lives, and we're grateful. I know Hattie Rose isn't what you want for a mate, you being a lawyer and all, but you shouldn't be so hard on my little girl. She's in love with you. I'm not asking you to treat her like your intended, but you don't have to be so—"

"Distant?"

Tears brimmed Pap's eyes. "She was once a happy seventeen-year-old girl, Mista Frank. Ever since she came back from the Lumpkin farm, she's changed."

Frank's axe fell to the ground.

"She came back pregnant. There was a hurting inside her which ran so deep, even I couldn't reach it.

But, after you came, I saw her become better than her old self."

A driver on horseback appeared and struck the ground between them with a bullwhip.

The men jumped apart.

"Get back to work."

CHAPTER TWENTY
I Shall Be Free

"Chester, in here." Dayton discovered Frank in the library.

Upon hearing the name "Chester," Frank cringed.

"Why are you in the library?" Dayton's frown deepened.

"Er, sorry, sir. I made a wrong turn. Still learning my way around, Master."

"Of course." Dayton raised an eyebrow. "We're waiting for you in the parlor. You will address me as 'Massa'. I trust I won't have to correct you again."

Frank nodded. "Yes, Massa."

The first time he had been invited to enter the mansion, Frank was determined to find the library. He held the violin and bow in his long slender fingers and followed Dayton into the parlor. In his breast pocket was a thin pamphlet he had "borrowed." He could hardly wait to read *How to Make a Slave* by Willie Lynch.

His fear subsided as he joined his fellow musicians, who made up the chamber music ensemble.

Luke, the eldest slave, played the viola, and his son, Thomas, the cello. Abe, the youngest at twenty, played the violin. With a nod from Luke, the musicians began one of his favorite pieces by Mozart, "Eine Kleine Nachtmusik."

Frank learned the musicians had been kidnapped for their musical skills. His own musical skills were like icing on the cake for Dayton. Orchestral music was Frank's favorite, but he also enjoyed playing spirituals, gospel, and the new syncopated tunes they practiced for their own enjoyment.

~~~

Several weeks earlier, while mending fences, Frank's ears were assailed by screeching violin notes. He couldn't resist the chance to impart some advice to the player.

He followed the sounds to the back of the house. There stood a white boy of about eight-years-old holding the instrument.

Frank approached him. "Young man, I can help. The violin is like the human voice and can evoke a myriad of emotions."

The child surrendered his instrument without a word.

Frank lifted the violin to his chin. "If it's sadness you're trying to convey, make it moan like this."

The bow glided across the strings, and the corners of the little boy's mouth pulled down.

"Or, if you want to kindle happiness, make your instrument laugh, like this."

Frank's bow soared across the strings, and the child laughed and clapped his hands.

Dayton appeared and applauded with enthusiasm.

"You must teach my boy how to play as well as you do. I insist." He looked at his son. "From this moment on, Charles, he will be your teacher. We'll fire Mr. Brownley straightaway. What is your name, boy?"

"Frank."
~~~

"Frank?" Dayton frowned and shook his head. "It will never do. From now on, you'll be known as Chester. Yes, Chester, now that's a proper name for a violin teacher." Satisfied, Dayton put his hands on his hips and rocked on his heels. "If you can improve my son's playing, I'll give you wages of your own, Chester. Would you like that?"

"Yes, indeed, Master Dayton.

Dayton frowned.

"I meant to say Massa Dayton."

Dayton smiled.

Money would enable a successful escape.

Frank relished his thoughts of escape but knew he had to be careful when to leave and decide where he would go. There was talk amongst the slaves of an agent of the Underground Railroad amongst them, but he had no idea who the person might be. He couldn't ask around. Some slaves were spies for their masters and racked up privileges and rewards for themselves for their betrayal.

Frank noticed the parlor for the first time upon his return. The room was painted eggshell white. The cornices and chair rails were made of hand-carved ebony and shone like glass. A two-tiered cake with creamy icing dominated the center of the dessert table. Delicate bows of blue and yellow dotted Dayton's birthday cake. Other confectionery delights included a sweet potato pie, two apple pies, English plum pudding, and a box of chocolates.

Upon a nearby table, decanters of spirits and wine set alongside an exquisite display of crystal glassware, Davenport English china, and a sterling silver coffee service. Frank took a closer look at the china since Hattie Rose appreciated its beauty.

After several musical selections, the players were allowed a break to enjoy refreshments in the kitchen.

Frank welcomed the respite.

“What are you hiding, Hattie?” Frank had slipped into the pantry behind her.

She jumped at the sound of his voice. Pretty Hattie’s furtive glances had aroused his suspicion.

“Oh, it’s you, Chester.” She breathed a sigh. “I thought you were old Wallace. He’s Massa’s spy, you know.”

“I can keep a secret. Hattie, in our own society, will you please call me Frank?”

She looked puzzled. “All right, *Frank*, if you like.”

“It’s my identity, a link to my past. What are you hiding?” He glimpsed a newspaper, and his excitement grew.

“Nothing.”

At one time, Frank had admired Pretty Hattie. She sometimes wore her hair loose. The abundant ringlets fell to her shoulders in a most attractive way. He noticed she had more than one dress, and the material was finer than what the other women wore. However, once he learned she had replaced Mary as Massa’s bedmate, he felt nothing but pity.

She fluttered her eyelashes and waved the newspaper in front of him.

The word *Liberator,* flashed before his eyes. *Is it William Lloyd Garrison’s newspaper?* Maybe it contained an article about him. He grabbed the periodical out of Hattie’s hands with lightning speed.

“That wasn’t very nice.” Pretty Hattie pouted.

With trembling hands, he scanned the words. It was *The Liberator* with a picture of Carrie on the front page. She was accused of murder. She was a fugitive, like a common runaway.

"May I have this? I'll give it back."

"Go ahead. Take it. I can't read it anyway."

"Maybe I'll teach you, one day."

Pretty Hattie smiled.

Carrie had become a faint memory, like his freedom. *How strange.* He and Carrie had lost their freedom at the same time. *Does she know about my misfortune?*

Frank hid the newspaper under his shirt and bolted through the kitchen door. He lingered in the hall, to listen to the whites' conversation. With his nerves on fire, he needed a little time alone before he had to don the vacuous mask of an obedient slave.

"I've seen a few of her kind in my day, Lucius." A woman's voice reached his ears. "Damn near white, like those New Orleans octoroons, pretty, and speaking like a college graduate. My cousin couldn't take his eyes off her."

Frank peeked through the half-closed door to see the speaker. He recognized Susan Johnson, the mistress of Twin Oaks. She exemplified the model of the Southern belle, whose beauty and character were at odds. Her violence toward her slaves, who labored for her benefit, was legendary.

"A damn shame about John." Dayton moved closer to the woman. "I knew his antics would someday catch up with him."

Susan's eyes blazed in contempt, and then she smiled. "Did you hear about the death of Carrie Bennet's Aunt Mary, Lucius?"

"Of course. Sheriff Coffe sent a telegram before my deputies got back. Damn fool woman."

"Any survivors?" A young brunette turned to join the conversation.

"Yes, my men brought back two of her children, a boy and a girl." A faraway look clouded his eyes. "She was a damn good slave. Born here, she'll be missed by many."

Susan nodded with a smile. "I'm sure she will be."

~~~

Frank took the long way to his cabin, reliving the facts of his kidnapping. He remembered the events with clarity.

Calvin. Calvin was missing. Three white men had attacked them after they left the Fraunces Tavern. They had kidnapped his boyhood friend into slavery. The realization hit like a bolt of lightning. What had the white man said? Calvin looked like a slave who had fled from a Virginian plantation. What else had they talked about?

Frank tried hard to remember. It was something terrible. Now their words came back. They had killed a slave, and Calvin was the replacement.

Frank had headed home for his horse, Gold Nugget. A five-minute run had brought him to his front door. Mounted on Gold Nugget, he galloped south.

Instances like these had motivated Frank to become a lawyer. In 1850, when Frank was twelve-years-old, the Fugitive Slave Law had passed. Frank reasoned if escape to a free state was no longer a sanctuary, then
~~~

free Negro men and women were also at risk. Any white person could challenge their freedom.

Like Solomon Northrup, a free man who was kidnapped into slavery in 1841 had spent twelve years on a southern plantation. His determination to get justice through the courts was thwarted at every turn. Had he been successful, the courts would have been flooded with cases such as his, a threat to the institution of slavery.

"Liberty and justice" were not for all.

When will the stalwarts of justice abandon their hypocrisy and provide those very same democratic principles it extols for its white children for its dark children as well? Have we not shaped this country from our own sweat, blood, and bones? Let freedom ring in the slave cabins, the courtrooms, and the plantations. His heart cried out for justice. When will America listen?

Frank had been riding for more than an hour. With each step of his horse, his spirits sank.

Then he heard the deep rumble of masculine voices. He slowed his horse. Crickets sang. Frogs croaked. Two opossums scampered across Frank's path.

The glow of the moonlight revealed the slave catchers at their campfire, about a thousand feet away. The firelight illuminated their white faces, and Frank recognized the giant who had carried Calvin across his shoulder. Searching the area, his eyes rested upon a dark figure huddled against a wagon. It was Cal. He was tied to the spokes of the wagon wheel. Calvin's head rested upon his chest as if in slumber.

Frank planned to approach Calvin after his captors had fallen asleep. He sat on the cool ground and rested his back against a huge rock. The aroma of bacon and coffee spiked his hunger. He watched the slave catchers eat, smoke, and drain a whiskey bottle. After a while, they drifted off to sleep.

The young lawyer waited a full hour before he made his move. Frank crept toward Calvin. When he reached his friend, he put a hand over Calvin's mouth.

Calvin started.

"Quiet, old buddy." A scarlet bandana cut across Calvin's mouth with tight cruelty.

Frank produced a knife and freed his friend. The two men stole away from the campsite.

A horse whinnied. Within minutes, the slave catchers roused.

"We can't afford to let those niggers get away." Big Red fumbled for his pistol as Scott dashed off after their quarry.

"We've got to hurry." Fear stabbed Frank's chest. "Gold Nugget is just beyond the big oak."

They raced ahead, but just as they glimpsed the oak tree, Frank twisted his ankle and fell to the ground. Calvin stopped to help him.

The three white men appeared.

Without a word, Calvin ran for his life. He grabbed the reins of Frank's horse and mounted. Fear sped him away from slavery and the cries of his boyhood friend.

The men turned on Frank like a pack of wild dogs. He was struck from all sides. The butt of a rifle slammed into his chest.

"Mighty kind of you to offer yourself in your friend's place, fancy nigger."

Frank was stunned. Calvin had deserted him after he'd risked his life to save his friend.

Frank fought his attackers, but a vicious punch to the midriff brought him to his knees.

Big Red slammed his fist into Frank's face, and he'd plunged into darkness.

CHAPTER TWENTY-ONE
Moses Delivers

Carrie opened her eyes and beheld strange people staring down at her. The family was dressed in worn clothing and threadbare coats.

Field hands, Carrie surmised. Her hand sought her charm, and comfort flooded her. She looked around and found her carpetbag a few feet away. She scanned the contents. Nothing had been taken. She thanked God the fugitives were honest people.

There were two men: one tall and muscular and the other short and fat. His pudgy cheeks were like a chipmunk's. A tall, thin woman stood behind the men with worry in her eyes.

With every heartbeat, an angry pain throbbed inside Carrie's head. Her memory returned as she sat up. Lawmen took Cole, and she'd sought refuge in a shack.

The chipmunk man walked toward her. "Don't be frightened, Miss Lady." He picked his teeth with a stick.

Carrie noticed the chewed-off fingernails of his dirty hands.

The man next to him stepped closer to the woman, and Carrie could see farther. Sitting fifty yards away, she saw a figure leaning against the crook of a huge tree. Moonlight cast the figure in silhouette.

The other man finally spoke. "Dis here our guide. She gonna lead us to Canada. We couldn't leave ya behind. Seen yo wanted picture up on da broadsides, so I knowed ya best be comin' wid us."

The woman nodded. "Yeah, we couldn't let ya be caught."

Carrie frowned.

"I was 'bout to gib up on y'all. Y'alls late." The shrouded figure stepped forward. "Glad to see you, Chloe, Joe, and Felix." The woman addressed the people who surrounded Carrie.

Felix waved.

"Who is dat ya got wid ya?"

"Sorry, ma'am. We got sidetracked. Dis here da girl day all lookin' for." The woman pointed. "Carrie Bennet, she done kilt a white man. She fought back. Amen. We had to knock her out, 'cause she was gonna git us caught."

"Carrie Bennet, heh?" The guide smiled. "Not gonna take her lessen she wants to come."

Carrie groaned and touched the painful spot on her head and found a bump. "Ow."

"We sorry, ma'am. You was gonna get us kilt by shootin' at dem mens." The tall man stood next to Chloe, who shifted the bundle in her arms, and Carrie realized she held an infant, swaddled in tattered blankets.

"You're da one dat hit her." Felix looked at the other man, whom Carrie surmised was Joe. "I'd never hit a lady." Felix lifted his head and smiled at Carrie.

Is he flirting?

Of the clan, he was the most ragged. His jacket sleeves were too short, and his feet were clad in broken shoes. His appearance displayed the poverty and neglect common in slavery.

Joe lowered his head and stared at the ground. "I's sorry, ma'am." He raised his head and turned regretful eyes upon Carrie. "But I ain't had a choice."

"What happened to Cole, my friend? One of the fugitives was going to—cut his throat."

Chloe stepped toward her. "It looked like dey did, right before we stopped ya from shootin'. Couldn't see it directly."

Carrie sobbed.

"Dey aimed to cut every white man's throat dey come across who lay on de ground. After dey left, de white mens put dere dead in a wagon and a coach. I'm sorry 'bout your friend, miss. He's most likely dead, so you best come wid us. Here yo gun."

Carrie's hands shook as she took the pistol and shoved it into her bag.

"Only if ya wants to." The guide moved forward away from the tree.

Her head was wrapped in a bandana under a wide-brimmed hat pulled down low. Over her coat, she had draped a large shawl. In her gloved left hand, she held a sturdy walking stick.

Carrie wiped her eyes with a handkerchief and then nodded. What else could she do? At least this group had a plan to leave the south. Like Cole had said, settling in Canada would circumvent the arms of southern jurisdiction.

The guide offered her right hand to Carrie, who clasped it and rose to her feet. "Thank you." Carrie was surprised by the strength of the petite woman's grip.

She introduced herself. "I's Harriet."

Carrie did likewise.

"We bes' get going."

The slender woman joined Carrie. "I'm Chloe. The handsome one is my husband, Joe." She nodded toward the tall man. The couple appeared to be in their early twenties. "And the pudgy one is Felix, my brother-in-law."

Chloe rejoined her husband. Carrie walked behind the guide with Felix in the rear.

Twinkling stars studded the inky black sky, and the full moon dappled its light upon Harriet's secret path.

Oh God, for aiding me Cole has paid the highest price. I'll never forget him. Carrie shivered. The tears turned cold on her cheeks.

As she followed the group, an indescribable feeling seized her. *Chloe didn't seem sure he was dead. If by some chance he survived, he'll go to Mr. Stephens's home.*

Carrie stared at the guide and felt strength radiating from her. A surge of hope engulfed her.

"Dat's Harriet Tubman." Chloe fell into step beside her. "Dat's da woman everybody calls Moses." Chloe spoke with pride. "We be safe like we's under Michael's wings."

Carrie stared at their guide in wonder.

Harriet stood no more than five-feet, two-inches tall. She strode over the forest floor as if it was her backyard. Dark-skinned with plain features, easy to overlook, Harriet's face belied the bravery and resolute allegiance to freedom she possessed.

Guiding enslaved people to freedom time and again had made her a living legend. For some, she was the Lord's disciple, her name spoken in whispered reverence. For others, her masterful escapes evolved from a powerful, nefarious talent, belonging to some other world. For both supporters and detractors, the similarities of Moses and Harriet guiding their people out of slavery were impossible to ignore.

The group trudged along the secret corridor. A whiff of fragrant Virginia pines invigorated them. A spicebush with yellow pungent flowers glowed in the moonlight.

A whimper from the baby punctured the silence.

Chloe told Harriet she had to feed her daughter. When they reached a clump of winterberry bushes, they rested.

"Let's eat." Joe looked around. "Who's got the food?"

"There's no guessing about dat." Chloe chuckled. "Your brother, Joe, and let's pray he's left a bite or two for us."

As the baby suckled, Felix rummaged through his carpetbag and produced a loaf of bread. He passed pieces to the group.

Harriet added fruit and nuts. Carrie found portions of cured bacon and ham Alma had packed. She also shared the canteen of water. Inside the carpet bag, lay *Romeo and Juliet* with Cole's poem written inside. Carrie caressed the book. Once again tears fell. She closed the bag and shut her eyes. Cole's handsome face loomed in her memory. She opened her eyes and shook her head. This wasn't the time to think about her loss but she wouldn't give up hope. She clasped the talisman around her neck and whispered a prayer. If he were dead, she was sure she'd feel it in her heart. *We are kindred spirits.*

In the far distance, they heard the sound of barking dogs.

"Dem dogs be comin' after us." Fear widened Felix's eyes.

"I knows what to do 'bout dat." Harriet summoned the fugitives. They cornered a squirrel, killed it, and smeared its blood on some old clothing Harriet had with her for this purpose. She walked away from their secret trail and dropped the clothing near a pond, making sure several pieces fell in the water.

"Dem dogs will lose our scent and latch on to dat squirrel's. When dey see dem clothes in de water, dey will think dat we done swum through de pond. Dogs can't follow a scent through water."

As the group continued their journey, they heard the barking grow faint. Another hour passed and then another. Drunk with exhaustion, they begged Harriet for a few minutes' rest.

After about twenty minutes, Harriet ordered them on their feet. They had to reach their destination before daylight.

Felix saw a tree stump a few feet ahead and ambled over to it. He sat down and sighed. "I can't move. My feet's too tired to walk."

Chloe stood and stared at him. "Alla us tired, Felix. Get up."

"Well, you best move 'cause ain't nobody gonna carry ya." His brother took the baby from Chloe. The discussion went on for another few minutes. Everyone sympathized, for their feet were sore as well.

Harriet finally spoke. "Come on, Felix. We is all dead tired. When we get to the hidden camp in the woods, you can sleep all day long. We're less than two hours away."

"Don't dat sound wonderful?" Joe scowled.

Felix still wouldn't budge. He then uttered something detestable to all. "I may as well wait here, till dey comes and I can go back. Cain't move my feets no mo', Harriet."

"Felix, I can't believe whatcha done said." His sister-in-law looked at him with wide eyes.

"Did I hear, right?" Harriet glared at him.

Everyone eyed their guide with worried looks.

"Harriet, I'm too tired to walk any mo."

"Too tired? With a bounty on my head, I risk my life to come back for ya, and ya too tired?"

Her laugh sent shivers down Carrie's spine.

"I never heard of a slave too tired fo' freedom. Ya too tired to walk to freedom but ya ain't too tired to go back to slavery, where dey work ya like a mule, a horse, and an ox all at de same time?"

"I'm sorry, y'all, my feets is bleedin'. Dey is mighty sore. De white folks ain't gonna leave us alone, no how. I'm gonna go back, and I won't tell dem nothin' 'bout where y'all is. Y'all have my word."

"You can keep yo word. If you can't stand the pain of bleedin' feet walkin' to freedom, you won't be able to stand de lash on yo back." She leaned close to him. "Deys gonna whip ya till yo skin slips off ya back. Do you know pain like dat? The pain of swollen feets don't come no way close. Dey'll whip ya as an example to others. Let me tell you something, Felix, I know yo gonna give us away."

The scar on Harriet's forehead was joined by a frown between her eyes which produced the shape of a snake. She'd been struck by a two-pound iron weight intended for a runaway slave at twelve years old, which left her a sufferer of narcolepsy,

"Dey'll torture ya till ya tells dem what dey wants to know." Her voice got lower and softer and she leaned in, inches from his face. "Like, what road we done took. Where we're headin'. I ben goin' up and down des here same road, time and time again. And when ya tells dem, if I let ya go back, I can't use dis road no mo'. Dis road be crawlin' with slave catchers. Ya gonna give us away and I can't let ya do dat. I'm responsible for alla us. And I can't let one person spoil de chance of freedom for de rest of us." She pulled a revolver from under her coat, aimed it at Felix, and cocked it. "I may as well shoot ya right now."

The look in her eyes caused the fugitives to step back.

Shaking, Felix raised his hands in the air. "Now, Miss Harriet. Don shoot. I can do it. I knows I can do it now. My feets just needed more rest than de rest of y'alls." Felix got up to prove that he was able to walk.

Carrie looked down at his bare feet. His shoes had fallen off some time before.

Carrie offered to wrap his feet and extracted the extra shirt from her carpetbag.

"Thank ya, Miss Carrie."

She ripped the garment and bandaged his feet.

CHAPTER TWENTY-TWO
A Hidden Camp

Word of the slave revolt had spread across the nation. Newspapers carried the story in various detail. Few called it what it was: an uprising. Generally, the white press described it as a riot to suggest it was spontaneous. The description downplayed its dynamic. It took forethought and bravery to execute this well-planned revolt. For slave owners, this represented a frightening concept. It proved slaves could suppress their hatred and delay their vengeance in order to catch their masters unaware. Smiles and cordial nods by the enslaved to their masters were suspect.

The Negro press took a different slant. *The National Era* warned the slaving community uprisings would continue until all slaves were free.

Floyd's insurrection had alarmed even the most sympathetic white supporter. Black hatred was revealed as a reality to be reckoned with. The capture of runaway slaves and criminal fugitives was given the highest priority by law enforcement. Half of the rebels were caught and hung, but Floyd escaped.

As Harriet Tubman and the fugitives headed north, they saw an increasing number of wanted handbills on broadsides. Carrie bemoaned how many she saw of herself. She ripped them down wherever they appeared.

By the time daylight had chased away the night, the exhausted fugitives neared safety. Several days into the journey, they had reached Maryland. Five men stood guard as the tired group approached the clandestine camp. The guards saluted Harriet upon sight.

A camp vibrant with life appeared in the midst of a dense forest. Huts built against hillsides had been camouflaged by vermillion winterberry bushes and evergreens. Each contained several rooms dug into the earth. The camp's inhabitants had created a source of refuge for hapless runaways on the road north toward freedom.

Mundane pleasures took on monumental importance to those deprived of even the simplest comforts as they traveled, always in danger: a comfortable chair to sit upon, warm food, and a supportive community.

A group of children played blind man's bluff. Knots of adults sat inside the huts conversing. Lovers huddled in corners together sharing dreams.

The expectation of good food, a long rest, and the company of fellow runaways was like an elixir to their beaten souls. They smiled at the happy brown, tan, and pale faces of their ethnic kin.

Harriet led her charges into the largest hut. Over sixty people welcomed them.

Carrie was surprised when she learned some slaves had been residents of this camp for a decade. Despite its crude way of living, they could work and rest at will. Whatever the hardships, they were free from the master's whip, the mistress's belt, and the overseers' hot branding irons. Moreover, they had escaped the incessant verbal abuse of their masters, which corroded their self-worth.

Outside, where the campfire blazed, people milled about. Several cooked breakfast and prepared dishes to be eaten later.

Inside, the residents greeted Harriet with kind words and hugs. She was escorted to the most comfortable chair. A crowd gathered around the woman many saw as their savior. Kisses were bestowed upon her nut-brown cheek, and she was offered gifts, including quilts, clothing, and money. She made good use of the gifts. She changed her clothes, stuffed the money inside a pocket, and wrapped a quilt around her shoulders.

Harriet Tubman might as well have been royalty. Men, women, and children were eager to comfort the woman called Moses. Some greeted her with tears in their eyes. Others thanked her for saving their kin.

"The Lord is great. He never fails you, sister."

A man appeared with a tub of warm water and submerged Harriet Tubman's feet in its contents.

The residents invited them to sit and rest. A tub of warm water was brought out for each of the runaways.

Harriet sighed with pleasure as she wiggled her toes in the tub. Then, she introduced them. A woman had come to Chloe and offered to care for baby Gloria as she rested. She looked to Harriet, who gave a nod, and then Chloe surrendered the child to the woman. Harriet introduced her to the rest of the fugitives.

Huge plates of campfire food were set before Felix, Joe Harriet, Chloe, and Carrie. The meals were delicious, and the fugitives ate their fill.

Feeling relaxed for the first time in days, Carrie took off her hat and was surprised by the gasps and laughter her action produced.

One young man stepped closer and examined her. "I thought you were a boy."

"It was my intention." Carrie shook her hair and ran her fingers through it to smooth out the tangles.

A man fastened hard eyes on her.

Goosebumps rose on her arms.

He leaned against the wall in one corner of the hut with a newspaper in his hand, but his eyes focused on her. Carrie's fingers traced the contours of her charm.

I'm with Harriet Tubman. Why can't I be trusted? Once again, Carrie felt her skin color was a barrier between herself and the others. Anger stirred within her, and she returned the man's cold stare.

Above the hubbub of conversation, a single voice rang out. A disheveled man entered the hut and moved from person to person with questions about his family. "Have you seen Mama and da babes?" He addressed a child who screamed at the sight of him.

"Come on now, Randy." A white-haired woman steered him to a nearby table. "How about getting something in your stomach?"

A woman in a blue-checkered bandanna crept up to Chloe and Carrie. "Dat's Randy, a field hand from de Marlboro plantation. Got here 'bout two days ago, rambling on 'bout his wife and kids. Dey say deys dead, but he just won't accept it. She died under the lash after her plan to run off was discovered. When

Massa sold the children, Randy ran off to search for them."

Carrie understood him. His tragedy was so extreme he created a different reality where hope was possible. *What had Mason said at Twin Oaks? Plantation life is full of uncertainties.*

The man who had been staring at Carrie came over and sat next to her.

She eyed him and prepared to defend herself.

"You're the girl I've read about in the newspaper." He spoke in flawless English. "Carrie Bennet, isn't it?"

Carrie felt the blood drain from her face.

"Good luck, sister." He gave her the newspaper. "I'm sure you'd like to read about yourself."

Carrie took the paper. It was *The Richmond Enquirer.* A hand-drawn picture of her dominated the front page. The article recounted the same details of the crime she had read in *The Richmond Times.* However, it listed a one-thousand-dollar bounty for her capture. The reward was offered by the law firm of Liftman and Stevens. Carrie wondered who had put up the money for the bounty.

Carrie knew the reward would entice more bounty hunters.

Another article caught her attention, an editorial about the anniversary of Stuart West's murder. She recalled the pain in Cole's voice as he recited the events which led to his father's death. Now, he too was gone. A longing for him stirred an ache in her heart. She placed a hand on her chest and took a deep breath as a current of grief ran through her. She would miss the feel of his big hands holding hers and the sparkle she saw in his eyes whenever he looked her way. Her inner voice whispered a revelation to her. *You loved him.* Tears rolled down her face. She mourned the love lost to her forever. Yet, their kindred spirits were entwined for eternity.

When darkness fell on the second night of their stay, Carrie was awakened by a firm hand. She opened her eyes, and Harriet stood over her.

"I've got a feelin' we needs to be quittin' dis place now. I seen it in a dream. Dis place is no longer safe. Deys been warned, but some said deys gonna stay and fight, if necessary."

Without a word, Carrie rose to join her.

CHAPTER TWENTY-THREE
A Safe Haven

When the fugitives passed the sign, Byberry, Bucks County, Pennsylvania, in early March, their cheers jarred the late afternoon serenity. Their two-hundred-thirty-three-mile journey had been lengthened by inclement weather and traveling with an infant. At times, the fugitives traveled by buggy and wagon which some conductors provided.

Although this was not their final destination, Harriet told them people of color had made extraordinary gains here. They were curious to see for themselves what freed people had accomplished.

The Quaker founders of the state abolished slavery in 1780, and prior to the Fugitive Slave Law, refused to return fugitives to their masters. Thus, a Tubman favorite, this long-established, colored middle and upper middle-class community abounded where a fugitive could disappear and create a new identity.

Their destination was Harmony Hall, a sprawling homestead, which rivaled the beauty of any southern plantation. The sight raised their spirits as their pains seemed to melt like icicles in the sun.

Harriet Tubman hurried along the path, bordered by English boxwoods, and climbed the front steps of the house. The brass knocker formed a calligraphy designed as an initial P. The fugitives followed, passing winterberry trees dotted with tiny fruit, glowing red in the sunlight.

Music spilled through the massive door. The man who answered Harriet's knock was the embodiment of high society. His attire was exquisite and his good looks, exceptional. Shiny black, wavy hair with a touch of gray at the temples contrasted with his white complexion and European features. His dignified bearing led Carrie to put his age at around forty.

Had Harriet Tubman not informed her, Carrie would have thought his lineage all European, which would have vexed him. She could identify with his sentiment. She, too, walked a tightrope between the two Americas.

"Welcome, cherished friend." His radiant smile was cast upon Harriet. Then he added, "and guests."

Harriet sank into his arms. She had praised Robert Purvis's accomplishments to her charges. A passionate abolitionist, he served as president of the Philadelphia Underground Railroad, charter member of the American Anti-Slavery Society, and president and vice president of the Philadelphia Vigilance Committee and the Pennsylvania Anti-Slavery Society.

His home was affectionately called "Saint's Rest" by the abolitionist community, where more than nine-thousand fugitives passed through on their road to freedom.

Once inside, a tall, handsome, tan-skinned man filled the doorway. Tears filled his eyes. "Once more, Moses has delivered God's children from bondage. God bless you all."

"Frederick, its mighty good ta see you again, mighty good."

Harriet turned to the group. "This here's my friend, Frederick Douglass."

Behind him, appeared a middle-aged, white man, who grinned at Harriet. "Thomas Garret, the fugitive slave has no kinder friend than you."

"Hello Harriet." He nodded and clasped her hands. "I brought thee a new pair of shoes and a collection from the Society of Friends." He gave her an envelope.

"Thank you, Thomas." Harriet slipped the envelope inside her pocket. A servant appeared and offered to take the shoes to the bedchamber she'd occupy. Harriet peeked inside the box before she thanked the dainty little maid. She introduced the fugitives to Mr. Garret.

"Why are so many prominent people here?" asked Carrie.

Mr. Purvis responded. "My wife's society is sponsoring their annual fundraiser tomorrow. Each year, it becomes more elaborate than the previous year. There will be noted guest speakers, games, races and a ball. The money will fund the activities of our various anti-slavery societies. Frederick and Thomas are amongst the guest speakers. Harriet will speak as well. It's why she brought you here before going on to Canada. Come in, everyone." Mr. Purvis led them into a vast parlor.

The arrivals soon realized they were in the presence of many celebrated defenders of liberty. The fugitives stared open-mouthed as they were introduced.

Chloe shook Mr. Douglass's hand and stared at the regal halo of black and silver hair.

Felix's hand trembled as he greeted Mr. Douglass.

Joe wore a sheepish grin as he told the renowned abolitionist he was his hero.

"I feel so ashamed," Chloe whispered to Carrie, as she stared down at her clothing. They had left what was left of their footwear in the vestibule. "Meet'n Mr. Douglass in dese dirty rags and bare feet."

Carrie smiled and put her arm around the young mother, whose sleeping infant started to stir. "Don't be ashamed, Chloe. Mr. Douglass was once a humble slave who traveled to freedom by foot and boat. I'm sure his clothes got dirty, too."

Chloe smiled at the young maid who offered to take her daughter off her hands.

A beautiful fair-skinned woman headed towards them. She was dressed in a royal blue silk tea gown. Mr. Purvis introduced her, as he held her hand. "May I present my wife, Harriet Forten Purvis, one of the founding members of the Philadelphia Female Anti-Slavery Society."

"...and suffragette," Mrs. Purvis added. She shook hands.

Felix was the first. He wiped his hand on his clothing before grasping Mrs. Purvis's soft hand, one which had never felt the blood-ripping assault from picking cotton.

When it was Carrie's turn to meet their hostess, she inquired, "Forten, any relation to James Forten, the sailmaker?"

Mrs. Purvis nodded. "He was my father, an extraordinary man. He walked to Philadelphia at fourteen after being released from a prison ship in Brooklyn, New York after the Revolutionary War."

Her husband added, "He was one of the most successful businessmen, white or colored, in Philadelphia."

The entire Purvis family had advocated for emancipation and universal suffrage, including Harriet's niece, Charlotte Forten, Mr. Purvis's brother, Joseph and sister-in-law, Sara Louisa Forten Purvis, Harriet's sister. The brothers shared ownership of the family estate, which consisted of several thousand acres, worth over a quarter of a million dollars.

Also present were William Wells Brown, the famous writer, and the anti-slavery poet Frances Harper, whose poetry Carrie admired. When she spied a familiar face, she crossed the room. William Still, secretary of the Philadelphia Vigilance Committee, greeted her and stepped back to appraise Carrie.

"Mr. Still, I'm a mess." Carrie understood how Chloe felt.

"Despite your recent perils, it's evident you've grown into a beautiful young lady. How is your family?"

"They're all well, except for mother." She frowned. "Consumption has taken hold of her, but she's getting the best of care. Sammy is growing like a weed."

Mr. Still conveyed his wishes for Sarah's improvement. "I'll pray for her recovery."

Carrie's eyes were riveted on a handsome woman in conversation with Mrs. Purvis. She wore a dark green gown, which set off her deep brown complexion. The woman's cultured voice was distinguishable amongst all others. When Mrs. Purvis's eyes met Carrie's, she led the stranger to the newcomers.

"Carrie, Joe, Felix, and Chloe, may I present our special musical guest for our benefit concert tomorrow, Miss Elizabeth Taylor Greenfield, the renowned opera singer. Perhaps you've heard of 'The Black Swan,' as the press calls her?"

The travelers looked puzzled, all except Carrie. "Oh my, Miss Greenfield, I'm delighted to meet you. I've read about you, but never had the pleasure of attending a concert." She curtseyed and Miss Greenfield responded in kind.

"It's a pleasure to meet you." The artist clasped Carrie's hand.

Carrie gushed. "I saved the *Richmond Enquirer* article about your Command Performance at Buckingham Palace for Queen Victoria, in my scrapbook."

The singer smiled at the compliment.

Joe, Chloe and Felix looked at their feet as Miss Greenfield stood before them.

"Please don't be embarrassed if you've never heard of me. Although, I've led an extraordinary life, I too was born into slavery."

Chloe, her husband and brother-in-law raised their heads and stared open-mouthed at the performer.

"I was blessed to have had a mistress who freed me as an infant. I fight injustice through music by donating a portion of my salary to Negro charities and churches. God bless you all for your courage. We are all inspired by it."

"You got that right, Miz Greenfield. We was in plenty danger, but we were brave." Felix wiped the sweat off his brow. "I almost turned 'round, but Harriet encouraged me, and I soldiered on."

Chloe rolled her eyes at Carrie, who suppressed a giggle.

The trio of musicians switched the musical selections from classical to spirituals. When their instruments played Tubman's favorite, "Steal Away," she started singing, and others joined her.

Sadness crept over Carrie. The song reminded her of the loss of Cole and her kin. This was the same song Mary and Joshua sang when they chose to end their lives. However, when Miss Greenfield's voice rose and fell throughout the song, adding color and texture, Carrie found she was held spellbound. A rich tenor joined in, its powerful depths rolling underneath the singing voices, anchoring the melody with dramatic waves of its own.

All eyes turned to the foyer and beheld the commanding presence of a tall, broad-shouldered man, who walked toward them as he sang.

The song ended, and Miss Greenfield hurried to welcome the handsome golden-skinned gentlemen. She hugged him and clasped his broad, sculpted hand in hers. The singer turned to the crowd and she introduced him with high-spirited accolades.

"May I present Mr. Thomas Bowers, my former protégé. Now, he's an accomplished concert singer in his own right."

Applause erupted throughout the room.

"Thomas, will you join me in a selection or two from our previous repertoire as my surprise guest at the concert tomorrow night?"

Mr. Bowers nodded and smiled.

Moments later, Mr. Bowers was surrounded by new admirers. After each introduced themselves to him, they implored him to sing again.

He pleased them with a familiar Spiritual, "Free at Last," which he dedicated to Tubman's charges. He signaled for all to join in. Soon, a wall of voices resounded.

When the song ended, the former fugitives hugged one another, some were teary-eyed. The last leg of their journey was before them but the most dangerous part was behind them. A solemn hush spread over the crowd as they watched in reverent solidarity.

Refreshed after scented baths, the travelers were transformed by the formal attire loaned to them by their host and hostess.

At dinner, Carrie wore a yellow silk gown, which complemented her lustrous chestnut-colored hair.

Joe looked dashing in tails. Chloe sent him doe eyes across the table. She was delighted by the pink gown she wore, which flattered her cinnamon-brown complexion.

Felix, who was shorter and stouter than Mr. Purvis, borrowed a suit from the butler. On his way to dinner, he stopped to preen at every mirror along the way.

Carrie enjoyed the dinner conversation. It was a fountain of intellectual thought. Subjects abounded, from slave uprisings to culture and politics.

"Uncle Robert, what did you think of Mr. Lincoln's speech at Cooper Union?" Charlotte's eyes widened as she looked at her uncle.

A gleam shone in Mr. Purvis's eyes, and he clenched both his fists and raised them in the air before he launched into a description of Abraham Lincoln's address. "He refuted Stephen Douglas's misinterpretation of the founding fathers' intentions about the expansion of slavery in the territories. He denied the Democrats' assertions that Republicans and the anti-slavery sector are responsible for John Brown's raid and all slave insurrections. Lincoln said Brown wasn't a Republican, and slave insurrections have always been a part of our history. Moreover, the cruelties of slavery are reason enough for folks to flee from it or fight against it." He paused and cocked his head. "Lincoln possesses a sound mind, capable of logical thought. He uses facts to form his opinions and arguments not fearmongering and falsehoods, as does Douglas. He'd have my vote if my voting rights are restored before the election." He clenched his jaw and shook his head.

The Purvises expressed an interest in the personal histories of their guests. One by one, the fugitives gave a brief description of their lives. The host family appeared riveted by their accounts.

Carrie had intended to recount the tragic deaths of her family and Cole, but her voice faltered and her eyes filled. She fingered the charm which rested on her chest.

Charlotte Forten, who sat next to her, laid a hand on Carrie's arm. "You don't have to continue. We understand."

Carrie cleared her throat. She blinked back tears, and turned her attention to Harriet Tubman, the hero of the hour.

Carrie raised her glass to offer a toast. All the fugitives followed her example, as each thanked Tubman for helping them arrive at the "City of

Brotherly Love and Sisterly Affection." The rest of the diners raised their glasses for the toast.

After dinner, the ladies retired to the drawing room, where libations and sweets awaited. The men enjoyed cigars and pipes before joining the ladies. Carrie informed Mr. Purvis she needed to send Thaddeus Stevens a note about Cole's death and get word to her parents. He escorted her to the study.

"Carrie, I'm sorry to hear about Cole. His father and I worked together on the Underground Railroad. I heard he had followed in his father's footsteps."

"Yes, he was a stationmaster." Carrie's throat tightened and her eyes watered as thoughts of Cole rekindled her grief.

"I know Mr. Stevens well. We're blessed to have his support, as a United States Congressman and leader of the Radical Republicans."

Carrie expressed a desire to visit the ailing titan before she left for Canada. She hoped against hope Cole had contacted him.

"I'll send one of the servants to post your letters." Before he returned to the drawing room, Mr. Purvis offered to accompany her on a future visit to the politician's home.

Alone in the study, she wrote to her parents, using her middle name. Then she penned a letter to Mr. Stevens. She informed him of Cole's death, at the same time saying a prayer of hope that he might somehow have survived. With her messages in hand, she returned to the drawing room.

Mr. Purvis offered her a chair and handed her a snifter of brandy.

Carrie sipped the warm topaz-colored liquid.

Mr. Purvis rang the servants' bell, and the butler appeared.

Carrie handed him the missives but was astonished when he returned moments later. Behind him she spied the outline of a tall, well-built man. His face was obscured but his bearing seemed familiar. Intrigued, Carrie rose to get a better look.

It can't be.

She felt faint at the possibility, while her heartbeat thumped in her ears. The butler stepped aside, and the man came into view.

"Oh, she doth teach the torches to burn bright." The man beamed with joy.

"Cole," Carrie whispered. The crystal glass slipped from her hand, and its golden liquid melted into the carpet. Heat rushed through her body, and the floor rose to meet her.

"My goodness, she's fainted." Charlotte's far-away voice penetrated her consciousness.

Cole knelt by her side and patted her cheek.

Her eyes fluttered open.

Cole held her hand.

He's alive. She stared up at him. "I prayed you had survived. I felt in my heart you were alive. Am I dreaming?" She clutched his muscular bicep for confirmation.

"No, I'm here. We're together again."

"Take her upstairs." Mr. Purvis ordered. "I'll send for the doctor. By the way, sir, you are...?"

"Cole. I'm Cole West, Stewart's son."

"There's no need for all this fuss." Carrie rose with Cole's help. "The last time I saw you, a man was about to cut your throat." She leaned against Cole.

He swept her up in his arms and carried her upstairs.

Dizzy, she nestled her head against the expanse of his chest and thanked God he had survived.

Charlotte rushed up the stairs ahead of the pair and opened the door to a spare bedchamber. Cole gingerly laid Carrie upon the counterpane and sat on the edge of the bed.

Thank you er—er...."

"Charlotte Forten. It's nice to meet you, Mr. West. "I'll leave you two alone to get reacquainted." Carrie saw concern on Charlotte's face. "You can expect a visit from the doctor, Carrie. Don't bother to protest. My uncle can't be dissuaded."

She closed the door behind her.

Carrie and Cole were in each other's arms in an instant. Relief swept over her even as she felt her body tremble. Carrie released him and searched his face. She felt the tears run down her cheeks.

"What happened to you? I thought you were dead."

"I got caught up in the melee and was knocked unconscious. A man slapped me. When I came to, Floyd was looking down on me. He told me he'd spare me because of my father."

"Why?"

"Floyd was accused of insolence by his master. Frederick Wilson at the Mayfair plantation wanted to make an example of him so his punishment was severe. He gave Floyd thirty lashes and hung him by his wrists for more than a day. When my father heard about it upon his return from a business trip in Washington, D.C., he appealed to Wilson for mercy. He persuaded Wilson to release Floyd, which saved his life."

"Your father sounds like quite a man."

"He was, and a better orator you'd be hard-pressed to find. After Floyd spoke to me, I soon lost consciousness. When I awoke, I was lying on a pallet on the floor of a plantation house. There were other wounded white men present, as well. A local doctor looked after us along with the mistress of the house, a young widow. She offered me an interesting proposition."

"What kind of proposition?"

"She asked me to marry her and run her plantation."

Carrie laughed and Cole joined her.

"Most of her field hands had run off to join Floyd's rebellion."

Carrie looked up at him with a crooked smile. "So, the widow wasn't attractive enough to tempt you?"

"Oh, she was attractive all right, but I couldn't wait to get out of there and find you." He caressed Carrie's cheek.

A soft knock interrupted them. The door opened to reveal Charlotte. "My uncle would like a word with you, Mr. West."

~~~

"So, you're Stuart's son. At last, we meet." Mr. Purvis held out his hand. Cole quickly shook it.

They waited in the drawing room for the doctor to arrive while Mrs. Purvis and Charlotte comforted Carrie upstairs.

"I worked with your father." Mr. Purvis expressed his condolences.
~~~

"Thank you, Mr. Purvis. I've continued his work as stationmaster and legal counsel for the enslaved and freedmen."

"Glad to hear you're carrying the torch. Your father would be proud. Since when does a stationmaster escort *cargo* across state lines?"

Cole reddened as he tapped his long fingers on his knees. He cleared his throat. "Well, after the deaths of her family members, Carrie was very distraught. I wanted to assure her safety, so I planned to escort her to Canada, myself."

"You've fallen in love with her, Mr. West?"

Cole shook his head. "Is it so obvious? And, please call me Cole."

"Very well, Cole, it is. Whenever you mention her name, there's a spark of affection in your eyes, my young friend. You would not risk your career and freedom, if it were not so."

Cole's brows knit. "I confess." He shook his head. "She's a fugitive of the law, which I've sworn to uphold. There's little chance for us." He looked away, and then back to his host. "What future could we have, even if she'd have me?"

"Let me tell you about my parents. My mother's name was Harriet Judah. Her mother was African, and her father was a European Jew. She was born free in Charleston, South Carolina. My father, William Purvis, was a native of Northumberland, England, born to wealthy parents. He met my mother while in South Carolina on business. They married in 1810 and had three sons."

CHAPTER TWENTY-FOUR
Love Finds a Way

As the sun sank in the sky, the slaves' spirits rose for a kind of freedom was at hand. From Saturday evening to Monday morning, field hands were given time off. Household slaves were expected to be available to their owners day and night. However, if a social event occurred in the quarters, most were allowed to attend.

"Y'all young folks just go on to dat dance at Junior's," Matilda told Frank and Pretty Hattie. She shooed them out the door. Matilda whispered to Pretty Hattie, "You 'bout to bring the handsomest man in the quarters with you. Sweet on him, ain't cha? Go on, 'fo' Massa be lookin' for ya."

Pretty Hattie gave Matilda a hug.

While walking toward the quarters under the stars, Pretty Hattie turned to Frank. "Are ya goin' to Junior's?"

"No, I'm going to my cabin."

"Black Hattie be there waitin'. Oh, excuse me, Hattie Rose. Everybody says she be sweet on you, Frank. How you feel 'bout her?"

"Mind your business Hattie. Enjoy the dance. Goodnight."

"Humph." She faded into the darkness.

As he neared the cabin, eagerness seized him. He knew Hattie Rose would have a pail of water ready so he could wash up before supper. As he opened the door, an appetizing aroma greeted him.

Pap stood at the hearth stirring a pot. "I've prepared supper tonight, so my little girl can study longer. It's rabbit stew. She's mighty nervous about taking your test, Mr. Frank."

"If she studied well, she has nothing to worry about."

Pap wiped his brow. "This stew will be ready soon."

After several months of study, Hattie Rose was taking her first series of exams in mathematics, American history, English grammar and literature, in addition to an oral exam.

"I'm taking supper next door so you and Hattie Rose can have the cabin to yourselves."

"I appreciate it, Pap. Where's our scholar?"

"Studying."

He saw the pail of fresh water by the wall. She'd once teased him that no one was cleaner than an educated man. He washed up and donned his Sunday clothes.

"Well, it's ready now." Pap took a portion for himself. "I'll go get my daughter."

"Hello, Hattie Rose." Even to Frank himself, his voice sounded curt. The sight of her unnerved him. She wore her Sunday dress and matching head wrap, in a purple and gold print.

"Hello, Professor Frank." She'd bestowed this title upon him since the first lesson.

Heat ran through his body, which left beads of perspiration on his brow.

They had never spent time alone. Pap had provided a buffer. Now, alone with her, it would take all his strength to harness his feelings. He must be stern, aloof. The fence must always stand between them.

"We'll eat first, and then the exam." Frank bowed to Hattie Rose. *What's come over me? Why is she wearing her best clothes and me, my best?*

They sat down and reached for each other's hand to say the blessing. Tonight, the sizzle of their fingers was stronger than ever. His withdrawal was quick. Frank said the blessing with his hands on the table.

She held hers folded in her lap.

"You've got a couple of tests tonight, three written and one oral." His voice sounded sterner than he had intended. "I've borrowed a sheaf of paper from Dayton's office, along with an ink bottle and quill pen. I must get these back to him before he misses his extra set. I hope you're prepared." He arched a brow.

"I been studyin' hard."

"I've been studying hard," corrected Frank.

She swallowed and then corrected herself.

A deafening silence filled the cabin. Neither spoke as they ate, except to say "pass the salt," or "pass the pepper." In time, they finished.

The sound of the fiddler's music intruded. Peals of laughter seeped through the door, mocking them. When the bowls had been washed and stowed away, Hattie sat down to take her tests.

"You'll have fifteen minutes for each section. To mark the time, I'll practice some musical pieces and stop when the time is up. If you should finish before I do, please use the time to check your answers. Then, you can raise your hand to signal me. When I start playing again, you will start the next test. Is that clear?"

Hattie Rose nodded.

Frank opened the violin case, which he kept on a shelf. He caressed the shiny dark wood of the 1825 baroque-style instrument before he placed it under his chin. Dayton was delighted with Frank's musical abilities, so the master purchased the violin for his use.

"Your first test is in mathematics. I'll play Mozart's 'Violin Concerto No. 5 in A, Second Movement'. I hope it inspires you. Good luck. You may begin."

Frank slid his bow over the strings, and the stirring melody soared.

Hattie Rose took a deep breath and started. She was quick to fill in the answers and review her test. She raised her hand.

Frank nodded and ceased playing.

Next, she started the second test.

Frank walked around as he continued to play the piece. "I'll take off points for misspelled words."

Hattie Rose's eyes flashed. She finished and reviewed her answers. At last, she tackled the combined English grammar and literature test. There were questions about the many stories they had read, including *A Tale of Two Cities, Macbeth,* and the banned book, *Uncle Tom's Cabin*—all borrowed from Dayton's library. Hattie Rose had finished before Frank stopped playing.

While he checked her answers, she walked the floor.

"Stop pacing, please, you're distracting me."

Hattie Rose sat down and rocked in the chair. She glanced at him from time to time.

He re-checked her answers. Looking up, his eyes bored into hers like a hammer driving a nail.

"What year did the East India Trading Company land at Plymouth Rock?"

"1606?"

"1607," Frank snapped. "1607." He flung the test papers at her.

She sank to her knees, and snatched the papers off the floor. Each one had a "C" in front of the answer. Blinded by her tears, she questioned her vision. "C" meant correct. Frank offered to help but she shook her head. She picked up the last piece of paper. It was the first page of the test. At the top Frank had scrawled the letter grade "A+" and "99% correct."

Hattie Rose studied each page. Her one error had been the date when the East India Trading Company landed at Plymouth Rock.

The lawyer looked at his student with something akin to fear.

Hattie Rose pulled herself up to her full five-feet, four-inches, as her anger threatened to consume her. She struggled to control her shaking hands and ragged breaths. "Oh." She panted. "I didn't fail. I passed. I thought from the way you responded, I had failed." She swallowed hard; and then put the papers in order.

"I—I want to thank you from the bottom of m—my heart for teaching me and my father how to read and write and count. You have given me a gift, which I could never have fathomed would have been mine—a precious education.

"When you first came here, injured and lost, I took care of you. As time went on, we became friends. And then, you started to pull away, like you couldn't see me. It felt like I was mud on your shoe, which you couldn't rub off. I asked myself why. What had I done to garner such a response? I hoped by becoming an accomplished student, I could transform myself into a woman whom you could consider a friend again. I wanted you to be proud of me.

"I hoped you would look at me like you used to look at me and really see *me* and not a slave. I know I'm not your equal. You would never think of me as such, but I hoped—I—hoped."

Tears streamed down Hattie Rose's face as her words stopped.

In a few strides, Frank closed the distance between them and gathered her in his arms.

"Hattie Rose, I'm so sorry I've hurt you, my darling Hattie Rose."

She looked up at him, and a tear slid down her cheek.

He cupped her face. "I've tried so hard to keep you at a distance." His voice faltered. "But the truth is I—I love you. I love you, my beautiful Hattie Rose. I've been in love with you from the first time our hands touched to bless the food at the table." He dropped his hands from her face and hugged her. "I knew you were the most loving woman I have ever known, but I couldn't admit to myself that I was falling in love with you, a slave."

Hattie Rose wiggled out of his arms and stepped back, the hurt evident in her eyes.

"No. What I meant is falling in love with *any* woman here might delay my plans to escape. I've never abandoned my desire to flee, but I've wrestled with the dilemma of when to escape. I've learned freedom for colored people is circumstantial, at best. I must regain my freedom and light the path for you, as well. I promise you, darling, we will be free."

"Frank, I've waited so long to hear you say—you, at least, appreciated me."

"I was fighting the love I felt for you with all of my strength, but my heart is yours. Can you forgive me?"

She stepped toward him and flung her arms around his neck.

Frank kissed her forehead, her nose, her round cheeks and her lips over and over again. He tugged her headpiece and released a head of thick, soft hair, which coiled around his fingers. "Your hair is beautiful." He started to run his fingers through it, but they were caught.

"You can't run your fingers through this head without a catch," Hattie Rose teased.

"You've caught me already, woman. Never let me go."

They laughed.

"By the way, regarding the oral exam, Hattie Rose, your elocution was impeccable." He planted a kiss on her cheek. "Your delivery was succinct." His lips found her eyelids. "Your composition had beauty, tone, and clarity. You've passed the oral exam."

Their laughter filled the room.

"I've never been scolded with such dignity." Frank kissed her lips.

Hattie and Frank held each other for a while. Infectious music from the fiddler blared through their door, which prompted them to dance. Their bodies, so close, inflamed their passions. Her scent intoxicated him and his desire mounted.

"I want to make love to you, Hattie Rose."

She answered him with ardent kisses.

Frank led Hattie Rose to bed.

His lips trailed the smooth skin of her shoulders as he pulled down her dress. He finished undressing her and then freed himself from his garments. Frank aroused her to a fever pitch, which sent their passions soaring until their ecstasy crested.

Afterward, as Frank cradled Hattie Rose, he queried her again about the child she never mentioned.

"Hattie Rose, whose child are you caring?"

"I'm carrying your child, Frank." She looked away. "Please don't ask me."

"What we did makes us family. I want to marry you."

"You do, Frank? Not if you knew what I did."

"I won't judge you."

Her eyes traveled from his face to the mask on the shelf, which depicted the god of truth. A moment or two passed, and then she shrugged.

"Whenever Massa tried to marry me off, I'd hide. He wasn't satisfied until every young woman was either pregnant or had just given birth. One day, he had his men rounded up some of us to take to the Lumpkin farm."

Frank's body stiffened.

"Robert Lumpkin has the biggest breeding farm and jail for slaves in Virginia."

"I know."

"The men who brought you here were the same ones who took me there. When I found out what they wanted me to do, I refused. Big Red slapped me so hard he knocked me out. When I came to, he threatened to do it to me himself if I didn't go in the barn with all those naked men and women. They blindfolded me so I wouldn't recognize the man. I heard the elders say this was done because there was no effort made to prevent relatives from mating with one another. Since I found out I was pregnant, I've been praying—"

"They took me there, too." Frank's voice held sorrow. "They split the money between them for treating me like an animal. Like you, I refused until Big Red threatened to cut off a few toes or fingers." Frank lowered his head. "I forced a woman, just to get it over with. I had no choice. Blue eyes were watching through the peep holes in the walls."

"Even though I was forced to do it, I can't rid myself of the shame." Hattie Rose wept.

Frank drew her closer to him. "We did what we had to do to stay alive. Our very survival is a victory. They didn't break us."

"I've been told some of our own in Africa sold us."

Frank nodded. "Not all Africans were from the same tribe or spoke the same languages. "Europeans often instigated wars, which yielded prisoners of war, who were sold to slavers to fill their demands for plantation labor. For centuries, slavery was a common social condition in many countries. In Rome, slaves could marry into the ruling class, buy their freedom despite the master's wishes, become citizens, and own land. A child of a slave woman and free man was free. In Africa, slaves could marry into the family which owned them. But slavery in America is chattel slavery. Slaves can be sold, beaten, and burned alive, hung, raped, or bred like livestock. There are no laws governing a master's treatment of his slaves."

Frank shook his head. "When the slave trade began, Willie Lynch, a slaveholder in the West Indies, stood on the banks of the James River in 1712 and delivered an address, which was printed in a pamphlet, entitled, *How to Make a Slave.* He promoted violence, murder, and rape as tools of controlling and demoralizing slaves.

"When Thomas Jefferson terminated the North Atlantic slave trade in 1808, he incorporated protectionism to control the domestic market. This resulted in an increase in the value of slaves. Since the foreign slave trade was prohibited, breeding farms have played a role in keeping up with the demand.

"The leading commodity in our country isn't tobacco or cotton, it's people. Slaves are mortgaged to banks, which package that money into bonds or other monetary instruments to sell and expand their investments. Slavery is a three-point-five-billion-dollar industry."

A long pause ensued. Frank took a deep breath. "I hope I haven't sired a child who could be born into slavery."

"I hate the child I'm carrying." Hattie Rose wailed. "I wish I could rip it from—"

"No darling. I wouldn't want you to, 'cause..." His throat tightened, and he grew hoarse. "It's my child you're carrying, just like you said. It's my child."

Crying, they clung to one another.

At dawn, Hattie Rose retrieved a thick, white leather-bound book from Pap's cabin.

Frank queried her about the book.

"This diary belonged to Massa's daughter, Isabella. She used to read it to me. Now, thanks to you, I can read it for myself. She would have wanted me to have it, I'm sure."

In time, Frank was invited to join the elders who settled disputes and set rules among the slave population. The single most desirable attribute Frank possessed, which his fellow men and women in bondage wanted, was an education.

He started to teach them in secret. After a few weeks, Frank and Hattie Rose jumped the broom. Dayton performed the ceremony and gifted the newlyweds with homemade sweets.

Frank regretted he didn't have a wedding band for Hattie Rose. He thought of his ring on Carrie's finger. He finally admitted she'd worn the ring to please her mother, which was the same reason he had given it to her. It was expected of him by her parents and his.

CHAPTER TWENTY-FIVE
News from Virginia

Doctor Lange finished his examination and left Carrie's room.

Glad to be alone, she reflected upon the doctor's diagnosis. She was fatigued, but otherwise healthy. A good night's sleep was all she needed. However, her worst fears had been put to rest she wasn't pregnant by her attacker.

After resting, Carrie heard a soft knock on the door. "Come in." She hoped it was Cole.

As if he'd read her mind, Cole entered and smiled at her.

She patted the bed, and he sat down.

"I'm so happy to see you again." Cole leaned down, hesitated, and then kissed her forehead.

Carrie was overjoyed. He wasn't dead, but alive, against all odds. She had not lost him after all. Aware of her attraction to Cole, she moved back and leaned against the pillows.

They looked into each other's eyes as if to assure themselves of the reality of their situation, and exchanged self-conscious smiles.

"God bless Floyd for sparing you." She touched his cheek.

"What happened to you?"

She felt her eyes water and blinked the tears away. "I was going to shoot Floyd, but someone knocked me out. A family of runaways was hiding in the barn, too. When I regained consciousness, they had taken me somewhere deep in the woods to meet their guide, who was none other than Harriet Tubman. They said they had witnessed your murder. I had no choice but to join them."

"You were right to go with Harriet. Surely no one better could have guided you to safety."

"Cole, what led you here?"

"Once I recovered and left the widow's plantation, I went to the next safe house, where I was told Harriet Tubman was escorting a family north. She would stop in Philadelphia to speak at an anti-slavery fundraiser, hosted by the Purvises, before leaving for Canada. I prayed to God you were with them."

Cole told Carrie he had heard from Allan Pinkerton about the goings-on at Twin Oaks and reported Olivia had fully recovered.

"The Lord answered my prayers." Carrie wept for joy. "Does Mr. Pinkerton know what made her sick?"

"No, but he's asked Mason to keep an eye on things at Twin Oaks."

"Has Mr. Pinkerton made any progress in finding out who killed your father?"

He told her Pinkerton had identified the gun which killed his father. "Nothing more has come to light. Once we get some material evidence, we can ask the judge to open Missy Dayton's sealed testimony. It may contain a clue about his death."

Seeing the puzzled look on Carrie's face, he explained. "Missy Dayton is...was Lucius Dayton's daughter. Her father spirited her out of town so she couldn't testify against him, but she gave testimony in a sworn affidavit. It helped my father win the case. She died from typhoid fever."

"It must be terrible to have a loved one murdered and the assailant unknown and unpunished."

"Justice can be evasive, but not out of reach. I won't rest until my father's killer stands trial."

Carrie squeezed Cole's hand. "You can rely on me to help you in any way I can."

CHAPTER TWENTY-SIX
The Philadelphia Elite

The morning sun splashed gold across the Purvis estates. Clumps of snow hugged the tree limbs and bushes until the sun loosened Old Man Winter's grip. Droplets fell to the ground like a steady March rain. Green shoots emerged from white patches of snow.

Carrie was delighted to help with last-minute preparations for the grand fundraiser.

The brothers decided Robert would accommodate the dignitaries with private bedchambers and home-cooked meals, while Joseph would host the activities on his land.

Mrs. Harriet Purvis, her niece Charlotte, Carrie, and members of the Philadelphia Female Anti-Slavery Society supervised the finishing touches before the events were to commence at ten o'clock on Saturday morning.

The women entered the Freedom House, a two-storied structure where Joseph and Robert held routine meetings. They surveyed the grand Americana ballroom on the first floor. Here, a musical concert and elegant ball was scheduled to take place in the evening. The featured orchestra was the famed Philadelphia Treble-Clef, a Negro classical music society.

Upstairs, the Philadelphia Room was arranged for the speaker's bureau and auction. Across the hall, the Louisiana Room would serve as the dining space. There, the wait staff and cooks were busy with their preparations.

Joseph's estate included a lush park with landscaped gardens and paths. A fountain occupied the center of the square. Its cobblestone pavement would provide a space for vendors to set up their wares. Each had pledged to donate twenty-five percent of their sales to the society. The proceeds would provide food and clothing, education and housing, and legal fees for fugitives and freed people in need.

Popular activities planned for children included foot races and games. The velocipede or bicycle race was sure to draw a large crowd.

Once the women were satisfied with the preparations, they ate breakfast at Robert Purvis's residence.

The day began with the speakers' forum, which included William Still, Harriet Tubman, Frederick Douglass and William Lloyd Garrison.

Harriet Purvis, addressed the audience:

"My fellow Philadelphians, visitors, friends and family, our next speaker has a long history of championing emancipation and universal suffrage. On December 9, 1833, our speaker and twenty-one women, myself included, met in a schoolroom to found the Philadelphia Female Anti-Slavery Society. On December fourteenth, we finalized our constitution. At that moment, her voice shaped our mission, and I quote: 'We deem it our duty, as professing Christians, to manifest our abhorrence of

the flagrant injustice and deep sin in slavery by united and vigorous exertions.'

"The society got right to work. Schools for colored children were founded. We boycotted manufactured goods by forced labor, and collected 3,300 signatures of women demanding emancipation, and submitted them to congress.

"On May 17, 1838, a mob of pro-slavery protestors, enraged by the presence of white women in public with Negroes of both sexes, burned down Pennsylvania Hall, the setting for the second Anti-Slavery Convention of American Women.

"In 1848, she helped to pen the Declaration of Sentiments during the historic Seneca Falls Convention.

"Her detractors are many. One religious leader described her as 'evil itself.' A statesman denounced her as a dangerous 'amalgamator.' Yet, her work to acquire universal suffrage and emancipation is an effort to stop the hemorrhaging of American morals, which erodes the integrity of this great nation. It is my pleasure to introduce a friend and sister in the cause of liberty, Lucretia Mott."

Enthusiastic applause accompanied Lucretia Mott, as she walked to the podium. Slender, aged and dressed in her plain Quaker attire, she at once delved into the crux of her subject:

"For close to thirty years, Philadelphia's free colored male citizens have had their voting rights revoked. These men have been voting since 1776. It isn't surprising the Philadelphia legislature enacted this policy soon after the Nat Turner rebellion..."

The event was well attended by the colored society of professionals and entrepreneurs, as well as cooks, waiters, and household staff. At times, strong discussions ensued about how wide-spread equality of the races should or would go. Some liberal-minded white and colored people supported universal citizenship and suffrage but frowned upon colored and whites socializing or marrying.

Carrie was enthralled by the speakers. She sat in the front row, between Charlotte and Cole, and enjoyed the intellectual foray. Dressed in Jonah's clothes, she had agreed to Charlotte's suggestion to add a pair of blued steel spectacles to her disguise.

Several donation baskets were passed among the audience. By the look of the donations, Carrie knew the sums would delight Mrs. Purvis.

When the speakers' forum ended at two o'clock, Charlotte grabbed Carrie's hand and proposed they all attend the wheel races. "We've got to be on the south side of the park where the Meteor Wheelman will race. It's the most exciting thing you'll ever see." Charlotte guided them through the crowd. "They race once a month, if weather permits."

Carrie looked at Charlotte. "I've never seen a bicycle race, nor rode one. Someone told me the inventor is a Scottish blacksmith."

"You're quite right. The modern bicycles you'll see today were invented in 1839 by Kirkpatrick MacMillan. Racing is not considered a sport for women because the velocipede weighs about fifty-seven pounds with its wooden frame and iron-rimmed wooden wheels."

Cole walked alongside Charlotte. "I've never ridden one of those contraptions, either."

Once in the square, they scanned the various activities in progress. Children squealed with delight during relay races or as they played nine pins. Vendors sold baked goods, homemade wines, candies, and a wide array of foodstuffs. Carrie stopped to look over the cakes, but Charlotte led her away.

"Don't mind the food. My aunt has a sampling of everything being sold. Let's hurry."

A crowd of spectators formed where the colored bicycle club, the Meteor Wheelmen, was gathering. In twenty minutes, the first race would commence. The bicyclists wore uniforms of black pants and green long-sleeved shirts.

As Charlotte approached them, she pointed out a very attractive young man among the riders with golden-brown skin and wavy hair.

"His name is James Le Count. His family owns a store, a hotel and a tavern on 92nd Street and Second. Isn't he handsome?" Carrie nodded. When Charlotte offered to introduce her, she declined.

"My voice would reveal my gender. We'll stand back here and watch." Carrie nudged her forward.

Charlotte's face glowed as she greeted James Le Count.

Carrie turned toward Cole, but he had disappeared into the crowd. Not seeing him, she approached a knot of noisy men. She tapped the arm of one, who admitted her into the circle.

There stood Cole staring at the collection of MacMillan bicycles. Pedals on both sides of the front wheel propelled the machine forward, unlike its predecessor, the hobby horse, which required the rider to use his feet to advance the vehicle.

When Charlotte and James appeared at Cole's side, she introduced them. Cole couldn't hide his excitement. "I'd like to give it a try after the race."

"Certainly." James smiled.

James steered his bicycle away from the crowd as the announcer ordered all racers to get behind the starting line. He raised a flag, and shouted into a megaphone, "On your mark, get set, go."

Thirteen men mounted their machines and dashed off.

By far, Mr. Le Count was the swiftest of the group in the three-mile race. In record time, he rolled across the finish line amid a chorus of cheers.

Charlotte celebrated his win by jumping up and down.

He was declared the official winner, and a sterling silver medal was pinned to his shirt.

Carrie looked around at the crowd and spotted the faces of her fellow fugitives. She tipped her hat to greet them. She spied Harriet Tubman, as well, dressed in quiet colors, a hat resting low on her brow.

Carrie glanced back at the riders and was surprised to see Cole riding a bicycle. He pedaled smoothly until a crowd of people turned a corner and faced him. They parted in haste as he rode by them. Suddenly, the water fountain appeared, and Cole's tire hit the base.

He was thrown off the bicycle, tumbled in the air, landing on the grass near a vendor's tent.

A crowd gathered around him, and a few people yelled for a doctor.

Carrie pushed her way through to see him crumpled on the ground, unconscious.

~~~
~~~

Doctor Lange was called once again. Some family members and Carrie gathered outside the chamber where Cole had been carried while the examination was in progress. James Le Count was among them.

When the doctor emerged, he said Cole felt nauseated, complained of blurred vision, and couldn't remember the accident.

"When a patient has a concussion, we'd like for them to stay awake after the incident for the first few hours. Could one of you—"

"I'll stay with him," Carrie volunteered. "Can we see him now?"

Carrie's heart lurched at the sight of him.

He sat up in bed against several pillows. Half of his forehead was covered by a thick, white bandage, which the doctor said concealed a nasty cut above his left eye. Below the bandage, a bruise began to color his skin. His bare chest was swathed in bandages over broken ribs. A dark curl fell over his forehead. His hair, loosened from its tie, reached his shoulders. Cole looked tired and as if he could barely keep his eyes open.

Mr. Purvis told Cole he was welcome to stay during his convalescence.

Charlotte and Joseph wished him a speedy recovery before they left to resume their duties at the fundraiser. James Le Count offered to give him a few pointers on bicycle riding once he recovered.

"He'll need a lot of rest." Dr. Lange addressed Carrie. "He'll be laid up for a month or so."

"Just in time to defend Mr. Stevens' defendant." Cole shook his head. He winced. "My head hurts." He raised his hand to massage his forehead, and then realized his right hand was also bandaged. Carrie sat on the bed and obliged him. She massaged his temples with gentle circles.

"You have a concussion," said the doctor. "You've got to stay awake for a few hours, just to be safe, or you might lapse into a coma."

"What's the verdict, doctor?"

"Son, you have a few broken ribs, your right hand is sprained, and your knuckles are bruised, and a black eye is a certainty."

"When I do anything, I go whole hog."

"I will help him, doctor." Carrie grinned at Cole's self-assessment.

Satisfied his patient was in good hands, the doctor left Carrie with a few instructions.

She noticed his eyelids start to close. In her attempt to help Cole stay alert, she told him her favorite jokes. Each time, she told a dud, Cole seemed to find her failed attempts hilarious. He begged her not to continue because it hurt when he laughed.

They played memory games until Cole asked her to sing. She obliged him with one of his favorites, "Swing Low, Sweet Chariot."

After a few hours, Carrie ceased all conversation, and the patient drifted off to sleep.

Later, he awakened and saw her still sitting in a chair at his side. "Carrie, yesterday, I heard Harriet Tubman say she would soon leave for Canada. You must go with her."

"There's no way I would leave you here in the condition you're in, Cole."

Cole sighed. "You must grab your chance at freedom the first opportunity you get. I appreciate your concern for me. But every minute you stay in America, you're at risk of being captured."

"I'm safe here as long as I stay on the estate."

"I won't allow you to put your life in jeopardy for my sake."

"It's no more than what you've already done for my sake. If you're caught, you would certainly be disbarred and jailed."

"If you're caught, you could be hanged. I doubt the Richmond courts would hang me for helping you."

"There's no way you can be sure they won't."

~~~

The following day, Carrie found Cole delirious with fever. The bandage had been pulled from his head wound, which had swollen overnight.

Dr. Lange returned and verified her worst fear: Cole's wound was infected. She helped the doctor change his bandage.

"There's nothing I can do now." Dr. Lange shook his head. "We'll just have to wait it out. He may recover, with any luck, but I won't lie to you. The infection is a threat to his life."

"I'll look after him, doctor. I won't leave his side."

When Harriet Tubman came to visit Cole, she advised Carrie to prepare teas made from ginger and echinacea and sweeten them with honey to help fight the infection.

~~~

The charity event was a great success. The coffers of the various charities were overflowing. Harriet Tubman was given a healthy sum of money for the continuation of her work. Her charges, Chloe, Joe, and Felix, were given funds for their settlement in Canada. They were overjoyed at the prospect of living in a thriving community of ex-patriots of color without being persecuted for the color of their skin.

The following day, Mr. Purvis drove Harriet and her charges to the train station. Well-groomed and dressed in clean garments, the fugitives boarded the train with their heads held high. To act as if they were free by a show of confidence in their carriage and manners, Harriet Tubman advised, was one of the best disguises a runaway could employ.

When the train rolled out of the station, it left without Carrie Bennet.

Harriet had left a note for Carrie which contained an alternate plan. Disguised in men's apparel, Carrie was to board a stagecoach before it reached the courthouse. There, an associate of Harriet's, a Mr. Goldman, would board the coach, and the two would travel by train. When Carrie mentioned his name to Robert Purvis, she was relieved to find they were acquainted.

~~~

It was touch and go for a while, but on the third day, Carrie found Cole awake and in good humor. She had kept him full of chicken broth and herbal teas. She made sure his wounds were cleaned and dressed. He often fell asleep as she read from her favorite books, of which she found many on the well-stocked shelves of the Purvis library.
~~~

CHAPTER TWENTY-SEVEN
Captured

Late afternoon, on Monday, the second of April, Cole found himself sitting on the opposite side of the crowded courtroom in Philadelphia from Prosecutor Dennis King. He rose to address the court. Several more men entered, and an attendant brought chairs so they could be seated along the wall.

That morning, Cole had bid Carrie farewell. This was the day she would carry out Harriet's plan. Cole was grateful Carrie would be leaving for Canada, but he wasn't comfortable with her traveling with another man, no matter how highly he was regarded.

As soon as the trial was over, he planned to intercept them and pay for Mr. Goldman's passage home.

Cole eyed the newcomers: Sheriff Coffe and his deputies. A chill seized him.

"When you brought your slave, Pepper, to Philadelphia, Mr. Bloomington, did you suspect he would escape?" King inquired.

"I had no reason to believe he would steal himself. I made all of my people aware of the Dred Scott Decision and the Fugitive Slave Law."

"Once you prepared to return to Maryland, what happened?"

"Some miscreants sent a note saying Pepper was taking his freedom since he was on free soil. Well, right away I enlisted the aid of the sheriff. We caught him, but he ran away again."

"According to the Dred Scott Decision, a slave who runs away from his master must be remanded to his master in the state from which he came. Pepper was brought to Philadelphia, attempted an escape, was caught, and brought before a tribunal, where your ownership was proven. Is this a fact?"

"Yes, sir." Bloomington nodded.

"Your witness, Mr. West." King turned to Cole.

Thaddeus Stevens, the Radical Republican and abolitionist whose face wore vestiges of his illness, nodded at Cole, his co-counsel.

The young attorney rose. "When did you acquire the slave known as Pepper, Mr. Bloomington?" Cole pronounced the slave's name with disdain to protest the degrading moniker.

The slaver's chest expanded. "He was born on my plantation, The White Oak. Pepper was one of five-hundred slaves I inherited from my pappy, Colonel Gerald Taylor Bloomington."

"Did you take the slave Pepper straight to Maryland, Mr. Bloomington?" queried Cole.

"Well—er—no." Bloomington answered in a weak voice. "I didn't head for Maryland right away."

"I didn't quite hear you." Cole cupped his ear. Then, he raised an eyebrow to add another layer of sarcasm.

Mr. Bloomington cleared his throat. "We didn't head for Maryland right away."

"You had some business in town. Is this right?"

"It had nothing to do with this case." Mr. Bloomington shifted his weight.

"Was it your intention, Mr. Bloomington, to take Pepper back to your plantation?" He walked toward the defense table.

"Of course, it was." Mr. Bloomington blustered.

Cole retrieved a document and handed it to Judge Clifford B. Jones. "Your Honor, I'd like to enter this bill of sale as Exhibit A."

The prosecutor jumped up. "Your Honor, I object, counsel didn't produce the evidence prior to trial. This is highly irregular."

The judge looked at Cole. "Mr. West, would you care to respond?"

"This document came into my possession just now, Your Honor. I'm surprised counsel had no knowledge of it."

"Counselors, please approach." The judge read the bill of sale then handed it to Mr. King. The prosecutor's forehead furrowed as he studied the document. He angrily handed it back to Cole.

"I will allow it into evidence, in light of Mr. West's explanation."

He walked to the witness stand, his voice, ominous. "Mr. Bloomington, didn't you sell Pepper on February twenty-eighth after identifying him as your property?"

"I did no such thing, Mr. West, Pepper is lying."

"Didn't you tell Pepper you would sell him 'down the river,' after you caught him the first time?"

"No matter what lie he told you, Mr. West, a slave cannot testify against a white man in court about *anything*."

"I am prepared to call Mr. Stanford Bell to the witness stand."

Mr. Bloomington's eyes bulged in his fleshy face.

Cole continued. "This bill of sale from you to Mr. Bell verifies that you sold Pepper to him for eight-hundred dollars, soon after he was declared to be your property. You assured Mr. Bell you would transport Pepper to his Mississippi plantation, once he was in your custody. But your plans went awry when the Philadelphia Anti-Slavery Society hired Thaddeus Stevens to represent Pepper in a lawsuit for his freedom."

"They don't have a case in hell to interfere with my property rights." As Bloomington shouted, his heavy jowls quaked.

"Although, you schooled your *people* on the facts of the Fugitive Slave Law, it seems you don't quite understand the law yourself, sir." Cole squared his broad shoulders and strolled across the floor toward the defendant. His voice boomed throughout the courtroom. "According to the Fugitive Slave Law, 'a slave must be remanded to his master and brought back to the state from which he came.' If a slaveholder sells a runaway before returning him to the state *from which he came,* he would be in violation of the law." His lips turned in a crooked smile as he faced the defendant. "You should have sold him *after* you took him back to Maryland, not before. Pepper ran away after you sold him illegally to Mr. Bell. What was your intention after this trial? To sell him to someone else if Mr. Bell had gone back to Mississippi?"

Bloomington's face contorted with anger.

"You bloody lying bastard." A man jumped up from his seat and pointed a finger at Bloomington.

The judge struck his gavel. "Quiet sir. Who are you?"

Cole answered. "I believe we have met Mr. Bell."

"Precisely." Mr. Bell pulled on the lapels of his jacket.

"I must beg the court's compassion, Your Honor." Cole addressed the judge. "I ask you to declare the defendant free, since his master is guilty of violating a federal law."

The judge struck his gavel. "So be it. Pepper, you are free to go. Mr. Bloomington, give Mr. Bell his money back, and you'll pay the court fees as well."

Bloomington sputtered his protest. Spittle stretched down his chest.

"You're lucky I don't throw you in jail. This case is adjourned." The sound of the judge's gavel echoed through the courtroom.

Applause broke out from the abolitionists in the crowd. As the spectators stood up and began to file out of the courtroom, Pepper blinked in confusion. The stocky, dark-skinned man remained immobile.

Well-wishers came up to congratulate him and his counselors.

He jumped up from his chair and hugged Cole. "I'm free?"

Cole nodded his head. "Do you have people in Philadelphia who will assist you?"

"The Anti-Slavery Society."

"You'll need a new name, sir."

"From now on, I'm Johnny West, if it's okay with you, sir. If it hadn't been for you...." His voice thinned.

~~~

Cole heard a commotion outside the courtroom. He looked for the lawmen, but they had left. In the open doorway, he could see a stagecoach. Was Carrie
~~~

inside? His heart hammered in his chest as he made his way through the door.

A crowd of people stood around with shocked expressions on their faces. In the center stood Carrie in men's clothing. Her long hair hung down around her shoulders and spilled down her back. Deputy Larson stood near her. He waved her hat above his head.

She cried out and clutched her head. Horror stamped her features.

"This is Carrie Bennet, the murderer." Deputy Larson shouted her name, over and over. His eyes blazed with manic glee.

"Pipe down, Larson." Coffe frowned at him. "Carrie Bennet, I arrest you for the murder of Captain John Pierce." He handcuffed Carrie.

Judge Anderson emerged from the crowd. "What's going on here?"

Cole moved to the other side of Carrie.

"She's my prisoner." Coffe glared at Cole.

"Your Honor," cried Cole. "I'd like to offer my legal services to this young woman."

"Are you Miss Bennet?" The judge stared at her.

Carrie looked at Cole, who shook his head. "You've no need to answer the question now, ma'am."

"Do you wish to have Mr. West represent you, young lady?"

"Yes, I do, Your Honor." Carrie answered.

Larson countered. "Of course, she's Carrie Bennet. I have a picture of her right here." He thrust the faded drawing in Cole's face.

Cole slapped his hand away, and the sketch fell to the ground.

"Let me see that sketch." The judge held out his hand.

Larson picked up the drawing and handed it to the judge.

"There is a strong likeness. I don't see why the lawmen can't take the prisoner into their custody."

Cole addressed the judge. "Your Honor, I beg you to allow me to place the accused in my custody for her own protection."

"Why would you defend her, Cole?" bellowed Coffe. "She killed one of our own."

"Everyone deserves a defense, Sheriff. It's constitutional law." Cole glared at the lawman.

Coffe took a step toward the judge. "Your Honor, I'm Sheriff Benjamin Coffe, and these two men are my deputies." He waved a hand at Larson and Jedidiah. "This gal escaped from Virginia, probably with the help of abolitionists. We've tracked her all the way from Richmond."

Cole moved forward. "Your Honor, it has been well-documented by newspapers across the country that the fugitive, known as Carrie Bennet, is being pursued by bounty hunters, men of dubious reputation, such as these men who stand before you. I live in Richmond and know of Mr. Larson's unsavory character. No young lady would be safe with men of his ilk."

"What does he mean 'men of his ilk'?" Larson's face reddened.

"How the hell would I know what crazy lawyer talk means?" responded the sheriff.

The judge looked at the picture again and then at Carrie. Then he returned it to Larson.

Judge Jones looked at Carrie "The likeness between the young woman and the picture appears to be very close. The courthouse is already closed. I can't do anything now. Therefore, I am going to put her in the protective custody of our county jail until nine o'clock tomorrow morning, and then I'll handle the question of extradition."

He turned to Cole. "Counselor, I assure you, she will be safe. Court is adjourned until nine o'clock tomorrow morning."

"Your Honor, I can hardly believe you are subjecting a female prisoner to spending a night in the county jail. How can you guarantee a woman's safety?"

Judge Jones paused and then nodded. "Counselor's remark is duly noted. The prisoner will be sent to Mrs. Rutherford's House of Correction for Females."

CHAPTER TWENTY-EIGHT
Extradited

Carrie's night at the women's correctional house proved unforgettable. Mrs. Amelia Rutherford, the matron, enjoyed a reputation as a savior to misguided girls and young women, who found themselves inmates at her three-story brick home. At fifty-two years of age, Mrs. Rutherford espoused it her Christian duty to reform these creatures and bring them back into the church-going community. After all, she believed most of them were victims of their own immaturity. Some confessed to being lured into misadventures by foolish young men for amusement or found rebellion against parental authority and social decorum irresistible.

Never had a woman of color been allowed to step across the threshold of her establishment. It was once the home she had shared with her beloved husband, Sheriff Nathanial Rutherford. The widow was flummoxed at being expected to house a colored prisoner. However, she had no choice.

Before the prisoner appeared, a female friend had rushed to inform her of the judge's unprecedented decision. So, when Carrie and her entourage arrived, Mrs. Rutherford met them at the door and forced her lips into a smile.

As Carrie entered the house, her female companion turned to her. "I'll come back with your toiletries and a change of clothing for your court appearance. I'm sorry I won't be able to stay for the trial. We have to return to Philadelphia this evening on business. Commitments have been made. Everyone involved is dependent upon us to do our part."

The prisoner smiled at the young woman. "I understand, Charlotte. Thank you for coming here to support me and all you have done on my behalf." Carrie turned to Mr. Purvis. "Thank you as well, Mr. Purvis."

The prisoner's friend hugged her, and left, teary-eyed with Mr. Purvis.

The sheriff handed the widow the court order.

It shook in her hands as her smile dissolved into tight-lipped anger.

"I'm sorry about this, ma'am."

"Mrs. Rutherford." Cole bowed. "I'm Cole West, this young woman's attorney. I assure you she is a law-abiding person and a teacher by profession. She is innocent of all charges. I entreat you to afford her the same kindness you bestow upon other young women who have found themselves in serious circumstances. I hear this is a respectable and safe establishment. May I have your word t—"

"I have never had a woman of color stay here. If the judge says I must, then I must. Not to worry, Mr. West, she'll be well-treated." She pasted a smile upon her face and showed them to the door. "Good day, gentlemen."

On his way out, Cole turned and announced he would arrive for Carrie at eight o'clock the following morning, and reminded the widow Charlotte Purvis would return later with a change of clothing and personal toiletries for Carrie's courtroom appearance.

"Very well." Mrs. Rutherford slammed the door and dropped her smile.

~~~

Carrie stood in the vestibule trembling. She studied her jailer. The tall, thin woman wore a white blouse with a stiff collar and a black skirt. Her hair was pulled back into a severe bun. Not a strand escaped.

"Come along, er— What shall I call you?"

"Jane," Carrie replied. Her middle name would suffice.

Mrs. Rutherford lit a lamp and led the way.

Carrie followed the woman past the parlor into a hallway. She could see bright daylight from the room at the end. Perhaps, this was where she would sleep.

Her stomach growled, reminding her it was dinnertime. She guessed it must be nearly noon.

The widow stopped in front of a door on the left and turned the knob. It led to a stairway leading downward. Carrie's heart stopped.

"Follow me, Jane."

In the dingy basement, a cot piled with well-worn bedcovers sat against one wall. Carrie scanned the items, which crowded the room. It was obviously used as a storeroom.

"Do you expect me to sleep down here—in the basement, ma'am?"

"You'll be fine down here. I can't allow your kind to sleep in beds intended for white folks." She gazed at Carrie and smirked. "You could pass for white, you know."
~~~

"I wouldn't dishonor my heritage by passing. May I have something to eat, Mrs. Rutherford?"

"Sure, dearie. I'll get you a bowl of soup and some rolls. Hope they're still warm."

The widow turned and started to ascend the steps.

When Carrie followed her, she spun around. "You wait here. I'll bring it down."

Taken aback, Carrie stumbled down a step or two before regaining her balance. She walked to the bed and plopped down on the dusty, threadbare coverlet. When the widow closed the cellar door, Carrie heard an unmistakable click of the lock. She was going to be locked in the basement all night.

She got up and moved the piles off the bed and shook the dust from the coverlet. Tears streamed down Carrie's face as she sat upon the lumpy cot and waited for her jailer's return.

~~~

Her stomach was full. She appreciated the food, and she found the soup and rolls delicious.

After dinner, she followed Mrs. Rutherford upstairs. Her entreaties for an explanation went unanswered. A broom was thrust at her with an order to sweep the kitchen and hallway floors.

Carrie did as she was told. When she swept the last pile into a dustpan, she heard a knock at the front door. Mrs. Rutherford ordered Carrie to return to her quarters.

She locked the basement door, and Carrie heard her steps as she walked to the front door. Carrie stood on the top stair, put her ear to the door, and heard Charlotte's voice.

Mrs. Rutherford had very little to say.
~~~

Charlotte asked to see her, but Mrs. Rutherford refused and slammed the door. The widow's steps were audible as she crossed the parlor to the hallway. Carrie descended the stairs and sat on the cot. Her nerves were rattled as she waited for the matron.

"You are the lucky one, dearie." Mrs. Rutherford descended the stairs with a suitcase in hand. "That pretty gal must have brought you plenty if she needed a suitcase. Very well-spoken and poised she was, much like you. Educated girls, so unlike my usual inmates. Now, let's see what she's brought us."

Carrie's stomach churned with fear. Did Mrs. Rutherford intend to steal Charlotte's belongings?

The matron opened the suitcase and extracted fine clothes, which included a tailored gray suit, a chemise, a shift, pantaloons, several petticoats, stockings, a bonnet, a comb and brush, and a beautiful gold-rimmed, hand mirror. A small box held a pair of pearl earrings. Carrie didn't know if they were genuine or not. She hoped they were imitations.

Mrs. Rutherford held them up to the lamp to admire them. "What a nice friend you have, Jane. This mirror is the finest I've ever seen. The design is reminiscent of Chippendale. I think I'll keep it. Don't look so surprised. I should be paid more for housing prisoners. I get a pittance from the city, but it doesn't cover my expenses. Winter is a lean time for wayward girls. Let's hope April will be busier. Now, follow me upstairs, dearie, there are more chores to do. Bedtime is eight o'clock."

The day passed with Carrie performing housekeeping tasks. She mopped the floors, washed dishes, and dusted the downstairs rooms. She changed the linen on the upstairs beds, which gave her a chance to see where white inmates slept. There were four bedchambers on the second floor. The wallpaper was peeling, and the paint was chipped. However, the beds held sturdy mattresses.

At eight o'clock, Carrie undressed while the matron laid out Charlotte's clothes on a table.

"Get into bed, dearie, while I read my favorite passages from the Bible."

Carrie stretched out on the cot and within minutes became drowsy as she listened to Mrs. Rutherford's monotone.

Quick footsteps approached.

Carrie's eyes flew open as a shadow fell across her bed. As quick as a blink, her jailer handcuffed her right wrist to the bed rail. Fear pounded in Carrie's chest.

"No. No. What are you doing?" She yanked the cuffs in a futile attempt to free herself. "Please, Mrs. Rutherford, there's no need to chain me to the cot. You're going to lock the door anyway. I've done nothing to deserve this kind of treatment."

"A body can't be too careful in the company of a criminal. I'll do what's necessary in order to feel safe in my own home."

The room plunged into darkness. Carrie called the matron to please bring her an oil lamp, but her cries went unanswered. She shivered with fear until, exhausted, she fell asleep.

~~~

Cole hadn't liked the look on Mrs. Rutherford's face as he left. He knew she had little concern for the plight of Negroes, and feared Carrie might be in for a rough night. He hated leaving her there. However, he knew
~~~

she would persevere no matter what shenanigans the old girl invented. If she was too severe, Cole would see to it that she'd be held accountable.

Robert Purvis extended his invitation for Cole to stay at his home, and he accepted.

Cole headed to the telegraph office to send several important wires: one to Carrie's parents, whom he invited to stay at his ranch during the trial. He hoped Carrie's mother would be well enough to travel. In the wire to Tim Weeks, he inquired about Mrs. Weeks' health. There was a telegram waiting for him as well from Mrs. Tubman. She and her charges had arrived at the headquarters of The Anti-Slavery Society of Canada.

Had she gone to Canada instead of caring for me, Carrie would be safe now.

Although Cole regretted her decision to stay behind, he had to admit it had been some of the most precious times he had spent with her.

He had much to do to prepare for the most important case of his life.

I must save the life of the woman I love.

~~~

The following morning, the methodical wheels of justice turned fast for the former school teacher. The young woman was identified as Carrie Bennet based on her own declaration. Extradition to Richmond, Virginia was ordered.

Cole petitioned the judge to remand Carrie to his custody until they reached their destination, on the same grounds as his previous petition. Once in Richmond, he would surrender her at the sheriff's
~~~

office into Coffe's custody. He suggested they travel by train where Coffe could keep an eye on his prisoner.

The judge acquiesced.

After breakfast, Cole and Carrie waited at the station to board the eleven o'clock train. To their astonishment, they heard the sheriff arguing with his deputies. In a clandestine move, Coffe had arranged for the lawmen to escort several extradited outlaws from Philadelphia to Virginia in a prison coach along with two local deputies.

The deputies feared Coffe would collect the reward money before they reached Richmond. He promised they would go to the law office together to obtain the one-thousand-dollar reward.

Cole and Carrie sat next to each other on the train.

It whistled and clanged before it rushed down the rails.

Carrie drifted off to sleep. Her head leaned toward Cole and finally rested upon his shoulder. Her night at the Rutherford establishment had been anything but restful. However, she had managed to reclaim Charlotte's mirror without her jailor's knowledge.

CHAPTER TWENTY-NINE
Mason's Sacrifice

Richmond, Virginia
April 3, 1860

"Please, Aunt Olivia." Tears welled in Mason's eyes. "Stay with me." His baritone voice faltered. "I can't bear to lose you." He hovered over the woman whose labored breathing frightened him. Then he knelt beside her bed and reached for her hand. When another wave of pain and nausea swept through her, she gripped his hand with all her might.

Mason had bought his freedom but instead of leaving Twin Oaks, he had decided to stay and protect Olivia. It was a sacrifice he was willing to make. However, it seemed Olivia had been poisoned again.

Once the pain faded, Olivia beckoned him with a gnarled finger, and he leaned toward her lips. What she told him caused him to gasp.

Mason had lost his mother as a child, and this aged woman had taken her place. Her hands had tended his childhood injuries and bruises. She had sat with him through illness and childhood trials. Her words shaped a positive self-image, and her courage strengthened his. She'd assured him freedom would someday welcome him. Her plea convinced a young Massa Robert to educate a handful of slaves, and he had been among them.

Master Johnson entered Olivia's living quarters. The crowd of household servants who stood by the doorway parted to admit him. His steps hurried as he made his way to her bed and sat on the edge. It creaked under his weight. On the other side, Mason held her hand.

Master Johnson greeted Mason with a nod. He placed a hand over Olivia's wrinkled one. "Gabriel has gone to fetch the doctor." He patted her hand. Closing his eyes, he recited the Lord's Prayer, and others joined him. Once the prayer ended, they all wished Olivia a speedy recovery and left Master Johnson and Mason alone with the woman who had shaped their lives.

Olivia's chamber in the servants' area of the house was roomy and furnished with cast-offs from the Johnsons' household. She hadn't resided in the slave quarters since she was midwife to Master Johnson's mother.

His was a difficult delivery. When the doctor arrived, he credited Olivia with saving the lives of the sixteen-year-old mother and her firstborn son. This gained her fame, and her talents as a midwife were heralded in the countryside among the neighboring plantation families as well as a few society matrons in the City of Richmond. Olivia believed her work was a calling from the Lord. She believed this was why she had been born: to save the lives of mothers and infants. She taught herself the healing properties of herbs, plants, and flowers. Moreover, she soaked up information from benevolent medics and apothecary merchants.

Aunt Olivia's practice had also given her valuable insight into the lives of folks in the slave quarters and leaders in the county. She kept the secrets of many. It made her a powerful ally to some but the presumptive enemy of those who feared she would someday betray their vulnerability and expose the darker side of their natures.

"Been poisoned, again. I jest know it, Massa Robert. Arsenic. I use it in my gardening. I seed its effects on peoples."

"Aunt Olivia, I promise you I will find out who is responsible. Until then, we're all at risk."

"It was da cake. One of de mens brought me a little cake in a basket. He told me it came from one of da people from another plantation. It was made just for me to eat. I love cake and tried some. When I felt sick, it made me think of da candy. I put it in a drawer afta I got sick some time ago and never minded it again."

Mason became excited. "Let's have the candy and the rest of the cake analyzed. It must be the source. I'll take the sweets to the apothecary tomorrow." Master Johnson nodded to Mason and patted Olivia's hand.

"I'll prepare your food, myself," offered Mason. "Don't eat anything from anyone, other than me. Promise?"

Olivia nodded.

Master Johnson touched Mason's shoulder. "An excellent idea. I think Lulu should move in here with her." He addressed Olivia. "She would be the last person I'd suspect of trying to harm you, since her own child died."

"I would like that, Massa Robert." Olivia spoke in a hoarse whisper. "She is a comfort to me, always has been."

~~~

Dr. Witherspoon emerged from Olivia's room with a wrinkled brow. "I suspect Olivia's been poisoned, again. She's experienced the same symptoms: cramping and stomach pain among others. Thank God, she's still alive. It's a wonder, at her age. This is a matter for the law. Have you contacted them?"

Master Johnson shook his head.

"You should before your own family's lives are threatened. I've given her some medicine to ease the pain and a sedative." He pulled Master Johnson aside. "At her age, I can't be sure if she'll pull through."

Mason was given permission to return to his cabin. As he walked to the slave quarters, the daylight began to dim. He eyed the faint outline of a crescent moon in the April sky.

At twenty-years of age, Mason had made a promise to himself not to marry. Acquiring his own freedom was easier than having to raise funds to purchase a family's as well.

Entering the dwelling, he walked straight to his secret place. He took off his shirt and began to dig. In a corner, hidden deep under the packed dirt floor was a colored cigar box faded with age. It had once belonged to Master Johnson's father, Ebenezer. As a child, Mason coveted the box, which had sat on his former master's desk as he dusted the room. The picture of several garrulous gentlemen sitting around a table drinking and laughing with glee drew his eyes like a magnet. They all held cigars between their
~~~

fingers or lips. Like the men in the picture, he wanted to be well-dressed, well-fed, and living a life of freedom.

Amused by the child's fascination, Ebenezer gave it to him when it was empty.

Now, the box held his life savings. As Massa Johnson's favorite, he had been allowed to earn his own money from the age of fourteen. His newspaper delivery route took him miles beyond his home. Gratuities from the occasional odd job increased his savings.

Every time he opened the box, warmth spread through him, as if he had drunk a glass of sunshine. The sum was nearly two-thousand dollars. His freedom would cost him one-thousand. The remainder could provide him with a financial enterprise, what kind of business he had yet to decide.

He lifted the bills out of the box and thumbed through the thick sheaf. He took the money to the table and counted it with care. He enjoyed the feel of the bills in his hands. With the money counted and stacked according to the denominations, he returned the bills to the cigar box.

Tomorrow would have been his day of emancipation. All had been arranged between him and Massa Johnson. But now, with the illness of dear Aunt Olivia, he had decided to wait to see if she would recover. If emancipated, he'd have to leave the state. Now, he understood why she had refused her freedom when her daughter Sarah had offered to take her when she left. Olivia couldn't leave Mary behind.

On her sickbed, she revealed she had saved a lot of money. Her math skills were limited, so she couldn't count it all. She had confided in Mason. Mothers often slipped her bills to thank her for delivering their babies. Mason had counted the money when they were alone. It amounted to three-thousand dollars, all of it earned from her midwife practice.

She asked Mason to promise he'd give the money to Mary, once she and her family obtained their freedom.

He must get word to the funny little man, Allan Pinkerton. The Scottish detective had visited him more than a month earlier, asking him to keep a journal of the comings and goings of those around Aunt Olivia. After tomorrow, he would have definite information to report.

The next morning, Mason collected the candy, cake, dishes and utensils from Olivia's room. He waited at the shop until the analysis was determined. Arsenic in both the candy and cake was confirmed.

CHAPTER THIRTY
Pinkerton Investigates

"Come in, sir." Miss Barbara Dayton stepped back to admit Pinkerton, who had identified himself in his letter as Gavin Carmichael, a biographer. A wide grin lit up her eyes as she appraised the Scotsman, whose red-bearded face and blue eyes twinkled with kindness. Dressed in a brown tweed suit, Pinkerton handed his matching derby hat to his delighted hostess. She hung it on the coatrack standing in the foyer. She offered to take his leather briefcase, but he demurred.

Miss Dayton addressed her colored maid. "Please see to the refreshments, Mae."

The young servant retreated.

"I received your letter, Mr. Carmichael. I can't tell you what an honor it is to have a noted biographer write about one's family. Just think, you've come all the way from Richmond to interview me in St. Louis, Missouri about my famous brother."

She proffered a thin, damp hand and curtseyed. "I'm delighted to meet you."

Pinkerton bowed and kissed her hand. "The pleasure is all mine."

She batted her eyelashes and giggled.

Pinkerton laughed to himself. He often used an alias to glean information from those who might be reluctant to be questioned by a detective.

"Your accent is quite attractive, Mr. Carmichael. Where are you from?"

"Glasgow, Scotland, it's a charming city with a busy port."

Miss Dayton led Pinkerton to the cluttered parlor, brimming with antiques and expensive trinkets; many appeared to date before the Revolutionary War. She offered Pinkerton a seat on a plush chair of pink and green opposite the matching divan, upon which she sat. Next to her was a servants' cord. She rang it. "We'll have some refreshments, Mr. Carmichael."

Soon, another young maid entered with a sterling silver tea service. Trailing behind her, Mae carried a silver tray adorned with scones, biscuits, and cookies.

Over tea and baked goods, Miss Dayton apologized. "Mr. Carmichael, I'm embarrassed to admit I've never read any of your books." A frown appeared between her blue eyes.

"Not to worry." Pinkerton smiled. "Most people read to escape their predictable lives and prefer the popular novels of Dickens or the poetry of Walt Whitman, but my readers like to read about real people."

Pinkerton opened the thick briefcase and extracted several biographical volumes. He smiled as he looked at the book jackets. Miss Dayton may have attributed this to pride in his authorship. However, it was due to his admiration of Mason's clever ruse. The book jackets were fakes, produced at the newspaper office by Mason's friend, Jimmy. The titles were authentic, but the title pages, artwork, and byline, fictitious. He handed three volumes to his hostess, who perused them with a satisfied smile.

Now convinced he was a bonafide author, Lucius Dayton's elder sister appeared overjoyed by the attention of a distinguished writer.

After Pinkerton had quizzed Miss Dayton about the privileged childhood she'd shared with Lucius, he guided the conversation through various subjects, eventually leading to what he had come to discover.

"I heard Dayton's wife died several years ago."

"Yes. I wasn't invited to the funeral. He never explained to my satisfaction how she died. They had a tumultuous marriage. Lucius, as so many other southern gentlemen did, maintained relationships with slave women. Southern wives have been trained to look the other way, but Camille was too much the idealist to tolerate his indiscretions. She pleaded with him to leave the slave women alone. She told me so herself. She didn't grow up around here. She came from a rich family in Paris, France, Mademoiselle Camille Marie Bizet. She was so glamorous when Lucius brought her here. I suppose our customs were strange to her. She never really fit in."

"Much of my book, Miss Dayton, will explore the celebrated cases Lucius tried in his time. However, details of his private life, although interesting, are not the subject of my book."

Pinkerton leaned forward. "My focus will be on his trials. I expect the legal community will comprise the core readership of this book. It goes without saying his is one of the most brilliant legal minds in the State of Virginia or perhaps, the country. I've researched the

Pennington case, the Chisolm trial, and the Elderbee case.

"The case of the Elderbee School for Boys shocked us all." The aged woman's hands fluttered in her lap, and then she pressed her palms against her cheeks. "Five, well-to-do boys kidnapped a fellow classmate and held him for ransom. Then they killed him." She lowered her hands and fisted her right hand. "I tell you, folks were in an uproar." She reached for her cup.

Pinkerton added he had discovered minute details about the case but very little on the case involving a slave on Dayton's plantation: the grand larceny trial he prosecuted against Thomas.

At the mention of Thomas, Miss Dayton pressed her lips together and began to fidget with the buttons on her blouse.

"I know your niece, Isabella, stayed with you during her testimony for the defense." Pinkerton kept his tone friendly. "Those records are sealed." Pinkerton leaned forward and whispered, as if to conspire with his hostess. "Did you happen to hear any of her testimony?"

Miss Dayton's eyes darted back and forth until they focused on the wart on her right hand. "Poor, poor Isabella, she was so distraught when she came here. Her father said it was to protect her from the newspaper reporters and gossipmongers."

"Did she discuss the case with you?"

"It would have violated the law, I believe." Miss Dayton lowered her voice to a whisper. "It's not anything she said, but *what she didn't say,* which I found alarming. She loved that colored boy. They grew up together, you know."

Dayton's sister explained children of the slaveholding family and their personal slaves often formed close ties, which sometimes extended beyond childhood. Those ties were severed before puberty. Both were schooled to accept the social realities of the society. However, when a friendship continued, it threatened the divide. "Mind you, I don't agree with how they treat their colored." She pressed her lips together in disdain. "Slavery degrades both slave and master, making one the victim and the other an un-Christian tyrant, in many cases. I hire only free people, white or black, makes no difference to me as long as they are clean, polite and capable. I pay my help a little better than the average, so they won't be enticed to leave me for greener grass."

Miss Dayton described visits to her brother's plantation. She said she always found Isabella and Thomas together. "Lucius tried to keep them apart, but by age twelve, it was too late. Isabella had taught Thomas how to read, write, and do mathematics. She shared everything with her childhood friend. They were like the couple in that novel by Emily Bronte, *Wuthering Heights*, separated by class and in this instance race but still drawn to one another like love birds. She told me they were distant cousins. Thomas's father was Dayton's second cousin."

Miss Dayton lowered her voice even further and dropped a bomb. "She was pregnant when she was here, but she never admitted it. Her appetite was poor. She was nauseated and sick every morning. No one needed to tell me what was ailing her. One time, she fainted, and I saw by accident, what was inside the locket Missy always wore."

Pinkerton felt confused and it must have shown on his face.

"It was the pet name her father called her. I'm no snoop, mind you. I took off all of her jewelry before the doctor examined her. The gold locket popped open in my hand. I must have opened the clasp by mistake and there was an inscription inside. Let me see...."

She raised her eyes to the ceiling in an attempt to recall the words. "It simply read: 'Thomas,' I still have it."

Pinkerton sat up straight in his chair and rubbed the side of his nose. He was about to see direct evidence of Isabella and Thomas's relationship. He asked to see the locket.

He waited for Miss Dayton to return with the jewelry.

Once it was in his hand, he flipped open the locket and read the inscription his hostess had quoted.

"I heard Mr. West, the defendant's lawyer, came to visit Isabella."

"What a nice man he was." Her lips turned down. "I was sorry to hear of his death. Murdered, you know. The papers named Thomas as the killer, but I'll never believe it. Mr. West was defending him. He was Thomas's singular chance for freedom. Mr. West spoke privately with Isabella. I wasn't allowed in the room when he recorded her affidavit."

The spinster added more information about her niece. Isabella was calmer after Mr. West left. "He must have assured her Thomas would benefit from her testimony."

"Was she happy to accompany her father to Virginia?" Pinkerton leaned forward.

"The poor child was terrified. I tried to stop him, saying she was better off with me, but he wouldn't hear of it. A curious thing though, she left a suitcase here and said she'd come back for it later. Since she's dead, I should have sent it to her father long ago. I didn't because for some reason, I felt like it would have been a betrayal. Isn't that odd?"

"May I have a look?"

"Yes, of course." Miss Dayton left the room and returned with a leather suitcase. They searched its contents, but only found clothing.

"I'm staying at the St. Louis Hotel if you want to contact me again. By the way, Miss Dayton, I'd be glad to take Isabella's things with me and give them to her father."

"Would you? It would save me an expense. Thank you."

"Oh, one more thing, did you see any symptoms of typhoid fever in Isabella before she left with her father for Virginia?"

"Typhoid fever? Bosh. Lucius concocted a story to explain her death. Isabella was pregnant, I assume by Thomas. My guess is she died in childbirth. Typhoid fever didn't hit this part of St. Louis until months *after* Isabella left for Virginia."

CHAPTER THIRTY-ONE
A Plan for Liberty

Frank barged into the cabin and slammed the door. The books on the shelves shifted. Some fell over and hit the floor.

"Hattie Rose, you must never leave books on the shelf. What if Green saw them? He'd whip us for certain."

"Well, hello to you."

She hid the books inside a trapdoor in a corner of the floor, which Frank had crafted to secret the crimes of reading and pilfering volumes from Dayton's library.

"Is something else the matter?" Hattie Rose stared at him. The look in her husband's eyes frightened her. She had never seen him so angry.

"We have to get away from here before I kill him or do something to get me killed."

"Please, darling, tell me what's the matter?"

Frank plunged into the sordid tale. That evening, Dayton's spring ball was in full swing. Frank, attired in formal wear, led a quartet of musicians through classical and popular tunes. Richmond's finest were in attendance.

"It was somewhere between Mozart's 'Violin Concerto No. 1 in B-flat major' and 'Violin Concerto No. 2 in D major' when I heard old man Dayton's conversation." His voice cracked and rose an octave.

"He haggled with two other planters over the cost to breed slaves. They talked about what a fine specimen someone was, his physical strength, his civility. Dayton described him as a standout among other men. Another said he'd appreciate a supply of slaves whom he could teach carpentry or other skills. 'Perhaps, your Chester could give them music lessons. After all, they would be his progeny. Talent like his is inherited.' Hattie Rose, they were talking about me."

Frank's thumped his chest; and then, loosened the top button of his shirt. "They wanted to stud me like a prized bull. I had to leave the room before I exploded. I will not condemn my descendants to a life of degradation to enrich the coffers of immoral men, not while I draw breath." His eyes darted around the room before they rested upon his wife. "We had just ended the first concerto. I hurried to the library in a panic." He gripped her by the shoulders and pulled her toward him. "While standing there shaking with indignation, the answer came to me. It's time for us to leave. Once my mind was made up, I was able to compose myself and continue. We must leave before daylight."

Hattie Rose's face brightened. "Mason will be on his way to pick up the Sunday paper for his paper route. We'll catch a ride with him."

Feigning illness, Frank had convinced Dayton he wasn't able to play and was allowed to retire.

They had to leave at once. It was then Saturday evening. Since slaves were given Sunday off, the couple wouldn't be missed until Monday morning. Frank and Hattie Rose packed their meager belongings. Frank intended to disguise himself as a woman.

After rising before dawn the next morning, they waited behind a tree off the main road.

Before the sun rose Sunday morning, Mason drove Massa Johnson's horse-drawn wagon toward town to pick up the next day's delivery of *The Virginia Enquirer.* As he rounded a bend in the road, he found a wood pile across his path. He had no choice but to clear the way. Mason alighted from the carriage, and Frank appeared from behind a tree and aimed a gun at him. He ordered the frightened man to raise his hands.

Hattie Rose came out of hiding and stood next to Frank. The pair of would-be outlaws wore long coats, hats pulled low across their brows, and kerchiefs over their noses and mouths. Frank ordered Mason to clear the road. Afterward, he helped Hattie Rose into Mason's wagon, and they threw their bundles on the floor.

"You're helping us escape north, brother," Frank announced. "Don't turn around, Mason, or I'll blow your head off."

Mason disregarded the threat and turned to face his kidnappers.

He studied them and then burst out laughing. His shoulders shook with mirth. "You couldn't pass for any woman I've ever seen." He burst into a new round of chuckles.

Hattie Rose looked at her husband and giggled, releasing the pent-up tension the escapade had sparked. Frank's tough exterior melted as his merriment gained momentum.

"There's no need to force me to help you. I do this all the time. I'm a conductor on the Underground Railroad. To whom am I speaking?"

Frank lowered the gun and introduced Hattie Rose and himself.

Hattie Rose studied Mason. “So, you’re the conductor? I suspected there might be one on either the Mayfield or Johnson plantations because they’ve had the most recent escapes, but I didn’t know who it was. Your paper route provides a good cover.”

“May I ask a question? Frank, where did you get the gun?”

Frank handed it to Mason. “I made it out of wood and painted it black.”

Mason whistled. “Well, I’ll be. Good job. It looks real.” He turned the gun over in his hand then returned it to Frank. “Where’re you folks headed?”

Hattie Rose looked at Frank. “We just had to run.”

“No worry, I know of several safe houses. What’s your final destination?”

“New York City, my home town. Have you heard or read anything about a fugitive named Carrie Bennet?”

Mason revealed how he had driven Carrie Bennet in Dr. Ashley’s carriage off the Johnson’s plantation, thinking his passenger was the doctor. He described the inquest and recalled an article which detailed her capture in a Philadelphia courtroom. Since then, she had been extradited to Richmond to stand trial. He asked Frank how he knew Carrie.

“We were childhood friends. I’ve known her all of my life. We went to the same schools. There was a time when I thought we’d marry. I’m sorry to hear she’s on trial for murder.”

Frank could see insecurity in Hattie Rose’s eyes. “I wouldn’t change a thing, my dearest Hattie Rose.

When we get to New York, we'll have a proper church wedding. Would you like that?"

She nodded.

"I've often asked God why he put me on the Dayton plantation. Now I believe it was to marry you. I am a changed man. Before I met you, making money was my only goal. Now, I intend to use my legal talents to free my enslaved brothers and sisters and to fight for equality." Frank lifted his wife's chin and kissed her lips with tenderness.

~~~

Hattie Rose closed her eyes and laid her head upon her husband's chest. She slipped her hand into the pocket of her coat and clutched the diary of her former mistress, Missy Dayton, whom she'd felt was a dear friend. It was the last thing she grabbed before she vacated their cabin. Tears slid down her face, tears of joy. She was free. Free. Somehow, the greenery before her was more vivid, the air, sweeter, and her love for Frank burned brighter than ever.
~~~

CHAPTER THIRTY-TWO
The Sexual Politics of Slavery

Sarah Grimké and her sister, Angelina, cast their eyes over the solicitous members of the Philadelphia Female Anti-Slavery Society. Both women were euphoric by the swelling ranks of members, who crowded her parlor and answered the call to act.

Sarah called the impromptu meeting to order. She first acknowledged the absence of notables. Mrs. Mott and the Purvis women were unable to attend due to family obligations. Her parlor overflowed with members, Quakers and non-Quakers, colored and white alike.

"The agenda in front of you is limited at best." Sarah held up her copy. "In light of the immediate crisis, which faces Miss Carrie Bennet in Virginia, I thought it best to put a proposal to you now."

The women, some of whose husbands were present, listened to Sarah with rapt attention. "No recent public incident has pushed the inequalities of race and sex to the forefront of social and political thought as Miss Bennet's arrest and impending murder trial."

Sarah looked at the assemblage. "Here, we have a young, Negro woman, born free in New York City, who is accused of killing a white man. The newspapers have implied she is a Jezebel, but I've heard from sources I trust that this young lady was protecting herself from rape and a vicious beating because she refused his sexual advances. She struck back to protect herself from further assault. He died from his injuries, but his death was *not* her intention.

"None of the journals describe Miss Bennet's actions as self-defense. The decedent had a reputation in Virginia for abusing women in bondage and jeopardizing the reputations of white women, whom he pursued under the guise of courtship. This is an opportunity for us to gather more supporters against the brutality of slavery and the subjugation of women.

"Angelina and I propose we journey to Virginia to give Carrie Bennet our support. If Miss Bennet had been white, would she be standing trial today? I doubt it. Her right to refuse to have sexual relations would have been protected under the law. Well, as a colored female, born free in the United States of America, Miss Bennet is denied citizenship and equal protection under the law. In the face of this appalling contradiction, 'in the land of the free and the home of the brave,' we must protest this flagrant violation of Christian values and moral decency."

Angelina stepped up. "Let us be *brave* in our protest and *free* in our right to rally against this brazen injustice in which Miss Bennet finds herself. This is an affront to our rights as women."

Grace Bustill Douglass, a founding member of the society and past vice president of the Convention of Women in New York, a free colored woman and entrepreneur, was recognized. Her head was covered with the thin white Quaker cap of her religious sect. She began to chant. "Free Carrie Bennet. Free Carrie Bennet."

One by one, others stood up, and the chant grew and reverberated throughout the room.

After a few minutes, Sarah waved her hands, indicating they were to take their seats. "We will now choose a committee to create a plan of action. It is our mission to educate the citizens of our country, to persuade them to take action by joining the anti-slavery society to fight for the freedom of all America's people."

"May I speak?" Mrs. Douglass stood.

Sarah smiled in affirmation as she bit into one of the delicious pastries Mrs. Douglass had brought from her father's bakery to share with the society.

"I'm drafting a pamphlet I've entitled, *The Sexual Politics of Slavery,* which will depict how sex is used by the slaveholding community to wield power, demean, and abuse people in bondage. Rape, incest, and the breeding farms are weapons to expand the numbers of enslaved people for economic gain, since importing slaves from Africa has been outlawed. This is what the economy of the United States flourishes upon, the tragic devastation of the lives of so many.

"I would be remiss if I didn't mention enslaved men suffer sexual abuse by slaveholders of both sexes. If a white woman of means fancies an enslaved man, he could not refuse her advances, and she could accuse him of rape, whether or not he complied. He would be lynched for certain. Can you imagine how enslaved people feel being forced to share the most private parts of their bodies and emotions with those who have degraded them and their family members?"

"Grace, this a subject most people prefer not to acknowledge, but it is as much a part of slavery as being forced to work in the fields or plantation households." Sarah Grimké nodded. "We look forward to adding your pamphlet to our literature."

Next, Sarah asked for volunteers, and members responded. Among the various activities they listed was to provide a speakers' forum to tell the truth about Miss Bennet's arrests in front of the courthouse and to sell and distribute literature. Among the pamphlets for sale would be: Sarah's *Letters on the Equality of the Sexes,* articles from *The Liberator* and *The North Star,* Angelina's *An Appeal to the Christian Women of the South* and *An Appeal to the Women of the Nominally Free States,* written by Isabella Maria Child and Sarah Mapps Douglass. Through the sale of anti-slavery and pro-feminist literature, as well as jellies, preserves, scarves, shawls, bonnets, gloves, and baked goods, the women intended to raise funds for Carrie's defense and the costs incurred due to her imprisonment and trial.

CHAPTER THIRTY-THREE
Carrie's Trial Begins

At the arraignment, a formal charge of murder was entered into the court record against Carrie. She entered a plea of not guilty. As Cole expected, bail was denied. After all, Carrie had fled the jurisdiction of the law.

For over a week, she awaited trial at the House of Corrections for Females. Matrons were on duty twenty-four hours.

The trial began at ten o'clock on Friday, April 13, 1860. The courtroom was filled to capacity. The mood outside mimicked a carnival. Children played tag, vendors crowded the sidewalk, and protesters touted women's suffrage and emancipation, amid shouts from hecklers.

Cole's carriage arrived at the courthouse with the Walkers in tow. His thoughts were on Carrie, as he assisted the couple from the carriage. He had visited Carrie's cell last night and brought a change of clothes and words of support from the Walkers.

"Free Carrie Bennet. Free Carrie Bennet." A female protester started the chant, and others joined her. Cole looked at the cluster of women and smiled.

Cole noticed the plaque on their table which read: The Philadelphia Female Anti-Slavery Society. He had received five-hundred dollars from them for Carrie's defense. He walked over to their table and introduced himself. He met Charlotte Forten and thanked them all for their support.

~~~

Carrie's throat tightened as she waited with a matron behind a door which led to the courtroom. A small window in the door allowed her to watch the courtroom fill. She spied Cole and the Walkers enter, and a lump gathered in her throat. Soon after, Charlotte Forten entered along with her fellow anti-slavery members.

She came all the way from Philadelphia to support me. I'm going to take it as a good omen.

Inside the courtroom, all watched Carrie's slender form as she walked to the defense table. She knew she looked elegant in a gray skirt and matching jacket. She wore a bonnet of gray and lavender, edged with black lace.

Across the aisle sat Lucius Dayton, the revered Chief Prosecutor of Richmond County, himself a slave master. Carrie heard he owned nearly one-thousand slaves who worked on tobacco and rice plantations in Virginia and South Carolina, respectively. He fastened his penetrating dark blue eyes on her. Carrie learned his reputation as a brutal courtroom combatant earned him the nickname: "The Hawk." His needle-sharp, close-set eyes, bony narrow face, hooked nose, and pointed chin contributed to his predatory countenance.

Carrie returned his stare.

She saw an undercurrent of amusement flicker in his eyes, spiking her fear.
~~~

He's enjoying this. He's circling overhead, like a bird of prey, ready for the kill.

"Order, order in the court." Judge Anderson struck his gavel. The noise died. "Is the prosecution ready?"

"We are, Your Honor," responded Dayton.

The Hawk stood to his full six-foot, two inches. He was immaculate in a crisp black suit as he approached the jury.

Twelve white faces stared back.

Turning his body to include the spectators, he began his opening statement. "Ladies and gentlemen, and gentlemen of the jury, the prosecution will show how Carrie Bennet, the defendant, with intent and malice plunged a wooden stick into the eye of Captain John Pierce. Afterward, she struck him on the back of the head with a rock, killing him."

He paused and stared at the defendant. "Look at her. She appears demure and as prim as a lady, a cultivated lady, as I understand. But appearances can be deceitful. The defendant isn't what she appears to be. *This* is the basis of our case. Miss Bennet is anything but demure, anything but a lady, and anything but innocent.

"She arrived at the Twin Oaks Plantation with the intention to free her grandmother, so she says. However, her attraction for Captain John Pierce upset those plans. The defendant admits she went to the barn in the middle of the night, according to the inquest record. Why? To meet the Captain or was it for a more sinister purpose, to steal the property of Master Robert Johnson and others by providing aid to runaways?

"On the night in question, when Captain John Pierce met his demise, the prosecution believes Carrie Bennet's plan to free slaves was discovered by the deceased. When he threatened to divulge her secret, she killed him.

"An investigation into the activities of the defendant has proven she has been attending anti-slavery meetings in her native city of New York. Purchasing her grandmother's freedom wasn't enough for Carrie Bennet. She still had an aunt and uncle, as well as nieces and nephews enslaved on the Dayton plantation. The family managed to escape but was captured by Sheriff Coffe and his deputies. The aunt and uncle died by their own hand. The mother smothered one of her children and drowned another."

Gasps were heard from the spectators.

"This is what Miss Bennet's abolitionist's motive has led to: the death and destruction of her own kin and another's property.

"After an encounter with Carrie Bennet, Captain Pierce was found dead. An inquest was conducted—the state's Exhibit C. The defendant was charged with first-degree murder. Before the sheriff could take custody of her, she disguised herself as Dr. Carolyn Ashley and escaped in the doctor's waiting carriage. This alone attests to her artfulness as a master of deceit.

"If she were innocent, why would she have fled? This in itself is an admission of guilt."

Dayton spun around and pointed a finger at Carrie. "Carrie Bennet is guilty of fraud. Guilty of theft. And guilty of murder. If the defendant is found guilty, nothing but the death penalty would suffice for this vicious murder of Captain John Pierce."

Newspaper men, seated in the front row, hastily scribbled on their pads.

Carrie surmised possible headlines: *The Prosecution Asks for the Death Penalty,* or *The First Woman to Hang since Ann Bilansky in St. Paul, Minnesota for poisoning her husband.*

Carrie sat up straighter and held her head high, denying how she felt inside. Her heart pounded against her chest. *I have to be a moral and believable witness.*

Cole stood, ready for battle. He strode from the defense table. Audible gasps from several ladies in the courtroom echoed as he turned toward the jury and spectators. His deportment was estimable, a perfect match for his handsome face and muscular physique. His black shoulder-length hair was tied back. An errant lock fell over his forehead. Green-blue eyes glittered. The young attorney wore a black suit. His white shirt blazed against his tanned complexion, his collar set off by a black cravat.

Carrie looked up to the balcony at the sea of black, brown, white, and tan faces.

A man looks familiar.

His face was drawn, and a thick beard covered his chin. His bony shoulders looked sharp under his coat. He stared as if he knew her. More puzzling was the shame she felt. Then, the answer hit her. *It's Frank. Yes, it is Frank. Oh, how he has changed.* She looked up again, and Frank leaned forward and waved.

She scanned the faces in the balcony and almost cried with joy at the sight of her parents and brother. At the end of the aisle she spotted Charlotte, flanked by white women from the female anti-slavery society, who must have refused to be separated from their colored members. A lump gathered in Carrie's throat as tears brimmed in her eyes.

The night he'd visited her cell, Cole had revealed he had received a telegram from her family accepting his invitation to stay at his ranch. For the first time in months, Carrie would see her family.

The telegram also heralded good news: Sarah's condition had improved. Although, a cough still seized her on occasion, the doctor felt there was reason to hope she'd make a full recovery. Her prayers had been answered. Hopefully, the deadly disease would never reappear.

"Appearances are what Mr. Dayton says this trial is about." He began to pace before the jury. "That, gentlemen, is a scheme to divert your attention from the truth. Fabrication, a cover-up, and slanderous falsehoods are what you have heard from the prosecution." He waved a hand toward Carrie. "I assure you this young woman, Carrie Bennet, came to Twin Oaks, for one purpose and one purpose only, to purchase her grandmother's freedom. She encountered the deceased when he lured her into the barn with a cryptic message: '*Meet me in the barn. I need your help.'* Fearing an enslaved relative may have been injured or in dire need, she heeded the call. To her surprise, Captain John Pierce was waiting for her in the dark. Ready to force her to his will.

"Miss Bennet would not be on trial for her life had she been a white woman. If a free woman of color is compromised, to whom can she appeal for justice? Not the law, because her place in society isn't recognized.

Moreover, citizenship is denied her in the country where she was born. Thus, she has no rights. No state in the union prosecutes any man for assaulting a woman of color. This is the shame of our country.

"Yes, Captain John Pierce committed an act for which he *knew* he'd never be prosecuted. Women like Miss Bennet are fair game in a society where the color of one's skin excludes one from the protection of the law.

"Exploitation, of all kinds, within the institution of slavery is an economic ploy to increase prosperity and morally bankrupt the enslaved, but it is *never* acknowledged in public. These same abuses would be considered crimes if the victims were white.

"'Children of the plantation' is what racially-mixed offspring are called." Cole whispered his next words with theatrical effect. "And Carrie Bennet, the product of a white father and an enslaved woman, would have been called a 'child of the plantation' had she been born here.

"As a colored woman, she'd have had no legal rights. But she has moral rights. She has a right to govern her own body and refuse any man's proposition. She *is* a free woman and has *no* master, but therein lies the rub. S*he isn't free at all.* She wasn't free to refuse *him* because our society dictates *all* white men are her masters.

"Miss Bennet refused his advances, and this must have enraged a man like Captain Pierce. A mere colored woman, with no citizenship or legal rights, had no right to refuse a man of his stature.

"Miss Bennet is unique. She was born free in New York City in a middle-class family and attended college. She was promoted to head teacher in an institution where she worked to educate orphans. Her stepfather is a successful entrepreneur, who has provided a fashionable home for his family. He has earned some privileges and opportunities by his own endeavors and fortitude, which whites have inherited because of the color of their skin. A woman of this caliber must have been irresistible to a man like Pierce, noted for his womanizing ways."

Dayton jumped to his feet. "Objection. Counsel is trying to sully Captain Pierce's reputation."

"Your Honor, may I address the court?" Cole turned to face the judge.

"Please, Mr. West."

"Captain Pierce's reputation as a 'ladies' man,' is legendary. Scandalous behavior toward the opposite sex has been the subject of rumors for years."

The judge responded quickly. "This may be the case, but until testimony of your assertion has been entered into the court records, please refrain from utterances which could be construed as prejudicial against the deceased. Objection sustained. Your remark will be stricken from the record."

The judge looked at the court reporter who recorded the legal proceedings by the use of the Pittman phonemic orthography shorthand.

Dayton's features softened as he flashed Cole a victory smile.

"Very well, Your Honor." Cole walked over to the jury.

"Yes, the defendant presented an irresistible challenge for the captain. He wanted to put Miss Bennet in her place—a place subservient to himself.

"After he had brutalized Miss Bennet, he continued his assault. So, to protect herself, she fought back. She was afraid for her life. She was protecting herself, and for this she should die? It was self-defense. Gentlemen of the jury, I beg you to substitute Carrie Bennet for your own daughter or wife in the same situation. Would you fault her for protecting herself and send her to her death? Where is the justice? For the sake of decency, in our Christian society, I beg you to find the defendant not guilty."

Cole walked to his chair.

The courtroom was still. Never had a white lawyer pleaded with such passion for the equal treatment of a person of color. The balcony exploded in applause, people cried and hugged one another, and then pandemonium broke out.

The whites below shook their fists at the balcony. Some hurled racist epitaphs at Cole. Some applauded with passion.

Judge Anderson lifted his gavel and then noticed it had cracked under his assault. After five minutes, the cacophony began to subside. All stared at the red-faced judge.

"Deputies and officers, there will be a fifteen-minute recess."

CHAPTER THIRTY-FOUR The Prosecution Presents its Case

Sheriff Coffe rose from his seat and was sworn in.

"Sheriff, please tell us about your encounter with Miss Bennet on New Year's Eve," instructed Dayton.

Coffe adjusted his girth in the too-small chair. "We were relaxing in Master Johnson's study after the ball, invited to taste his best wines and spirits. It was a tradition. Miss Bennet rushed into the study. She was a mess. She said Captain Pierce needed assistance."

"Please describe to the jury the scene of the decedent's death?"

"We found the body of Captain John Pierce in front of the manor. A bloody stick with skin and eye parts clinging to it lay next to him. What a nasty sight. His head lay upon a rock with blood on it, too."

Dayton advanced to the exhibit table and retrieved the rock and the stick, Exhibits A and B.

Coffe examined and identified the weapons.

Dayton returned them to the exhibit table.

"Did the defendant confess?"

Coffe leaned back and stroked his chin. "Yes sir. She told us she struck him because he had—"

"Please answer the questions without embellishment, sheriff. So, there was an inquest. Please tell us about it."

"From her testimony and the evidence collected, there was a strong case she was responsible for the captain's death."

"I have the transcript of the inquest, Exhibit C, for your perusal." Dayton walked over to the exhibit table picked up the document, then handed it to the sheriff. Coffe looked it over then returned it to Dayton.

"Yes, that's the document Robert Johnson signed."

"What happened next?"

"She needed to change her clothes. They were blo—"

"You're doing it again, sheriff, embellishing your testimony." Dayton stared at the witness. His eyes narrowed.

"Oh, you mean was she arrested?"

"Yes, that's what I mean." Dayton pasted on an insincere smile, as he returned the document to the exhibit table.

"Well, no. She escaped. She put on Dr. Ashley's cloak and left in the doc's carriage. We were waiting for the defendant to change her clothes. It did seem odd the doctor would leave without saying goodbye. That was one thing that rubbed us the wrong way." A ripple of laughter emanated from a few spectators. "We soon learned it was the defendant escaping right under our noses. It was the darndest thing." He shook his head.

"How did you discover she had fled?"

"Mrs. Walker, who was with the defendant, came into the study as if in a daze, asking us had we seen Carrie. Doctor Ashley came from the kitchen asking where her carriage was. That's when it dawned on us the girl had fled in the doctor's carriage."

"And thus, your four-month long ordeal to capture the defendant began."

The sheriff nodded. "In all of my twenty-three years as a lawman, nothing like this has ever happened."

"How did you discover Miss Bennet's whereabouts?"

Coffe explained they had traveled north to Philadelphia and stopped by the jail to ask the sheriff if he had any news of the fugitive. They were told the sheriff was attending a trial.

"We sat in to listen as well. Just as the trial was ending, we went outside for a smoke. A stagecoach stopped and a gentleman boarded. There was a young man seated inside. He turned to look toward the courthouse and his features reminded Deputy Larson of those in the sketch. Deputy Larson often said the fugitive had pretty lips which reminded him of a bow. He told me what he suspected, so I ordered everyone out of the coach. Larson was dead to rights. He put the sketch up to her face. She had on men's clothing and glasses, but the lips were identical. He snatched the hat off her head, and down came the hair.

"Cole West volunteered to defend her while she stood in the middle of the street bareheaded and female for all to see." Sheriff Coffe grinned.

"So, Mr. West just happened to be present at the time of Miss Bennet's arrest. How lucky for Miss Bennet?"

"I don't believe it was a coincidence, either." Coffe frowned.

Judge Anderson addressed the witness. "Sheriff Coffe, do not make any insinuations about Mr. West. Just answer the direct questions of the prosecutor. Your opinion, no matter how right or wrong, isn't evidence in this case. The jury will ignore the witness's opinion about Mr. West. It'll be struck from the record."

Coffe squirmed in his seat while Dayton addressed the court. "I have no further questions. Your witness, counselor." Dayton sat down.

"I have no questions of the witness at this time." Cole spoke from his seat.

"Very well." Dayton stood up. "The prosecution calls Doctor Edward Stevens."

Doctor Stevens rose from his seat, was sworn in, and took the witness chair. Dayton asked the witness to state his name and profession. His next question was to describe the captain's body and the results of his examination.

Stevens described the disarray of the decedent's clothing, his injured eye, and the bleeding wound on the back of his head. He testified the head injury from the rock killed Pierce, but he couldn't say whether or not he was struck or he fell.

"Thank you, Dr. Stevens. Your witness, Mr. West." Dayton regained the chair at the prosecution table.

Cole rose and walked to the witness box. He asked Dr. Stevens to describe the decedent's clothing. The prosecutor jumped to his feet and objected.

"During direct examination, the prosecutor asked for a description of the body. The witness stated the deceased's clothing was in disarray. I would like a more detailed description."

The judge overruled the objection.

Dayton sat in his chair.

"Would you please clarify the condition of his clothing?"

"The doctor cleared his throat. "His clothes revealed there had been a struggle. They were wet and soiled with mud as if he had been rolling on the ground. A small patch of hair had been yanked from his head, which caused his scalp to bleed."

"Was the decedent dressed?"

"Yes, he was. Although, his shirt was out of his pants, if that's what you mean."

"What about his pants? Were they buttoned or unbuttoned?" Cole faced the jury and walked toward them.

"Unbuttoned."

"Could you tell if the deceased had engaged in sexual intercourse before his death?"

The courtroom was still. Dayton jumped up from his seat, wagging his finger at Cole. His face turned scarlet. "The deceased is not on trial. I see where this is going. I object to this type of questioning."

"Your Honor, the defense must establish the state of mind of the defendant at the time of the captain's demise. If he assaulted her, and she killed him in a struggle to get away from him, it would have a direct bearing on her guilt or innocence."

"Objection overruled."

"But, Your Honor," Dayton stuttered. "Defense counsel is attempting to smear the reputation of the deceased with this line of questioning."

"I have already ruled, Mr. Dayton. Besides, it was you who opened this line of questioning when you described his attire."

Dayton resumed his seat and scowled.

The judge turned his attention to the witness and asked him to answer the question.

"I couldn't say. Er—er. Yes, his pants were unbuttoned and it seemed unusual."

Cole thanked the doctor and dismissed him.

"The prosecution calls Mrs. Elizabeth Johnson to the stand."

Robert Johnson stared open-mouthed at his Aunt Betty, who sat at his wife's side. Susan Johnson turned to look at the prosecution's witness. Her lips inched upward in a slight smile.

Their hands touched on the seat between them.

Clad in a tan linen dress with a matching jacket, the Johnson matriarch sat until her nephew rose to escort her up the aisle. Moments later, she took the oath and Mr. Johnson returned to his seat.

"Mrs. Johnson, please describe your first encounter with the defendant."

"She came to the home I share with my nephew and his family on New Year's Eve. She was accompanied by my nephew's uncle, the retired New York Senator Eldridge Walker and his wife, Laura."

"Your nephew is Robert Johnson, master of the Twin Oaks plantation?"

"Yes."

"What was your impression of Carrie Bennet?"

"She deceived us from the start."

"How so?"

"She passed herself off as a white woman."

Dayton looked at the jury. "How did the other members of your family react to the defendant?"

"They all treated her in a manner above her station. We all thought she was white until the senator introduced her."

"Had your nephew informed you in advance of her visit?"

"He did not, which wasn't surprising." A blush appeared on her cheeks. "My nephew never confides in me about plantation business or his personal matters."

"Were you formally introduced to the defendant?" Dayton took a few steps toward the jury and then turned his attention to the witness stand.

"Yes, he introduced her to me on the evening of the New Year's Eve ball as Carrie Bennet."

"Did he explain why she had come?"

"He didn't but his wife did."

"What did Susan Johnson say?"

"It sounded innocent enough; she told me the purpose of

Carrie's visit was to purchase her grandmother's freedom."

Dayton frowned. "You don't sound convinced. Did you suspect Carrie Bennet had another reason for visiting Twin Oaks?"

Cole stood up. "Your Honor, I object. Counsel is asking the witness to speculate on my client's intentions."

"I'll allow this line of questioning. The witness is a pillar of the community and as such the court is interested in her observations." The judge stared at Cole, who stiffened.

Dayton smiled broadly and looked at Cole. “Go on, Mrs. Johnson, you may answer the question.”

“I believe she came to obtain money from my family.” Mrs. Johnson pursed her lips.

“What led you to this conclusion?”

“I overheard her talking to Laura Walker, my nephew’s aunt. Carrie said her mother was dying of consumption, and she claimed to be a member of my family. I feared Carrie had planned on making a claim on my son’s estate. Robert is the executor.”

Exclamations rose from the spectators. The judged rapped his gavel against his bench and the noise subsided.

“Were her claims valid, Mrs. Johnson?”

“I would say not.” Her lips tightened. “All of my son’s children were born from his marriage, and I can say the same for the rest of the family. I assure you, there are no pickaninnies among them.”

Loud whispers were heard in the courtroom. The judged used his gavel to restore order.

“Mrs. Johnson, how did Carrie Bennet react when she was introduced to Captain John Pierce?”

“She became flustered. So much so that when she clutched the necklace around her neck, it broke.”

“Mrs. Johnson, I want to ask you a question and before you answer, please give it your honest opinion. Do you think Carrie Bennet is guilty of murder?”

“Your Honor, I object.” Cole shot up from his seat.

“The witness will answer the question on the same grounds as before,” The judge looked at Cole.

“Yes, she must be. I didn’t attend the inquest, but I read the report. She confessed to killing Captain Pierce.”

"Why do you think she murdered the captain?"

Cole shot up from his seat. "Your Honor, the liberties counsel has allowed this witness to take is outrageous. Mrs. Johnson's opinion isn't fact."

"The court is interested in this witness's opinion. You may answer the question, Mrs. Johnson."

"A tryst gone awry is how it was reported in the inquest. It was evident upon meeting the captain, Carrie Bennet was smitten. She met him in the barn, and he ended up dead. His loss will be greatly felt by the community. God rest his soul."

"I have no further questions." Dayton looked at the judge.

"Do you have any questions of this witness?"

"I do indeed, Your Honor."

The judge raised an eyebrow. "Go ahead, Counselor."

Cole rose and faced the witness.

He smiled at the elderly lady, who returned a smile. "Mrs. Johnson, you said Carrie Bennet passed herself off as a white woman. How did she do that?"

For the first time, Aunt Betty's eyes darted around the room. "It was her deportment—how she carried herself and how she spoke." Her hand swept her brow.

"In other words, *you* perceived her as white because of her manners and elocution, and somehow this is her fault?"

Mrs. Johnson shifted in her seat. "Well, she was putting on airs, which led me to believe she was white."

"Now, this was the first time you had met Carrie Bennet. How could you deduce she was putting on airs? You had never seen her before. Therefore, you have nothing by which to compare her behavior. Why couldn't her speech and mannerisms have been natural due to her education?"

"It wasn't just her manners. The senator and his wife allowed her to walk with them through a main entrance of Twin Oaks. Coloreds, servants and merchants are prohibited from using those entrances." She shook her head. "New Yorkers, they overlooked our rules of civility." She pressed her lips together and sat up straighter.

"Mrs. Johnson, please describe the captain's response to Carrie?"

"He was polite, too polite."

"How could you deduce she welcomed his attention when you must have seen him force her to dance with him?"

"She was enjoying herself. After all, why would a colored woman decline to dance with the captain at the year's most elegant social event? She shouldn't have been there at all. The captain was impulsive. It was his way of amusing himself."

"Could you tell whether or not he was inebriated?"

"The captain enjoyed a drink now and then. I won't deny it. He was very sociable and popular with the ladies. Yes, he had a few drinks, but he wasn't slurring his words or stumbling about the dance floor."

"Mrs. Johnson, you stated you had read the inquest report. Then you know the reason my client fought with the deceased. She was defending herself against rape."

Mingled conversations rose from the spectators.

"I know nothing of the sort." Mrs. Johnson's voice cracked.

"Your Honor, I object." Dayton jumped from his chair.

"I have no further questions of this witness," Cole snapped.

Dayton rose. "The prosecution calls Mr. Tucker to the stand."

"Your Honor, the defense was not aware of this witness."

"He arrived this morning. I wasn't able to inform counsel in time for trial."

The judge nodded. "Carry on."

Mr. Tucker, tall and lanky, advanced to the witness stand was sworn in and seated.

"Mr. Tucker, please state your full name and occupation."

"Harley Aaron Tucker, investigator."

"Mr. Tucker, where is your office?"

"Here in Richmond."

"Were you recently employed by the prosecutor's office in Richmond County?"

"Yes, you hired me."

Laughter rippled through the spectators.

"Yes, we did, Mr. Tucker," Dayton cleared his throat. "Explain your assignment."

"I was hired to investigate the defendant's political activities. She is an associate of an organization which raises funds for escaped slaves."

"In other words, she aids and abets criminals." Dayton turned to look at the jury. "Was there any other pertinent information you discovered in your investigation, Mr. Tucker?"

Dayton looked over at the defense table with a smile.

"Yes, a will in the deceased's papers. Seems his father purchased a young slave woman who lived at Twin Oaks from Ebenezer. Old Eb was about to lose his farm due to a bad crop year. He couldn't make payments on his bank loans so he sold her to the deceased father."

"And who is the young slave woman you are referring to?"

"Sarah Johnson, Carrie Bennet's mother."

Gasps were heard from the balcony. Sarah grabbed her chest and stood up in the balcony. Jonathan put his arms around her. Carrie dropped her head and cried into her hands. Cole's face lost all of its color.

"When did this purchase occur?"

"I have the bill of sale right here. It's dated June 20, 1840." He handed the document to Dayton.

"So, this transaction occurred before Ebenezer accepted Jonathan Bennet's payment for Sarah's freedom, in December of 1840. In other words, Ebenezer had no legal right to accept money for Sarah's freedom because he no longer owned her. This makes Sarah and all of her descendants the property of Captain John Pierce, the heir to the Senior Pierce's estate."

"Exactly."

Loud exclamations were echoed.

"Now, if Captain Pierce told Carrie Bennet about the will, which claims she and her mother are enslaved to the Pierce heirs, would you say, Mr. Tucker, it would be a motive for murder?"

"I certainly would."

"I submit this will as the prosecution's exhibit D"

"Counselors, approach," the judge said.

Dayton jauntily advanced to the bench while Cole appeared in a daze. The judge looked over the document and handed it to Cole. The paper shook as he read the shocking news. It was authentic.

"You may submit the document and continue your examination, Mr. Dayton."

"I have no further questions. Your witness, Mr. West."

Carrie's heart lurched in her chest. She grabbed Cole's arm and spoke to him in a shaky voice.

"Cole, I swear I had no knowledge of this. What's going to become of me? Whether or not I lose in this trial, my life is over."

He patted her hand. "I can't address that now without further investigation. The document could be a forgery, but I can refute his previous insinuations." He took a moment to consult with Carrie.

Cole rose and walked over to the witness. "Mr. Tucker, isn't it true the society of which you've characterized as one where criminal activity is conducted, is the New York Asylum for Colored Orphans?"

He scratched his head. His blue eyes darted around the courtroom. "Yes, it's the official name, but you can bet there are plenty of runaways hiding out there."

"The orphanage houses children under the age of twelve, who were placed there by destitute parents unable to care for them. Did you inquire about the circumstances of all of the children living there?"

"I didn't have the opportunity. When I questioned Mrs. Murphy, the director, about them, she wouldn't cooperate. She said I needed a warrant to check the files of specific children. I didn't have time to get a warrant. Mrs. Murphy didn't allow me access to any of the files, so I couldn't tell which ones were runaways and which ones were true orphans. Some of those little nigras must have been enslaved to somebody. There are heaps of 'em living there."

"I have no further questions of this witness, Your Honor, but I reserve the right to recall him at a later date."

"Yes, Mr. West. Mr. Tucker, you may stand down."

"You may call your next witness, Mr. Dayton."

Dayton rose from his seat with a broad grin on his face. "The prosecution rests."

The judge announced the court would reconvene Monday morning at nine o'clock. He tapped his gavel, and the spectators began to exit the courtroom.

"Cole, I'm terrified. This makes my mother and me legally slaves." Carrie wrung her hands.

"I've got to find a way out of this. Carrie, don't give up hope. Twin Oaks is where I might find some answers."

CHAPTER THIRTY-FIVE
Family Ties

Rising from the defense table, Carrie took a step and almost lost her balance. Cole's strong arms steadied her. She had to compose herself. She didn't want to appear vulnerable to the spectators. Curious onlookers anxious to glimpse the face of a murderess would judge her every move.

Her nerves were on edge. The first day of trial was behind her. Nothing could have prepared her for the tumultuous emotions which twisted through her while she listened to the testimony of the prosecution's witnesses. Among the sea of faces, she discerned a look of empathy from Robert Johnson, but his Aunt Betty glared at her with unsympathetic eyes. Next to her sat Susan. The hatred in her eyes was unmistakable.

To her left, a group of people approached her. She was sure Frank was among them. However, her eyes fell upon her mother, father, and brother. Frank held the hand of an unknown pregnant woman. Behind them were the senator and Laura Walker.

Carrie felt overwhelmed. She caught her breath. "Praise God."

Exuberant salutations erupted from her family and friends as they talked at once.

Sarah, supported by Jonathan, advanced with her arms outstretched.

However, a deputy stepped in front of her, curtailing her reunion with her daughter.

The joy on Sarah's face vanished, replaced by frustration.

The lawman, accompanied by a prison matron, ordered everyone to keep away so he could handcuff the defendant.

"Is this necessary?" Cole put his arm around Carrie.

"I'm afraid so, counselor. You know the rules. I'm Chief Deputy Davenport." He shook Cole's hand. The lawman stroked his mutton chop whiskers before he introduced the prison matron. She was a plump middle-aged woman clad in a dark grey uniform. "This is Mrs. Sawyer."

She gave Cole a curt nod and took her place beside Carrie. She gripped one arm as the deputy took the other.

Deputy Davenport addressed the visitors. "We have to escort the prisoner to her cell. You folks are welcomed to visit her at the House of Corrections for Females, located in back of the sheriff's office, just a quarter mile west of the courthouse. It'll have to be brief. Prisoners are served dinner at six o'clock, about an hour and a half from now."

Oblivious to the conversation around her, Carrie's eyes were riveted on her mother. Tall and graceful, she appeared to have shrunk from her illness. She still looked ill, and worry lines appeared between Sarah's soft gray eyes as she looked upon her daughter in handcuffs. Sarah's golden complexion appeared luminous under the courthouse lamps. Only faint dark circles under her eyes marred her beauty. Although her slenderness was sharpened by disease, she looked regal in her elegant beige traveling suit. Sarah appeared to have recovered from her bout of consumption, until a cough racked her shoulders.

Fear overcame Carrie when she saw her mother hold a handkerchief to her mouth. She glanced at the cloth, which was free of blood. Carrie knew the disease could return with a vengeance and reclaim the life, which had appeared to escape its clutches. She hoped her mother's fate would be otherwise.

Carrie realized how difficult it must be for her family to see her handcuffed and on trial for murder. This caused her deep grief, but she smiled to reassure them.

Flanked by Mrs. Sawyer and Chief Deputy Davenport, she headed for the exit. Her supporters followed. Carrie feared the mood of the onlookers beyond the courtroom. Before the deputy opened the door, a din of voices could be heard.

Outside, throngs of people flowed from the top of the stairs to the bottom. The square below swarmed with the curious. Cole moved ahead of the entourage and scanned the masses, looking for troublemakers.

The crowd parted, like the Red Sea, as they descended the stairs. Angry faces glared at her. Sympathetic ones smiled and nodded. Carrie cherished their empathy.

Relief flooded her when she stepped into the prison carriage, unmolested. She was safe from prying eyes and hate-filled stares. Drawing the curtain across the windows, her attorney sat beside her. His private carriages followed with Sarah, Jonathan, and Sam in one, and the Turners and Walkers in another.

When they arrived, a small group of protesters surrounded them. A cadre of lawmen gained order and waved their rifles at the crowd to make way. Once inside the gate, the lawmen locked it. The mob surged forth, shouting racial epithets as the visitors alighted from the carriages and entered the building.

The matron escorted Carrie to the visitors' room. Cole followed. Once alone, they spoke in hushed whispers, as they held hands and waited for the others to arrive.

"Carrie, my darling, I'm so sorry about the will. I had no idea. I never thought there would be a trial. I never thought you'd be caught." He shook his head. "I was supposed to see you to the Canadian border. I've failed you." Cole's eyes were glassy.

"Cole, you can't blame yourself, no matter how this ends."

Cole wiped a tear from her cheek. "I can't lose this case." His chest rose and fell. His breath quickened and warmed her face. "I promise you. I'll win back your life for you—and for me, because without you, there is no life for me. I love you."

"Cole, I—I—"

The door creaked as it swung open. Her family and friends rushed to her side. Loving arms embraced her as kisses brushed her cheeks.

Sarah's tears ran freely down her face. She held out her arms to Carrie.

"What does it mean? This will? I never knew any of this. Ebenezer betrayed me on so many levels."

Mother and daughter stood hugging one another. The rest of the family put their arms around them.

Cole walked over. "As far as I know, Pierce had no heirs, but there might be distant kin who could lay claim on your freedom. This is a terrible blow. There has to be a way out of this. I promise you all, I will find it. Carrie will walk out of here a free woman, or I'll die trying."

Carrie extricated herself from her family and moved near Cole. "I have every faith in you Cole. I know you will succeed. I trust you with my life."

They embraced one another without hesitation. Jonathan spoke first. "If my little girl feels so strongly about your abilities, then so do we. If there's anything we can do to help, please...."

Carrie moved out of Cole's arms and stared at her brother. She saw Samuel no longer as her little brother but as a young man of fifteen. She had to look up to see the sorrow in his eyes. "You look more and more like Pop, Sam." Carrie spoke through tears. "You're already taller." She caressed his smooth, wet cheek.

Turning to her father, she looked into his teary brown eyes. When a tear trailed down his cheek, Carrie wiped it away with her pale fingers, which contrasted with his dark skin.

"I'm sorry we didn't tell you about your heritage. It was a difficult truth to convey. Now, as for this will, I don't know what to think."

"Pop, you are the only father I have ever known, and I am so proud to be your daughter. You're the dearest father a girl could ever hope for. I love you." She put her arms around him, and both of them wept.

A few minutes later, Carrie greeted the Walkers with hugs. They pledged to pray for her acquittal.

Frank stepped forward. He put an arm around her shoulder and told her how happy he was to see her again. While he talked, Carrie eyed the pregnant woman beside him. "This is my wife, Hattie Rose." His arm circled his wife's waist. "Hattie Rose, this is my childhood friend, Carrie Bennet."

Carrie looked into Hattie Rose's deep brown eyes and saw kindness. "She is beautiful, Frank. I'm not sure you deserve her."

They laughed.

Sarah stepped forward and put an arm around Carrie. "My dear child, you must tell me—all of us—the trials you faced during these past months."

The room held a small table and a few chairs. Carrie sat down and recited a truncated version of her journey.

Soon, they heard a knock at the door. Not waiting for an answer, the deputy stuck his head in and announced visiting time would conclude in ten minutes.

"Before we say goodbye, Frank, you must tell us what happened to you. I saw an article about your kidnapping in *The Liberator*. How did you escape?"

Frank filled them in on the details, peppered with colorful insertions from his wife. "Our child will be born, well, any time now. Born in freedom."

Laura Walker had listened with rapt attention. "I was going to ask you when the baby is due."

Hattie Rose beamed.

Cole stood. "It's time for us to leave."

Everyone rose and moved toward Carrie for a final farewell.

Cole stood by her side and watched as her visitors hugged her once more with parting words of encouragement.

Sarah reached for Cole's hand and thanked him for taking care of her daughter.

Sam was the last to say goodbye. "Be strong. We're all praying for your release."

Cole stepped toward Carrie. She wouldn't see him again before the trial reconvened. He hugged her once again in front of everyone.

Carrie was lost in the depths of his eyes. They stared longer than necessary, causing Jonathan to clear his throat.

They all kept repeating their goodbyes until Carrie had left with the matron.

As she walked away, she heard Cole invite everyone to dine at his home.

CHAPTER THIRTY-SIX
The Wild Valley Ranch

The carriages rolled through the gates of the ranch. It hummed with activity. Gardeners tended flower beds and bushes. Cows lowed as they were milked. Pigs squealed and scurried for their feed. Two women scattered chicken feed in the fenced-in yard, as the birds squawked and jockeyed for position. Cattle and sheep grazed on the edges of the property, as cowboys looked on.

Jonah greeted Cole, who introduced his foreman to the guests.

The men helped the ladies down from the carriages, and Cole led his guests up the stairs to the front door, where the butler, Gerard, greeted them.

Cole gave Mrs. Parks, the head housekeeper, instructions to have rooms prepared for their guests and have the head cook, Mrs. Lindstrom, set eight places for supper.

The visitors were ushered into the drawing room for tea and light refreshments while the maids readied their rooms.

Later, they sat down to an excellent meal of stewed chicken, peas and carrots, baked potatoes, hot rolls with homemade butter, and an excellent Madeira.

"Cook tells me Louisiana gumbo is on the menu for tomorrow." Cole looked around the table for a reaction.

"Mrs. Parks, my head housekeeper, is quite a cook herself. She and Mrs. Lindstrom have a friendly rivalry about who's the best cook. It works to my benefit. I get to taste all kinds of dishes. By the way, Frank, you and Hattie Rose—all of you—are welcome to stay here for the duration of the trial."

"Thank you, Cole." Jonathan wiped a tear from his eye. He looked at Sarah, who nodded her head. "We couldn't bear to be away from her now."

"That's right, Pop." Sam nodded.

"How very generous of you, Cole." The senator agreed. "We'd like to accept your offer."

His wife smiled. "She can use all of the support we can muster at a time like this."

"Thank you, Mr. Cole." Hattie Rose looked relieved. "A real bed would be a nice change. We've been traveling on the road, sleeping where we can: in barns, on the ground, and on kitchen floors, along the Underground Railroad."

"Hattie Rose, it's just Cole."

Hattie Rose smiled. "Yes, Mr. Cole."

Frank chuckled along with the others. "Old habits die hard."

"Well, this is a station on the Underground Railroad." Cole's pride shown on his face.

"What do you know? This is the finest station we've encountered by a mile." Frank smiled at his wife.

"It's like sleeping in a palace, Mr. Cole."

Cole thought of Carrie, who would sit in a jail cell all weekend. He wished she was at the table beside him. He missed her with every beat of his heart. He'd make sure her family visited and brought Carrie a change of clothing for the trial.

Cole recalled how jealous he had been of Frank whenever Carrie had mentioned his name. It had been a relief to know Frank was married with a baby on the way.

Sudden laughter erupted from the guests. He wondered what had been so amusing. He had missed the entire exchange.

By half-past nine, some of his guests had retired. Jonathan, the senator, Frank, and Sam were in the drawing room playing whist.

Cole sat in his study and sipped a glass of brandy. He spread the trial notes across his oversized mahogany desk.

The door was ajar, and Gerard stepped in to announce visitors. Allan Pinkerton stood behind the butler. In one hand, he held a valise, and in the other, he twirled his bowler hat on his index finger. Cole chuckled. Henry Mason stood next to the Scottish detective.

Cole rose from his seat and shook hands with his friends.

Gerard walked to a corner, where decanters and glasses sat on a dropleaf mahogany bar cart, and poured drinks.

Cole led Allan and Henry to a sofa and several armchairs. He sat on the sofa, while his guests occupied the chairs.

Gerard carried a tray of brandy snifters and set the tray on the wooden table in front of the sofa.

Cole handed one to each man. Allan declined, but Mason accepted a glass. Cole swirled the contents of his glass a few times before he took a sip. “Ah.”

Holding his snifter, Mason imitated Cole's ritual. He took a swig of brandy, grimaced, coughed, and then pounded his chest as he tried to catch his breath.

Cole and Allan laughed. Allan gave Mason a few hard pats on his back.

"First time you've had brandy?" Cole retrieved a glass of water from the desk and handed it to the twenty-five-year-old Mason.

The latter nodded and took a sip.

Cole turned his attention to Allan and inquired if he had any news about his father's case.

Allan plunged into a lively account of his conversations with Miss Dayton in Missouri and the discoveries about Dayton's daughter, Missy.

~~~

Upon hearing Missy's name, Frank froze. He and Sam were on their way to bed when he heard the name of his wife's young mistress. He motioned for Sam to continue upstairs while he remained quiet and eavesdropped in the hallway. Allan divulged what he'd learned about the girl's condition. He told Cole the valise belonged to Missy. When the subject changed, Frank continued on his way to the bedchamber he shared with Hattie Rose.

~~~

The Scot complimented Mason. "The book covers you made for me worked like a charm. The old lady was eating out of me hands when she saw me name on the jackets. Mason, dear boy, I'd like to offer you a job as an operative with the Pinkerton's National Detective Agency."

Mason's eyes gleamed with joy even as his jaw dropped in surprise.

"You'll have to move to Chicago, where our headquarters are located, for training. Then, I might assign you to New York or Washington, D.C., if you can manage to extricate yourself from the hospitable south." Allan chuckled.

Mason remained silent.

"Are you a free man, now?" Cole looked at Mason with a raised eyebrow.

"Yes, I bought my freedom from Massa Johnson." He shook his head. "Mistress Susan argued with Massa something fierce about him accepting my payment. He could have charged me more, but he took the eight-hundred dollars I offered. Yes, indeed, Mr. Allan, I'll accept your offer. God bless you." Mason threw his arms up toward the ceiling with clenched fist. "Thank the good Lord. I've always wanted to see Chicago. I hear the women are mighty pretty up there."

"A married man doesn't notice." Pinkerton smiled.

Mason shook the hand of his new employer.

"Congratulations Mason." Cole leaned over and shook his hand, too.

Cole informed Allan once the deed of manumission was filed in the courthouse, he'd have to post a bond to ensure Mason would be a law-abiding citizen until he left Virginia. "It's the law. Our pro-slavery government sees a free colored man as a threat to their social order."

Mason said he could afford to pay the extortion fee himself, but Allan insisted the debt was his. "You're going to need what you've got for lodging. As a Pinkerton detective, I expect my operatives to shun all vices. So, if you accept my offer, enjoy the drink while you can. Once you're a Pinkerton detective, you can't play cards, drink, smoke, and curse, use slang, or spend time in disreputable establishments. We're officers of the law, who pride ourselves on integrity, truthfulness, and loyalty."

"Mr. Pinkerton, it's the way I've lived my whole life. Yes sir, I can do it."

"May I ask you a personal question, Mr. Pinkerton?" Allan nodded. "What brought you to America?"

A deep laugh rumbled from his chest before it reached his lips. "I'll tell you, if you promise what I'll say will never leave this room." Both Mason and Cole nodded. "There was a warrant for my arrest in Glasgow for being a Chartist. We were a workingman's organization who dared advocate for political and social reform. I'm a fugitive meself."

CHAPTER THIRTY-SEVEN
The Defense Presents Its Case

On Monday morning, at precisely ten o'clock, the trial resumed.

The judge addressed Cole. "Mr. West, you may call your first witness."

"I call Senator Eldridge Walker."

The senator rose, was sworn in, and took the stand.

Cole's first question established the witness's career as a State Senator of New York who served from 1846 to 1858. Now retired from public life, he testified he wrote a monthly editorial column in the *New York Tribune* and was a guest lecturer at colleges and professional societies about the political climate in which he served.

"Senator, you've heard testimony from the prosecution's witness, Mrs. Johnson, who swore Carrie Bennet, had an ulterior motive for her visit to Twin Oaks. You've known the defendant since she was born. Would you please tell the court your opinion of her character?"

"Yes, indeed I have known her since her birth. She was baptized at the First AME Church in New York in July of 1841. Furthermore, I'm her godfather."

This statement caused an audible stir amongst the spectators.

"Senator, will you elaborate on Miss Bennet's background?"

"Carrie is one of the most intelligent and industrious young women I have ever known. Her father is an entrepreneur. He's a successful cabinetmaker. Miss Bennet holds a degree in English and is currently the head teacher at the Colored Orphans Asylum of New York City. Her reputation was unblemished, prior to this unfortunate business."

"Did you accompany Miss Bennet to Virginia from New York?"

The senator nodded. "Yes, I did."

"Why?"

"Carrie had planned to purchase her grandmother's freedom and thought our presence, mine and Mrs. Walker's, would protect her from any mishaps. Unfortunately, it didn't happen."

Cole paced as he questioned the witness.

"While staying at Twin Oaks, senator, you had a chance to observe the relationship between the deceased and the defendant. How would you characterize it?"

"He was respectful at first. However, once he discovered she was Aunt Olivia's granddaughter, lust replaced chivalry. It was evident in his eyes and his behavior. I've known Carrie to be a truthful person. She wouldn't lie about being raped."

Discordant chatter rose from the spectators in response. The judge rapped his gavel against the bench. "Order, order in the court or I'll clear this courtroom."

Silence ensued within seconds.

"She's not responsible for his accidental death," continued the senator. "Just mark it as a reversal of the Casual Killing Act of 1669 and 1705, which exonerates slaveholders from felony charges if their slaves die during punishment. Likewise, Carrie Bennet shouldn't be held criminally responsible for the accidental death of her attacker while attempting to protect herself."

The judge slammed his gavel down as conversations swirled around the courtroom.

"The jury will disregard the witness's last statement, and it will be stricken from the record. Senator Walker, you will refrain from making any statements of your own. Just answer the attorney's questions."

"Thank you, Senator Walker. I have no further questions." Cole turned to his opponent. "Your witness, Mr. Dayton."

A pair of blue marble eyes bored into Cole's, as Dayton said, "I have no questions of this witness."

Cole called his next witness, Professor Franklin Delaney. The well-dressed, elderly gentleman had a crown of white hair and a bronzed complexion. He emanated a regal aura as he walked to the witness stand. Underneath his arm, he carried a portfolio. He was sworn in and seated.

Cole asked him to identify himself.

"I'm Professor Franklin Delaney, Dean of Teacher's College at Oberlin in the State of Dayton, Ohio. I've served the institution in this capacity for twenty-odd years."

"Professor, do you know the defendant?"

"I most certainly do. Miss Bennet graduated with honors last year. She's a gifted student and exemplifies all the qualities we stress at the college. We teach our students to set high goals and achieve them by hard work and sacrifice."

"You've heard the testimony of the prosecution's witnesses, who have attempted to dishonor Miss Bennet's reputation. Are you in possession of documents which will verify your assertions?"

"Indeed." The professor nodded. "I have a copy of her bachelor's degree, as well as several articles about Miss Bennet from the school newspaper. Some have drawings of her image. I offer them as evidence."

Cole walked to the jury box, took the portfolio from the professor, and passed it to the jurors.

The contents—the degree and articles—were perused and passed among the jurors.

"Professor, please summarize the articles while the jurors review your portfolio."

"The first article names Miss Bennet as the winner of the English Department's poetry contest. The second lauds her distinguished academic record."

Cole concluded his examination, and Dayton addressed the judge. "I have no questions of this witness."

Cole approached the bench. "Your Honor, may I request a short recess?"

"Due to the late hour of the morning, we'll adjourn for dinner and reconvene at one o'clock."

Cole patted Carrie's shoulder to reassure her before the guard returned her to her cell.

Cole needed time to reassess his strategy and beckoned Allan and Mason to join him outside for a discussion.

Cole led the men quickly down the steep courthouse steps. They encountered Frank Turner smoking a cigarette. He nodded in greeting and disappeared around a corner.

Before Cole spoke to his friends, he heard a commotion. Cole and Allan rounded the corner in a hurry to investigate. What they saw surprised them.

Two white men held Frank's arms back while another stood in front of him with a tight fist ready to repeat a blow to Frank's midriff.

"What's going on?" Cole confronted the strangers.

An immense, red-haired white man turned to Cole. "This here niggah is an escaped slave from the Dayton plantation, and we're about to take him back."

"These are the men who kidnapped me," shouted Frank.

Suddenly, Mason appeared and stood between Cole and Allan.

"Oh really?" Mason winked at Frank.

Frank grinned. In short order, all seven men were embroiled in a fistfight.

Frank fought hard. He was determined to make the kidnappers wish they had never laid a hand on Frank Harding Turner, Esquire.

~~~

"The defense calls Mr. Robert Johnson to the stand."

The Master of Twin Oaks, a handsome man whose high-born status was evident in the sway of his shoulders and the dignified gait of his walk. Mr.
~~~

Johnson appeared impeccable. His fashionable attire included a charcoal gray suit and cravat, a white shirt with a high collar, and light gray waistcoat. The ensemble was set off by a charcoal gray town coat with deep pockets. The gold fob gleamed across his waistcoat as he took the oath.

Cole's face had been altered since he left the courtroom for the dinner recess. The scar above his left brow had reopened and a small amount of blood had surfaced. In addition, a strawberry-colored bruise blossomed on his right cheek.

His associates, Allan and Mason, had a few bruises after combating the slave catchers, too. The three bounty hunters were now in jail for assaulting an officer of the court.

"Mr. Johnson, when did you first encounter the defendant?"

Mr. Johnson leaned back in the witness chair, crossed his long legs, and set his hat upon his knee.

"I received a letter from Miss Bennet, the fall of last year, asking to purchase her grandmother's freedom. Aunt Olivia, her grandmother, had been a slave in my family since before I was born. She was my mammy."

"Had you ever seen the defendant prior to her arrival in Richmond?" Cole paced before the witness stand.

"No. I had never seen Miss Bennet, but I knew of her existence."

"Did you ever become suspicious of the defendant's motive?"

Robert turned his head toward the jury and directed his answer to them. "No, but I did inquire about her. In her letter, she mentioned she was head teacher at an orphanage in New York City. So, I wrote to the institution to verify her statement. I received a letter from the head mistress verifying Miss Bennet's employment, along with a physical description."

"Thank you, Mr. Johnson. I will ask you to return to the witness stand after I examine other witnesses. You will still be under oath."

Mr. Johnson nodded.

Cole turned to the prosecutor. "Your witness, Mr. Dayton."

"I have no questions of this witness." Dayton did not look up.

CHAPTER THIRTY-EIGHT
Carrie Testifies

Cole rose. “I call Miss Carrie Bennet to the stand.”

She caressed the amulet which hung from her neck before she rose and took the oath.

Can I hide my love for her? Cole knew her family had detected it. *Would the judge, spectators and jury see it as well? If so, she would be doomed.* Her freedom depended on his hiding his love behind his official persona of Cole Bartholomew West, Esquire.

As Cole approached, their eyes locked. He smiled first, and then, she. They were kindred spirits, a united force.

“Miss Bennet, would you agree with the testimony of Senator Walker about why you visited Twin Oaks?”

“Yes, I came to Twin Oaks to purchase my grandmother’s freedom. It was my only motive.”

“Carrie, Mrs. Elizabeth Johnson said she overheard you speaking to Laura Walker. Is it true?”

“Yes, I was speaking to Miss Laura about a personal matter. Once I finished, I realized the door was ajar and glimpsed a lime green frock flash by the door.”

“Who wore a lime green frock that evening?”

“Mrs. Elizabeth Johnson. We were introduced earlier in the evening. Her frock was a lime green shade.”

“What were you and Mrs. Walker discussing?”

"My father, m—my biological father." She grasped the amulet.

"And who is your biological father, Carrie?"

"Preston Johnson, Mrs. Elizabeth's son."

Several audible inhalations were heard as all eyes fastened on the Johnson matron. She trembled as the murmurs from spectators swirled around her.

"Take me home." She turned sad eyes on her nephew. The Johnson matriarch stood on unsteady legs. Mr. Johnson was soon at her side and offered his arm. However, when she slumped against him, he grasped her around the waist, and then assisted her down the aisle.

Laura Johnson averted her eyes from settling on any of her neighbors and trailed her husband and his aunt out of the courtroom.

Once order was restored, Cole resumed his examination.

"Did Mrs. Walker identify Preston as your father?"

"She didn't have to. Miss Laura confirmed what my mother had already revealed to me before I left home."

"Were you planning to ask any of the Johnsons for money to help your mother or for any other reason?"

"Of course not. My only plan was to free my grandmother and take her to New York to see my mother before she grew worse. I was there to fulfill, what I thought at the time was, my mother's dying wish. She has since recovered."

Cole walked toward Carrie and stood by the witness box. "In the record of the inquest, you testified you went to the barn in the wee hours of the morning. Why?"

"I was awakened in the dead of night by an enslaved child. He gave me a note. I thought one of my relatives in the quarters had taken ill."

"Tell us what happened in the barn?"

Carrie took a deep breath and paused before she spoke.

"It was pitch-black, except for the streak of moonlight across the floor. Then, someone struck a match. Light flared from a lamp. It was then I saw Captain Pierce. He had tricked me so I would be alone with him." Carrie swallowed hard and bit her bottom lip.

"Go on, Miss Bennet."

"Again, he asked me to be his mistress, as he had done at the ball. I declined, but he countered by saying I wasn't really free. He said he could have me, and no one would do anything about it. So, I might as well submit. I realized he was right. The same thing happened to my mother on the Twin Oaks estate. The law would turn a blind eye. I feared for my safety."

Her hands shook. She grasped her skirt and took a deep breath.

"He came toward me. I ran and threw the lamp onto a pile of hay. It caught fire. While he extinguished the fire, I escaped. Outside, the rain drenched me. My cape wrapped around my legs, and I fell. By then, he had caught up to me. He lifted me up and carried me. I thought he'd take me to the house but he took me toward the oak trees. I begged him to let me go. He punched me in the stomach, threw me down, and raped me. I found a stick and intended to stab his back to make him stop. But he raised his head, and the stick penetrated his eye. He screamed and rolled off me. I got up and ran into the house."

"Did you consider the consequences after you stabbed Pierce?"

She shook her head. "My only aim was to try to stop his attack."

"Miss Bennet, was it ever your intention to kill Captain Pierce?"

"No. I never intended to kill him. I just wanted him to stop, but he wouldn't. He told me he wasn't through with me and continued to assault me. He tore my dress. I just wanted him to stop." She sobbed as her voice rose in anguish. "But he wouldn't stop."

Tears rolled down Carrie's cheeks. Cole handed her his monogrammed handkerchief, and she dabbed her eyes. "Thank you."

"Take a few moments to regain your composure, Miss Bennet," instructed the judge.

Carrie struggled to stop sobbing and after a few minutes she was able to compose herself.

~~~

The courtroom was dead silent.

Cole scanned the spectators. He thought the southerners would be in an uproar upon hearing testimony which questioned Pierce's reputation, but they weren't. He felt they saw Carrie as a credible witness.

Once composed, Carrie nodded when the judge asked if she was ready to resume the examination.

Cole walked to the defense table and picked up a garment. He carried it to the witness box, where he displayed it to the jury and spectators. Exclamations buzzed around the room.
~~~

Carrie's tattered frock was stained with mud and blood. The rip in her gown nearly reached the waistline.

"Miss Bennet, this dress is identified as Exhibit A. Is this the dress you wore on the night in question?"

"Yes," Carrie looked down and fidgeted with Cole's handkerchief.

Cole returned the dress to the table and picked up the cloak. He displayed it in the same manner, pointing to the torn hem.

"Exhibit B is this cloak. Miss Bennet, did you wear this cloak to the barn?"

"Yes."

"And can we deduce from the creases in the hem that this garment twisted around your ankles, causing you to fall?"

"Yes."

A juror beckoned for Cole to let him examine the cloak. Cole passed it to him. The man checked the garment and passed it along.

One of the jurors held it up. "Excuse me, Mr. West. There's something in the pocket."

Cole spun around and in quick strides was in front of the juror. He searched the pockets until his hand felt a crumpled piece of paper. His heart beat like a drum when he extracted it. *Could this help or hurt Carrie?*

"Counselors, please approach," ordered the judge.

Cole handed the evidence to the judge. He read it and passed it on to Cole. He skimmed its contents then passed it to Dayton.

"I object," shouted Dayton. "The defense is required to hand over all material evidence prior to trial. I believe Counsel planted this note."

"On my life, Your Honor, I had no idea anything was in the pocket of the defendant's cloak. The juror asked to examine the cloak of his own volition."

Dayton looked livid. "I call for a motion to suppress this so-called evidence, Your Honor."

Judge Anderson ran his fingers through his salt-and-pepper hair. "I agree with your opponent, Mr. Dayton, I'm going to allow it to be entered into evidence."

Cole suppressed a smile. "Thank you, Your Honor." He walked over to Carrie with a spring in his step. "Miss Bennet, do you recognize this?"

Carrie grasped the paper and read its contents. "Yes. This is the note the child handed me."

"Please read it."

Carrie held the familiar note with unsteady hands. Some of the ink had faded. "It says, '*I need help tonight. Meet me in the barn, now.*'"

The signature was illegible. Only the letter 'a' was readable. Cole precluded her from testifying about the signatory and interrupted her testimony.

"Your Honor, I would like to call another witness before I conclude with Miss Bennet."

"I object, Your Honor." Dayton rose. "I haven't had a chance to cross-examine the witness."

The judge looked at Cole. "Counselor?"

"Your Honor, it's imperative to my defense to bring another witness to the stand now."

"Go ahead."

"Carrie, you may stand down."

Carrie nodded.

Cole helped her step down.

"Your Honor, I call Doctor Carolyn Ashley."

Doctor Ashley rose to take the stand. The attractive woman was sworn in and seated in the witness box.

"Doctor Ashley, state your name, place of residence and credentials."

"I'm Doctor Carolyn Ashley. I received my medical degree from The Female Medical College of Pennsylvania in 1852. I moved to Richmond a year ago, married, and began a medical practice."

"Doctor Ashley, when did you meet Carrie Bennet?"

"I was introduced to Carrie at the New Year's Eve ball by Captain Pierce. The next time I saw the defendant, Carrie was disheveled, bruised and soaking wet."

Cole looked pointedly at the witness. "Did Miss Bennet divulge what had happened?"

Doctor Ashley sat forward in the witness chair. "Miss Bennet said Captain Pierce had raped her."

"Was there an occasion to prove her claim?"

"Yes, before the inquest, I volunteered to examine her."

"And what was your conclusion?"

"It appeared she had been a virgin before she was assaulted. There was considerable blood and tears in her private area. I also found bruises on her upper torso, and a partial imprint of fingers on her face."

"What became of Miss Bennet after the inquest?"

"The decision at the inquest demanded she be charged with first degree murder. While she was given a chance to change out of her wet clothes, she fled. Oh, she was quite clever about it. She escaped in my cloak and carriage while I was in the kitchen and the gentlemen were gossiping and drinking in the den."

Dr. Ashley was dismissed when Dayton declined to cross-examine her.

CHAPTER THIRTY-NINE
An Unlikely Witness

"The defense calls Robert Johnson to return to the stand."

Whispers rose and fell around the courtroom.

Cole cast grateful eyes upon the witness. "Your aunt testified for the prosecution, on Friday. Your presence here must have put you in an awkward position at home. Why have you agreed to be a witness for the defense today?"

Mr. Johnson took a deep breath and was slow to exhale. "It will undoubtedly put a strain on my relationships with some family members. However, I must act in accord with my conscience. I cannot sit by and remain quiet while a young woman's reputation has been slandered with suppositions which could lead to a conviction. I hope the evidence I am about to present will cast a new perspective upon Miss Bennet's intentions for visiting Twin Oaks."

"After you prepared Olivia's emancipation document, what else did you discuss?" Cole walked toward the jury, and then slowly made his way back to the witness.

"Miss Bennet asked me to intervene on her behalf to keep Captain John Pierce at a distance. First, I apologized for his ill-mannered behavior, which was on full display at the annual New Year's Eve masquerade ball. I assured her there was nothing to worry about because I had seen him leave with other guests at the end of the evening. I regret to say, I was mistaken. He must have returned or engaged himself somewhere else on the estate without my knowledge."

"Did you discuss anything else?"

"Yes, she presented me with a Christmas gift. It was a signed copy of a first edition of *A Christmas Carol.* I was delighted, as a collector of first editions to receive one by Dickens." He smiled and leaned back against the chair. "I was about to tell Miss Bennet I had something for her as well when we were interrupted by a man in my employ. Thus, the meeting concluded."

"Please, continue, Mr. Johnson." Cole nodded.

"Subsequent events of which we are all aware precluded me from my duty in regards to Miss Bennet."

"Mr. Johnson, what had you intended to discuss with the defendant?"

"Preston Johnson, my cousin, named me executor of his will. He asked me to make sure Carrie Bennet received the inheritance he had set aside for her."

Low murmurs followed his statement. Cole looked at Carrie, and his heart went out to her. Shock cemented her features. Her shoulders trembled while she twisted the handkerchief around her fingers. He longed to reach out to her. A wave of regret hit him as he saw the pain in Carrie's eyes.

I wish I could have prepared her for Mr. Johnson testimony. I hope she forgives me for this courtroom tactic. Everyone can see she is as surprised by these facts as they are.

Judge Anderson made use of his gavel to quell the rising sounds from the spectators.

"Mr. Johnson, have you brought the items your cousin entrusted you with to the courtroom?"

"Yes, I have."

"Please hand them to me and detail the contents."

Mr. Johnson complied. He reached inside his coat pocket and extracted a drawstring pouch, from which he brought forth a small black box and two envelopes.

"He provided her with a generous inheritance. In his will, which I have here among other legal documents, he acknowledged his paternity and bequeathed to her one-thousand dollars, along with some jewelry, valued over five-hundred dollars."

"Please, Counselor, bring those items over to the bench."

"I object, Your Honor." Dayton bellowed as he shot up from his seat.

"Your objection is overruled. The court is interested in seeing these items and the will." Judge Anderson gave Dayton a stern look.

"But Mr. West has neglected to provide the prosecution with these items before trial."

"Your Honor, I only became aware of their existence yesterday evening."

"Let's have a look." The judge beckoned Cole forward.

Dayton had sat thorough Mr. Johnson's testimony with astonishment on his face. He walked with a stiff gait to the judge's bench.

Cole, with his hands trembling slightly, laid the items on the bench. The judge picked up one of the envelopes, extracted the will, and read its contents.

Next, he opened the pouch and withdrew a sheaf of bills, totaling one-thousand dollars. He reached for the black leather box. Inside were several emerald and ruby rings, a simple gold chain necklace, diamond earrings, and a brooch sprinkled with tiny diamonds. The judge opened the other linen envelope and extracted two documents of the same stock. His eyes widened, and his jaw dropped and remained so, as he read each one. Judge Anderson handed the papers to Dayton.

As the prosecutor read them, his brows furrowed and his features seemed to sharpen. He resembled a hawk, more than ever.

"Counselor, you may enter these items as exhibits." Judge Anderson nodded to Cole.

"Yes, Your Honor."

Cole turned to the witness. "Mr. Johnson, I have one more question. Did the deceased ever mention to you he had a bill of sale for Sarah Bennet?"

"Yes, he did. At the ball, he told me he possessed the bill of sale. I told him Preston had bought the bill of sale and drew up an emancipation document to free Sarah. Pierce laughed and said he had planned to go to court and contest Preston's documents. Since he was better known and Preston was deceased, he believed the court would rule in his favor. I tried to discourage him, but it was futile."

"Thank you, Mr. Johnson. Your witness, Counselor."

Dayton rose and walked over to the witness.

"Mr. Johnson, did your cousin suffer from any mental defect?"

"None whatsoever."

"What caused his death?"

"A heart attack. All the days of his life, my cousin was in full possession of his faculties. If you doubt my opinion, let me read the letter he wrote to his daughter."

"I have no further questions of this witness, Your Honor." Dayton turned on his heels and headed for the prosecution table.

"Mr. West, call your next witness."

"I recall Carrie Bennet to the stand."

The judge reminded Carrie she was still under oath.

Cole read the fear in her eyes. She seemed to tremble all over. Cole was quick to offer his hand as she stepped up to the witness stand. She still held the damp handkerchief and dabbed her eyes and nose on occasion. Grief had altered her appearance. Her creamy complexion was blotchy. Her swollen eyes were like tiny apertures.

"Carrie, I'm sorry you had to learn about these revelations in a public forum. I have one more request to ask. Will you please read the letter your father addressed to you?"

"I'd rather not. I want nothing from him. He raped my mother, and she bore me in shame. I was raised by a wonderful man who married her and treated me as his own. He is my father, not this—this white man who exploited my mother because of the color of her skin. He means nothing to me."

"Carrie, your response is understandable but if you consider it for one moment, by leaving you a part of his wealth, it may have been his attempt to make amends. Please read the letter. It's important." He extended it toward her, but she ignored it, so he lowered his arm and held it by his side.

"Nothing he could write would ever make up for what he's done." She lowered her head and took in a deep breath. "Living on the cusp of a society which defines itself by color often made me feel like an outsider." Her voice grew shaky. She swallowed and sniffled. "He did that. He made me feel alienated in my own skin."

Her fingers sought the ivory charm beneath her bodice.

"Carrie, are you a Christian?"

"Of course, I am." She snapped and turned hard eyes on Cole. Her cheeks burned with indignation.

"Christians forgive those who have trespassed against them." Cole moved closer to the stand. He held the letter between his thumb and index finger, extending it toward her. "Are you going to hold a grudge against your father for the *rest* of your life?"

Carrie didn't respond. She avoided Cole's eyes and stared at her hands. She took a deep breath and exhaled.

She looked up to the balcony and searched for her mother. All those who occupied the balcony were on their feet, watching below. Carrie spotted her mother in a brown suit. Sarah held a handkerchief to her mouth. Her shoulders gently shook. Carrie couldn't see the tears but she knew they were there. Carrie saw her mother look at her and nod her head.

Without a word, she looked at Cole and reached for the envelope. She opened it and extracted the letter.

"Read it aloud, please." His voice was tender.

Her voice, soft and hesitant, filled the courtroom as every audible sound was held at bay. No one sneezed, coughed or whispered.

August 5, 1859

My Dearest Carrie,

Enclosed is your inheritance to which you are entitled. I am forever indebted to Robert for ensuring my wishes have been carried out. So often, children like you are disinherited or unacknowledged by their father's relations. When your mother left Richmond, I feared I would never see you. But I did find you. On a business trip to New York, I watched you carry out your normal day's activities: shopping, attending school, and such.

I must confess I was the mysterious benefactor who paid the dinner bill for you and your mother at the Astor House Hotel restaurant last summer. I remained anonymous because I didn't want to upset you or your mother. She could not have spoken of me with kindness over the years, and I didn't want to see the same hurt in your eyes, which I put in hers. For what I did, I am truly sorry. In my youth, I was selfish and callous per the dictates of my society.

You are very beautiful and have made me proud by finishing college and teaching those who are less fortunate. In time, I believe people of color will stand on an equal footing with whites.

I loved your mother, and if things had been different, we could have been a family. However, I hadn't the courage to defy society. I hope this inheritance will bring some measure of joy to your life and lessen the animosity toward me, which you must feel.

There's another matter which might haunt you one day. I discovered that your grandfather, Ebenezer, sold Sarah to a Lieutenant Robert Pierce in order to pay an installment on a bank loan to save Twin Oaks. A conniving fellow, Pierce only agreed to the purchase in order to have Uncle Eb in his debt. This occurred before Sarah left for New York. Pierce has since died but before he did, he bragged about the transaction to me, knowing how I felt about Sarah. I begged him to let me buy Sarah. After much haggling, to his credit, he did. I wasted no time in drawing up an emancipation document for Sarah. Now, she and her descendants are forever free and no longer entailed to the Pierce estate. The documents are in Robert's possession, if ever you need to prove these facts in a court of law. I've learned the lieutenant has an heir, a son, named John Pierce.

You'll remain in my heart forever.

Your Father,

Preston Johnson

Carrie identified the other papers as a bill of sale from Lieutenant Pierce to Preston Johnson for Sarah and the emancipation document her father had prepared to free Sarah. Overwhelmed, she turned her head and struggled to hold back tears.

The courtroom again rumbled with conversation.

Judge Anderson called for a fifteen-minute recess.

During his cross-examination, Dayton hammered at Carrie about her motives for visiting Twin Oaks. He accused her of being an agent of abolitionists whose mission was to steal and liberate slaves.

"Carrie, when you learned Captain Pierce intended to contest Preston's will and enslave you, your mother and brother, you committed an act, which you felt compelled to commit, and act of murder, which freed you and your family from a life of slavery. Isn't that a fact?"

CHAPTER FORTY
The Trial Ends

Dayton rose to present his summation to the court. "Ladies and gentlemen and men of the jury, the prosecution has proved the defendant is a scandalous flirt. This unmarried woman met Captain Pierce in the barn for a tryst.

"She claimed Captain John Pierce attacked her. The only corroboration to her assertions is a female doctor who graduated from a *female* college. How expert is her expert testimony?"

A conspiratorial smile seemed to cross his lips as he looked at the twelve male jurors.

"The defendant admits to fleeing the law after the inquest. She claims she feared she wouldn't get a fair trial. This is a definite insult to the men of this jury and shows the defendant's lack of faith in our judicial process. Or was she motivated to flee by a guilty conscience?

"You heard the testimony of the respectable Mrs. Elizabeth Johnson. She said Carrie was attracted to the Captain. The attraction was so strong when she met him that she snapped the necklace she wore. He revealed to her she was his legal property, and why would he not tell her? She killed him to maintain her freedom and her family's. Preston's letter, although sentimental, doesn't exonerate Carrie Bennet from murder.

"If there are heirs to the Pierce estate, might they have a claim on Miss Bennet, her mother, and brother? Yes, they very well could challenge the bill of sale. It would be their legal right.

"So, to prevent such a possibility, she killed Captain Pierce. The idea of being a slave after living a life of freedom was a reality Carrie Bennet couldn't face, so she took the matter into her own hands. Now, I ask you, gentlemen of the jury, to return a verdict of guilty in the first degree."

Lucius Dayton turned on his heels and sat down at the prosecution table.

~~~

Cole rose from his chair and walked to the jury box. "Gentlemen of the jury, you've heard testimony which corroborates my client's assertion she was raped by the deceased. Dr. Carolyn Ashley is a qualified doctor. The medical college from which she graduated is an accredited institution, certified by the State of Massachusetts.

"Gentlemen, you saw the ripped garments which could only have been torn by human hands. The doctor testified there were bruises on the defendant's body. Her undergarments were ripped and torn, bloodied by the rape. There were impressions of fingerprints on the defendant's face. All of this testimony speaks of a brutal assault, not of consent.

"What happened under the oak trees where the captain met his demise? Carrie Bennet has given testimony which the facts and exhibits prove. She was assaulted. Pierce must have fallen back on the rock
~~~

and struck his head so hard, he died. This is the only reasonable explanation given the facts.

"The prosecution contends the defendant ran because she was guilty of murder. Come now, how can his assumption be plausible? Think about it, she fled *after* the inquest was conducted, which resulted in an accusation of first-degree murder. If she had intentionally murdered the captain, why would she wait? Why not flee right away? Why go into the house at all? She returned to the house to tell Robert Johnson what had happened. She returned to the house because she's innocent of murder. She fled after the inquest because those who sat in judgement of her didn't believe her. She feared she wouldn't get a fair trial since the inquest had condemned her. Given the defendant's race, it was a reasonable assumption.

"She didn't trust the law with her life. She was born into a society where she's denied citizenship, where she can't testify against a white person and must obey all whites as if they were her master. Yet, she's legally free. Where's the fairness in those laws?

"The defense has proven its case by Mr. Robert Johnson's testimony. Carrie Bennet visited Twin Oaks only to obtain her grandmother's emancipation. But she got more than she bargained for. Pierce, believing she was his legal property, raped her. She had no idea her father had left her money and jewels, let alone purchased her mother's freedom. She was not aware of the transaction between Ebenezer Johnson and Lieutenant Robert Pierce, the sale of her mother to the senior Pierce. You saw her surprise at the information contained in her father's letter. Pierce didn't divulge these facts to her, so they cannot be a motive for murder.

"In his letter, Preston Johnson acknowledges his paternity. Mrs. Elizabeth Johnson's testimony of denial of Carrie's heritage was proven false by her son. Being a pillar of society is neither synonymous with telling the truth nor knowing the truth.

"The defense has proven Carrie Bennet was raped by Captain Pierce. The defense has proven Carrie Bennet didn't flee because of guilt, but fear—fear she wouldn't get a fair trial. The defense proved Carrie Bennet, by the testimony of others, is an upstanding, law-abiding person, who has never been in trouble with the law. The defense has proven she fought the deceased to protect herself from further assault, and he died, accidentally. The coroner said her only blow, which she admitted to, was the strike to the deceased's eye. This blow would have rendered him blind in one eye but alive.

"I ask you, gentlemen of the jury, should a young woman die for defending her person from assault? Is this fair? Virginia law exonerates a woman of murder if her attacker dies while she attempts to protect herself against rape. It's time the law included women of color as well. I beg you to find the defendant innocent of all charges and render a decision of not guilty."

The jury deliberated for only one hour.

They returned to the courtroom with a verdict of not guilty. It was unanimous.

Carrie Jane Bennet walked out of the courtroom as a free woman.

CHAPTER FORTY-ONE
There Are Many Kinds of Freedom

Carrie, her family, and friends returned to the Wild Valley Ranch with Cole. They filled the drawing room and spoke to one another in quiet tones. Victory was theirs. Carrie was free. However, the emotional turmoil it had produced had created a surreal atmosphere.

Carrie addressed her attorney. “Cole, I was so angry with you at first for making me read my father’s letter aloud on the witness stand. However, now I want to thank you. I know it was a dramatic scheme to have me read the letter instead of Mr. Johnson. Now, I can understand why. You wanted the jury and spectators to see the surprise on my face as I read the contents. It’s been an incredible discovery to know my father thought of me—accepted me.” A tear crawled down her cheek and clung to the square jaw she inherited from her biological father.

“I can’t describe my feelings. Since I’ve learned of his existence, he’s been an enigma. Now, I feel I have some answers where he is concerned. He acted like a typical slave holder to my mother, but he changed. He protected us by securing our freedom for generations to come. This journey to emancipate my grandmother has been a voyage of self-discovery of my own freedom as well, a different kind of freedom.

"My existence blurs the color lines. Life's challenged me to erase those lines and feel comfortable in my own skin. Initially, this new information about Preston Johnson found me grappling with who I am all over again." A fresh tear slipped down her cheek. "But, I know who I am. I am a woman of mixed-race, and I make no apologies for my heritage. I am finally free to feel comfortable in my own skin."

Sarah moved to the sofa, sat next to her daughter, and hugged her with all of her might. "Carrie, I am so glad to know you have come to grips with the past and no longer find it an obstacle to how you feel about yourself. Please forgive me. I did my best to protect you."

"I didn't need protection from the truth, Mother. Don't blame yourself for what happened to you at Twin Oaks. It was not your fault, and it is not your shame to bear. It belongs to the slaveholding culture and the individuals who perpetuate it."

"How wise you have grown, Carrie." Sarah hugged Carrie again. "I love you so much. Your words have freed me from a shame I felt was mine to bear, but I no longer own it."

Gerard entered the room and announced visitors.

They guessed who the evening caller might be.

"Robert." Cole rose from his chair. "What a pleasant surprise. "To what do we owe the pleasure of your company?"

The men shook hands. He congratulated Cole on winning the case and then smiled at Carrie. He expressed his happiness at her acquittal.

As she acknowledged his kind words, he looked past her and froze.

"Robert, it's good to see you." Sarah smiled and walked toward her half-brother.

Speechless, Robert clasped her hand and then pulled her into an embrace.

"I've brought someone, who is very anxious to see you all." Robert's gray eyes gleamed. He gestured toward the entrance and an elderly woman appeared.

Sarah Bennet, put her hand over her heart as she saw the woman's face. "Mother."

Everyone froze, until Olivia flung her arms wide, breaking the spell as her family rushed into her embrace.

CHAPTER FORTY-TWO
Olivia's Story

Cole winked at Carrie, who sat next to him at the dining table. He had insisted that Olivia occupy the seat at the head, upending custom, to mark the close of her more than sixty years of slavery.

An assortment of desserts and after-dinner liquors were available. Olivia accepted a glass of Madeira from Sarah. Intrigued by the glassware, she held it up to the chandelier, admiring its starburst design.

"This is original Waterford crystal, Olivia, named after the town in Ireland where they were manufactured. My family has some dating back as early as the 1790s. The glass you hold is about twenty-five years old."

"Den, I bes' be careful wid it." Olivia sighed. "Evethin' would be perfect if Mary and her family were wid us."

At the mention of Mary's name, some exchanged furtive glances or averted their eyes.

Robert Johnson cleared his throat and excused himself saying it was getting late. He had sat at the table, sipping a glass of Madeira and entertaining them with stories about the privileged class of his society. He walked over to where Olivia sat, bent down, and kissed her cheek.

Olivia's lips trembled. Her life at Twin Oaks had run the gamut, from her loss of liberty, to fear of punishment, and Robert's occasional success of safeguarding her from his father's abuse or later, his wife's methods of "handling these people." Former master and former slave clasped hands and wished each other well.

After he left, Sarah rushed to describe the wonders of New York City to her mother.

"What's it like for colored?" Olivia looked wary.

Sam leaned toward her. "Grandmother, the New York State Assembly voted on Negro suffrage."

"You kiddin'. Did it pass?" Olivia raised an eyebrow.

"No, but it was 197,503 votes in favor and 337,984 against."

"As I 'spected." Olivia shook her head.

"But Grandma, at least it was considered. Do you think 197,503 Virginians would vote for Negro suffrage?"

"You've got me there, Sam." Olivia nodded. "Carrie, did you meet up wid Mary at da Quaker woman's house? I needs to know where my daughter is." Olivia's tone was strident.

"We'll talk about it when we get upstairs, Mother. You must be exhausted. I'll take you to your bedchamber." Sarah rose and bid everyone goodnight.

~~~

Sarah escorted Olivia to her room. "Mother, where did you get this trunk? It's lovely." A servant had placed it in the room while Olivia had enjoyed the company of her family around the dining table.

"Massa Johnson gave it ta me as a gift." Olivia smiled as she surveyed the bedchamber. Large yellow
~~~

roses against a white background adorned the wallpaper, bed linens, and curtains.

Sarah opened the trunk, and her eyes widened at the sight of the many frocks it held.

"Dese belonged ta Missus. I never want ta see dem old shifts I wore again." A belly laugh erupted.

Sarah joined her mother's laughter. "We'll buy you new clothes, Mother. I know you don't want to wear Ole Missus Susan's castoffs."

"I sure don't." Olivia shook her head and spoke in a whisper. "She was a mean and spiteful woman, and I'm glad I don't have to see her no mo'."

"Mother, you don't have to hide the way you feel anymore."

Olivia shouted, "She was a mean and spiteful woman and I'm glad I don't have to see her no mo'." Then Olivia and Sarah collapsed in laughter.

Later, dressed in her shift, Olivia lay back against soft pillows. "Now, tell me 'bout Mary." A crease lined her forehead. "I wants the truth." She smoothed the coverlet around her. "I figger since you holding back, it ain't no ways good."

There was a knock on the door. Olivia called, "Come in."

Jonathan and Sam entered the room. Carrie followed.

The men stood near the bed, while Carrie and Sarah sat on each side of her bed.

Sarah started to speak, but Carrie intervened. "I—I'll tell her, Mother." Carrie related the sequence of events which led to Mary's death and those of her family members.

Sadness settled upon the room like dusk shutting out the day.

Olivia sobbed.

Carrie put her arms around her grandmother.

Sarah did likewise.

Jonathan laid a hand on Sarah's shoulder, while Sam began to recite the twenty-third Psalm.

Soon everyone joined in.

Olivia grew calmer by the time she uttered, "Amen."

"My poor chillens." Tracks of tears lined Olivia's cheeks. "And I don't remember the faces of half of dem. Deys taken from me when dey was so young. No matter how bad it was for me and Sarah, we all know'd dat Mary suffered mo' at Dayton's hands. Where's Mary's chillens?"

"The sheriff returned them to Dayton."

Jonathan touched her shoulder. "He won't hurt those children. We must try to win their freedom."

"Oh, no." Olivia shrieked. "Carrie, you've got ta get dem back as soon as possible fo' he kill or sell dem ta spite me."

"Why would he want to spite you, Grandmother?"

"There ain't no reason for me ta keep quiet now—now dat Mary's gone. I'm free ta tell it all."

"Tell what?" Carrie stared at her grandmother.

"I knowed a secret. Lucius Dayton swore he'd kill me if I ever told. Dat's why he poisoned me, ta warn me. Maybe he feared I'd tell you, Carrie."

Olivia began to relate a tale of a corrupt man's ambition and desperate attempt to regain control of his life. The result left his daughter dead and his own grandchild to live a life of slavery.

"Grandma, wait." Carrie shouted. "I have to get Cole. He has to hear this, too."

Before Carrie returned with Cole, she begged him to see what he could do to obtain Mary's children's freedom. She doubted Dayton would allow anyone in her family to pay for their emancipation.

Cole promised he'd see to it.

Moments later, everyone was assembled in Olivia's chamber. Carrie retrieved paper, pen, and ink so she could record the story.

Olivia's voice was solemn as she spoke:

"It was late dat night, in '57. It had rained hard. Jordan, from Dayton's plantation summoned me. It was Mary's time. I grabbed my midwife bag. No sooner had I jumped from da carriage when Jordan said, "It's Missy Dayton's time, too."

"I didn't know Missy was in da family way.

"Matilda let me in. I was scared by the screams I heard comin' from da billiard room. Missy was lying on a mountain of linens, on da billiard table.

"Matilda followed to help. Massa Dayton was yellin' at Missy.

"Outside, Mister Green, de overseer, had tied Thomas to da whippin' post. Massa Dayton say he only have ta wave his hand for Mister Green to start lashin' Thomas.

"I looked out da window and saw Thomas tied at de wrists and naked to his waist. His flesh shone white in the torchlight.

"Dat's why Missy in de billiard room. So she could see Thomas suffer. Her bedchamber was on da opposite side of da house.

"Massa Dayton say he send her to a wimmen's college, so she can forget Thomas. Den he made a terrible threat.

"He pulled a tiny bottle of poison from his coat pocket. He say if she refuse, he promised to poison her baby and whip Thomas to death. He set de vial on a nearby desk 'fore Missy pushed her daughter out into de world. I slapped de baby's bottom, and da child wailed. Then I bathed her in warm water, dried her, and wrapped Missy's newborn in soft linens. Then I handed her to Missy.

"Da sweet new mother cradled her baby and looked contented. Her baby girl got red skin, wisps of blonde hair, and blue eyes. Missy touched da mole on de right side of its mouth, like hers.

"Missy promised to obey Massa. Next, she asked him why did he have Thomas arrested for grand larceny?

"He say to stop her from running off wid Thomas.

"She tell Massa dat when he filed a complaint against Thomas, dey sent bloodhounds. She glad he got to Mr. West, 'fore dem dogs got him.

"It was da sheriff's decision, he say, to send da dogs, not his.

"Den she say she love Thomas. Dat deys plannin' to live in Europe, where no one knows dem.

"He done yelled at her sayin' plenty of peoples he know live in Europe. Folks be saying he got a nigra for a son-in-law. He'd be a laughing stock. Dat would ruin his chance to win a seat in congress. So, he admit, he done sent the dogs.

"When he say dis, Missy accused him of wantin' to kill Thomas.

"De devil got in him and he admitted it all. He say a dead Thomas is de only way to be sure he out of her life forever.

"When Missy reminds him of his promise, he say he can't trust a body who would go behind his back and testify against her own daddy.

"She say since he intended to kill Thomas anyway, she wanted to die, too.

"Den, he slapped her.

"My heart was full of pity fo' her. Massa hit her so hard dat she fell off da table. Da baby went a-flying, but I grabbed her, 'fore she hit da floor.

"Massa went to da window and raised his arm. When Missy heard da whip snap in da air, and da crack as it hit Thomas's back, she begged her father to stop. Missy fell to da floor in a heap.

"I laid da baby in my big midwife bag on the floor. Den I helped Missy up. She ran to da window, and begged for Thomas's life. She jumped at every crack of da whip.

"Massa thanked God da baby look white so they can keep it. Say it belonged to a relative who died. She could marry a planter's son, he says.

"Dat's when she shouted she couldn't do dat."

Olivia bowed her head, and tears started to flow. She made use of the handkerchief Carrie offered before she continued.

"Dat's when she say, 'If Thomas die, den so will I.' She grabbed da bottle of poison and drank it. She moaned and frowned until she was still, like a child asleep. Den, he ordered me to take da baby and say

Mary gave birth to twins. He warned me if I ever tell, he kill me.

"I told Matilda da baby died as I hurried through da kitchen to da quarters with da sleeping baby in my midwife bag.

"I made Joshua leave da cabin before I tended Mary. I looked up and saw Massa Dayton on horseback. He got da reins of another horse. Thomas was on it swayin' from side to side. His hands likely tied to da horn of da saddle. His shirt flappin' in da wind.

"Mary gave birth to a girl by Dayton. I drugged her. When she woke, she believed me when I told her she had birthed twins. The baby girls looked alike, 'ceptin' Missy's got a mole near her lips.

"When Joshua returned, he wasn't surprised da twins looked white. Since dey was Mary's children, too, Joshua accepted dem as his.

"Before Mason came back for me, I saw a lone figure on horseback headin' toward da house. It was Massa Dayton, bringin' the other horse back to the stable."

Exhausted, Olivia asked for a glass of water. Then she lay back and drifted off to sleep.

"Will Olivia's story help you, Cole?" Hattie Rose asked.

"Olivia is a witness to the birth of a child born to Missy and Thomas. Her statements prove Dayton's intent was to kill Thomas."

"If only Thomas could be found." Hattie Rose frowned.

"Even if he were, he couldn't testify against a white man, and neither can Aunt Olivia." Mason frowned.

Cole stood. “True, it’s why I need material evidence. I’ll start writing the brief tonight, so I can get a search warrant for Dayton’s property. Thomas’s remains and the murder weapon are most likely buried there.”

“Let’s not forget Missy’s valise,” Allan said.

“Right. I’ll get it.”

Cole had left the bag Allan brought in his study. He returned with the bag in moments. He opened the valise on the desk and extracted a white dress and other fine garments. Sarah surmised these might have been Missy’s wedding apparel.

Allen brought forth the locket with Thomas’s name engraved inside from the bottom of the case.

Cole looked disappointed. “There’s nothing else.”

Carrie peered inside the bag. Her fingers felt a small tab in the lining on one side. She pulled the tab, and a drawer sprung open.

Everyone gasped when twinkling jewels appeared.

“These must be the gems which belonged to Missy Dayton’s mother. Now they belong to Dayton.”

“Dey belong ta his granddaughter.” Olivia had awakened at the sound of their excited voices. “Missy Dayton inherited dem on her eighteenth birthday, which she lived ta see. If da child dat survived has a mole on her face, den dat’s Missy’s daughter and dat’s who da jewry belongs ta.”

CHAPTER FORTY-THREE
A Plan of Action

Cole went to his office to start on his brief. He looked over Carrie's notes. The vivid details of Olivia's story were all there. Excited by the new developments and the success of the trial, Cole couldn't concentrate. He'd just have to rise early the next day and complete the report. So, he retired for the night.

His thoughts turned to Carrie. Although he knew she cared for him, she had never declared her feelings. After being assaulted, it was unrealistic to expect her to trust him so soon. Someday, he hoped, she would be receptive to his love.

~~~

At seven o'clock, Cole knocked on the Bennets' chamber door.

Jonathan opened it and saw Cole and Carrie standing before him.

"Good morning, Mr. Bennet, I'm sorry to wake you at this hour, but I need your help." Cole was dressed in work clothes. He held his black cowboy hat in one hand.

"'Morning, Cole, Carrie. No matter. Whatever you need, you can count on me."

"We think—Carrie thinks Thomas's remains may be buried on my land."

Jonathan stared at his daughter.
~~~

"Yes, Dad, remember Olivia's account of what happened on the night Mary gave birth?" Jonathan cocked his head. "Grandmother said Dayton left with Thomas on horseback but returned to his plantation alone. We just spoke to her, and she affirmed her statement. If Dayton killed Mr. West, and we're pretty sure he did, then he went to Mr. West's home. That's where he took Thomas."

"Dayton left my father's body to swing on the porch for all to see. Thomas's disappearance produced the desired effect. Everyone thought he had killed Dad in retaliation for his failure to win his freedom. Sheriff Coffe closed the case based on this assumption." Cole swallowed hard and shook his head.

Carrie looked from Cole to her father. "Dayton didn't care if Grandmother saw him return without Thomas, for she couldn't testify against him, no matter what she saw."

"I'm going to round up the men in the bunkhouse and start searching. Will you help?"

"Yes, of course, Cole." Jonathan nodded. "You've got seven thousand acres here. How are you going to narrow it down?"

"Well, I'm not sure. My guess is he was probably buried somewhere near the house, or in one of the nearby structures. Besides, Dayton, an elderly man, would have been exhausted both mentally and physically, after the trial and fighting with my father. I can't see him riding many miles away, late at night to bury Thomas.

"I'm going to start searching today. No matter how long it takes, if I have to turn over every inch of soil on this place.

"I'll get dressed and join you in a few minutes."

"Thanks, Mr. Bennet."

Carrie looked farther into the room and saw her mother still fast asleep.

CHAPTER FORTY-FOUR
A Secret Revealed

Within an hour, Cole and Jonah had assembled all the men on the estate, twenty in all. They grabbed shovels from the barn. Jonah organized the men, sending them out to various structures on the estate. Some began to dig around the porch, barn, and chicken coop.

"What exactly are we looking for?" Sam dislodged some dirt with his shovel near the porch.

Cole didn't expect Sam, at fifteen, to be allowed to participate. He looked quizzically at Jonathan.

"A decomposed body," Jonathan answered.

Sam's eyes shifted.

"If you don't have the stomach for it, don't worry. We'll understand. Being buried for a couple of years will make him pretty hard to look at."

"We're looking for Thomas?"

Jonathan nodded.

"Then, I'll help." The boy's voice rang with conviction. "From what I've heard, he got a raw deal. If I can help prove he's not a murderer, then I can stomach it. Where do I start?"

Cole smiled at the boy's sense of justice. He put his arm around Sam's shoulders and told him they would dig together.

"Where do you want to start, Sam?"

"How about the barn? It's where Mr. Dayton would have gotten the shovel. If he was tired, he may not have had the energy to go any further."

"Man alive." Cole smiled at the lad. "It's a pretty logical reason to start there first."

They walked toward the structure. When they reached the barn, Cole started in one corner and Sam in another.

After the men had dug for an hour, Allan called out. "I've hit something."

A few of the hands yelled for the others to come over to the site. They rushed from all directions to where the detective stood, about ten feet outside the carriage house. Some went down on their knees to assist Allan and began to dig with vigor.

Soon, an object began to emerge.

Moments later, Allan yanked a broken wagon wheel up from the ground. A round of robust laughter erupted from the men. The subject of their good-natured jeers and bantering, Allan turned a tomato red.

By now, all the men were bare-chested. Sweat glistened on their backs. They stopped digging to wipe their faces with their kerchiefs or shirts before resuming the back-breaking work.

~~~

After breakfast, Carrie and her mother helped the maids prepare trays of refreshments to take out to the men.

Carrie was about to pick up a tray when her mother touched her shoulder. "I'd like to have a word, Carrie. Let's use the drawing room."
~~~

Carrie didn't hesitate but her stomach clenched with anxiety. The tone her mother used always prefaced an important conversation.

Sarah sat across from her in a matching mauve and striped, cream-colored, silk-upholstered arm chair.

Sarah got right to the point. "Carrie, I've noticed your attraction to Cole and his to you."

"What? Mother, I'm not attracted to Cole." She cleared her throat. "Yes, I do like him, but that's all."

"You might deny it but your feelings for him are as plain as day. As for Cole, he isn't able to hide his feelings for you, either. I agree he is an attractive man."

"Mother, no matter what you think I am not interested in any man."

Sarah reached out and held her daughter's hands. "I know you have been hurt deeply by the captain and the trial, but as time goes on, you will heal. I just don't want you to think Cole...." She stopped and shook her head. "Carrie, I think the world of Cole. He's done so much for you, and our family. He saved your life. He's a generous and kind man, but he can't offer you any place in his life except as his mistress. He won't—can't marry you. When we get back home, and only when you're ready, there will be plenty of marriageable young men in your...."

"Mother, the last thing on my mind is being with a man. When we get back home, nothing will change. I just want to feel safe again. People will be staring at me. I'll be little more than a curiosity."

Sarah put her hand on Carrie's arm. "Honey, don't think that way."

Carrie sniffed as a tear threatened to fall. "What man would want me? I'm damaged goods and the world knows it. I have my work at the orphanage, if they'll take me back, and my poetry to comfort me and give my life meaning. I really don't need anything else. Well…my family of course."

~~~

At noon, Carrie and her mother joined the group out on the porch where a long table stood, burdened with trays of food and glasses of water. Famished men crowded around the tables and helped themselves to the scrambled eggs and buttered biscuits, ham and turkey sandwiches.

Once all the men had drunk their fill, the women returned to the manor to refill the trays with cakes and fruit.

Carrie emerged from the house a while later with the ends of her skirt tucked in her waistband and a straw hat on her head. She was anxious to see whether or not her hunch about Thomas was true. She picked up a shovel an older ranch hand had laid aside as he sat down on the porch steps to rest.

Some of the men clapped and nodded her way.

"This is no work for a woman." Cole walked up behind her with a glass of cool water in his hand.

Sam ran toward the manor. His voice rose in alarm. He waved his hands high in the air. Naked from the waist up, his copper-toned skin glowed from perspiration. "Hey, I hit something. I may have found Thomas."

The men came running from all directions.

Once inside the barn, Sam pointed to a spot where a leather-like object had been exposed. Cole knelt down and pushed the dirt with his hands. In a few
~~~

minutes, the leather object was identified as the heel of a foot. Audible expressions of horror resounded.

A short scream erupted from Carrie. She clasped a hand over her mouth and turned away for a moment before she was able to look again.

Cole let out a long, labored breath.

Without hesitation, a few of the crew got down on all fours and joined him, foraging with their hands, while the others looked on.

In minutes, more of the decomposed body appeared. Their mood changed from fear to reverence as they continued to push away the dirt and more of the corpse was exposed. The shirt was tucked into the waistband, producing an uncanny appearance of neatness.

Frank was the first to examine the skull. The cheekbones jutted through the leathery skin, the eyes were absent, eaten long ago by parasites. Maggots slithered over bones and clothing. A rotting rope was tied around his neck and hands.

The sight caused Sam to turn his head away. He choked back a sob. “He was a prisoner all of his life.” He ran off, and Jonathan followed.

Gently, Cole, Frank, Allan and Mason, examined the remains. The pockets of his pants yielded nothing.

Frank ran his fingers over the shirt and felt a hard object underneath. He started to unbuttoned the garment, but the buttons fell into his hands. He pushed the decaying material aside. A chain appeared with a heart-shaped locket attached. He rose and pointed it out to Cole, as the others closed in to get a better look.

Cole knelt by the corpse and reached for the locket. He popped the catch. The inscription inside read: *Isabella.*

Allan looked at Cole. “This one is a match to the locket in Missy valise.”

Cole stared at the locket. “There’s no doubt this is Thomas’s corpse.”

Cole and Allan resumed the search. A bullet rested on the ground near the spine. He passed it to Allan who rose and went outside to hold it up to the sunlight. Cole got to his feet and joined Allan.

Allan pulled a suede pouch from his breast pocket. He loosened the drawstrings, and shook the bullet into his hand, and compared them.

They appeared identical.

“This is a match to the bullet that killed Mr. West.”

As they cleared more dirt from the remains, one of the men touched a solid object.

“There’s something else here.” Chester Rollins, a ranch hand pushed the dirt away with his hands. His voice rose in excitement. “It’s the butt of a rifle.”

Once it was unearthed, Allan examined it. “It’s the Army issue used in the Texas Wars.”

Cole stood silently as a myriad of emotions roiled through him. All around him remained quiet. He looked at Carrie.

“Now, we have to prepare for the legal fight. Dayton’s political influence won’t make it easy.” He shook his head. “If he ends up a free man—after all we’ve done and have yet to do to get a conviction—Carrie, I swear to God, I’m not going to handle it well.”

Allan placed a hand on Cole's shoulder. "What we've discovered ought to be good enough to persuade the judge to reopen the case. If he objects, we'll know he's on the take." His Scottish brogue colored his English.

"I'm going to make him confess, no matter what it takes." Cole cracked his knuckles and turned to Chester. "Ride into town, please, and bring the sheriff and the coroner."

CHAPTER FORTY-FIVE
Dayton's Story

The next morning, Cole marched into a municipal building and headed for Judge Matthew Anderson's office at eight o'clock with his briefcase in hand. Trailing him were Allan, Mason, Frank, and Carrie.

A law clerk tried to turn them away, but Cole insisted he couldn't wait. They ignored the irate clerk and walked past him with unhurried steps.

"What in tarnation are you people doing in my office without an appointment?" The judge stood. "I have to be in court in an hour." He glanced at the case clock, which stood in the corner.

"I beg your pardon, Your Honor, but we have discovered something of extreme importance, and it can't wait. I beg you to read my brief and take a look at this diary." Cole's voice was firm. "Judge Anderson, with all due respect, sir, fifteen minutes is all I ask, and if you don't think this is urgent enough to act upon, we'll leave."

~~~

Dayton blinked in disbelief when the black-robed judge led Cole's party and Sheriff Coffe through his office door thirty minutes later. Before the judge acted, he waited to receive confirmation about the remains from the coroner.
~~~

"I hate to do this to you, Lucius, but I've just issued a warrant for your arrest." Coffe pulled the document from his breast pocket and showed it to Dayton.

"What the hell?" Dayton jumped up from behind his desk, and the chair banged against the wall. He recoiled from Coffe's outstretched hand showing the warrant. The blood rushed to his face in seconds as a scowl rumpled his uneven features. "You all must be mad."

Cole outlined the evidence against Dayton, showing him Missy's diary, and informing him they had discovered Thomas's remains and the murder weapon. "You caused the death of your own daughter."

"You killed my father with the same gun you used to kill Thomas." Cole's voice shook with fury.

"It's a lie." Dayton's eyes darted between the faces before him. He settled on the judge. "How can you let them in here and corner me with those insane accusations?"

"Lucius, I have no choice but to have you arrested on suspicion of the murders of Stuart West and Thomas. The evidence is too strong to be ignored."

Cole slammed his fist down on Dayton's desk. "Confess. Admit you killed my father to my face."

"And you poisoned my grandmother and killed Janie." Carrie pointed at "The Hawk" with a shaky finger. She grabbed the diary from Cole's hand and opened it to one of the dog-eared pages.

Dayton grabbed a heavy law book and raised it as if he meant to throw it at Cole.

Coffe threw up a hand to stop him, while Frank, Allan, and Mason went into a stance, ready to subdue the chief prosecutor, if necessary.

"Come on Lucius, surrender, you can straighten this out later." Coffe brought out his handcuffs.

Carrie started to read a passage in a voice filled with heart-wrenching emotion.

Dayton lowered the law book. It slipped from his hand and hit the floor with a thud.

"I love Thomas with my whole being. He is a kind and gentle man, who possesses a heart, the purest of all I have ever known."

"Stop it." Dayton demanded, as he covered his ears to drown out Carrie's voice.

Carrie read on:

"We devised a plan for our escape to Europe and get far away from the cruelty of my father, the man who put my mother in a lunatic asylum and deprived me of her love. He lied to me all of these years by telling me she was dead. She's in an asylum in Paris, France. I look forward to introducing her to her grandchild."

Carrie turned the page.

"Somebody stop her." Dayton's pitiful cries ensued. "I can't stand to hear anymore."

"The life growing inside of me is a miracle. My father will never make me forsake Thomas, the love of my life. I'd rather die first."

Dayton snapped. His eyes darted about the room, as if crazed. "Don't you see? I couldn't allow a daughter of mine to slip off with that worthless nigger. I'd be the laughing stock of the whole state. How could I, Lucius Dayton, chief prosecuting attorney who owns hundreds of slaves, count one as my son-in-law? Just like her mother, she wouldn't listen to reason, and look where it got her."

"What led to my father's death? Tell me, you miserable bastard." Cole's voice was low and menacing.

Dayton looked at Cole, the son of his nemesis.

"If Thomas hadn't gone to West, I never would have sworn out a warrant for his arrest. But West insisted upon representing him in court to win his freedom. Then, I had to charge Thomas with grand larceny in order to get custody of him again, even though the jewels were never stolen.

"When it looked as if everything was going my way in court, West found Missy and visited her at my sister's home in Missouri. He persuaded her to testify against me. She admitted she took the jewelry from the safe to finance their trip to Europe. Jewelry, she inherited from her mother. I charged Thomas with grand larceny to bargain for Missy's future."

He glared at Cole. "I took your father's life for revenge. Although West got him cleared of the charges, he couldn't win Thomas's freedom. Judge Francis Paine was a man of traditional values. God rest his soul. So, he remanded Thomas to my custody.

"After I had Thomas, West offered to purchase him. Thomas wasn't for sale."

A strange laugh bursts forth from Dayton. "Beyond that, he was of no use to me. I told my daughter I would save him from a whipping if she agreed to my demands to give him up.

"Once Missy killed herself, I gave the wretched child to Olivia. It was dead, anyway as far as I was concerned." He glanced at Carrie.

"I had Thomas taken down from the post. He could barely stand. I put him on a horse and tied a rope around his neck and hands then secured the other end to the horn of his saddle. I took my son's Army rifle down from the display case and headed for West's place."

His face assumed a maniacal grin. "I wanted the glorified defense attorney to see what had become of his ridiculous crusade to save the slave's life. The irony was too funny not to milk it for all of its worth. I could do whatever I wanted with Thomas, and West could do nothing about it."

Cole was so angry his friends had to restrain him from attacking Dayton as he tormented Cole with the details.

"Cole, take it easy." Allan took his arm. "If you hit him, it's assault and battery."

"I don't care."

"He's about to be arrested and tried for his crimes."

Dayton continued his story. "I paraded Thomas around West's yard and taunted him with my absolute power over the slave. I had a whip and struck Thomas just to watch West cringe. By then, the nigger was unconscious. West pleaded with me to stop and threatened to report me to the federal marshal if anything happened to Thomas.

"We fought, and when he fell, I struck him in the head with the butt of the rifle. He lost consciousness."

Cole lurched at Dayton, but Allan and Mason held him back.

"I hung him on his own porch. It was an execution: a public lynching of a nigger-loving traitor to the white race. And then I shot him with the Army rifle because he was the enemy, and we were at war. *This time, I won.*"

Dayton thrust out his chest.

"He took my daughter from me—him and Thomas. I couldn't let them live. I had killed the great Stuart West, the most feared and loathsome abolitionist in Richmond. People rejoiced and gave parties when they heard of his death."

Tears slipped from Dayton's eyes. His chest heaved as if every breath was painful. He leaned down and retrieved a gun from his ankle holster. He aimed it at Cole.

Allan pushed Cole out of the way, then drew his revolver, and aimed it at Dayton.

"Damn you, Cole West. Damn you to hell." Dayton placed the pistol against his own temple.

Mason and Frank rushed toward Dayton in an instant and wrestled him to the floor.

Carrie stepped on Dayton's wrist, and Cole kicked the gun from his hand.

Frank and Mason pulled the prosecutor up from the floor and turned him around. Sheriff Coffe stepped forward and handcuffed Dayton.

Cole stood face-to-face with the disgraced prosecutor. "Suicide is too good for you. You're going to face a jury of your peers and then serve time with the mudsill of society."

Flanked by Allan and the sheriff, Dayton was escorted out the door.

CHAPTER FORTY-SIX
A New Beginning

The evening after Dayton's arrest, they all returned to the Wild Valley Ranch for supper. Ella and Ingrid had prepared Cole's favorite dishes. The atmosphere was subdued as the day's events took hold.

Carrie noticed Hattie Rose was unusually quiet. The young mother-to-be rose from her chair with the speed of a sloth. Carrie guessed the cause. Hattie Rose's face was suddenly bathed in perspiration. "I think the baby's coming." Her eyes grew wide in wonder.

Carrie and her family helped the maids prepare Cole's father's room for the birthing chamber, as he had directed. She retrieved her grandmother's midwife bag from her upstairs guest room and followed Olivia's instructions.

The menfolk crowded around the door.

Sarah shooed them out, but Olivia told Frank he could stay for a few minutes. "I done seed it time and time again. A woman has an easier time when she has a supportive husband." Olivia smiled at the anxious father-to-be.

Frank knelt by the bed and held his wife's hand.

Carrie watched the loving couple. She envied the ease with which they had pledged themselves to one another.

"I love you, Frank, and I thank you for accepting this child as your own. You kept your promise. Our child will be born in freedom."

"My love, I live only for you. You've brought joy and purpose to my life. Otherwise, I'd still be the pompous knucklehead you met." He reached for his handkerchief in his breast pocket and wiped her damp brow.

She took it from him and twisted one end of the cloth around her fingers. "This is something I can hold on to, so, I can keep you with me in spirit while the baby comes."

He leaned over and kissed her lips. He rose and turned to leave.

Hattie Rose grimaced as another contraction gripped her.

Olivia put her hand on Frank's shoulder. "Don't you worry none, Mr. Frank, we gonna take good care of Hattie Rose."

~ ~ ~

"Ooh, he's adorable." Carrie stared at the plump baby Hattie Rose cradled in her arms. The young mother's smile, like a sunbeam, lit up the room. Hattie Rose sat up and laid the baby down on the bed. She un-swaddled the sleeping infant and passed him to her husband. Her chubby baby had golden-brown skin and a head full of silky black curls. Frank held him with tenderness as a tear crept down his cheek. He swaddled the baby and laid him in his wife's arms. He leaned toward her as they whispered to one another.

"What will you name him?" Carrie looked at the beautiful child.

The infant started to whimper and shook his tiny fists. Dimples appeared on both cheeks.

"When everyone's here, we'll make an announcement." Hattie Rose's brown eyes sparkled.

Once everyone was assembled, Frank announced, "Ladies and gentlemen, meet Franklin Stuart Cole Turner, the third. I'm a junior." Frank looked proud enough to burst.

Cole dropped his chin and shook his head. When he raised his head, his eyes were glassy.

"The name honors my father, your father, you, and me, Cole." Frank beamed. "It takes bravery and a high sense of justice to put one's own freedom in jeopardy to help others. As an attorney, like you, your father, and mine, I will fight for the liberty and justice for the less fortunate."

Applause filled the room.

Cole thanked Frank and his wife for the honor.

When Sarah asked Cole if they could plan the christening at his chapel, he complied swiftly.

Carrie smiled as Sarah took charge, assigning everyone a role, which included shopping, knitting and sewing and decorating the chapel.

Carrie watched her mother become stronger as the weeks passed.

Sarah declared she and Olivia would knit the baby's layette. Laura would make a dress for Hattie Rose. Carrie and Cole would decorate the chapel and drawing room where the reception following the ceremony was to be held.

When the new mother heard of their plans, she wept. Her brown eyes showed her gratitude. "I've never had a new dress before. You women are more than friends."

"Yes, Hattie Rose." Carrie smiled. "We're your family."

As they readied the chapel, Carrie suggested to Cole they plan a surprise wedding for the couple to take place before the christening.

Cole was delighted with the idea.

Carrie told Cole she had returned Frank's engagement ring since Cole had given it back to her after he had received his attorney's fee from the female anti-slavery society. She smiled as she thought of how much joy the ring would bring Hattie Rose.

"Who will officiate?" Carrie looked at Cole.

"Need you wonder? The Reverend Cornelius Jones. No one else will do. I've already sent him a telegram. There is something else we have to attend to besides."

"What's that?"

~ ~ ~

A few days prior to the ceremonies, Carrie waited outside in the carriage while Cole visited Dayton in his jail cell to sign the necessary papers to free Hattie Rose and Mary's surviving children.

When he returned to the carriage, Cole told Carrie how he had been unprepared for the ease at which he had acquired Dayton's cooperation. "My greatest adversary is a beaten old man. He seemed to have shrunk since I last saw him."

They drove to Dayton's plantation to pick up Joshua and Mary. Matilda admitted them through the back door of the kitchen. She expressed joy upon hearing the children were emancipated and would be reunited with their grandmother. "Soon, they'll be on a train, heading to New York City." She beamed with happiness. However, tears filled her eyes.

The housekeeper roused the two sleepyheads from their pallets in the kitchen. She tied their meager belongings in a bundle. Matilda gave the children some hard candy to take along. She lifted one at a time and kissed their round cheeks. Both children shed tears as they waved goodbye to their Aunt Matilda.

As he passed through the door, Cole stuffed some bills into an empty jar on the kitchen counter.

~ ~ ~

Hugs, kisses, and tears greeted the children as soon as they crossed the threshold. Aunt Olivia seemed to find new life with them there.

Carrie asked about clothing for the christening for Joshua and Mary.

Laura agreed to make a dress for Mary with the leftover material she used for Hattie Rose's dress. Carrie asked the housekeeper if she would ask the staff if they could borrow clothing for a little boy, which Joshua could wear to the service.

Before nightfall, Ella had received a white linen shirt and dark pants for Joshua from one of Ingrid's grandsons.

~ ~ ~

On Friday, May fourth, at noon, the assembled guests gathered in the foyer as Hattie Rose descended the stairs wearing the new cornflower blue gown and slippers, Sarah's gift. Her head was wrapped in a lovely blue scarf, which Sarah had lent her for the occasion.

"This is your day, Hattie Rose." Sarah beamed at her.

Frank followed her down the stairs, carrying the baby.

Cole had outfitted Frank with formal English morning attire: a black cutaway coat, black-and-gray striped trousers, and a pearl-gray waistcoat, white shirt with French cuffs, a four-in-hand tie, and a black top hat. Cole gifted Frank a pair of formal black shoes to complete his ensemble.

The Reverend Jones provided religious sanctity as well as humor to the wedding ceremony.

Henry Mason and Allan Pinkerton were also in attendance.

During the christening, Sarah and Jonathan were chosen as the baby's godparents.

~ ~ ~

As best man, Cole toasted the newlyweds with champagne. Soon the Turners, Walkers, Bennets, and Sam, along with Mason and Allan enjoyed the delicacies arrayed on the banquet table. Bottles of champagne sat in ice buckets in the drawing room. Carrie was surprised when Cole reached for her hand and led her out a side door.

"Where are we going?" Carrie had noticed how quiet Cole had become as the day wore on. His face held no clue. She guessed it had to do with the announcement Jonathan had made at the reception. They were to return home tomorrow. The prospect of leaving Cole and the Wild Valley Ranch saddened her as well.

"There's something I must ask you." He escorted her down a path which led to a gazebo. He led her to the bench inside the structure.

"I know your parents plan to return to New York tomorrow." He took in a deep breath and exhaled slowly. "I can hardly express how sad I am."

Carrie turned toward him. "I will miss you, too, Cole. I mean, I'll miss you—very much." She squeezed his hand.

He reached for both of hers.

"If you hadn't defended me, we wouldn't have this moment."

"Well, you had the good sense to hide in my barn in the first place." He grinned.

"Yes, thanks to Mason. He advised me to go to your house. Although, I thought he meant your father." She shook her head. "He didn't tell me Stuart had died nor had a son who was an agent of the Underground Railroad. Otherwise, I would have trusted you from the start. Well—maybe."

"You didn't trust me. I saw it in your eyes. You assumed I was like Pierce." He looked down at their hands. "I—I don't want you to go, Carrie."

"If I had my way, I wouldn't leave. This place has become like a second home to me. I feel safe here—with you. I've never known a man like you." A tear slipped down her cheek. She wiped it away with her finger.

"You're crying. Does this mean you care?"

"Yes, of course I care for you." She turned her body in his direction. "I have great affection for you, Cole. You mean so much to me. I'm going to miss you terribly." More tears threatened to fall.

"I—I want you to stay here with me. I can't bear to live here without you. This place would be a tomb with you gone. Every moment we've spent together has been heaven to me. I love you, Carrie. I don't want to go back to being alone. Don't go to New York. Marry me and live with me at the ranch."

"Cole, how wonderful life would be if I could live here. But I can't. I could never be happy in Virginia. After the trial, I'd be a target. I would only feel safe within these walls. Confined to a place, even a place of beauty, is no life at all. I'm sorry, Cole. I can't."

She rose from the bench. Tears streamed down her cheeks as she hurried back to the house.

~ ~ ~

At eight-forty-five in the morning, everyone was packed and ready for travel.

Cole called the servants into the drawing room so his guests could thank them for their hospitality.

Hattie Rose expressed her gratitude for the care they had provided for her and her newborn son.

The staff wished the visitors a speedy and safe return to their homes.

Cole welcomed all of his guests to return to his ranch at any time they wished. "My home is your home." His eyes had turned more green than blue as he looked pointedly at Carrie.

The sadness she read in his eyes tore at her heart. How would she go on without him? She loved him, but she couldn't put herself through the harsh reality that was the life for people of color in Virginia. And she wouldn't make Cole a target of local derision. How could she bear to see coffles of slaves treading through the town on her way to buy material for dresses or to meet her kin at the station? The trial had announced her abolitionist activities, and both she and Cole would pay dearly for their views.

Carrie knew everyone had seen how much she cared for Cole. She smiled her brightest when she was in his company. He had been her rock of support for every path she had walked for months. He had defended her and saved her life. She knew he loved her, and she loved him, but what good was it to speak of it to him when she knew they could never be?

It took two carriages to accommodate them all. The Walkers and the Turners occupied one, while Carrie, her parents, Sam, Olivia, and the children occupied the other.

The servants came outside to stand and wave as the carriages moved out.

Carrie looked back to see Cole with the saddest look on his face she had ever seen. Her heart wept for the love lost.

Jonathan patted Carrie's hands, which lay folded in her lap.

Tears stung her eyes. "Papa, I probably won't miss him so much when I'm in New York."

She looked at the landscape of the Wild Valley Ranch as they rode by for the last time.

"Time heals all wounds," Jonathan assured her.

As soon as they arrived at the depot, they had to hurry to board the train. Once their bags were loaded, everyone sat in the section for people of color, even the Walkers. Several passengers as well as the staff frowned at the sight.

The train moved down the tracks, away from Virginia, away from the Wild Valley Ranch and away from Cole.

~ ~ ~

Not more than twenty minutes had elapsed when excitement buzzed through the train. Something outside drew the passengers to the windows.

Carrie's curiosity rose. "What's going on?" She rushed to the window to see for herself.

A rider on horseback raced alongside the tracks in a cloud of dust as if the fires of hell lapped at his horse's hooves. He kept pace with the train.

Carrie's heart jumped in her chest.

Cole waved as she peered out the window. He reached the depot as the train entered the Fredericksburg station.

Once it stopped, Carrie and her family rose from their seats and crowded the door to greet him.

"Cole." Carrie took his hand when she reached the door. He lifted her off the train, and spun her around before he set her down upon her feet.

They stared into each other's eyes for several moments.

The passengers looked on in astonishment as they peered out the windows of the train or streamed down the steps to stretch their legs and gape at the couple.

"Cole, you came to say goodbye." Carrie studied his face.

"No. I came to reclaim the joy in my life."

"What do you mean?"

"Carrie, I'm miserable." Cole looked at his feet and sighed. He turned his eyes upon her. "Without you, I'll go mad."

"I've been miserable, too. I never told you, but I love you, Cole Bartholomew West."

Cole's lips spread into a wide grin. "Man alive, you don't know how long I've waited to hear you say those words. I felt it all along. I spoke to Jonathan this morning and asked him for...."

"What are you talking about?" Carrie frowned.

"Well, why don't I show you? Please sit down on the bench, Carrie. I want to do this right."

He led her to a bench on the platform and she sat down. Her heart gained speed as she waited for him to continue. He withdrew a black box from his pocket and knelt before her.

"What are you doing? You've asked my father for my hand? He never said a word."

Cole nodded. "Carrie, will you marry me?"

"Oh, Cole, I would say yes but I can't live with you in Virginia."

"That's what I've come to tell you. Since you won't live with me in Virginia, then I'll have to come with you to New York."

"Are you sure you can give up your life here? All you've built?"

"There's no life for me here without you." His eyes pleaded.

"Well, then yes, I'll marry you." She hugged Cole as the breeze carried her laughter.

He opened the box.

Her hands flew to her cheeks. She gazed at the lovely ring, a luminous pearl, surrounded by tiny diamonds. Cole slid the ring on her finger. Then, her right hand clutched her grandmother's talisman. Her heart soared with the joy of freedom, just like the bird she wore, its journey now complete.

EPILOGUE

Saturday, April 6, 1861
Hudson Valley, New York

Carrie stood in her own backyard.

After the trial, Cole realized it might be dangerous to remain in Virginia, and he could no longer live in a place with such inhumane laws. Even though Carrie had protested, he had sold his ranch and purchased acreage and a house here in this beautiful valley. Their estate sat on two-hundred acres, not including the vineyard. In addition to his law practice, Cole was now a vintner.

He now practiced law in New York, much of it focused on injustice, just as his practice in Virginia had been.

The kiss of spring ushered in a new birth upon the Hudson Valley. Her eyes swept over a collage of green grass, bushes and an array of foliage bursting with colorful blossoms bordered by mountains and a glassy lake.

Jonathan appeared at her side.

The first notes of "The Wedding March" summoned the guests to their feet. A perfect blue sky canopied a perfect wedding day.

~ ~ ~

By early afternoon the following day, the couple had embarked upon a steam ship en route to their honeymoon destination: Paris, France. Now, sitting on deck, side by side, Carrie read *The Legend of Sleepy Hollow* while Cole slept. Carrie put the book face down on her lap and looked out into the blue horizon. She recalled her wedding night and couldn't help but smile. At times, she nearly laughed aloud as she remembered her awkwardness and fear of the marriage bed.

When Cole first broached the subject, it had thrown her nearly into a panic. It was at their reception. They were dancing.

"I can't wait until we are alone so our wedding night can begin." Cole had whispered as a smile claimed his lips. They had just locked arms and turned in a circle as they danced the Virginia Reel.

Carrie was surprised he had brought up the subject on the dance floor. It had caused her a great deal of anxiety as their wedding date drew near. She felt her cheeks flame with embarrassment.

When they held hands and turned in a circle, he'd whispered: "We need not consummate the marriage tonight."

She felt instant relief. "Oh, Cole, thank you for being so considerate." She thought he must have read the anxiety on her face.

She didn't want to disappoint him. She only wanted their first night to be perfect. She was afraid her anxiety might spoil it. She feared when it was time to consummate their marriage she would start weeping or cry out for him to stop.

Their perfect day would end in a perfect disaster.

They were the head couple in line and were about to skip down the aisle, flanked by dancers, when he made an unusual proposal. "I only have one request."

"Of course, anything."

"Promise me, we'll share the same bed."

"Yes." She'd swallowed hard.

"And."

"There's an 'and'?"

"We'll sleep without any garments."

"Not a stitch?" Her eyebrows had shot up.

"Not a stitch. You said, you'd promise me—anything." He'd grinned.

He had tricked her into lying next to him—naked. She was sure she'd feel vulnerable. He could have taken her easily, but Cole had always been trustworthy. He would keep his word.

"Don't look so distressed, Carrie." His gentle tone reassured her. "We'll take it step-by-step. You'll feel more comfortable, and gradually your fears will subside. Then, one day you'll come to me of your own accord. Tonight is a compromise. I get to hold you in my arms all night; and you get to choose the day and the time we'll truly become man and wife."

"However long it takes?" Her brow knitted.

"However long. I'm a patient man because I know the wealth of love my bride has for me is worth waiting for."

"Cole, you're melting my heart." She waved my hand to fan her face and cool the flush on her cheeks. She was relieved she wouldn't feel pressured into performing her wifely duty right away. *Certainly, he didn't mean no clothes at all.*

~ ~ ~

Later, she opened the door to their bedchamber Theirs was the most beautiful she had ever seen. Cole had spared no expense in remodeling and decorating their home.

Once she stepped over the threshold, her eyes were riveted to the form of her magnificent husband. He sat upright against the pillows, the sheet pulled up under his arms. Dark curls fell over his brow. He smiled.

The sight of her no doubt amused him. She had never looked more modest.

"Come over here," he'd beckoned.

She walked toward the bed with measured steps.

"Why don't you light the candles? We'll talk for a while before we go to sleep."

His suggestion was music to her ears. *Of course, he'll keep his word..*

Her hand trembled as she lit the three candles set in a miniature brass candelabrum. She walked to the other nightstand and lit those candles, as well.

All the while, her bridegroom didn't take his eyes off her. To say she was nervous would be an understatement.

He patted the side of the bed for her to sit down.

She did.

He reached for the string, which tied the bun on the top of her head, and pulled it loose. Her waist-length hair tumbled down.

"Shake your head."

She did, and the twists, which had formed the chignon, fell out and covered her back like a blanket.

"You're a bit overdressed." He smiled.

She wore a nightdress with buttons fastened from her neck to the floor. "I didn't think you really meant for us not to wear any clothes."

"I did." The smile hadn't left his lips. "Come lie next to me."

He pulled back the covers and she could see his body down to his washboard stomach. He was completely naked.

She had made a promise, which she was obliged to honor. She slipped under the covers, which he pulled up high. Her heart beat so loudly, she feared he could hear it.

He opened his arms and invited her into his embrace.

She put her head on his shoulder, and his arm rested on her waist. The warmth of his body felt comforting. Something else was happening, too. She began to feel a tingling sensation in the nether parts of her body. She had felt similar feelings before when she'd been near Cole. Sometimes when they had held hands or when his thigh had grazed hers as they rode in a carriage. Now, those feelings were magnified. Since they were under the covers, she decided to undress before he made reference to their agreement. She didn't want him to think she was going back on her word or didn't trust him to keep his word.

She started to unbutton the buttons.

"May I?"

She nodded, not wanting him to think she was afraid.

He reached for the buttons and slowly undid each one.

Every time she felt the brush of his fingers against her skin, the tingling sensations intensified. She struggled to control her breaths, which had become pants.

The same thing was happening to Cole. By the time he had reached the middle buttons, they were kissing passionately. To Carrie, it felt as if they were caught up in a storm. She no longer had control of her own body. She welcomed his touch and dreaded when he lifted his hands from her skin. Before she knew it, she didn't wear a stitch.

They rolled under the covers, and then Cole stopped.

"Carrie, if we are to wait, we must stop now." His voice sounded raspy, and his wet curls stuck to his brow.

She looked into his eyes filled with love and desire. She spoke from her heart without forethought. "I want to consummate our marriage now. Otherwise, wondering when to do so would keep me in a constant state of anxiety."

~ ~ ~

Now as she looked at the ocean, Carrie thought how little she'd had to fear. The brief moment of discomfort soon dissolved into a tempest of pleasure. The result produced contentment and serenity Carrie had never experienced before.

She was truly happy. No matter what the future brought, her dreams had already come true.

~ ~ ~

Cole awoke, and after lunch, he escorted her to their cabin where he presented her with a gift. Carrie recognized it as a book before she held it in her hands. She tore off the wrapper and read the title. Carrie was astonished. She held the volume, *On the Wings of Freedom*, in her hands.

"Cole, when did you...?" Tears started to fall. "I had no idea."

Cole had submitted her poems for publication to the Hudson River Valley Publishing Company. Now, she was a published author. She opened the ninety-page book and read the familiar titles of poems she had shared with Cole for some time. On the last page, Cole had added his sonnet, “The Faithful Groom,” as a tribute to his wife.

~ ~ ~

The following week of their honeymoon voyage, Captain Bernard Wilson summoned all of the passengers to the dining salon. The voyagers arrived, most in a jovial mood with expectations of some new amenities.

The captain’s face, haggard and drawn, dispelled any hope of frivolity.

Carrie and Cole grasped each other’s hands and moved closer together.

In an uneven voice, Captain Wilson announced: "On April 12, Confederate troops captured Fort Sumter in South Carolina. A number of southern states have seceded from the union. If this is the beginning of a civil war, God help the United States of America."

STEAL AWAY HOME

3
THE PATH TO GLO-RY SEEN, AND WHEN THE NORTH STAR SHINES,
AND MY LORD HE CALLS ME. HE CALLS ME. HE CALLS ME. HE CALLS ME. HE
CALLS ME. HE CALLS ME HOME!
CHORUS
YOU'VE GOT TO STEAL A WAY STEAL A WAY STEAL A WAY HOME TO JE- SUS.
STEAL A WAY. HEY! STEAL A-WAY HOME!
I AIN'T GOT LONG TO STAY HERE.
NO, NO, NO, OH!
SLOWER LIKE BEGINNING
I AIN'T GOT LONG TO STAY HERE.
STEAL A-WAY, STEAL A-WAY, STEAL A-WAY HOME; STEAL A-WAY HOME TO
JE - SUS.
STEAL A-WAY, STEAL A-WAY, STEAL A-WAY HOME. STEAL A-WAY HOME TO JE- SUS.

ACKNOWLEDGEMENTS

This book could not have been written without the encouragement of so many supporters. Thanks to my editor Lorna Collins, who inspired me to write a much better novel than I first presented to her. To Larry Collins for finding the right art for the book cover. To the readers for taking the time to read the work in progress: Albert Nickerson, Maxine Clark, Bronwen Chisholm, Robin Coppock, Mabel Gantt, and Madeline Bickel for crafting a sonnet from my poem. Thanks to Doug Shultz for editing an early draft. Thanks to the Riverside Writer's Group, the Ladies of Literature book club, Paula Chow, and photographer Susi Darr. Special thanks to my wonderful family: my husband and sisters, niece and stepdaughters. And in loving memory to my mother, grandmother, and brother; and to Carrie McKissick, a cousin who passed before I was born, who was the inspiration for my heroine's name.

I give God thanks for all of my blessings.

This book focuses on the exploitation of people held in bondage. Slavery is now called human trafficking. Like racism, it doesn't go away, but adapts to the ever-changing world. Please consider supporting reputable organizations that fight slavery and champion the dignity and respect for all people.

ABOUT THE AUTHOR

Malanna Carey Henderson has written and produced ten plays which have been performed in Brooklyn, New York; Culpeper and Fredericksburg, Virginia. For the past two years, she has worked with members of the Friends of the Wilderness Battlefield, Shiloh Baptist New Site, the United Methodist Church, and St. George's Episcopal Church to produce vignettes under the title: *Untold Stories.* These vignettes focused on little-known historical events featuring the contributions of African Americans as spies and military heroes to celebrate Black History Month. The one-act plays included *To His Excellency George Washington, Camp Casey, It Was a Matter of Pride, Democracy is a Weapon, Secret Codes and The Pension Office.*

In 2009, she won first place in the One-Act Play Festival sponsored by Stage Door Productions for *The Eclipse.* She won a first-place award sponsored by the Tulsa City County Library for *A Question of Color.*

A native Detroiter, she earned a Masters of Fine Arts degree in Creative Writing from City University of New York, Brooklyn Campus and a Bachelor of Arts degree in Liberal Arts from the University of Detroit.

On the Wings of Freedom is her first novel. She lives in Fredericksburg, Virginia with her wonderfully supportive husband.

Made in the USA
Middletown, DE
04 May 2023

29558524R00229